MW00943186

Mistress Spy

WITHDRAWN
BY
JEFFERSON COUNTY PUBLIC LIBRARY
LAKEWOOD, CO

PAMELA MINGLE

This book is a work of fiction. Names, characters, places, and incidents are the product of the author's imagination or are used fictitiously. Any resemblance to actual events, locales, or persons, living or dead, is coincidental.

Copyright © 2018 by Pamela Mingle. All rights reserved, including the right to reproduce, distribute, or transmit in any form or by any means. For information regarding subsidiary rights, please contact the Publisher.

Entangled Publishing, LLC
2614 South Timberline Road
Suite 105, PMB 159
Fort Collins, CO 80525
rights@entangledpublishing.com

Amara is an imprint of Entangled Publishing, LLC.

Edited by Erin Molta
Cover design by Yellow Prelude Design, LLC
Cover photography by Kiselev Andrey Valerevich/Shutterstock

Manufactured in the United States of America

First Edition August 2018

AMARA
an imprint of Entangled Publishing LLC

For the Twain Book Club
Twenty-one years and counting

Chapter One

February 1570

She charged into battle with the zeal of one who demands justice and will accept nothing less.

They had been riding all afternoon on the old Stanegate Highway, from Carlisle east toward Naworth Castle, where the rebels were mustering. There were five of them besides herself—two friends she had persuaded to join the fight and three others they had picked up along the way. It was a frigid February day, piercing deep to the bone with an unforgiving cold. When the beacons came into view at last, their flames a call to battle, she glanced at her companions triumphantly.

They scarcely had time to give their mounts a rest and let them graze and drink before the order was given to move out. She kept the bright red banners, adorned with white gryphons, in view, and hoped her friends were close by. A fellow riding alongside her leaned in and said, "What about the reinforcements?"

At a loss, she said, "What reinforcements?"

He glanced around, as though fearful of being overheard. No chance of that, in the din of hundreds of men mustering for battle. "Word is, more than a thousand Scots are supposed to be joining up with us. Far as I can tell, they're not here."

She shrugged. Why did they require more men? There were infantry and horsemen as far as the eye could see, though they looked like a ragtag lot. Nobody in mail or armor. She rode on, keeping her eyes on the banners ahead, from time to time searching the crowd for her friends. But to no avail.

They could see the queen's forces in the distance. It was almost as though they wished to sneak past. No judge of the difference between brilliant or foolhardy military strategies, she accepted chasing after an enemy who clearly did not wish to engage as part of a plan. Lord Dacre was their commander, and in her vengeful fervor she would follow him anywhere. On his orders, they gave chase until finally, circling ahead of the queen's southern army, they lay in wait near the Gelt River where Hell Beck joined it.

In mere moments, her belief that justice would triumph shattered.

Hundreds of horsemen at the rear of the queen's army began a vicious attack, pushing Dacre's troops out onto the heath. She dismounted, electing to take her chances as one of the infantry. Within minutes, mayhem ensued. Mounted troops wielding lances made short work of the men, most of whom carried nothing more than dirks. A lucky few were armed with pikes. Arrows flew, and she ducked every time she saw a bow raised. But before long, the smoke from the harquebuses was so thick, she could see nothing, nor could she hear anything other than the screams and shouts of both the rebels and queen's men. What a fool she'd been, expecting an orderly military action. She'd gotten chaos instead.

Their footmen broke through and tore into the rebels with pikes, and cavalrymen attacked with lances. She looked on helplessly as men around her were run through with rapiers or felled by blows to the head. The darkness helped to mask the grievous wounds, but when she dropped to the ground to avoid a hit, a nearby cry for help pierced the frigid air. Crawling in the direction of the sound, she located the injured man. With blood foaming at his open mouth, he tried to speak.

"Finish me." Though the words were garbled, his meaning was clear. Knowing she couldn't do what he required, she began backing away. "Pray, help me," he said, a note of desperation in his voice. Feeling cowardly, she continued to edge away, and when it seemed safe, sprang to her feet and lunged onward. She was too fired up—and apparently too brainless—to sense the inevitability of the outcome, or even the extreme peril she was in.

Having removed her travel cloak, she shivered in her thin shirt and doublet. Neither did much to ward off the bone-chilling cold. Ahead, mist rose from the river like a curtain of gauze. She tripped over more than one lifeless body, both human and beast. Shouts of command and cries of the wounded were muted in the dense air. Clutching the handle of a dirk that had belonged to her brother, she longed for the chance to put it to use. If she could surprise one of the queen's men, catch one of them unawares…a life for her brother's life. That was all she wanted.

The wind rose, clearing the smoke. Glimpsing an opening, she plunged forward, straight toward a giant of a man wearing the queen's badge and without a weapon to hand. She was ready for him. With an upward thrust, she aimed for his heart. But with one step back, he was out of reach. She was stabbing at the air. He brought a beefy fist down on her wrist and knocked the dirk out of her hand, then gave a low chuckle before grasping the back of her doublet and hoisting her a few feet off the ground. "God's wounds, you're no bigger than a wench," he said.

"Because she *is* a wench, fool," a second man said, stepping out of the darkness. This one wore a short beard. Or perhaps it was only stubble—she couldn't tell in the dark. He reached down and picked up her dagger.

"We could have some fun with her, I'll warrant," the giant said. He still held her aloft as though she weighed no more than a cloth doll. While he mulled it over, she kicked him in the groin, as hard as she could while swaying in the air. He doubled over and dropped her, and the second man laughed. She leaped to her feet and ran.

Unfortunately, she managed only a few steps before an arm hard as stone and every bit as unyielding wrapped around her. It was the bearded man. The terror, the panic, all the unacknowledged dread she'd been holding inside now burst out in one long, agonized plea. "Let me go, I beg you. I have a family to look after."

He snorted. "A bit late to think of that, is it not?" He ordered the giant to bind her hands behind her back, and they dragged her, one on each side, to an area where prisoners were being held, and dumped her to the cold ground. But not before they'd spotted the scabbard tied at her waist and relieved her of it.

The next day they marched to Carlisle Castle, and she, Madeleine Vernon, daughter of Philip and Blanche Vernon of Carlisle and sister of the executed Robert, found herself thrown into a dank, stinking cell, fit only for murderers, thieves, and rebels.

. . .

The days slipped by in a shadowy nightmare. Maddy had not even a pallet, only a meager pile of straw to lie on, and a thin woolen blanket for cover. It provided little warmth but was better than nothing. Though her ankles had been chained when they arrived here, the chains had been removed, thank the Blessed Virgin. They had caused her to stumble on the crumbling, narrow steps that led to the cells, twisting her right ankle, and each time she rose to pace her cell it burned with pain.

Among the other prisoners she'd not seen either of her friends who had accompanied her to join up with Leonard Dacre. They were neighbors, a brother and sister, Ann and Charles Dodd. Fear that they might have been killed in the battle gnawed at her while she was awake and allowed her only a restless sleep. *If I was responsible for their deaths... better to have lost my own life.*

At the end of each day, she'd been setting aside a stalk of straw to keep track of how long she'd been held prisoner. Six stalks now lay in the little pile, and she wondered how much longer it would be before she was summoned for questioning. She was frightened, of course, but ironically, she didn't like being ignored. Left to rot in a cell forever seemed worse than any torture they could subject her to, although she would no doubt change her mind, if that came to pass. The cell was reasonably clean, if she overlooked the stink of urine and feces. Even if the place were scrubbed down with boiling water and lye, the smell would linger. The straw was fresh— there were no bugs in it, and it smelled clean—and despite the dripping water pooling in one corner, she might have been held in far worse conditions.

The jailer, who was appropriately called Wolf, brought her breakfast—the usual hard crust of bread and thin porridge— and then thrust a bucket of water at her, hard enough that most of it splashed onto the floor. "Wash yourself. The master wants to see you." Though curious, Maddy knew he would ignore her questions. Better to keep silent. Hastily, she broke her fast and afterward washed her face in the meager amount of water left in the pail and dried it on her shirt. At least the water was warm, which surprised her.

Very soon thereafter, Wolf returned to deliver her to his master.

• • •

Nicholas Ryder sat at his desk awaiting the prisoner. The one they intended to put to work to further their cause. His father's and the queen's. Not his. The brawny jailer, Wolf, pushed the lass forward. A more bedraggled woman he'd not seen in his thirty years. Nor smelled. God's blood, had they not allowed her to wash in the week they'd held her captive?

After a cursory look at her, Nicholas dismissed Wolf and glanced down at the papers he'd been studying before she entered the room. They provided him with the bare facts. Name: Margaret Vernon. Age: Unknown, but probably mid-twenties. Unmarried with no issue. Daughter of the late Philip Vernon, a Catholic, but never a trouble-maker, and one Blanche Vernon, a deceased French woman. Sister of the recently executed—for his part in the northern rebellion— Robert Vernon.

A flash of movement made him raise his eyes. He would not tolerate an attempt to escape. There were other female captives whose services they could draw upon. It did not have to be this one. But she was quite still, save for a quick swipe of the back of her hand over her face. When he looked a little closer, he could see a trail of tears carving a path through the grime on her cheeks. She was weeping, then. That bode well for coming to terms swiftly.

"You are Margaret Vernon?"

"My Christian name is Madeleine, spelled in the French way."

Fools. He made the correction with his quill. "And your

age, Mistress Vernon?"

"I am three and twenty."

"And you are the daughter of the late Philip and Blanche Vernon of Carlisle, and sister of Robert, lately executed?"

She winced but remained silent. Nicholas took the opportunity to study her. Not only was she filthy, but she was still dressed in a man's hose and doublet, the clothes she'd been wearing when they'd captured her. Her hair looked like a serpent's nest. Like Medusa. No wonder she stank.

"Pray answer the question, mistress."

"Aye." Now his captive was weeping in earnest, and for the first time Nicholas noticed she was balancing on one foot, her face racked with pain. Obviously, the lass had been injured.

"You are not well." He hauled his chair from behind his desk and set it down near her, then circled her waist with his arm. "Allow me to help you." God's breath, her smell nearly made him gag. After she was seated, he rose and strode to the door, yanking it open. A guard stood watch outside. "Find Joan and bring her to me."

"Master?" Joan said when she entered the room. He'd been standing at the windows, surveying the sere winter landscape. The cold had been bitter and relentless. The windows were frosted over every morning, and when he roused himself at sunrise, he had to poke through a thin film of ice in the ewer before he could pour any water.

He could hear the question in Joan's voice. Why was he standing with his back exposed to a prisoner? The answer was simple. Because he did not care to look at Mistress Madeleine Vernon. Her countenance bore an odd mix of vulnerability and strength, and he didn't like seeing what had been done to her. Her actions had been rash and foolhardy, but he was awed by her courage.

"Pray escort Mistress Vernon to one of the chambers

and help her wash. I cannot have her stinking and miserable while I am questioning her. Make sure the fire is stoked and the room warmed first. While you are waiting, give her some cheese and bread and hot wine. And God's mercy, find her some clean apparel. Fit for a female."

"Aye, Master Ryder." With Joan's help, the prisoner limped slowly to the door.

"How were you injured, mistress?" Nicholas asked.

She glared at him defiantly but did not answer.

He nodded at Joan. "Take her. And do not return her until she is clean, fed, and clothed in something that does not reek."

The door slammed shut behind them. Nicholas unleashed a sigh. So this was not to be swiftly done after all.

Chapter Two

The servant, called Joan, led Maddy back to her captor. This time the woman didn't hold on to her. She must have decided Maddy wouldn't try to escape, since she hadn't shown any signs of doing so while eating, bathing, or dressing. Her pace was slow due to her sore and swollen ankle, but Joan was patient and did not try to hurry her along.

Maddy sighed with relief when she saw that a settle had been brought in and placed before the table, evidently for her benefit. For the moment, she was alone in the chamber, dark save for the fire burning in the hearth and the meager light slanting in through the arrow slits. Free of the hunger pangs that had plagued her for days, her mind felt clear and sharp. She'd been able to think about the questioning she must submit to and had devised a strategy. Her interrogator had revealed various facts he knew about her; perhaps she could bargain with him. A pardon in exchange for information, though if indeed she'd committed treason—and Maddy was reasonably sure she had—she would be lucky to obtain one. As far as she knew, nobody had yet been pardoned for taking part in the rebellion that had occurred last November, the debacle that had forced her onto the path that had ended here at Carlisle Castle. Indeed, punishment had been meted out using martial law, which granted the queen limitless powers during wartimes. Maddy's brother had been hanged within a month, without even a trial. He and scores of others. Where was the justice in that?

But she was no outlaw, merely a woman with a grievance. Her strategy was to plead her case as the sole protector of her sister-in-law and niece and nephews. Not only had they lost a brother, husband, and father, but their land and most of their goods had been confiscated. Maddy's family needed her, and it was her duty to care for them.

The door opened and in strode her captor. Master Ryder, as Joan had called him. He was a tall, imposing figure. She had already taken note of his clear, green eyes, and had she felt more herself, she would have found him quite attractive.

He nodded at Maddy before taking a seat behind the big oak table, which, thank Our Blessed Lady, was pushed close to the hearth. Carlisle Castle was a cold, damp fortress, not fit for human habitation, in her opinion.

"You look..." His voice tapered off. "Did you eat something?"

"I did, sir. I am most grateful for the food and drink and the clean clothing. And even more so for the chance to bathe." She glanced down at her plain bodice and skirts. Nothing fancy, but warm and serviceable, and not that far removed from her usual attire. He was being kind, the better to induce her to talk. She understood that, but for now she would behave in an appropriately obliging manner, even though she knew his kindness was simply a means to an end.

His gaze was fixed on Maddy's face. "Will you talk to me now?"

She inclined her head, very slightly.

"Tell me how you were injured. You are limping."

Maddy smiled sheepishly. "I twisted my ankle when I was descending the stairs to the cells. Clumsy of me, but in my defense, the steps are crumbling away to nothing, and even without shackles on my ankles they would have been difficult to manage."

He made no answer, merely studied her. A massive log on the hearth split apart, shooting sparks up the chimney. After a time he said, "It should have healed by now, since it cannot have been put to much use this week. We shall have a physician look at it."

"Do not trouble yourself, sir."

"It is no trouble. There are several residing in the town." He took up his papers and examined them.

She waited mere seconds, then said, "May I know your name, sir?"

"Ryder. Nicholas Ryder."

He set his papers down and pinched between his brows, as though he had a headache. "Perhaps the most efficient way to approach this is for you to tell me how and why you became involved in Leonard Dacre's raid." He leaned back in his chair and waited.

Maddy thought for a moment. It would do no harm to tell the truth if she left out names. "You know what happened to my brother?" When he nodded she went on. "Then there is nothing much to tell. I had not wanted him to get involved in the rising, but he'd always been—from childhood—impulsive, even reckless. And Northumberland made rash promises to those who would join with him, including rewards when it was over. Robert thought every able-bodied man in the West March should show loyalty to the lord." Maddy could feel her gorge rising, so she paused to calm herself before proceeding. Master Ryder was leafing through his papers, head down. She was an annoyance to him—a fleabite or a persistent itch. "I begged him not to take part, to consider what it could mean for his family, but in the end he ignored my counsel. I believe it is almost obligatory to disregard the advice of a woman, especially one's sister.

"When the rebellion ended so speedily, the leaders, as you well know, escaped to Scotland. The poor foot soldiers were left to the queen's retribution, which was immediate. And harsh."

Master Ryder's head snapped up. His eyes, now gone cold, lanced into her. "What would you have expected? Those men, your brother included, were traitors."

"I could perhaps forgive the queen for her brand of justice had it been meted out without consideration of money, rank, or land ownership. Those who possessed such attributes have not been executed."

"With the wealthier families, nobles among them, the workings of justice proceed more slowly." He resumed looking at his papers and making notes, but Maddy thought she detected a note of unease in his tone.

"Do enlighten me, then, sir. I had always believed justice was blind. Why should it be different for the wealthy?" Time in the cells must have dulled her wits. Otherwise, she would never have spoken thus to him.

Ryder dropped his quill and rose. He began pacing, hands behind his back. The room, drafty and dark, was growing cold. As if sensing Maddy's discomfort, he went to the hearth and placed a few small logs on the fire, then spent considerable time adding kindling, poking at it, and even using the bellows to encourage it to catch. At last he returned to his desk.

Apparently, he was not going to address her concern, because he said in a flat voice, "It is not for you to question the queen's actions. Pray continue with your tale."

Her comments had made him uneasy rather than truly

angry. She had feared he would punish her for challenging him, return her to her cell to rot. But instead, she sensed only annoyance and his own disquiet. Most interesting. "My sister-in-law and I, and my niece and nephews, were forced to leave our home—which has been in the Vernon family through many generations—and take up residence with her parents. Their home is small. While they, of course, welcomed their daughter and her children, they were less than pleased to do the same for me. I was a Vernon, after all, and shared the disgrace my brother had brought down upon them. At times, it felt as though I was the only one who truly mourned him.

"I did what was required of me and more. The care of the children was left almost entirely up to me. They—including my brother's wife—began treating me like a servant. So when I heard rumors, I took note. I was not usually inclined to listen to gossip, but I did so now, discreetly. It did not take long to discover what was afoot."

"And where did you hear the rumors?" He had been recording Maddy's words but paused and looked up at her.

"The usual places. The marketplace, fairs, the alehouse—even at Sunday services. After a time, I heard of clandestine meetings and I began attending them."

"Had you no care for the safety of your family? Of yourself?" he asked sharply.

"Sir, I witnessed a beloved brother hanged in the market square, even though I pleaded for his life before the Council of the North." That had been one of the worst days of her life. The councilors had been contemptuous, dismissed her before she had even finished her statement. It had been her last chance to save Robbie's life, and she'd failed him.

Ryder's eyebrows lifted, but he made no comment, only gestured at her to continue.

"I stood by, helpless, while rude soldiers from the queen's army stole my household goods, and I considered myself lucky they did not rape me." She was standing now, leaning into the table with her hands propped on the desk, glaring at him. The words were out before Maddy realized what she'd said, and she ducked her head in shame. The room was silent. *He* was silent. Before he could command her to do so, she lowered herself to the settle and continued, more subdued.

"And then the queen's 'other' agents came, the ones dealing with land and property, to inform me that we were to be deprived of our house and land. Even our livestock. That we must find somewhere else to live. I suffered all this, and you ask if I had no care for the safety of my family? By the time of these meetings, I had no care for anything but revenge. I was mad for it."

• • •

Was she indeed mad? Nicholas would need to reconsider his plan if that were the case. Her eyes glittered with a fervor he'd never before witnessed in a lass. She was bold; he would concede that. "Ah. So you admit it was revenge you sought rather than justice."

She took so long to answer, he finally prompted her. "Well?"

Now she appeared more rational. "Aren't revenge and justice sometimes the same thing? Was the queen seeking justice when she ordered the execution of the rebels? Or was that retribution?"

Rational but saucy. Too saucy for her own good. But by God, she made a good argument. Judging from her smug expression, she knew it. "It is not for you to question the queen's actions," he repeated.

He needed to change tack. Regain control of this interview. "Tell me, pray, what weighed more heavily with you in seeking revenge? The loss of your land and goods—

and being treated like a servant—or the summary hanging of your dear brother?"

Madeleine Vernon's reaction was immediate. Her blue-green eyes shone, but she blinked away her tears. Turning her gaze to one side, she said, "All of it. It all weighed heavily with me." Her voice was so soft, he had to lean forward to catch her words. That peculiar mix of courage and vulnerability struck him again, and he regretted having to hurt her.

"And you believed joining up with Dacre and his band of outlaws, reivers, and the like would provide you an opportunity for what you sought?"

"Have you never been so angry your reason goes begging? Your actions belie common sense and good judgment? That is why I joined Dacre's rebellion; that is why I remained, even though I could plainly see we would fail. It was madness, I know that now, but—" She stopped speaking abruptly, as though she'd run out of words.

In the sudden silence, voices drifted in from outside the door. Nicholas grasped his quill but only stared at the sheet of foolscap before him. He had, on rare occasions, abandoned good sense and judgment and allowed anger to rule him in his dealings with his father. But unlike the Vernon lass, he'd never risked his life. When she spoke, her words surprised him.

"Sir, is there any hope of a pardon for me?"

Could it be so easy? He schooled his face to blandness. "I believe, mistress, under certain circumstances, a pardon for you may be possible."

She gawked at him, looking skeptical. "In exchange for what?"

"I have a job for you. If you perform well, do what is required, you will be granted a pardon."

For a moment she said nothing, and he feared she would drive a hard bargain.

"If I refuse?"

"Under martial law, it would not go well for you, I'm afraid. You would most likely suffer the same fate as your brother."

She flinched, and he heard her quick, indrawn breath. "I would be hanged? But I killed no one, hurt no one! How could this be a hanging offense?"

"As I believe you are aware, Mistress Vernon, you committed treason. You conspired against the queen. Whether or not you succeeded is beside the point. You had the intent."

She seemed stunned, and her words tripped over each other in a jumble. "But I did not...I never meant to...I am indeed sorry for what I did."

"I sense you need some time to think on this, mistress." Nicholas walked to the door and called for the guard. "Escort Mistress Vernon back to her cell. And mind you go slowly. She is injured." He gave her a practiced look full of mockery and contempt.

And now for the final blow. "You say your actions harmed nobody. Yet you have not inquired after your friends, the Dodds. Do you not wonder what became of them?"

She stilled. "Pray, tell me, sir."

"Mistress Dodd's head was split open by a lance. If it makes you feel any better, I believe death was swift."

"Oh, no." Her words emerged on a moan. "And what of Charles?"

"Young Charles told me all I needed to know about you. How you persuaded him and his sister, through lies and trickery, to join the raid. I sent him home. He did his duty." Nicholas opened the door and motioned to the guard to take her.

Despite tears spilling out, she held her head high, and he admired her for that. His words had been cruel, but he suspected they'd had the necessary effect. Nicholas needed to bend her to his will. He did not like doing so, but it was the only way to convince her to cooperate.

• • •

Maddy lay on the straw and wept for a long time. The jailer had brought her a meal, but she felt no hunger, only a deep sadness. Instead of being content with pursuing revenge on her own, she had convinced her friends to join Dacre's raid along with her. The Dodds were younger than Maddy and easily influenced. They too had been outraged by the injustice of Robert's hanging, and, with the impulsivity of youth, had agreed to join, seeming enthusiastic about the plan. Ann, sweet, kind Ann, looking forward to marriage and a family. Maddy didn't blame Charles for revealing whatever secrets he thought he knew of her or embellishing the truth about why they had participated in the raid. He probably hated her as much as she hated the queen and her henchmen. Perhaps it would be for the best if they hanged Maddy; then she would not have to see Charles ever again. All the years she had suffered through Robert's ridiculous and irresponsible schemes, and all the times she'd tried to talk sense into him, had she learned nothing? In the end, she'd been as foolish and impetuous as he.

Why had she not listened to her sister-in-law, Kat, the only person Maddy had confided in, the only one with whom she had shared her intention? Kat had begged her not to do anything so capricious, had even asked if she wanted to end up like her brother. At the time, the vehemence of her reaction surprised Maddy. Now, she realized Kat had had the sense to see where this would lead—down the same path trod by Robert. She wished to God she'd listened to her.

She slept fitfully, rising only to relieve herself. After a

long time, she heard voices and smelled food. Morning, then. What difference did it make? Morning, afternoon, night, they were all the same in a cell. Her door opened and her meal was brought in, but she stayed as she was.

"The master says you're to eat," the jailer said.

"I'm not hungry. Take it away."

"Master says we're to feed you if you won't feed yourself."

At that appalling statement, Maddy pulled herself up. "What, force me to eat? You can't do that!"

He cast her a threatening look. "Oh, aye, we can. I'll hold you down while another guard spoons the food into your mouth. You'll either choke on it or swallow it."

"Leave it. I'll eat it."

"I'll stand right here while you do." Implacable, he did not move. She lifted the bowl and drank some of the soup, then dipped the hard bread into the broth and bit off a piece. Then another, until she'd consumed most of it.

"That is all I can eat."

"You're to eat some of the meat." He took a menacing step toward her. "Go on. Don't make me shove it down your craw."

Repulsed, Maddy picked up a chunk of the meat. It shone with grease and was gristly in the bargain. She'd vomit if she ate it. Letting it drop back into the bowl, she said, "Pray you, good sir, my digestion is unsettled. If I eat this, I'm sure to cast up everything I've already eaten. Surely Master Ryder would not be happy about that."

He wrapped his filthy fingers around a piece of the meat and stepped closer to her. "Open your mouth, wench."

She shook her head and kept her mouth closed.

"Damn you, open your mouth!"

Maddy pictured what it might be like. She would choke, first on the food itself, then on her own vomit. Blindly, she reached out for the bowl, intending to feed herself a piece of the vile fare. Apparently, the jailer thought she was trying to do him harm, because he cuffed her in the face as hard as he could. She fell, howling with pain. He threw down the bowl, and it hit her in the chest, spilling onto her clean bodice. Rolling onto the straw, sobbing, she managed to scream, "Take me to Master Ryder! Right now, do you hear me? I demand to see Ryder!" The door slammed shut. She picked up the cursed bowl and heaved it against the wall.

Maddy lay there for what seemed a very long time, wallowing in pain and humiliation, before she heard the door burst open. The jailer grabbed her arm and jerked her to her feet. "You're in luck, wench. Master Ryder has summoned you."

Chapter Three

Wolf had tied Maddy's hands before bringing her to his master. Now he yanked her into the chamber and pushed her down onto the settle. Nicholas Ryder did not deign to look at her. Maddy didn't mind, since he'd previously looked at her as if she were lower than vermin squirming about in a dunghill. She held still and concentrated on keeping herself upright. Her face was throbbing from the blow, her stomach still roiling. And her ankle pained her fiercely, because Wolf had threatened to drag her to the chamber if she did not quicken her pace. After what seemed an eternity to her, but was probably no more than a few minutes, a small moan slipped out.

Ryder's head jerked up at that. He rose and skirted the table. "Allow me." He took Maddy's face in his hands and examined her injury. His touch was surprisingly gentle. Afterward, he went to the door and spoke quietly to the guard.

When he returned, she said, "Wolf forced me to eat—"

"He had no orders from me to treat you so roughly. I've

called for something to ease the swelling." Before seating himself, he untied her hands. "Now that you have had some time to think, are you willing to listen to my proposal?" Apparently, Ryder would waste no more time on her well-being.

Maddy nodded. She had caused the death of a friend by her reckless decision to join up with Leonard Dacre on his ill-conceived raid, and she was deeply sorry for it, but she didn't want to die. She should let them hang her, but her desire to live was too strong. Perhaps Master Ryder was bluffing about her fate being the same as her brother's. She could not tell. The man, with his inscrutable expression and unreadable eyes, revealed nothing other than his contempt for her. He reminded her of the Catholic priests now required to lead the Protestant church services, their eyes vacant.

"A wise decision. Striking at those who may have had a role in planning the rebellion might be a more effective way of avenging your brother's death."

She thought she'd misheard him. "How could I do that?"

"We have arranged to place you at Lanercost Priory, home of Lady Jane Dacre, wife of the late Sir Thomas."

She was incredulous. "You are sending me to a Dacre? Have you forgotten it was Leonard Dacre who got me into this situation in the first place?"

"Leonard is Lady Dacre's nephew by marriage, but the two branches of the family have been feuding for years and have had nothing to do with each other during that time. The Lanercost Dacres are the Protestant branch of the family."

Maddy was skeptical. "*Hmm.* And where is Lanercost?"

"Not far from Brampton. Do you know it?"

She nodded. Brampton was a small town about nine miles to the east of Carlisle, where her own family was from.

He went on. "You'll be employed there as Lady Dacre's personal secretary and companion. According to my information, you can read and write?"

"I can." For once she was sorry her father had insisted on teaching her those skills. "But won't she think it odd when I so conveniently appear at her door? And what did Lady Jane Dacre have to do with the rebellion?"

Ryder almost smiled. Even though he wore a short beard and moustache, she could see the slight tremor in his lips. Maddy gave her head a shake. She'd better pay attention to his words rather than his sensual mouth.

"As to your first question—she will be expecting you. We don't yet know the answer to your second question. That is where you come in. The Lanercost Dacres appear to be loyal subjects of the queen, but we have our doubts."

"And you expect me to somehow discover the truth?" She heard the rise in her voice, felt her eyes widen with disbelief.

"You lack patience, mistress. Among other attributes that might serve you well, were you to cultivate them." He studied her for a moment, scowling. "If you would prefer to return to your cell and risk going to trial…"

The top of Maddy's head was ready to explode. How she wished she could curl up in a ball and be left alone. Or somehow return to the way life was before the rebellion last November. Before Robbie had answered the call to muster and put all of this in motion. But she could not. She'd better humble herself. "Forgive me, sir. I am not practiced at this kind of work."

"You will not be required to undertake any task beyond your capabilities. May I go on?"

She nodded.

"I understand Lady Dacre is a bit of a termagant, so tread carefully with her."

By God's light, could she not be a saint? Or simply kind?
"How so?"

"Be patient. Do every task she assigns you without

complaint. I would not be surprised if she tested you in the beginning."

"And what will she require of me?"

"Lady Dacre put it out that she needs someone to help with her correspondence, and that is where we think you will be most useful, both to her and to us." He paused and rubbed the back of his hand over his bearded cheek, a habit of his. "She will most likely wish you to sit with her while she stitches. You should take needlework with you. If she does not read, she may request that you read to her.

"What—" He didn't allow her to finish her question.

"Be watchful for any information concerning the rebels who escaped to Scotland. The queen has a strong interest in their return."

"The earls? Westmoreland and Northumberland?"

He nodded. "And their families and cohorts. Primarily Westmoreland. Northumberland is being held by Hector Armstrong, and I understand he plans to sell the earl to the highest bidder."

Maddy's ire rose. "That is unfortunate. He is a good man, much respected here in the North, and many times has he shielded Scottish outlaws." The idea that a Scot would betray Northumberland galled her. Obviously, Master Ryder did not share that sentiment.

His brows arced up. "What about those rash promises he made to your brother? Getting him mixed up in all this?"

Ryder was right; it *had* been Northumberland who had stirred up her brother and made him join the rebellion.

"Best not to repeat such treason in the company of anybody else, Mistress Vernon." She probably should have kept her opinion to herself, but Ryder needed her. He would not toss her back into the cell now that she had agreed to do his bidding.

"They may be planning another raid, and the Scots over

the border are now their allies. Perhaps a raid of great import, or simply forays on the locals for cattle, sheep, and horses." He shrugged. "Whichever it is, we want to know about it. Do not record anything—you will have to memorize it. It would be much too dangerous to commit such things to paper."

"The leaders of the rebellion were Catholics. You said the Lanercost Dacres are Protestant."

"Indeed, they are. You need know nothing beyond the fact that we have reason to be suspicious."

She nodded. "And how do I get this information to you?"

"On market days, you will walk to Brampton, where I live with my father. Our home is located on Church Street, off the market square. The house is half-timbered, with a gabled roof. It stands by itself and is set back from the street."

"What time should I come?"

"It matters not. Be assured I will be there on market days."

"Won't Lady Dacre think it odd if I traipse off to town every week and return empty-handed?"

"No need to keep your visits to my father and me a secret from her. She does not know I serve the queen, and she believes you are a relation of mine. And you will have time to visit the market. Indeed, you should, so that the good citizens of Brampton will see you going about your business."

"Who else lives at the priory? Surely she does not reside at such a large estate by herself."

"In truth, I am not certain of that. Possibly Christopher Dacre, the late Sir Thomas's son from an earlier marriage. There may be guests. Find out whatever you can about them. They could be there for nefarious reasons. The usual cadre of servants, as well, and you must be alert for suspicious characters among them."

"In other words, I should not trust anybody. They are all suspect."

"At present, yes. After you have passed some time there, you'll be better able to judge who warrants your attention. There will not be more than a few, in any case."

"How will I know what information is useful? Surely I am not qualified to decide."

"Commit to your memory anything that seems out of the ordinary or unusual. It may be something you hear in conversation or glean from Lady Dacre's correspondence. Do not try this on your first few days, but at some point, you will need to search her chamber, or wherever she keeps her letters. Anything that must be kept secret could well be locked in a coffer."

"Am I to break the lock? Certainly that would lead to my exposure."

"Indeed, you cannot risk that. But you may be able to learn where she keeps the key. I do not want you to endanger yourself, for then you would be of no use to me."

Maddy's face ached fiercely, and she wanted these directives to end. So she moved on to what was, for her, the crux of the matter. "How long must I remain there? When may I expect to be pardoned?"

He clucked his tongue at her. "Your work has not yet begun and will most likely take several months. You must discover some useful information before you gain your freedom."

Maddy exhaled a long breath. There was always the chance she would not find out anything helpful, and then she would never be pardoned. Perhaps once she was installed at Lanercost Priory, escape might be possible.

Something must have shown on her face, because Ryder said, "Do not even contemplate running away. Wherever you go, we will find you, and then your fate would be sealed."

She gave no reply. He was right. Maddy's days of rash and thoughtless actions were at an end.

"Today you will be moved to new quarters, and tomorrow you will begin to prepare. A seamstress will fit you with appropriate attire. Beyond that, you will need a few days for your wounds to heal. When the time is right, I will deliver you to Lanercost Priory and then we shall see what happens."

He rose and escorted her to the door. "Ah, Joan. I was wondering where you were."

Joan, standing just outside, curtsied and handed something to Ryder. He in turn passed it to Maddy. "Some raw meat for your face. It should help the swelling." She accepted the bloody piece of beef, which was wrapped in a cloth, and barely suppressed the urge to gag.

Ryder spoke softly to Joan for a moment, then nodded for Maddy to go with her. She curtsied hastily and followed, feeling Ryder's eyes boring into her as they walked away. Though she wanted to, she did not dare risk a glance back. She would be a fool if she made the mistake of looking upon Ryder as her friend, even if he did possess those striking green eyes.

• • •

Nicholas threw his quill down, unease niggling away at him. Mistress Vernon would be a reluctant partner in this endeavor, that much was clear. Yet she possessed intelligence and courage, and he was certain, if only to save her own skin, that she would do his bidding. He would have to tread carefully; he was developing a degree of sympathy for her he could not afford to indulge. And a degree of attraction. Under the dirt and grime and the wounds, she was lovely. Any fool could see that. He'd hurt her with his harsh words, and damned if he wasn't sorry for it. If his father caught on, he would insist on choosing another lass for the job. And then what would befall Madeleine Vernon?

The door opened and the tall form of Francis Ryder entered. "Well?"

"She agreed. What other choice did she have?"

"But will she succeed? She will be our spy, and that requires presence of mind. Self-assurance. And most important, cunning. Does she measure up?"

Nicholas leaned back in his chair and tried not to show the annoyance he felt. Why assign him these tasks if his father did not trust him? If he questioned Nicholas's every decision? "In my judgment, yes. But we won't know for certain until she's in place and working, will we?"

"Nick? You are not telling me everything."

He rubbed the back of his hand over his short beard. "I threatened her. She's cooperating to save herself. Would you expect her to exult in her situation?"

His father stared at him a long moment.

"Mistress Vernon is astute, and I've no doubt she can carry off the ruse."

"Very well. We shall soon see what she can accomplish. When does she go to Lanercost?"

"Four or five days' time. Preparations must be made. I'll escort her there and assure matters at the priory are as we believe."

Francis Ryder nodded and made for the door. "Father, hold a moment. How does Daniel fare?"

"I haven't seen much of the lad. Too busy. But rest easy, I would have been informed were anything amiss." Nicholas interpreted that to mean his father hadn't bothered to spend any time with his grandson.

"After I've delivered Mistress Vernon to Lanercost, I intend to remain at home with the boy. I've been away too long."

Francis Ryder scowled, and Nicholas knew what his next words would be. "You spoil the lad. He needs to toughen up."

Nicholas sighed. "He has only six years, Father. And he's lost both of his parents. I'll follow through with anything related to this current business, but otherwise I wish to tarry in Brampton for at least a month. I must be there to receive Mistress Vernon's reports, in any case." When Nicholas's brother, Richard, had been killed last year, Daniel had become Nicholas's ward. The boy's mother had died in childbirth the year before, along with the babe who would have been his sister, had she lived.

The older man gave a brusque nod and exited, leaving Nicholas to ponder his future. He wished to be done with the queen's affairs but had yet to find a way to exit, and now he wished to see this business with Madeleine Vernon through to its conclusion. His father and the queen's satisfaction notwithstanding, Nicholas was determined to ensure that it ended well for Mistress Vernon.

• • •

Joan ushered Maddy up two sets of stairs to the withdrawing chamber, a large space that encompassed both sitting room and bedchamber. And, God be thanked, a fireplace, in which a fire was laid and ready to light. The floor was strewn with fresh rushes. Only then did she realize her prison had been the castle gatehouse, an enormous structure that seemed to contain an endless collection of rooms. From what she could tell, Nicholas Ryder's office was on the ground floor, and her cell had been just below. Joan directed her to sit on the settle and hold the hunk of meat to her face. She did so gladly, as the settle was before the fireplace. Joan set about lighting the fire.

After a bit, warm and temporarily free from worry, Maddy curled up and drifted off to sleep. All the nights she had been imprisoned she had not slept soundly for even one of them. If voices, footsteps, and locks clinking open and closed didn't keep prisoners awake, certainly fear did the job. Were those voices and footsteps heading toward her? Would her door be unlocked next? Then what? The rack? The scold's bridle, or iron maiden? Or perhaps they would simply crush her to death with heavy stones on her chest. *Peine forte et dure.*

She was deeply asleep when Joan pinched her, despite the fact that a tub had been brought in and servants were filling it with water. "Wake up, mistress! You must bathe. Master Ryder wishes you to sup with him tonight."

She rose so rapidly, spots danced before her eyes, and the piece of beef dropped to the floor. For a moment, Maddy couldn't remember where she was. She simply stared, her vision blurred, until gradually the chamber and its furnishings began to arrange themselves into a meaningful whole. Joan helped her undress and step into the water, which was blessedly hot. *Heaven.* It felt like heaven. Joan shoved a linen cloth into her hand, and said, "Scrub yourself, mistress. I'll be back to help you wash your hair."

The water smelled of herbs. Lavender and thyme. How astonishing. A bathtub, with hot, fragrant water, here in Carlisle Castle, the unyielding stone fortress. For what reason would the castle possess a bathtub? And sweet-smelling herbs?

For a blessed few minutes Maddy lay back in the water, luxuriating. When it occurred to her she did not know how soon Joan would return, she set about washing, scrubbing herself hard all over with the coarse linen cloth. Between the scrubbing and the hot water, Maddy was red as a ripe strawberry. When Joan bustled through the door, she was ready for her. The servant scrubbed her head with some kind of lye soap, so hard it was painful.

"Ouch! Is it necessary to be so rough?"

"Done," she said. "That should see to the lice. I'll say this, mistress, you do have a beautiful head of hair. That chestnut color—I'll wager you're the envy of all your friends."

Maddy tried to thank her, but she cut her off. "Now rinse your hair and get out. The master wishes to use the water from your bath."

She shot out of the tub at that. "But I must dress and sit by the fire to dry my hair. Why can he not bathe someplace else?"

"Have you not noticed that baths are a rare thing around here? We have one bathtub, and the only reason we've that is because Mary, the Scots queen, was our special guest for a time. Nothing but the best for that woman and her ladies. 'Tis not every day that we can bathe—in a tub, that is. So you can hie yourself into the sitting room while the master has himself a nice soak."

After Maddy had dried herself with another linen cloth, Joan helped her dress in a plain smock under a kirtle and skirt. She held out a bodice for her and fastened it. Maddy slipped on a pair of clean stockings, tied them with cloth garters, and accepted the slippers Joan held out. Had the queen and her ladies left these behind, too?

"He is waiting outside, so—"

"I'm going," she said, moving to the other room. "There isn't even a door!"

"See that you respect my privacy," a male voice said. Ryder's.

That silenced her. Although Maddy heard him splashing around, he didn't say another word. An image of a naked Ryder floated through her mind. His broad shoulders and chest. His narrow waist. Lower. Then his singing distracted her, which was a good thing. A rousing rendition of a popular Scottish ballad, "Jock o' the Side." She sat there running her fingers through her hair and laughing silently.

She had not laughed in months, it seemed, and Ryder was the last person she'd expected to evoke that response.

• • •

Nicholas cleared off his writing table, placing a branch of candles on one end, and asked the servant to set their trenchers on either side.

"Be seated, mistress," he said when Madeleine Vernon entered the chamber. He felt her eyes on him, but initially he did not look at her. Then she stepped into the candlelight, and he could not look away. God's breath, but she was a beauty. Dressed in men's clothes, her looks had been well concealed. Now he became only too aware of her voluminous chestnut hair, and the way it cascaded about her shoulders. Her porcelain skin and delicate cheekbones were marred by the bruise, but that did not detract from her loveliness. And under those serviceable clothes, a body to tempt a king was only too evident.

Jesu. He must rein in his thoughts before his cock stiffened to painfulness. And he needed to keep his wits about him.

He motioned her to the settle, which had been pulled close to the table, and after they were both seated, Nicholas raised his tankard and said, "To a safe and fruitful enterprise." She said nothing, only drank deeply, her blue-green gaze peering at him over the rim of her cup. A servant carried in a platter of roast capon, and then one of potatoes, turnips, and carrots. "Have some bread, mistress," Nicholas said, pointing to the freshly baked loaf resting on the table. She snatched the loaf and ripped off a piece. By God's light, her hands were shaking. She visibly controlled herself when she realized he was watching her. How long had it been since she had eaten a meal, something other than the disgusting victuals they'd served her in the cell?

"At present I am not prepared to trust you with a knife, so I will serve you," he said.

They ate in silence. Finally, she paused and Nicholas heard a stifled belch. He resisted the urge to laugh, while at the same time feeling sorrier than he should for her near-desperate hunger.

When the silence lengthened, he wondered if she had deliberately chosen not to speak to him. A way of retaliating against him. "I may as well have put you in a scold's bridle, mistress," Nicholas said after a long time, "you are so quiet."

"Have you ever seen a woman in a scold's bridle?" she asked, her head snapping up. "I have, and I shall never forget it."

"Alas, 'tis an uncommonly cruel punishment. We must discuss the details of your mission," he said, spearing a piece of capon with his knife. "That device would render you incapable of speech, as you well know." God's mercy, he sounded humorless.

She inclined her head slightly, and Nicholas interpreted that as a willingness to overlook his boorishness. "Pray, am I to use my own name with Lady Dacre?" She shoved a fatty piece of capon into her mouth and washed it down with a sip of ale. She looked as if she were in the throes of *la petit mort*.

"Is there any reason she would know you or your kin? Recognize your family name?"

"There is not."

"Then I believe it is safest to stick with as much truth as possible. Use your own name, and tell her about your family, if she should ask. Nobles are famous for their lack of interest in us common folk, however. I doubt she will show the slightest curiosity about you, beyond your name and the ways in which you might be of service to her." He sliced off more capon for her, then said, "Did you ever come to Brampton for market days? Would anyone there recognize you?"

She shook her head. "We attended the market in Carlisle. Who does Lady Dacre think I am? She must have made inquiries about me."

"She believes you to be a distant relation of my family. A cousin thrice removed. My father was acquainted with her late husband, Sir Thomas. Because of our supposed connection, if somebody sees you visiting my home, it will not seem suspicious. My father's name is Francis, in case you should need to know."

"She does not know of your...work, then."

"No one hereabout does, though there are those who may suspect. Now, as for a means of getting a message to me. Lanercost Cross is situated to one side of the priory church. At its base is a loose stone, which is easily removed. Place any message you may have there. You may need to wait until dark."

"Who will be checking for messages?"

"Somebody I trust. No concern of yours. Contact me only in case of imminent danger—something that would threaten your personal safety or compromise the mission."

"Pray have your minion check often, then, since I have no skills as a spy."

He raised a brow, knowing full well she was more than capable of taking on this work. Madeleine Vernon had a habit of denying her own wit and strength, but she wasn't fooling him.

"Your task is not a difficult one, and you're an intelligent woman. Listen, observe, and read Lady Dacre's correspondence. It should not be too demanding."

A servant entered, delivering a platter of marchpane, cheese, and dried apples. Nicholas gestured to the array, and Madeleine helped herself to some of everything. As with the other food on offer, she ate her fill.

Afterward, they both rinsed their hands and dried them.

Nicholas was rising from the table when she spoke. "Does my cooperation in this allow me a chance of getting Vernon land and goods back?"

He scowled, because it behooved him to be firm with her. His father expected nothing less. "You will be fortunate, mistress, to receive your pardon, if all goes well."

She got to her feet and looked him in the eye. "So my reward for this...service is simply to return to life with my sister-in-law and her family? I can never go back to my own home?"

"At least you will have a life. And, who knows, perhaps you will find a husband and he'll provide a home."

Mistress Vernon laughed humorlessly. "Nay. There are but few marriageable men left," she said, turning toward the door. "The queen executed most of them."

God's wounds, the warrior firebrand was right.

Chapter Four

Four days later, their small party set off for Lanercost Priory, home of Lady Jane Dacre. Maddy rode pillion behind Nicholas Ryder. Although she despised the man, she was happy enough to share his warmth. A footman accompanied them, leading a packhorse carrying her belongings. She wore a traveling gown with an overskirt to protect it, a woolen riding hood and cloak, and a scarf, leather gloves, and sturdy boots. The temperature hovered near freezing, but at least it wasn't snowing.

The past few days had seen a flurry of preparations. Maddy had been measured for a wardrobe, since she'd arrived at the castle with nothing wearable. She now possessed newly stitched smocks, kirtles, skirts (one slashed), and three bodices. She had done much of the sewing herself, having always been handy with the needle.

Ryder thought it would look odd if she arrived without any personal belongings, so he presented her with a coffer and instructed her to choose from an array of goods he had laid out on his table. She was uncomfortable with this, being quite certain everything had come from families like her own, whose beloved fathers, husbands, and brothers had been executed and their property seized. When she'd asked Ryder, a corner of his mouth ticked up, and he'd given her what she had come to think of as his do-you-truly-expect-me-to-answer look: a cold-eyed stare and a slight rise of his brows.

She chose a couple of goose quills, a penknife, and an inkhorn. "Is that all, mistress?" Ryder asked. "I'm sure Lady Dacre will provide you with writing supplies. What about this necklace?" He gestured toward a chain strung with enameled flowers, with pearls set in between. It was lovely, certainly of higher quality than anything she'd ever owned.

It was tempting, but she couldn't accept it. "Nay, I do not want it. Someone like me would not own jewels, and it must have been precious to the lady from whom it was stolen."

Ryder shrugged.

As Maddy's eyes swept the table one last time, she noticed some embroidery supplies. Linen fabric and a few hoops of different sizes. Next to them were a needle case and a hempen bag filled with silks of different colors. "I shall take these," she said, smiling in spite of herself. "If I must sit with Lady Dacre while she stitches, I may as well do the same." In truth, needlework was a great pleasure of hers. She did feel a pang, though, wondering what had happened to the lady to whom these once belonged.

"Good." He nodded in approval.

While she had sewed her clothing, Ryder had often circled the chamber, bombarding her with suggestions and counsel about her demeanor (sober), habits (circumspect), speech (submissive), and appearance (unremarkable). Now, as they rode alongside the sere fields, he told her a little of the Dacre family history.

"Sir Thomas married Jane Carlisle late in his life, only a

few years before he died. She was an heiress, thus enriching him further, and she inherited a generous portion of his estate. Your living situation should be quite comfortable. I don't believe you'll be treated as a servant, which you so disliked at the home of your sister-in-law." Puffs of frosty breath shot from his mouth as he spoke. Maddy was not sure if he was being sarcastic or merely stating a fact.

Ryder had turned his head toward the side so she could hear him, and this afforded her an opportunity to study his profile. His face was narrow, a young man's face—skin taut and unmarked. She judged him to have about thirty years, but he may have been younger. His curling hair and beard verged on black. Nose straight, except for a slight bump in the middle. Although she couldn't tell from his profile, she recalled the unusual clary sage color of his eyes. She had noticed that the first time she'd sat before him as his captive, because they were quite extraordinary.

"The Lanercost Dacres are Protestants, awarded the priory after the Dissolution for their loyalty to the king. They are estranged from the Naworth Castle Dacres, who remained Catholic. At present, nobody is living at Naworth. Leonard, as you know, has fled to Scotland, and his brothers have been banished for their suspected role in the rising."

"Ah, yes, banished, disgraced perhaps, but not executed. The queen needs the use of their land and property until their death. Not so for the rank-and-file foot soldiers."

He turned his head abruptly, spurring his mount into a canter, and she had to throw her arms around his waist to keep her seat. The warmth of his body felt better than it should have. She regretted her impulsive comments, because talking made the journey more bearable. Maddy again reminded herself that Master Nicholas Ryder was no friend of hers. She recalled his disdain for her, his cruelty when he'd told her of Ann's death. No, she should converse with him as little as possible, and most assuredly should not be admiring his handsome visage, nor enjoying his nearness.

There could not be much else that he had not already told her about the Dacres, in any case. They rode in silence until sometime later Ryder said, "We are near Brampton. Lanercost is not far."

"Aye." Her spirits were low. The thought of being left at the priory to fend for herself was daunting, since, despite the store of facts Ryder had drilled into her, she still possessed only a vague notion of what she was meant to accomplish. And Maddy much misliked helping the queen, who had given the order for the executions.

Not long after, they rode through Brampton. A few shopkeepers had their wares out under their signs, though they themselves were sheltering indoors. She glimpsed a mercer, glover, and shoemaker, and farther along, a carpenter, tinsmith, and wheelwright. Not many people were about; it was too cold. Ryder bestirred himself to point out Church Street, where his family home was situated.

And then, in the distance, there was Lanercost. They crossed over the Abbey Bridge and rode under the arch of the gatehouse. The gray stone buildings of the priory spread out before them. Farm buildings stood to the south of the road, and they passed those first. A few brindled mongrels gave chase, barking at their heels. The church, once for the use of the Augustinian canons in residence, was now a parish church, Ryder had said. It dated from several centuries ago. Ryder walked his horse up to a two-story building and stopped.

"I believe this is known as the vicarage. It was renovated by Sir Thomas as part of the residence for the family." After he dismounted and handed the reins to a stable lad, Ryder lifted Maddy down from the pillion.

She said nothing. Her stomach was quivering with

trepidation. Something occurred to her, and before he turned toward the entrance, she grasped his arm. "You said they were Protestants. Do they know I am a Catholic? Do they know about my brother and my participation in Dacre's raid?"

His expression briefly softened before assuming its usual mask of indifference. "No. I thought it best to let you decide if and when to inform Lady Dacre of your family history, or anything else personal in nature. If she seems sympathetic, you may decide to confide in her, but religion is a topic you should steer clear of." He looked at Maddy with bewilderment. "God's wounds, mistress, never tell anybody you're of the old faith! As I said before, I doubt she will be interested enough to inquire about such matters." He turned, then spun back. "Do not forget; she thinks we have ridden over from Brampton." Maddy nodded, and they ascended the circular steps to the entrance.

A female servant welcomed them into an entryway of small proportion. "My lady will receive you in the drawing room." They followed her up a staircase to a first-story gallery, hung with portraits that could only be of various Dacre ancestors.

They entered a comfortable-looking chamber with south-facing mullioned windows. Good. The room would be warm. Two upholstered chairs were positioned before the fire, and from one of them rose a woman whom Maddy took to be Lady Dacre. Two men were also in the room, sitting at a chessboard, and they got to their feet as well.

"Lady Dacre, I am Nicholas Ryder of Brampton. I do not believe I have had the pleasure of your acquaintance until now, although your late husband was well known to my father." He gave an impressive bow. Here was a side of him she'd not seen.

"Master Ryder. I trust your journey was safe and pleasant. As much as was possible in this dreadful cold."

"It was but a short ride from Brampton, my lady." He turned and, taking Maddy's hand, drew her forward. "May I introduce my relation, Mistress Madeleine Vernon? She is come to provide assistance in whatever way you should require."

Maddy curtsied low, as gracefully as her not-quite-healed ankle would allow. She could sense the older woman looking her over before she even rose.

"Mistress Madeleine, welcome," Lady Dacre said, surprising Maddy with the warmth in her voice. "I am glad you are joining our little household. You and I will talk later about your duties."

"Thank you, Lady Dacre."

She glanced at the two men, which apparently was sufficient inducement for them to come forward. "My stepson, Christopher Dacre, and his friend up from London, Thomas Vine."

Jesu. She knew this man, and his name was not Thomas Vine. She'd stake her life on his never having stepped foot in London. But she did not dare let on.

The men gave their requisite bows, and Maddy curtsied. Dacre was the elder, with mud-brown hair, sallow skin, and a sparse beard. But he had a pleasant enough smile. "Lady Dacre is in need of female company, mistress. Welcome."

"I'm happy to be of service," she said, keeping her gaze squarely on Dacre, feeling as though a wild animal had sneaked up on her, ready to pounce. Had Nicholas Ryder sprung this on her for some fiendish purpose of his own? Did he know who Vine really was?

"Will you take refreshments before departing?" Lady Dacre asked Ryder.

He hesitated, no doubt weighing up the advantages of leaving before the early winter darkness fell, against those of common courtesy.

Pray do not desert me yet.

Courtesy won out. "Most gracious of you, Lady Dacre," Ryder said. She opened the door and ordered food and drink, and Maddy risked a quick glance at Vine, whose true name was John Musgrave.

To her dismay, he was looking right back at her, his mouth curving in a brazen smile. Her heart quickened. The man was as fearsomely attractive as ever. He wore his dark blond hair long. It was streaked with lighter strands, most likely from his work being much out of doors. Running cattle, burning fields, and generally harassing innocent citizens usually took place outside. Although Musgrave had cleaned up for his visit to the vicarage, he still had the scruffy outlaw look about him. The look she had found irresistible at one time.

Maddy forced her gaze back to Lady Dacre.

Fashionably dressed in a slashed gown, she moved with an easy grace. She wore a partlet at her bosom and a small starched ruff around her neck. She was a short woman, her age hard to guess. Possibly as old as sixty, but she appeared to be in good health and not at all the termagant Ryder had warned Maddy of.

She led them to a small dining room, adjacent to the drawing room. "Our kitchens are in the tower, and we eat in the hall if we have a large number of guests. But with such a small party, we will sup here." After she sat down at the head of the table, the rest of the party slid onto the benches, Dacre and Musgrave on one side, Ryder and Maddy on the other. She must keep her eyes down or on Lady Dacre, even though she longed to fix her gaze on Musgrave.

The first course was a salad, with a variety of lettuces and herbs and boiled eggs. With a nervous stomach, Maddy was hard pressed to eat anything, but it would be rude not to. Drenched in vinegar, salty and sweet all at once, it was delicious, and her appetite revived somewhat. They ate in silence for a time, until the second course was brought: salmon in a dill sauce and cheese tarts. While it was served, Lady Dacre asked, "Was your family affected by the recent unrest, sir?" Grateful this was addressed to Ryder and not her, Maddy waited to see how he would answer.

"Not significantly, my lady. Unfortunately, I lost a few dear friends who had thrown in their lot with the earls."

Was this true? He had never said, but why would he share something like that with her?

"Fools, all," proclaimed Musgrave. "They deserved what they got." He banged his tankard down as if to emphasize the point, then wiped his mouth with the back of his hand.

Maddy itched to point out the irony of his standing in judgment of anybody else's wrongdoing. But of course she could say nothing. Ryder only shrugged. "I suppose they had their reasons."

"When men decide rashly to take up arms, it is their families who suffer," Lady Dacre said, her lips thinning in disapproval.

Especially when the queen's justice is cruel and wielded so swiftly. And when she steals your property afterward.

"And you, Mistress Madeleine? What of your family and friends?"

Maddy had just swallowed a sip of ale and coughed a little when she heard her name. *What to say?* She must tell a lie, probably the first of many. "No, my lady. I was not affected." If Musgrave had heard about Robbie, she prayed he would keep his mouth shut. In his fake identity as Vine, admitting an acquaintance with her brother surely would seem odd.

"What circumstances cause you to seek employment, mistress?" she asked. "Are your parents no longer living?"

"They are both dead. My brother is wed now, with children, and living with his wife's family. They were welcoming, but I could see there was not room enough for me. I wished to do something useful, in any case."

"No room for you? I would think they would have done anything to accommodate you. Your help with a growing family would be invaluable."

Maddy gave her a tight-lipped smile, having no idea how to respond to that. Let her interpret it as she liked.

Ryder asked if the rising had harmed their family, saving Maddy from further questions, at least for the moment. Christopher Dacre spoke between bites of salmon. "A few laborers and the son of a former cook joined with Northumberland. They've not been seen since. We do not know if they were killed, executed, or have fled over the border." He made no mention of his close relation, Leonard Dacre, or his raid.

Ryder fixed Musgrave with a hard stare, one he had often used on her. "What is the London gossip about these events, sir?" Given the outlaw's appearance, Ryder may be having doubts about his identity. Perhaps Musgrave had met his match.

The man took a long draught of ale before replying. "'Tis said the queen is furious and will send her army on raids into Scotland until she finds the rebels."

"The Scots will mislike that," Dacre said.

"Aye," Musgrave replied. "She has other worries, too. Now that Moray's been murdered, there is no regent. Who's going to protect the little king?" He spoke of the infant son of Mary, the Scots queen. The babe had become king after Mary abdicated. The Earl of Moray was her brother, and this was the first Maddy had heard of his death. Ryder must have known, though.

"He belongs with his mother," Lady Dacre said. The unfortunate Mary, after a series of scandals, had been taken prisoner in Scotland, her infant son torn from her arms. She stood accused of conspiring with the men who had murdered her husband, Lord Darnley, father of her child. Subsequently, she had married one of them, the Earl of Bothwell. Somehow, she had managed to escape and make her way to England, where she'd become Queen Elizabeth's prisoner. Lady Dacre's expression of sympathy for the Catholic Queen Mary was surprising.

"A new regent will be appointed in due time, I'm sure," Ryder said. "Any other news?" He was trying to act as though his interest was merely casual, but Maddy knew better.

"The French and Spanish are of great concern to the queen and her councilors. Whether they're right or wrong, they believe this rebellion might have provided reason for one or the other—or both—to think the time is ripe for an invasion of England."

Maddy was shocked, perhaps naively, and stared at Ryder to see if she could gauge his feelings on the matter. His bland gaze told her nothing, as usual. How in God's name was it possible that Musgrave was privy to any of this information? Was he inventing it?

Dacre broke in. "The rebellion was so ill considered, and such a failure, it is hard to see how the queen and her advisors could draw such a conclusion." Maddy had to agree with that.

"Surely the queen must take any such threat seriously until they can judge the truth of it," Ryder said with a lift of his brows. Dacre merely shrugged in response.

After a platter of figs and blanched almonds was brought in, along with wine, the talk turned to hunting, and the Dacres said they were having problems with locals poaching within the priory grounds. When the conversation began to flag, Ryder smiled and said, "It grows late. Will you excuse me? I must be on my way." Lady Dacre rose, and the others did likewise. Ryder turned to Maddy and said, "Perhaps you may visit my father and me on market days?" Then he hesitantly glanced at their hostess. He played the game well.

```
        Checked out item summary for
                CLARK, MARJERY G
              01-03-2020 04:55PM

ARCODE: 11518045909jcpp
OCATION: 9jcpp
ITLE: Mistress Spy / Pamela Mingle.
UE DATE: 02-14-2020  * RENEWED
```

"We shall bid you farewell, then, Master Ryder. Mistress Madeleine will have market day afternoons to spend as she likes." She turned to Maddy and said, "Join me in the drawing room when you've parted from your cousin, my dear."

"That is kind of you, madam. I won't be long."

A servant brought Ryder's cloak. He and Maddy spoke nary a word until they arrived at the outer door and she slipped outside with him. A lad was bringing his horse, and the footman who had accompanied them to the priory was already mounted and leading the packhorse. "We have only a moment of privacy," Ryder said. "Have a care around Master Vine. I do not trust him. He has the look of a border reiver about him."

Because he is one. Should she tell him the truth about Vine? Not now. It would take too long to explain.

"Anything you may learn about the Scots queen, take note of. Even if it does not seem relevant. You must go inside. You are shivering with cold."

Was she indeed shivering with cold, or was it apprehension? Despite her hostility toward Nicholas Ryder, she felt tethered to him. She understood how things lay between them. Maddy did not want him to abandon her to these people, especially not with John Musgrave in residence. Faint candlelight shone from the entryway window. It had begun to snow, and big, lacy flakes settled in his dark hair. "Will you ride all the way to Carlisle tonight?"

"Nay, only to Brampton. Are you well, Mistress Vernon?" he asked gently. His eyes reflected the candlelight, giving them a soft glow.

"I am...ready. Farewell. Go, before you freeze."

He mounted. "Until Wednesday, then."

• • •

The snow fell thicker, heavier as Nicholas rode toward
Brampton. He kept his mount to a trot, slowing to a walk
when the terrain grew perilous. In the darkness, he could not
see icy patches.

Several things about Lanercost made him uneasy, and he
misliked leaving Madeleine Vernon there. Lady Dacre, while
welcoming, lacked warmth. Her son Christopher possessed a
weak chin and a gimlet eye. But Thomas Vine topped the list
of his concerns.

The fellow was an outlaw, an obvious conclusion given
his unkempt appearance and rough manner. Nicholas had
caught him leering at Madeleine more than once. Jesu, he
should have given her a stronger and more specific warning.
The lass was not experienced in seduction, he was sure, and
may be too naive to know when a man wanted to have his
way with her. A thought flitted across his mind and gave him
pause. The first man to bed her, to teach her the ways of the
flesh, would be lucky indeed. In a different world, Nicholas
could be that man.

As he dismounted and walked into the house, he chided
himself with the reminder that the only matter he should care
about was the efficacy of the information she would obtain
to aid their goals. Madeleine Vernon was not young. Many
women were already wed at her age, and she was no fool. By
the end of his ride, he had concluded she could hold her own
with Thomas Vine. He threw his gloves, whip, and cloak to a
bench and went in search of a warm drink.

Chapter Five

Maddy made her way back to the drawing room. The men had returned to their chessboard, but she could feel Musgrave's eyes on her. She ignored him. Cold to the bone and annoyed that she hadn't been shown her chamber or given an opportunity to refresh herself, she addressed Lady Dacre, probably too brusquely. "Pray, madam, where is my trunk? I would like to have my short cloak to put around my shoulders."

She looked taken aback. "My dear girl, how thoughtless of me." Hurrying to the door, she summoned a servant.

The woman, whose name was Edith, appeared almost immediately, and Lady Dacre directed her to escort Maddy to her chamber. "Your belongings have already been placed there," she said. "You will please tell me if you are lacking anything."

"Thank you, my lady. Shall I return here?"

"Yes, for a short time. I know you must be tired, but I think it would be wise for us to talk about your duties before we retire."

She curtsied and followed Edith. To her surprise, her chamber was not in the vicarage. In fact, reaching it meant exiting the building and entering the hall through a side door, traversing its length, and finally entering the tower. The kitchen was on the ground floor, and she could see the potboy, still hard at work. A kitchen maid was sweeping up. They climbed a stairway to the rooms above. Edith opened a door, walked in, and lit a candle for Maddy from the one she held.

"I'll wait for you in the passageway, mistress."

Maddy breathed a sigh of relief when she saw that the windows were glazed and a fire was burning in the hearth. Spying on Lady Dacre, finding an opportunity to look through her letters, would be difficult at this far remove. She sifted through her trunk and pulled out her short cloak, then looked under the bed for a chamber pot. God be thanked, she found one, and after using it, poured water from a ewer into the bowl on the washing stand and washed her hands.

Back in the passageway she noticed there were two other chambers. "Is anybody else staying up here, Edith?"

"No, mistress. Only you."

Lady Dacre's head bobbed up when Maddy returned to the drawing room, and she thought the older woman must have dozed off. The two men were nowhere in sight. She invited Maddy to sit across from her in one of the chairs before the fire. "I am sorry you must stay in the tower, Mistress Madeleine. Because Master Vine is visiting, there is no spare chamber for you here." Since the vicarage seemed spacious, Maddy wondered if her location wasn't due to her status in the household rather than the lack of available rooms.

Since Maddy could not say how relieved she was to know that Musgrave's chamber was nowhere near hers, she merely said, "It will suit me well. Chambers above the kitchens are always the warmest."

Smiling, Lady Dacre picked up a leather-bound volume from a side table and handed it to Maddy. At first glance, she thought it was a Book of Hours, although a very austere one. "Open it," she said. Maddy did so and was shocked to see she was holding a Bible. She must have gasped, because the other woman chuckled. "Have you never seen one?"

"Of course, but only in a priest's hands." Roman Catholics did not own Bibles. Few people did. She turned the pages with the utmost care. There was no decoration, no illumination of any kind, not even for the names of the books, and it was in English.

After she'd had a chance to leaf through it for a few moments, Lady Dacre said, "I do not read, beyond a few words. I never learned, and I'm too old to start now."

"You would like me to read to you from the Bible."

"Yes. Not now, the hour is too late. We will begin tomorrow. I enjoy poetry, too."

"My cousin told me you may need my help with your correspondence."

"Christopher has been assisting me with that task, but I know he finds it odious. Since much of it concerns a lawsuit one of my other stepsons has filed against me, it is awkward for him. You do not need to know the details; I only need you to read the letters to me and record my replies."

Maddy nodded and Lady Dacre went on. "I am an early riser."

"So am I, my lady."

"Good. I say my prayers in my chamber, and you may do the same. Afterward, I break my fast in the small dining room where we supped tonight. You may join me there. I am a needlewoman, Mistress Madeleine, and I spend much of the morning stitching."

"I take great pleasure in needlework as well."

"I will want you to read to me while I'm sewing," she said,

"but I will also allow you time for your own stitching."

Maddy's face heated. "Aye, that is kind of you, madam."
So far, her employer had exhibited no lightheartedness or
sense of humor. The days would be long indeed if she was
always so serious. Maddy pictured herself nodding off while
reading a Bible story out loud.

"After dinner, which is served midday, I rest for two hours.
Some days I will have work for you to complete during that
time; other days, you may do what you like. When I awake,
I work on my correspondence. I will, of course, require your
assistance for that."

Nothing she had said seemed to require a response from
Maddy, so she remained silent. "We sup around six of the
clock, and in the evenings I like to sew, if there is sufficient
light. Sometimes I play cards with my son and his friend."

Maddy stifled a yawn.

"Enough for now," Lady Dacre said. "I am tired, and I
can see that you are, too."

In the passage, they both lit candles and went their
separate ways. When Maddy stepped outside into the cold,
a blast of wind laden with stinging snow blew in her face
and extinguished the candle. She would have to feel her way
through the hall. Hurrying inside, Maddy wondered if Ryder
had arrived in Brampton yet. The weather would slow his
progress.

The large expanse of the hall was dark as ink, and she
doubted the single candle would have been much help. She
wanted to run, to reach the stairway quickly, but she couldn't
see well enough. Suddenly, a figure stepped out of the
shadows, and Maddy froze. It took only a moment to realize
who it was. Musgrave. He towered over her. Before she could
speak, he reached for her hand. "Let me guide you to your
chamber, Madeleine," he said, in that low, seductive voice of
his. "'Tis difficult to see in the creeping darkness."

Outraged, she pulled her hand behind her back. "Mistress Vernon, to you. And I am not letting you anywhere near my chamber." Her voice was pathetically shaky.

"It would be easier to talk in private. And wiser."

"Say now whatever it is you came to say. There is no one about."

"I could force you there, Madeleine."

"Aye, you could. But what will Lady Dacre say when I tell her?"

He sighed and looked away. When he turned back, he seemed resigned. "What are you doing here?"

"I might ask the same thing of you. Thomas Vine, indeed."

He grabbed Maddy's arm and dug his fingers in.

"Lady Dacre desired a companion and secretary. I needed employment," she almost squealed.

His grip eased.

"She does not know about your brother."

So he'd heard. "No."

"Who is Ryder?"

This was tricky. Maddy wished she'd had time to think about what to say before he confronted her. "A distant cousin," she said. "He learned of my predicament."

"If Lady Dacre knew about your brother, she would probably rid herself of you faster than King Henry shed his wives. She's angry about the rebellion."

"I worked that out on my own. And what if she learns of your duplicity? Why are you calling yourself Thomas Vine?"

"That is none of your concern. And if you dare to reveal my identity, I'll tell her what a lying little whore you are."

"I can see you have not changed. Not that I would have expected you to, if I'd given you a moment's thought." Even though Maddy knew what he was—a thief and probably a murderer—his words still stung. She'd fallen under his spell at one time, had even childishly thought he loved her. There was one thing in her favor, though. Musgrave did not appear to know about her involvement in the Dacre raid. God be thanked for that, at least.

"Go about your work as a companion, and I will attend to my own affairs. See that you stay out of my business."

She nodded and started forward, wondering exactly what that business could be. Maddy had nothing more to say to him. For a moment, she thought he intended to block her way, but he stepped aside. It seemed to take forever to get to her chamber. Her legs were trembling so hard she collapsed onto the bed, pausing only to set the candleholder down. Was she in danger of being accosted by him every time she passed through the hall?

A servant had recently been in to add another log to the fire. When she felt strong enough, Maddy stood before the hearth and undressed down to her smock. Unlacing a bodice without help was difficult, but she managed. She'd done it before. She threw the cloak back around her shoulders and retrieved the coffer Ryder had insisted she bring with her. Since nothing inside truly belonged to her, Maddy wasn't sure why it drew her. The key was in the lock; she turned it and lifted the lid.

To her astonishment, her brother's dirk was resting on the top. The one that had been confiscated the night of the raid, in its scabbard. A sheet of foolscap was wrapped around it and secured with a string. She read the message: *Mistress Vernon, in the event you need to defend yourself, you should have possession of your weapon.* It was signed *NR.* No wasted words there. Throwing the note on the fire, Maddy watched it catch, curl, and burn to ashes. He'd taken a foolish risk, with both the dirk and the note. Anybody could have searched the unlocked coffer during the evening.

Her door did not have a lock—it would have been quite unusual if it had. Maddy was too exhausted to worry overmuch about it. She shoved the dirk under her pillow. In the morning, she would lock it in the coffer and tuck the key into a pocket sewn into her skirts.

• • •

Each time he returned home after an assignment, Nicholas had to reaccustom himself to life in Brampton. To hearing his father's endless barrage of criticism about how he was handling a prisoner. This time would be no different. Now, though, he had his nephew, Daniel, to distract him and buoy his spirits. Outside Francis Ryder's library, Nicholas kneeled in front of the lad and said, "You know you cannot come with me when I talk to your grandfather. Find Margery. She will be good company for you until I am free." Margery was a housemaid with whom Daniel had formed a special bond, and Nicholas trusted her absolutely. For a moment, it looked as though the lad might cry—his uncle had only just arrived home, after all—but in the end, he blinked away the tears and ran off.

Getting to his feet, Nicholas watched for a moment. At odd times, he felt a tightness in his chest, an overwhelming sadness for Daniel. He followed Nicholas about, from his study to his chamber, from the kitchens to the stables. He was always at his heels. Daniel's favorite place was the glass house adjacent to the kitchens. After a visit to the botanic gardens in London, Nicholas had begun importing roses from the New World. Now he'd progressed to growing them himself, an enterprise his father thought completely useless.

Nicholas spoke an endless stream of words to the small lad, but, sadly, Daniel never answered. He hadn't uttered a word since his father's death. A bright child, he clearly understood all that was being said. His lack of speech had nothing to do with his intelligence. Before Richard died, the boy had been articulate for his age, and in a typical childlike way, had not had any hesitance about expressing himself. But it was as if, when he'd lost his father, his words had been taken away from him, too.

Nicholas knocked on the door of Francis Ryder's inner sanctum and entered without waiting for permission.

"Coddling that boy again, are you?"

"Good morrow, Father," he said, ignoring the comment about Daniel.

"Is the Vernon wench in place?"

Nicholas glanced at the map pinned to the wall behind the desk. It was crude—he'd drawn it himself—and represented the clans over the border. He'd drawn Xs with a quill to show the suspected location of the rebels.

Pulling his eyes away, he said, "She is. I supped with them before taking my leave."

"Ah. Who else was present?"

"As we thought, Christopher Dacre. And a fellow who was introduced as a 'friend,' one Thomas Vine from London."

"Vine, eh? Never heard of him."

Nicholas shrugged. "It could be an alias. I did not like the look of him. We should delve into his background."

"Indeed. I'll send a messenger to London. What did this Vine have to say for himself?"

"He knew about the queen's intent to send her army on raids into Scotland to find the rebels, whom he condemned as fools. Neither Lady Dacre nor her son had much to say about the rebellion, although she took the part of the Scots queen as regards to her child being separated from her."

"How do you think the girl will get on?"

"Well enough. She seemed at ease during the meal, although she was quiet. She spoke only when someone asked her a question." Fleetingly, he recalled Madeleine Vernon's blue-green eyes and the look of vulnerability reflected in their depths when he took his leave. He hadn't wanted to part from her, but Nicholas could not afford to think of her as anything other than his spy. To successfully complete this mission and his service to the queen, he must focus on the task at hand. A satisfactory end to this business would ensure his freedom, and that was his ultimate goal. His fears had eased about her situation at Lanercost Priory. Apart from Vine's presence, it was a relatively safe situation, and they should soon learn more about the man.

"A proper young woman, then," his father said, "who knows her place. Lady Dacre will appreciate that. Does she have the resolve to carry out her instructions? That is what we should be concerned about."

"I believe so, but she is, of course, an unwilling participant in this endeavor. How far she can be trusted, I do not yet know."

His father banged a fist down on the desk. "Did you give her the ultimatum, as you were instructed to do?"

"I did," Nicholas said evenly. "I told you that at the castle." In the last year, he had found that the most effective reaction to his father's bursts of temper was to remain calm. "Mistress Vernon expressed an interest in remaining alive."

"Then she has every reason to do as you bid."

"So it would seem. She will come here on market days to make her reports. I do not expect her to find out much of anything helpful this first week."

Fingers steepled, his father looked thoughtful.

What now?

"I do not care for the unexpected presence of this Thomas Vine at the priory. We expected there might be a guest present, but not a suspicious one. It would behoove us to keep watch on that situation."

Nicholas's annoyance grew. "Meaning what?"

"I want you to pay a visit to Mistress Vernon in the next

few days. Clandestinely, of course. Find out how she's faring and what she's learned of this Vine character."

That was the last thing Nicholas wanted. He was Madeleine's spymaster, the man controlling her every move. He felt drawn to her in a way that gave the lie to that relationship, and further contact would only intensify his feelings. Any dallying with the spies under one's command was strictly forbidden by Cecil, the queen's chief councilor. "It is too soon, Father," he protested. "She won't know anything yet."

Francis Ryder leaned across his desk. "It matters not how you arrange it, but I want it done."

In no mood for an argument, Nicholas nodded. "I should go and find Daniel, if there's nothing more."

"That boy could talk if he wanted to," the old man said. "One of these days he'll speak, if he knows what's good for him."

"He will talk again in his own good time. The physician said we must not press him."

Impatiently, his father waved a hand through the air, which Nicholas considered a dismissal. He left his parent to his papers, dispatches, and maps.

It was yet too cold for Daniel to play outside, although Nicholas often led him about on his pony, even in the coldest weather, for the benefit of some fresh air for them both. He knew Margery would not have ventured out, so he headed for the glass house, trusting that Daniel would find him there. His plants no doubt had been sorely neglected during the weeks he'd spent at the castle.

He puttered about, watering, pruning, cutting away dead foliage, and thinking about Mistress Madeleine Vernon in a desultory way. She was an interesting creature. She had borne her imprisonment stoically, and once she had agreed to work for him, hadn't expressed any trepidation or hesitance.

He admired her for that. He was having difficulty dismissing her image from his mind. The glorious hair. The entrancing blue-green eyes...

Give over, man.

He dragged a barrel over and swept the detritus of his work into it. And then he heard a giggle, which he pretended not to notice. It was a game he often played with Daniel, his favorite. "*Hmm.* I wonder what that noise was. There must be a mouse in here. I shall have to call the mole catcher." Another partially stifled laugh. Nicholas rolled the barrel back to its place and turned to walk down the other side of the workbench. "Where could that diminutive, hairy pest be hiding?"

Daniel's small arse protruded from under a low shelf. "Ah! There's the mouse! Fie, away to the fields with you, Sir Mouse!" He pounced on him, gathering his squirming little body into his arms. Every time they played this game, he expected the lad to beg for mercy, but he never had. Nor did he now. Nicholas made as if to open the door and cast him out. Daniel stopped laughing and shook his head vigorously. The game was finished.

"What shall we do now, young Master Mouse?" Daniel shook his head, then swept into a bow. Odd that Nicholas understood him through his gestures and expressions. "You wish to be called 'Sir Mouse?' Are you a knight, Sir Mouse? Shall we do a bit of jousting?" A smile and nod from Daniel, and they were off riding their imaginary destriers.

For the remainder of the evening, Nicholas pondered ways to secretly visit Madeleine Vernon, until at last he concocted a viable plan.

Chapter Six

The following day passed exactly as Maddy's employer had described. In the morning, when she entered the small dining chamber, her mistress was already at the table. "Good morrow, my lady."

"I trust you slept well? Were you warm enough?"

"I was. And thank you for sending Edith to me this morning. It is difficult to lace one's own bodice." Maddy sat down and cut herself a slice of bread and a few slivers of cheese. Figs were on offer too, so she helped herself to a few. Since she'd been too tense to eat much the night before, her empty stomach begged for sustenance.

She was savoring a bite of the rich cheese when Lady Dacre spoke. "May I call you Madeleine? Mistress Madeleine is a mouthful, is it not?"

Maddy smiled. "Pray do." They finished their meal and then proceeded to the drawing room.

When they had seated themselves by the fire, Lady Dacre handed her the Bible. "Will you read the book of Ruth? It is my favorite Bible story." After Maddy began to read, the older woman collected her embroidery from a basket.

Maddy decided the only way to keep her mind from wandering would be to make a game of it, to challenge herself to become first Ruth, then Naomi. Apparently, her mistress enjoyed it.

"You read very well, Madeleine," she said. Maddy held back a smile and thanked her. At the lady's request, she moved on to Psalms. If she were doomed to read these stories and psalms all day, Maddy thought she might die of boredom. Finally, Lady Dacre said, "Go, rest and refresh yourself, and collect your sewing things. I must talk to the cook about the day's meals."

The path to the tower had been swept clean, and the fresh snow sparkled like the queen's jewels in the brilliant winter sunlight. If she'd had the time to bundle up, Maddy would have enjoyed a walk. Perhaps later, while Lady Dacre had her afternoon rest. She refreshed herself and returned to the vicarage. Climbing the steps, she heard male voices, so clearly they had to be coming from a chamber off the gallery. As far as she knew, no other men were in residence besides Christopher Dacre and John Musgrave. She stopped but did not dare draw closer. Even so, she could make out some of the words.

"…your scheme is ridiculous…Scots might capture…kill you." That was Musgrave.

Then Christopher Dacre's voice. "We need a leader…one of the earls. 'Tis said…Ferniehurst shelters…find him easily enough." From within the room, boot heels thudded against the floor, and Maddy hurried on. She half expected Musgrave to fling the door open and chase her, but she made it to the drawing room unimpeded and breathed a sigh of relief.

Lady Dacre was not yet there. Maddy stood by the hearth and whispered what she'd learned over and over so she wouldn't forget. She knew of Ferniehurst; he was a powerful

Scottish laird who, according to what she'd overheard, was
hiding "one of the earls," and maybe some of his men, at his
castle over the border. It had to be the Earl of Westmoreland,
if what Ryder had told her about Northumberland was true,
that he was Hector Armstrong's prisoner. A bit of news for
Ryder, if he did not already know. Was Christopher Dacre
planning a raid over the border to come to the aid of the
rebels? Musgrave had sounded as though he thought such an
idea was mad.

"Do you have your embroidery, Madeleine?"

She started. Lady Dacre had returned, and Maddy had
been so caught up in her musings she hadn't even noticed.
She must be more alert, or at least make sure her back was
never to the door. Falling so deeply into thought would not
serve her well. "Aye, madam, I do."

"Let me see your design and your stitching, then."

Maddy unfolded a canvas begun at Carlisle Castle. It was
a floral design of violets, cowslips, and gillyflowers, chosen
because of the colors of the silks she'd found in the hempen
bag.

Lady Dacre peered at Maddy's work. "You've made a
good start."

Hmm. Faint praise if she ever heard it, but no matter. The
room was finally beginning to warm. They sat quietly and
sewed for some time. Lady Dacre broke the silence with a
question. "Do you want to know why I like the book of Ruth
so well?"

"Of course, if you wish to tell me."

"With little care for her own wants or desires, Ruth
pledges herself to Naomi. Even when Naomi urges her to
return to her own people, Ruth is adamant. I like that."

"'Whither thou goest, I shall go also.' Ruth shows great
love and loyalty to her mother-in-law, it is true."

The older woman sighed. She did not say it, but Maddy

wondered if she was thinking of her stepson, the one who was suing her. Thus far, Maddy did not believe the woman's legal dilemma would be related to her work here, but it couldn't hurt to find out what she could about it. From Lady Dacre's description, it sounded as though it was the primary subject of her correspondence, so Maddy need only do what she was meant to be doing to learn more.

That afternoon she donned her long cloak with the hood and her warm boots and gloves. She walked the length of the hall—in daylight a magnificent room with its high, beamed ceiling, enormous fireplace, and colorful wall paintings—and exited at the far end nearest the church. Standing before the west front of the beautiful old building, she admired its arched door and tall slender windows. And of course, the statue of Mary Magdalene, its patron saint, nestled into the gable. Maddy held very still and imagined she could hear the canons singing their prayers.

Footsteps came crunching up behind her. Swiveling around, she fully expected to see John Musgrave. But it was Christopher Dacre who approached.

"How now, mistress?"

She curtsied. "Sir. I thought to explore while your mother rested."

He smiled. "Aye, 'tis a good time for it. She likes her afternoon respite." His glance swept upward, taking in the facade of the church. "Did you know it dates from the twelfth century? Made from the stone of the great Roman wall, as are the other buildings at the priory."

"I thought it might be quite old." And even though she already knew the answer, Maddy asked a question. "How did your family come to own the priory?"

He looked at her then, but not with any annoyance. "Ah. That was good King Henry.

"Sir Thomas's reward for his role at Solway Moss, and for

supporting the reformed church."

Solway Moss was a battle fought with the Scots a few years before she'd been born. Now that he'd raised the topic of rebellions, Maddy decided to try a bit of prying. "I collect you and your stepmother opposed the recent...trouble here in the north?"

"It accomplished nothing except to give the queen a stronger and more visible presence in these parts. And to make her more suspicious of all of us northerners."

"But you are loyal to the queen. Why should you be disturbed about that?"

He shrugged. "We like to keep our own counsel here. As with any monarch, there are certain laws and practices with which we take exception." Just as she was poised to ask him to elaborate, he inclined his head toward the church and said, "Would you like to go inside? It's quite beautiful."

"Another day. I do not want to be gone too long."

"Then let's go on. It is too cold to stand in one place." Dacre took her elbow and moved toward the Lanercost Cross. The very place she was meant to leave messages for Ryder if the need should arise.

The grand stone shaft arrowed above them. "It's quite imposing. What is the inscription?" It was in Latin, of course.

"It mainly tells us when it was made, 1214. When Innocent III was Pope, and John reigned in England and Philip in France." Maddy glanced at the base, but since it was covered in snow, she could not make out where the loose stone might be. She hoped she wouldn't be forced to employ it, in any case, since it would mean she was in trouble. Out here in the open as it was, Maddy did not see how she could place something there and not be found out. Ryder had recommended darkness, but how would she ever find the loose stone at night?

They turned and walked toward the gatehouse and

precinct wall. Had the snow been any deeper, they could not have managed. Dacre chattered on about the history of the structures, giving her an opportunity to study his profile. He possessed a receding chin, hidden by his meager beard. And when he looked at her full on, she noticed his eyes were very close set. The overall effect was not pleasing.

She did not listen closely to his lecture but managed to utter appropriate responses now and then. Following the wall, they eventually reached the stables. The blacksmith's forge was fired, and he loomed over it with his bellows. He was in shirtsleeves, and with every push of the handles, his huge muscles bulged. Dacre introduced her.

"Mistress Madeleine, meet Matthew, the best smith in the county."

Matthew had a hearty laugh. He bowed and said, "Welcome to the priory, mistress. Looking about the place, are you?"

"Aye. I hoped to get my bearings." Maddy edged closer to the blazing warmth of the forge.

"You'd best get her inside, Master Dacre. She looks half-frozen. And her feet are wet."

"No, I assure you, they are not. My boots are damp on the outside, but my feet are dry." She smiled sheepishly. "They feel like ice, though."

"Matthew is right, then. The sun is already low. Do you wish to return to your chamber, mistress, or to the vicarage?"

"The vicarage, sir. I am afraid your mother may be awake and wondering where I am."

After they bid farewell to Matthew, a couple of frightening-looking dogs appeared. Dacre called to them. "These are my coursers, Irish wolfhounds. I call them Devil and Prince. Beautiful, are they not?"

"They are indeed." They looked rather menacing to Maddy, and appropriately named. She knew coursers were

trained to stalk and trap their prey and go about it very
silently. She would steer clear of them. Another smaller dog
ran up behind them, a beagle.

"Oh, this one is more to my liking," she said.

Dacre laughed. "That dog is useless. For some reason,
her scenting ability has never developed."

"What is she called?"

"Useless. That is her name."

Maddy frowned. "Oh, no. You cannot be serious."

He laughed. "I'm afraid it is true."

They had crossed the courtyard. The two hounds had
run off, but little Useless still trailed along behind them. "I
believe I will stop off in my chamber," Maddy said. "Thank
you for showing me around, sir."

"Until supper, then, mistress." He opened the tower door
for her, and she stepped through. After a moment, Maddy
cautiously unlatched the door and peeked out. Dacre was
gone. Useless was sitting there as if expecting her, head
cocked to one side and floppy ears dangling.

"Come, little one," she said. The dog leaped over the
threshold and followed Maddy down the long hall and up the
stairs.

Our Lady Virgin be thanked, she had found a friend.

"Ah, there you are," Lady Dacre said when Maddy entered
her bedchamber. She was most grateful to see a fire crackling
in the hearth, warming the room. Her feet would thaw while
she worked.

"I hope I haven't kept you waiting, my lady. I was outside
exploring when I met your stepson, and he wished to show me
around the property." Maddy was surprised by the disarray in
Lady Dacre's chamber. Her sewing tools, her embroidery silks

and canvases, from what she'd observed, were sorted neatly, allowing her ease in finding what she needed. This room, by contrast, was disordered and messy. Stacks of foolscap lay on tables, on the settle, even on her bed. A few dusty tomes that looked as though they might be law books rested on a shelf. She certainly wasn't reading them, so Maddy assumed her stepson was.

"He is fond of the place and enjoys showing it off." She motioned to a stack of fresh paper, an ink jar, and some quills. "Use the small writing table. I must dictate a reply to a missive I received a few days since."

Maddy seated herself, dated the letter, and asked to whom she was writing. Lady Dacre told her the name of the solicitor and the direction, which was in York, then began to dictate the body of the letter:

3 March 1570

Sir:

The claim lately made by my stepson, William Dacre, that my husband was not of sound mind when he made his will, has no credibility. I am enclosing written and signed statements from several of Sir Thomas's friends and family members attesting to the fact that he was of sound mind, having absolutely no impairment, when he made his last will and testament. These offer unquestionable proof, and I trust will bring an end to this matter.

Maddy had to ask her to speak more slowly, and to repeat a word or phrase a few times, but for the most part, the process went smoothly. When they were done, she asked Maddy to read it out loud and make a note of the date and nature of her reply, so that she would have a record of her response.

"Now, I must locate the statements. Where did I put them?" She flung her arms up, looking so rattled that Maddy offered to help.

"Pray do. Look through the documents on the settle." Maddy picked up the stack she'd pointed to, and it was then that she noticed strands of embroidery floss adhering to each separate document in the pile. The papers she was leafing through were marked with green threads that had been glued on.

"My lady," she said, puzzled. "Why have you put embroidery silks on your documents?" And then she blushed, because she'd worked out the answer before she finished speaking. "Never mind. That was very ingenious of you."

Maddy feared Lady Dacre might be annoyed with the question, but she smiled. "I had to invent a system so I could keep track of which documents were in which stack."

"What color thread marks the statements?"

"Red."

Although she didn't see any red, Maddy glanced at each page anyway, trying to find clues that would identify the statements, but they all seemed irrelevant. "These look like they have to do with the priory. Expenditures and bills of sale," she said. "That sort of thing. And they are all marked with green thread."

Busy sorting through her own stacks, Lady Dacre merely grunted in response. Maddy moved to another pile, this one on the mantel. Just as she began examining the document on top, her mistress shrieked. "Cease! Put that down!"

Maddy complied immediately. "Pray pardon me, madam. I thought you wanted me—"

She raised her palms in exasperation, stopping her. "Let us be done for today. You are excused until supper."

"Aye, my lady." Maddy bobbed a respectful curtsy and hurried toward the door. Before she made her escape, her employer said, coldly, "Never look at any papers I haven't explicitly given you permission to examine."

Maddy nodded, trying to look contrite. She had dropped the letter like a hot coal, but not before noticing it was marked by blue thread and signed by Thomas Howard, Fourth Duke of Norfolk.

Maddy castigated herself for making such a foolish mistake. Now the woman would probably be suspicious of her. By God's light, she hadn't even been trying to snoop. She should have realized, she should have *asked* where to look next. Now she would need to sneak back into Lady Dacre's chamber and try to read the Duke of Norfolk's letter. And she should do it before her first visit with Nicholas Ryder in five days. If Maddy didn't provide him with the information he required, she could be sent back to her cell at Carlisle Castle and eventually tried for treason. The chances of that ending well were miniscule.

Chapter Seven

After her abrupt dismissal, Maddy returned to her chamber to find Useless curled up before the hearth. She stretched out on her bed, and the wee dog leaped up and lay down as close to her as she could possibly get. Her warm little body snuggled up against Maddy felt entirely pleasurable. She worried, though, that one of the maids would find the pup and shoo her outside.

Why would Lady Jane Dacre be corresponding with the Duke of Norfolk? It was common knowledge that he was the queen's guest—in the tower—for scheming to wed Mary Stewart, the Scots queen, without Elizabeth's permission. Ryder might have an idea. But when and how would she be able to gain access to Lady Dacre's chamber to find that letter? How unfortunate that her employer worked from there rather than a library or office. The only way Maddy could safely search would be if she were not at home, and Maddy had the impression that happened rarely.

Nothing foolproof came to her. This was only her first full day at the priory, and she would need to bide her time and get a better sense of how the days passed. Not only what Lady Dacre did, but also her son and John Musgrave.

The next few days afforded Maddy with opportunities to find out more about the activities of Masters Dacre and Musgrave, but she did not discover anything of great import. Or any import at all, truth be known.

Although the weather wasn't suitable for hunting or hawking, the two men rode every day. More than once, she spotted Dacre riding about the property, stopping here and there to speak to laborers. Where John Musgrave rode, she could not say. He disappeared for long stretches, only returning in time for the evening meal.

There was one thing that disturbed her about Musgrave, though it would be of no interest to Ryder. He paid an immoderate amount of attention to the very pretty serving girl who brought their meals, and she—her name was Cath— seemed to encourage it. Perhaps Maddy noticed it only because of her past with the man. A gentle teasing, a wink, that was all it amounted to. Until one night, quite deliberately, so that Maddy would see, he slid his hand up Cath's leg. He was staring directly at Maddy while he did it, taunting her.

What concerned her was Cath's innocence. She could not have been more than fifteen or sixteen, and Maddy feared she did not understand what dallying with Musgrave could mean. She would continue to observe and try to judge whether it was seduction or simply a foolish game he was playing, designed to exasperate Maddy. Perhaps he had asked Cath to go along with it.

If the men remained at the priory in the evenings, they played chess or primero, and Lady Dacre sometimes joined them in the latter. They invited her as well, but she had no money to gamble. They must have understood this, because they did not ask again. More often than not, the two men rode off in the evenings. Probably to the alehouse in Brampton. Drinking, gaming, and whoring, if Maddy had to guess.

Dacre was all affability with her, as he had been the day he led her around the priory, and God be thanked, Musgrave ignored her other than what the demands of politeness in front of others required.

Maddy and her mistress plodded along with their routine. The older woman had not raised her voice with Maddy again—indeed she'd given her no reason to—nor asked her to look through any of her stacks of documents, which were legion. One afternoon while Maddy waited at length for her to locate a letter requiring a response, she blurted out, "Madam, would you like me to sort your papers for you? You and your son could remove anything private that you did not wish me to see."

At first Maddy thought she was angry. Abruptly, Lady Dacre lowered herself to the bed, still rumpled from her afternoon rest. Her fingers rubbed the gold cross she wore about her neck. She seemed to draw comfort from it. "It's all become so daunting," she said.

Glancing about the room at the papers piled on every available surface, Maddy understood how that might have happened. "That is a marvelous idea, Madeleine," she said. "I grow weary of this arduous duty. It is a constant thorn in my side."

"You are tired, my lady. I can see that you do not feel well." Indeed, she was pale and drawn. "May I call for wine or ale?"

She nodded. "Spiced wine, pray." Maddy quickly found Edith, who brought the wine, and after Lady Dacre had drunk a glass, her color improved and she seemed to regain some of her strength. "Pray forgive me for behaving like an old woman," she said. This was the nearest she'd come to joking with Maddy.

"You are far from that, madam. This task is overwhelming."

"William makes one claim after another, and the estate cannot be settled until we have dealt with them all." Massaging her forehead, she continued. "Christopher has helped, but, as I told you, it is uncomfortable for him since it is his own brother making the claims. He is very circumspect in what he says. I am never sure if he remains with me because he hopes to inherit the priory someday, or if he simply believes Will is being wrongheaded."

Maddy made a sympathetic face. Indeed, she was sorry for Lady Dacre. She wondered if Christopher Dacre remained loyal for other reasons. Reasons related to the priory's location near the border, for whatever schemes he might have in mind. This information may not be useful to Ryder, but she would tell him nonetheless. As she'd warned him, she was in no position to judge whether something was significant or not.

"I'll need some time to remove certain documents. When I've done that, you may begin your organizing. I shall ask the steward to be on the lookout for suitable containers. I have a locked coffer for my personal and private papers. I keep the key with me at all times." Lady Dacre wore household keys attached to a girdle at her waist, and Maddy guessed it must be one of those.

Her spirits plunged. She'd never be able to see what was in that coffer unless she found a way to gain access to the keys. If Maddy could sneak into Lady Dacre's chamber before she had a chance to lock up the letter from Norfolk, that would afford her the best chance. She wouldn't need the key. But still, she did not think she could manage it before her first visit with Ryder, not unless everybody had occasion to leave the priory at the same time. Maddy prayed he would not expect too much in scarcely a week.

One evening Lady Dacre retired early, and Maddy did likewise. Lighted candle in hand, she made her way the length of the banquet hall and up the stairs to her chamber. Useless was curled up on the bed and whimpered with excitement when Maddy entered. It occurred to her that the little dog would need to relieve herself before settling in for the night. With a sigh, Maddy donned her woolen riding cloak, warmest boots, and gloves. She lifted the dog into her arms and retraced her steps from a few moments ago. Once outside, she set Useless down and hoped she would take care of her needs as speedily as possible. It was abominably cold.

To her dismay, Useless dashed around the corner of the building and out of sight. Maddy had no choice but to follow. She didn't want to lose the little scamp and be forced to track her down. As she rounded the corner, a figure dressed in dark clothing emerged from the shadows. She gasped. *Jesu.* Was it Musgrave?

The figure stepped toward her and removed his cap. It was Nicholas Ryder.

"By God's light, you gave me a fright," Maddy said. "What are you doing here, lurking about?"

"I might ask you the same question."

Useless, having finished her business, now pranced through the snow toward Maddy. Ryder chuckled. "You have a dog. How domestic of you. A sign you've settled in."

Maddy judged a response wasn't required and bent to gather Useless into her arms.

"I have endured a long, freezing ride, my horse losing his footing on the ice and nearly throwing me more than once. May we speak inside?" He glanced at the door to the hall.

"Very well, but we must be very quiet. We dare not risk waking anybody."

• • •

Nicholas followed Maddy into the hall, where the temperature was not a great deal warmer. No matter, this business would be concluded swiftly. They stood before the massive grate, and Nicholas could feel cold air blowing down the chimney. "Let us move away from this damnable draft," he said, proceeding toward the center of the hall.

Madeleine spoke in a low voice. "This is far enough. We dare not go any closer to the kitchen, where a few servants sleep by the hearth."

He nodded his agreement. "God's breath, it is darker in here than outside."

"Why have you come, sir?"

"The presence of Thomas Vine at the priory was unanticipated and is potentially a threat. What have you been able to learn about him?" His vision had adjusted to the dark, and now he could make out Madeleine's features. The luminous eyes. The flawless skin and perfect little nose. And when she lowered her hood, her glorious hair flowed around the column of her neck. He was mesmerized.

Get hold of yourself, man. Madeleine is a sweet morsel you will never taste.

"Nothing more. He and Christopher Dacre ride out during the day and play cards at night. That is, when they are not visiting the alehouse. I have seen very little of him."

Nicholas did not speak, merely waited.

"There is one thing, but it's nought to do with your concerns. He is attempting to seduce one of the serving girls."

"Nothing unusual about that."

She looked fierce. "Perhaps not, but the girl is quite young and surely still innocent. I am keeping an eye on the situation and intend to intervene if it continues."

"You?" He chortled. "What could you do? If anybody

interferes, it should be Lady Dacre."

"She has turned a blind eye, which I find puzzling. I'll speak to the cook if necessary. Perhaps the girl can be assigned other duties."

"This affair will be a distraction. You should be concerned with your mission, not Vine's philandering."

"If nobody else will speak up for her, I shall."

Nicholas had to admire her courage. She seemed to have an unending supply of it. A disturbing thought occurred to him. "He hasn't, ah, made advances toward you, has he?"

"No. He knows better."

"Meaning?"

"Meaning I give him no encouragement. I never look directly at him, and we barely speak beyond what is necessary for common courtesy."

Relief slid through him. "And there is nothing else you can tell me about him?"

"Why do you suspect him?" she said, deflecting his question.

"He claims to be from London, and indeed, knows the Town gossip, yet he looks rough. Not at all like a denizen of a great city. We had no intelligence that he was residing here."

She shrugged. "You can't know everything, can you? What you say of him is true, and I will be on my guard around him. But I'm afraid I cannot enlighten you further."

Madeleine seemed wary. Was she keeping something from him? He grabbed hold of her arm and pulled her closer. "If you are withholding information, it will only bring trouble."

"I swear, there is nothing."

They were at a stand, eyes blazing at each other. Neither moved. Nicholas softened his grip on her arm but was reluctant to let her go. In fact, he'd love nothing more than to kiss that insouciant mouth.

Suddenly, the dog wiggled and yipped, and Madeleine tugged her arm from his grip. "Goodnight, Master Ryder. Safe journey home."

Nicholas watched her walk through the hall and waited to leave until he heard her climbing the stairs. Outside, he mounted and guided his horse toward the road to Brampton. Coming here had been a risk. He could easily have been discovered. But that wasn't the worst of it. He'd known it would be a mistake to see her again. Her visits on market days would be torture at this rate.

• • •

Maddy felt Ryder's eyes on her as she traversed the hall. She'd been trembling so hard she could barely walk. At the top of the stairs she paused, breathing a sigh of relief when she heard his footsteps and then the door latching. While she undressed, she mused about his reason for coming.

Someday he would find out about her history with Musgrave, and then what would happen? She should have told him, but she hadn't had the courage. And her past with Musgrave had nothing to do with her reason for being at the priory. Perhaps she would confess during her upcoming visit to his home in Brampton. For a moment, when he was clutching her arm, she thought he wanted to kiss her. In truth, she might have let him.

Maddy must keep her mind off Nicholas Ryder's attractions. She had more pressing matters to attend to.

Musgrave's lecherous interest in Cath continued and grew more daring. He had progressed to rubbing a hand over her buttocks when she was serving him, and Maddy had noticed him brushing against her breasts when he walked past the girl. The serving girl's expression, indeed, her whole demeanor, had changed. Where before she'd played along with his flirting, laughed and blushed, now she cowered when he was anywhere near. Maddy determined to speak with her. She was afraid of Musgrave, and with good reason, as Maddy knew too well.

After services on Sunday, instead of hurrying upstairs to her chamber she stopped by the kitchen and asked the cook if Cath was about.

"Aye, mistress, she's at the vicarage readying the small dining room for dinner."

"Will you send her to me when she returns? I'll be upstairs in my chamber."

Cook turned a suspicious glance on Maddy. "Be something wrong, mistress? Has she misbehaved?"

"Not at all," Maddy said, knowing this was not a satisfactory answer, but unwilling to explain further.

After a short time, she heard a timid rapping on her door. When she opened it, there stood Cath, with a wary look upon her face. "Come, Cath, and sit by the fire for a moment."

She seemed rooted to a spot just inside the door. "I cannot spare the time, mistress. Cook will be angry."

"Nonsense. I've told her I wished to speak with you, and this will not take long." Useless sidled over and leaned against Maddy's leg.

Cath's expression changed when she spied the beagle. "What is he called? I miss my dog."

"She's called Useless. Master Dacre named her that because she didn't satisfy as a hunting dog." They spent a few carefree moments discussing animals, during which time Cath joined Maddy on the settle.

She paused a moment to gather her thoughts. "Cath, I have noticed that Master Vine has been trifling with you. At first I thought you welcomed his attentions, but lately I've come to believe you are frightened of him." Maddy grasped her hands to reassure her. "Am I right?"

The serving girl's face suddenly changed, grew wary. She lowered her head, and strands of her golden hair, held back by a vivid blue ribbon, fell loose. "I'll lose my place here if Cook finds out. Pray do not tell her." She began to weep.

Maddy handed her a handkerchief. "Answer my question, Cath," she said gently.

She raised her head. Tears spilled from her eyes and trailed down her face. "At first it was fun, the teasing. I thought it was harmless. He is a handsome man, and I was flattered by the attention. But now I've realized he wants to bed me. I am a virgin, mistress, and wish to remain that way until I wed." She lowered her head and began to sob into her handkerchief. "Pray help me. I know what happens to girls like me who birth bastards."

She was so young. "Look at me, Cath." She raised her head, her face wet and blotchy. "First, know this. You've done nothing wrong. You are a maid; he is an experienced man of the world." *And far worse.* "Do you understand? You are not to blame."

When she made no answer, Maddy went on. "You must tell Cook, I'm afraid." Cath cried harder but did not refuse. "I am certain she has dealt with circumstances such as these before. Simply assigning you to other duties in the kitchen should rectify the problem, and you must make sure you do not encounter Musgrave in any of your other duties."

At that her head bobbed up. "Master Vine, you mean?"

Jesu. In her eagerness to help, Maddy had made a dangerous error. She put a hand to her head and quirked up her mouth. "Aye, Master Vine. I was thinking of someone else. Now, you must speak with Cook before your courage fails you. You may tell her we discussed this. If she is not cooperative, I shall speak to her myself." Tearfully, Cath nodded her agreement and went on her way.

The next day, Peter served both the meals. Musgrave

was quiet, watchful, as though he suspected this had been arranged to thwart him. He narrowed his eyes at Maddy toward the end of supper. She looked away, but feared he'd somehow learned of her role in Cath's removal.

It happened the following night. She should have expected it, but she'd mistakenly believed Musgrave would move on to other, more willing, partners. Certainly, he could find women willing to lie with him in the village, for coin. In fact, Maddy was nearly certain that's exactly what he'd been doing. Naively, she had never considered the fact that he might have a spy in the kitchen.

He lay in wait for her in her chamber.

During the evening meal, Musgrave had cast Maddy a few odd looks. At first, his expression seemed menacing, but then it had changed into a smug look of derision. After they'd eaten, the men disappeared, leaving her and Lady Dacre to their reading and sewing. When her mistress nodded off for the third or fourth time, Maddy laid a hand on her arm and said, "Madam, it is late. We should retire."

She shook herself awake. "By the time Edith has gotten me ready for my bed, I shall be wide-awake." Maddy helped her up, but when she offered further assistance, Lady Dacre waved her off. After she'd returned books to shelves, put her sewing away, and snuffed the candles, she set off for her chamber.

As soon as she entered the room, she smelled him. He had a habit of keeping a few cloves under his bottom lip to sweeten his breath, and the scent was unmistakable. Maddy froze, and he grabbed her from behind, blocking any attempt to escape. "Do not scream, or I shall make this rather more unpleasant for you than it might be. I think you liked it when I bedded you before. I remember your cries of ecstasy."

Cries of pain. They were cries of pain. She felt a cold blade of steel pressed against her breast.

"You took Cath away from me. She was mine. So I'll have you instead." His words were slurred, and she realized he was drunk as a thrush.

Cath must have shared their conversation with one of the kitchen maids. "She was afraid of you." He tightened his grip on Maddy, so that the last few words, forced out, sounded loud and unnatural. Gasping for air, she tried to wrest herself from his hold, but he was far too strong, even in his inebriated state. He dragged her toward the bed. She resisted with every bit of strength she could muster. When that did not work, Maddy turned herself into a dead weight. He cursed, then simply picked her up. He threw her face down onto the bed and lifted her skirts. She heard the clatter of his knife as it fell to the floor and the drunken fumbling with his hose.

Rage possessed her, and for a moment, a darkness blotted out her vision. She remembered—her dirk was under the pillow. Each morning she straightened her own bedclothes and saw no reason to hide it. If she could reach it, she might have a chance to fend him off. Maddy scooted toward the head of the bed, but Musgrave did not notice because he was too busy finding his member. She slid her hand under the pillow and grasped the dirk just as she felt his fingers crawling up her legs.

Maddy exploded off the mattress, clutching the weapon in her hand and emitting a primal scream, low and guttural. The surprise of it was his undoing. He had expected her to be compliant, to accept rape as her due for depriving him of Cath. Before he could reach for it, she kicked his knife across the floor. Holding the dirk with both hands, she said, "Get out, or I'll sink this into your belly." His male organ hung limp, and she doubted it would have served him well.

Under normal circumstances, Musgrave would have seized the dirk as fast as the brawny soldier had during the battle. But he was too far into his cups. Maddy's voice shook.

"Go. Get out. If you so much as look sideways at me, I'll tell Lady Dacre about Cath. And that you tried to rape me."

Backing up, he tucked himself in and nearly fell over backward. He choked out a harsh laugh. "If you do, I'll tell her I've already bedded you. And there is the small matter of your brother."

"Leave. Now."

"This is not over, Madeleine." He stumbled out the door.

She dashed over and peered down the passage, watching him until he turned toward the stairs. Then she closed the door firmly.

Despite trembling and gasping for breath, Maddy dragged her small trunk over and shoved it hard against the door. It wouldn't be enough to stop Musgrave, but at least she would be warned of his approach. She undressed quickly, washed her face and hands, and climbed into bed. Sleep would be her enemy tonight. She would fight it off as long as she could.

She heard a sound from behind the wardrobe in the far corner of the room. Useless emerged and toddled over to the bed. In her terror, she'd forgotten all about the wee creature. She patted the mattress and the dog sprang up beside her. "You are not much of a protector, little one." In truth, Maddy was glad Useless had stayed hidden. In his rage, Musgrave might have harmed her.

Instead of blowing out the candle, she let it burn down, until her eyelids finally grew heavy and she dropped off into a troubled sleep, the dirk still clutched in her hand.

Chapter Eight

Market day was fast approaching, and Maddy was still undecided as to how much to tell Nicholas Ryder about Musgrave. Or indeed if she should tell him anything. If he knew about the man, it would complicate their dealings. He may think she was not up to the task of handling an additional person who might be at Lanercost for his own nefarious reasons. And to be honest, she did not want Ryder to know of her past relationship with Musgrave, did not want to be forced to explain it. She was ashamed.

The weather also concerned her. It was still bitterly cold, and she dreaded going on foot to Brampton. To her surprise, at supper the night before market day, Lady Dacre offered her a priory mount to ride. "It is too cold to walk," she said. "You must ride one of our horses."

"Thank you, madam. That is most kind of you."

Sipping her wine, she nodded in acknowledgment. "Christopher, it is time we visited the tenants. And we must stop at Naworth afterward to check on matters there."

Musgrave, whom Maddy had managed to avoid other than

at meals, looked up at that. Apparently, he was as surprised as she was to hear the lady talk about this in their presence. Christopher said, by way of explanation, "Naworth Castle is the home of the Catholic Dacres. Our cousin Leonard resided there until his late, unfortunate participation in the raid at Hell Beck. Now we don't know where he resides." He barked a cynical laugh, earsplitting in the small chamber.

Lady Dacre glared at him, and he was silent. They finished the meal talking of nothing more important than the weather, a horse that had gone lame, and the repairs to the roof of one of the outbuildings. Maddy looked up once to find Musgrave's steely gaze upon her. Would he follow her tomorrow? Set upon her on a lonely stretch of road? If so, he could easily overpower her.

If he revealed the truth about her and her brother, Lady Dacre would have no choice but to cast her out of the priory. And then she would be forced to throw herself on Nicholas Ryder's mercy.

• • •

When Madeleine Vernon arrived for her first visit, around midday, Nicholas and his nephew were dashing about the hall swinging wooden sticks at each other. Nicholas glimpsed her out of the corner of one eye. "Touché, Sir Mouse! You have me." There was a moment's silence, and a servant announced her.

"Sir, Mistress Vernon is here to see you." Only then did Nicholas turn toward her.

"That is enough swordplay for now," he said to Daniel. The lass appeared stiff and restrained. If he did not do something to ease her discomfort, they would accomplish little this day. He approached, bowed, and said, "Well met, Mistress Vernon."

"Sir," she said, curtsying.

His nephew stepped forward and Nicholas placed a hand on his shoulder. "Make your bow, Daniel."

Solemnly, he did so, and to Nicholas's surprise, Mistress Vernon bent down and held out her hand. "How now, Master Daniel? I am pleased to make the acquaintance of such a fine swordsman." He grasped her hand, a big smile breaking out, and nodded.

Nicholas failed to hold back his own grin. So his ward was not immune to the charms of a pretty lass. "Now run and find Margery." When Daniel hesitated, his uncle grasped him gently by the shoulders and turned him around, pointing him in the right direction. He watched the boy walk away. "My nephew. He is my ward." He made no further explanation, as it was none of her concern.

He led the lass to a small chamber off one end of the hall, his personal domain. It was neither drawing room nor study, but a bit of each. A fire was burning in the hearth, and Nicholas motioned her to a settle placed in front of it. After removing her cloak, she moved to the hearth to warm herself. A small oak writing table sat at an angle to the settle, and he situated himself there after gathering papers, quill, and ink jar.

"Do be seated, mistress. What news do you have for me?" He dipped his quill into the ink jar and waited, his gaze on his papers rather than on her.

Silence.

He raised his head at length and was shocked to see that she looked stricken. Almost pained. God's breath, it should not fall to him to lift her spirits. He softened his voice. "Pray, sit down, mistress." Perhaps matters at the priory were not progressing as he'd hoped. "Is something amiss? Are you having difficulties with your assignment?"

She stared at him for a moment, the pained look waning. "No. Where should I begin?"

"Anywhere. But leave nothing out. I need not only facts

but impressions as well."

Seated now, she paused to collect her thoughts. "Lady Dacre. She's a bit of an enigma. She seems highly intelligent, yet she does not read or write. She understands the complex legal problems surrounding her stepson's suit and dictates letters regarding these with nary a pause for breath."

Nicholas interrupted. "Do you think the suit has any bearing on...what we are concerned with?"

"It is too soon to know. I've learned the matter has caused some awkwardness between Christopher Dacre and his brother, William. That is why she needed somebody else to help with her correspondence."

He nodded. "Tell me how you pass the days."

She related her daily routine to him. It sounded as if the Dacre woman was a creature of habit. "Unfortunately, my chamber is in the tower rather than the vicarage. Another complication is that Lady Dacre never ventures out, or at least she has not during this cold spell. The men are frequently gone. If only they would all be away at the same time."

"Is that likely to happen?"

"She told her son recently that they must visit Naworth Castle. I assume they mean to take what they can haul away before it is all confiscated. I was surprised that she mentioned this in my presence—and Thomas Vine's as well."

"And I am surprised the queen's agents have not been there already. What do you make of Dacre?"

Mistress Vernon raised her hands, palms up, in a timeless gesture of perplexity. "He is always courteous to me. My first day there, he escorted me around the property and gave me a proper tour. He knows much about the history of the place. When I had an opening, I told him it was my impression that he and his stepmother did not approve of the recent rebellion."

"And?"

"He was vague and evasive. He said something about northerners liking to keep their own counsel, and that there were certain practices and laws that did not suit them. And then, unfortunately, we arrived at the forge, and I could probe no further. He introduced me to the smith, and that was the end of that."

"*Hmm.*" On the whole, disappointing, even though it was what he'd expected in the first week. He set his quill down and was surprised when she spoke.

"A moment, sir. I am not finished."

He waved a hand. "Forgive me. Continue."

"Two things. One you may already know. I overheard snatches of a private conversation between Vine and Christopher Dacre. Vine's voice was raised, and he said something like, 'The Scots could capture and kill you.' Dacre then said they needed a leader, one of the earls, and Ferniehurst was sheltering him. I think the earl he was referring to must be Westmoreland. It sounded like Dacre was forming a plan to bring the earl back." She broke off for a moment, then said, "Perhaps 'plan' is too strong a word. When I heard steps approaching the door, I made a hasty departure."

"We knew of Westmoreland's whereabouts. But this is more specific evidence that they are hoping to regroup and reignite the citizens to rise again. We suspected as much. And Dacre is involved in that somehow. Well done, mistress." He jotted a note on a piece of foolscap and glanced up at her. Her face was flushed with pleasure, enhancing her natural beauty. Had his compliment pleased her so much? At least that pained look had not returned.

"Perhaps he's only sympathetic to their cause. He seems so mild mannered and harmless."

"Make no assumptions about any of them, and above all, do not trust them. Report everything and let us decide what is significant." He knew he sounded like a stern schoolmaster, but to protect herself and safeguard the mission, she must remain vigilant.

She nodded. "What's in it for the Scots? Why do they benefit from conspiring in this? Elizabeth isn't their queen."

"But Mary Stewart is. Or was. The Scots over the border share mutual goals with our English rebels."

"They want to restore Mary to the Scottish throne?"

He nodded. "Aye. But it goes further than that. They want her cleared of her first husband's murder. Some would see her wed to the Duke of Norfolk."

"And I suppose they would love to return to the old religion."

"Of course. What they desire most, however, is to have Mary named as Elizabeth's successor."

A soft knock sounded, and a servant carrying a tray entered. She set it down on the desk and withdrew. "I thought you might like some spiced wine and a small meal," Nicholas said.

Madeleine's smile lit up her face, and a cold place within him warmed. "Indeed, I would. It is most kind of you." He handed her a pewter cup and she drank deeply.

He waited until she'd set her tankard down. "What of Master Vine? Have you learned anything useful about him?"

She pushed a lock of hair back, away from her face. That single gesture entranced him, drawing attention, as it did, to the delicate bones of her face and her lovely eyes. *Hold, man. This is a business meeting.*

Her eyes darted to a spot behind his shoulder. Odd, since she'd been facing him squarely throughout her reporting. "No. He appears to be Dacre's friend, but he goes off by himself for long periods. Other than the one conversation I happened to overhear, I am not aware of them plotting or planning anything. No sudden breaking off a conversation when I walk into the room, no huddled conferring. At least not in my presence."

"I still think he is lying about being from London."

"Aye. I don't trust him. He...I was forced to step in and help the servant girl I told you about."

"What was the outcome?" Nicholas busied himself laying out the food while she finished the story. Cheese tarts, apples and pears, and a whole salmon. He handed her a trencher with a generous portion of everything, then resumed his seat and watched her.

"The cook assigned the girl other duties." Another flickering of her eyes. She was either lying or giving him partial truths.

"You're not telling me everything. What are you leaving out?"

Now she looked directly at him. "He was quite angry with me. Somebody informed him of my involvement."

"Madeleine. Do not make me beg for information. Vine's actions could be important. I cannot believe he let the matter lie without seeking revenge on you."

A rosy color bloomed on her cheeks. Was it because he'd called her by her Christian name or because the subject was embarrassing?

"He threatened me, told me to keep out of his business."

Ryder sighed. "Precisely what was the threat?"

In an irritated voice she said, "Since I prevented him from having Cath, the servant girl, he thought he might have me instead."

There was silence while Nicholas took this in. She should not have to worry about that cur's unwelcome advances. The situation was dangerous and could ultimately compromise their goals. But why was she irritated with *him*? He rubbed his beard and sprang to his feet. "I mistrusted him from the first. What did you do?"

"I told him he wouldn't dare, that I'd tell Lady Dacre."

"That's not enough to stop a man like him." He stood now with his hands on his hips, looking at her in frustration. "Perhaps I should intervene."

She shook her head vigorously. "Pray do not, sir. How would it look if, at the first possible opportunity, I ran off to you and told tales on them? Because he is a guest in their household, it would shame them. Even anger them. I can deal with Master Vine on my own."

She was mistaken about that. "Can you? You, a wee lass, and he a behemoth?"

A smile tugged at her lovely mouth. "I would not exactly call him that. He is a large man, but I have my dirk. I sleep with it under my pillow. Besides, I am just beginning to find information that may be useful to you. Do you wish to give up on that so soon?"

"You haven't revealed much that persuades me your services there are required. We could find some other way."

"Oh, by God's light, pray sit down and calm yourself. Drink. Eat. I have more to tell you, but let us refresh ourselves first."

. . .

He looked taken aback that she had spoken to him in such a way. Indeed, Maddy shocked herself. Never had she been so bold with him. How would he react? To her surprise, he abruptly sat and shoved a piece of salmon into his mouth, washing it down with a long draught of wine. "Sit here." He motioned to her to share the small table with him. She did so but would have preferred to hold her trencher on her lap and keep a safe distance from him.

Her status had risen; she was allowed a knife. She cut into the cheese tart, breathing in the heady aroma. Whatever wine had been used in the recipe smelled of quince and something earthy. "I haven't thanked you for returning my dagger. I feel safer with it."

He grunted. "Vine could wrest it away from you before you even had a chance to wield it."

Not when he's three sheets in the wind.

She shrugged. "Maybe." They ate in silence for a time. When she'd had her fill, Maddy laid the knife across the trencher and said, "One day while I was assisting Lady Dacre with her correspondence, I accidentally found a letter from the Duke of Norfolk. I had only a moment to look upon it, because she recognized what it was and screamed at me to put it down. She dismissed me immediately and warned me never to look at any documents again without her permission."

Ryder had gone quite still. He finished chewing and set down his own knife. "Were you able to discern the subject of the letter?"

"No. As I said, I merely glanced at it before Lady Dacre realized what I was looking at."

Agitated once again, he shoved back his chair and got to his feet. "God's wounds. We must know what's in that letter! Do you think—?"

"I've been doing nothing *but* thinking about how to lay my hands on it. My best chance will be when she and her stepson ride off to Naworth. But I doubt Vine will accompany them, although it is possible he'll be off on one of his own mysterious ventures. Also, I have the servants to contend with. I must not be caught by one of them."

"How did you come across it in the first place? And if she does not read, how did she recognize it?"

Maddy related the story of Lady Dacre's stacks of papers and her embroidery silk system. And how she'd picked up one of the stacks when the letter, right on the top, had fairly jumped out at her. "A few days later, I offered to help her sort her papers. She told me she keeps important documents locked in a coffer and the key on her person."

Ryder began pacing. "That will make it tricky." Finally, he flung himself back into his chair and rubbed at his beard. She nearly smiled, having noticed this was a habit of his when he was puzzling over something.

"One thing is in my favor, however. Her papers are extremely unorganized. She has stacks of them all over her chamber, even on her bed. If I had to guess, I would say she's not yet done anything about locking up the letter."

"So the sooner you can undertake the search, the better."

She drank the last few sips of her wine, then set the glass down. "Lady Dacre has been kind to me. I believe this problem with her stepson—William, not Christopher—has worn her down. I dislike spying on her."

Ryder's expression grew hard. "But you like it better than the alternative."

Maddy had time only to scowl at him before the door opened. In walked the little boy, Ryder's ward.

"Daniel, what have I told you about interrupting me when I have a visitor?" The child hung his head but did not leave. "Come here," Ryder said, his tone softening. When Daniel was close enough, Ryder hauled him up onto his lap and jiggled his knee. That brought a smile to the lad's face. "Are we done, mistress?"

"Aye." She had no desire to leave, despite the implied threat in his last words. Seeing Nicholas Ryder with his nephew gave her an entirely different impression of the man. "Master Daniel, do you read? What is your favorite story?"

He shook his head. She once again wondered why he didn't speak, but decided it was best not to ask. Maddy didn't want to embarrass the boy—and Ryder had chosen not to tell her.

"He has but six years. But he has recently started with a tutor, so it won't be long. For now, he must put up with his uncle reading to him, eh lad? Tell—show Mistress Vernon your favorite story." The boy hesitated, clearly shy of performing before a stranger.

Maddy leaned forward. "Pray do, Master Daniel. I see the sun is lowering and I must soon depart. Won't you show me before I take my leave?"

He slid off his uncle's knee and walked over to the open space near the door. Then he motioned to Ryder, who said, "Oh, no. You must do this alone."

When Daniel glared at him, arms akimbo, Ryder relented and said, "Very well. It won't be the first time I've made an ass of myself." He walked over and lifted Daniel by grasping him around his upper chest. Then he hurled him, gently, to the ground. After this, Ryder pretended to lock Daniel up. As soon as he did so, he returned, got down on all fours, and made a great, roaring noise.

Maddy clapped with delight when she recognized the story. Daniel in the lion's den! How perfect. The little boy and the lion feinted a few times, and then Daniel crouched down and seemingly made a friend of the great cat, who now meowed like a kitten and rubbed his head against the child's legs. Daniel, while trying to remain true to his character, couldn't help laughing, nor could Maddy. When the enactment was over, she said, "Well done, Daniel. I understand why that is your favorite story. Might you slay a real lion someday?"

He seemed to think seriously about this. Then, quite solemnly, he nodded. "I do not doubt it," she said. Glancing out the window, Maddy saw that the sun was already low in the winter sky. "I must go. And I haven't left any time for the market."

"Where is your basket?" Ryder asked. Before she could even look around, Daniel had found it and now held it out toward his uncle. "Take the rest of these cheese tarts. You can say you bought them at the market. What else can I give you?" Daniel gestured toward the bookshelf. "Good idea."

He grabbed a volume and set it in the basket.

"Does the market have a bookseller's stall?"

"Aye." Ryder grabbed her cloak and wrapped it around her shoulders, his hands lingering, and she felt his breath at the back of her neck. Flustered, she stepped away. The two men, big and little, walked her to the door. A stable lad brought her horse around, and suddenly, Ryder held up a hand.

"One moment. Have you no groom or lad who accompanied you here?"

"Nay, sir. Why should I?"

When he spoke, she heard exasperation in his voice. "Because you should not be traveling these roads by yourself. It is not safe. I'll escort you home." He turned back to the house. Maddy grabbed his arm, stopping him.

"Do not concern yourself. No harm will come to me. It is not a very long ride, after all. Next time I'll talk to Lady Dacre about an escort."

He studied her, his eyes troubled. "As you say, then. But I mislike it."

Maddy had stepped forward, ready to mount, when she felt a little hand grasping her skirts. It was Daniel, gesturing at her.

"He wants to kiss you," Ryder said. "Do you mind?"

Did she mind? When she craved the touch of someone who cared for her, how could she mind? Rather, she welcomed it. She crouched down, and Daniel put his arms about her neck and kissed her soundly on the cheek. She did the same for him. Tears pricked her eyes. She needed to be off before she embarrassed herself.

Maddy and Ryder made their farewells. She did not want to look at him for fear he would notice her moist eyes. "Pray, give me a boost up." He did, and she walked her mount through the garth and out toward the road, glancing back once. Ryder had lifted Daniel into his arms. They waved to her, and she waved back.

Chapter Nine

Lady Dacre had lent Maddy a smart little palfrey, Eve, to ride to Brampton. Wrapped in her hooded travel cloak, her feet booted, Maddy stayed relatively warm even in the waning light. She'd strapped the dirk about her waist, but God be thanked, there was no sign of Musgrave. She yearned to be safely inside the walls of the priory. If the knave confronted her there, at least she wouldn't be on a lonely, isolated road.

There had been a slight thaw the past week, and in some places the ground was visible. Alongside the road, snow lay in deep, curving drifts. Now, as the day waned, the trees cast long, spidery shadows against the stark white. The sky, indeed, it seemed the very air, was the color of pewter. Maddy had always loved the quality of the light in winter. Despite her eagerness to be back at Lanercost, it was good to have some time to ponder her visit with Nicholas Ryder.

Upon her arrival, Maddy had thought it was going to be a disaster. She'd looked forward to this day. Though she had told herself not to think of Ryder as her friend, plainly she had not heeded her own counsel. In vain she had waited for a few words of kindness before they settled down to business. *How fare you, or are they being kind to you?* They had never come, and yet the day had turned out to be the best she'd experienced in a long while.

Why?

In large part, it was because of Daniel. The child was a delight. A mystery as well. Why did he not speak? Was it a physical deformity? Perhaps his tongue did not work as it should. When he laughed, though, she could not see anything wrong with it. He was a very loving—and lovable—child. Ryder seemed to be completely under his spell. Intriguing to learn that he had a caring, patient side. A side she hadn't seen before.

And, unexpectedly, Maddy had enjoyed her exchange with Ryder.

When he'd expressed concern for her safety, she had searched his face. She could not doubt his sincerity. But when she'd professed her sympathy for Lady Dacre, he'd threatened her. Indirect though it was, his words had conveyed the fact that if she weren't at Lanercost spying, she would be back in a cell at Carlisle Castle awaiting her fate. If Daniel hadn't entered the room, she would have challenged him on it.

And the man was too perceptive for her peace of mind. He'd guessed she was keeping something from him. Fortunately, he had accepted her recounting of the Cath episode without probing further regarding Musgrave. It had irritated her that he seemed concerned for her well-being, yet he was the one who had placed her in this position.

They hit an icy patch and Eve slipped, nearly tossing her to the ground. She must pay closer attention. Taking a firmer hold on the reins, for a time she kept all thoughts of Ryder at bay.

But gradually, her mind found its way back to him. In the coming week, when she thought of Ryder at all, she must remember the brutal way he had told her that Ann's head had been split open by a lance. How carelessly he had informed her that she would be hanged if she didn't cooperate with him. She would recall the contemptuous look in his eyes as he'd accused her of worrying more about her status as a servant in the home of her in-laws than of the fate of her friends. She would remember the judgmental look when he'd implied that she hadn't mourned her brother properly. That was the real Nicholas Ryder. Not this paragon of fatherhood she'd seen today. Not the person who seemed genuinely concerned about her safety.

Aye, she would do well to remember exactly what that meant. It was in his best interest to keep her safe. If something happened to her, he would be left without an informant. Then perhaps *he* would be in trouble. He reported to somebody, possibly to William Cecil, the Secretary of State, himself. If something awful were to befall Maddy, he would be forced to find another way to obtain the information she was now supplying. The more she thought about it, the more convinced she became that this was the only reason he was the least bit concerned about her welfare.

By the time she rode over the wooden bridge that crossed the river Irthing, twilight had fallen, and she was tired and chilled to the bone. But she had managed to banish Ryder from her thoughts.

Maddy stopped by the kitchen with her basket, which contained at least a half dozen cheese tarts. Perhaps Cook would like to serve them with supper. She had been cool to her ever since the episode with Cath, so Maddy had no idea how her offering would be received.

"Good even, Mistress Derby. Something smells wonderful." A joint of beef was roasting on a spit in the hearth, fat crackling as it dripped onto the fire. The potboy stood sentinel nearby, ready to turn it. Maddy had noticed the priory did not observe the usual strictures of the Lenten season, eating as much meat as they pleased. The cook did not acknowledge her comment.

"Mistress." She barely inclined her head. Tendrils of hair, damp from perspiration, peeked out of her cap. It struck her that perhaps Cook was the one who had informed on her. Musgrave could easily have persuaded her, more likely bribed her, to let him know when anything occurred that might be of interest to him.

"I visited the market on the way home. I thought you might like these cheese tarts for our supper."

She narrowed her eyes. "You think I can't prepare a proper meal, mistress?"

Her rudeness shocked Maddy. "Certainly not. I have been in residence here long enough to know you're an excellent cook. The stall was closing, and the tarts looked very tempting. They sold them to me at a bargain price. If you do not want them, I'll pass them out to the servants." As Maddy made for the stairway to her chamber, the cook spoke.

"I'll take them. Warmed up, they'll be a nice addition to the supper." Maddy walked back over and handed her the basket, and she began placing the tarts on the long wooden worktable. When she'd finished, she handed Maddy the volume Nicholas Ryder had given her. "You'll be wanting this."

"Aye." Maddy waved the book at her and said, "From the bookseller's stall." After tossing the volume into the empty basket, she fled. Mistress Derby did not thank her, but then she hadn't expected her to. Convinced the woman was Musgrave's spy, Maddy would be wary of her from now on.

• • •

On the whole, Mistress Vernon's first visit had gone well. She had discovered more useful information than expected. At supper, Nicholas reported her findings to his father, who was not impressed.

Francis Ryder quaffed his ale before commenting. "She'll need to do better than that, Nick. Most of this we already knew, or at the very least, suspected."

"Perhaps. She has been at the priory for less than a full week, you recall. Norfolk's missive is significant. Why would he be writing to Lady Jane Dacre?"

The elder Ryder drew his bushy brows together. "Significant it may be, but we don't yet know its contents, and we may never. Norfolk could be writing to her for any number of reasons. He's a wily bastard."

Nicholas swallowed a bite of quail. "She will find the letter, I assure you. The lass has pluck and no end of determination."

Francis Ryder cocked his head at his son. "If I didn't know better, I'd say you may be developing an interest there. Be careful. She may end up a casualty of this."

Not if I can help it. "I am well aware of the strictures placed on such familiarities by the queen and William Cecil," Nicholas said, with barely contained rancor.

"With good reason. Lust can distort judgment, cause otherwise intelligent men to throw reason out the window. The wench can't be your whore, Nick."

Nicholas rose so swiftly, he knocked his empty tankard over. "That is the last thing she is. I must see Daniel before he goes to sleep. I give you good night, Father." Nicholas threw his napkin on the table and strode from the room before Francis Ryder could say another word.

God's wounds, sometimes he hated the man.

Margery was with Daniel. Bedtime was still difficult for the lad, and either he or Margery stayed with the boy until he slept. Occasionally, this was impossible, and Nicholas imagined Daniel cried himself to sleep on those nights.

"What ho, Daniel! Still awake? Were you waiting for me?" Nicholas nodded to Margery, and she left the room.

He lowered himself to the side of the bed. "Would you like a pony ride tomorrow? Perhaps it will be a bit warmer."

Daniel nodded enthusiastically.

"I will be speaking to your tutor in the morning. Will I receive a good report?" The boy dipped his head once again, if less enthusiastically. Nicholas chuckled and ruffled the lad's hair. "Give me a kiss, then. It's time you were asleep."

Daniel made no move to kiss his uncle, and Nicholas waited patiently. He'd learned over the past year that sometimes the boy had to think about how to communicate. At length, Daniel arose from his bed and stood on the cold floor, imitating, Nicholas realized at last, a lass. By smiling, wiggling his fingers alongside his head, and hugging himself.

Nicholas watched, laughing. "I see. A big smile, long hair, a loving nature. You are referring to our guest, Mistress Vernon, are you not?"

Daniel nodded.

"Did you like her?" The boy's grin was so wide, his answer was not in doubt. After Madeleine had gone, Nicholas realized how good she'd been with Daniel. She had such an easy manner with him. Real and true. His nephew had sensed that, as children do.

Daniel set his hands on his hips and glared at his uncle. Then he mimicked kissing somebody, afterward putting his arms up in a question.

Nicholas got it. "You're asking why I did not kiss her goodbye. Because I am not a little lad, but a grown man. And we are not well acquainted. Come now, to bed with you."

Reluctantly, Daniel climbed back into bed, hugged Nicholas around the neck, and kissed him soundly.

"Good night, dear boy," he said.

As he sat, waiting for his nephew to fall asleep, Nicholas weighed matters. All things considered, he wished he *had* kissed Madeleine Vernon. If the opportunity presented itself again, he would. But how could he stop at only a kiss?

. . .

During supper, Maddy realized Ryder had been correct about her mistress taking little interest in her. She made no inquiries regarding her day. Maddy thanked her again for providing her with a mount, and the talk then turned to which day she and Christopher would visit tenants. They were to go two days hence. Maddy said nothing, certain that if they wanted her to attend them on their mission, one of them would say so.

"I have business in Carlisle tomorrow," Musgrave said. "I shall take my leave early and return late the following day." She could not help wondering what business he could have there, if indeed he had any, but she was more concerned that Nicholas might be there and they could accidentally meet. She supposed Ryder could invent a reason for his presence, but it might be better if he were warned. That meant she would have to write him a note and place it under the loose stone at the foot of the Lanercost Cross.

"A pity," Lady Dacre said. "Sussex dines with us tomorrow."

"So Christopher told me," Musgrave replied.

Holy Blessed Virgin. Sussex, Lord President of the Council of the North. He had presided when Maddy appeared before the council to plead for Robert's life. An astute man, he would recognize her before he took the first bite of game. He'd reveal all to Lady Dacre, and she would be forced to put an end to Maddy's service here. She should have told her employer about Robert from the beginning. Now that she knew the woman, she believed Lady Dacre would have been sympathetic. But to learn from Sussex that she'd been lying— she doubted she'd countenance her staying on. Could Maddy plead a headache? An unsettled stomach? Whatever it was, she would need to invent a plausible reason why she could not be present.

During the remainder of the meal, Maddy considered why the Earl of Sussex would be calling on the Dacres. She could not imagine what business he would have here, unless they were old friends. One thing came clear, however. Musgrave must have a reason for wishing to avoid an encounter with the man, which was why he was absenting himself.

After supper, Lady Dacre and the men played primero while Maddy embroidered in the dim light, straining her eyes to distinguish one color from another. At length, she tucked away her silks and canvas and fetched the volume Ryder had plucked from his bookshelf for her basket. Drawing a candle close, she opened the book. It was the poetry of Sir Thomas Wyatt.

Weary and hoping Lady Dacre would call an end to the evening soon, Maddy read only a few poems. They proved to be charming and whimsical, and best of all, made her chuckle. Did Ryder enjoy these poems, or did the volume belong to one of his parents? Or to Daniel's mother, perhaps. It was difficult to imagine Ryder with a sense of humor, although she'd caught glimpses of it here and there. She envisioned him at his home in Brampton and wondered what he and Daniel were doing. Perhaps he was reading the boy a story. Settling him for the night.

So deeply absorbed was she, Lady Dacre apparently had to speak twice before Maddy heard her. "Madeleine! Attend!"

She jumped to her feet. "Pray forgive me, my lady. I was

caught up in my reading."

She glanced at the book. "What is it?"

"Sir Thomas Wyatt. I purchased it at the bookstall today. I've never read his poetry."

"He's reputed to be quite the wit. Will you assist me in my chamber? Edith suffers from a gastric complaint. I sent her to bed."

"Of course." Before they left the room, Maddy overheard Dacre and Musgrave making plans to meet by the stables in a few minutes. Thank heaven they would be gone when she attempted to place her message at the base of the cross.

After helping her mistress remove her bodice, slashed petticoat, and kirtle, Maddy bent down to unroll her hose. She turned back the bed clothing while the lady performed her ablutions, pushing a few stacks of documents aside first. Lady Dacre climbed the set of steps at the side of her bed and crawled under the covers. "Will you move the warming pan over, Madeleine?"

She slid the pan, heavy with hot coals, to one side. "May I do anything else for you, madam?"

"You must dine in your chamber tomorrow, Madeleine. The earl wishes to discuss a private matter with me and my son."

Maddy prayed her voice would not give away her profound sense of relief. "Yes, ma'am. I'll ask Mistress Derby for a tray." A candle flickered next to the bed. The gold cross the lady always wore caught the light and reflected it back. Maybe someday she would explain why this particular piece was so dear to her.

"Sleep well, my lady," Maddy said, closing the door.

She hurried to her chamber, a candle lighting the way. Once there, she gathered foolscap, quill, and ink jar and commenced her note to Ryder, keeping it short and concise:

8 March

*Thomas Vine will be in Carlisle for a few days. Be on
your guard.*

She hesitated a moment before adding another line:
Sussex dines here tomorrow.

She did not sign it. In the time required to don her warm
cloak, boots, and gloves, the ink had dried. Maddy folded
the missive and tucked it into her sleeve, called to Useless,
and cautiously proceeded down the stairs. The potboy and
scullery maid had finished their work and, she hoped, had
found their beds. All was quiet as she walked—without a
candle this time—through the hall and out the door, the little
dog padding along beside her.

In seconds, the cold air wrapped itself around her. The
outline of the Lanercost Cross reared up into the night
sky, and she made her way toward it, hindered by the snow.
Comically, Useless kept sinking into the drifts beside the
path. In the end, she picked her up and held her in her arms
the rest of the way.

Maddy lowered the pup to the ground and began scooping
snow away from the foot of the cross. Then she examined
each stone until she finally located the loose one. But when
she tried to lift it, it wouldn't budge. Perhaps the bottom of
it was frozen to the earth. She leaned back on her haunches
in frustration, and that was when she heard something. The
unmistakable sound of boots crunching through the snow
and coming her way. Heart racing, she glanced around for
Useless, afraid the dog would bark. She was nearby, and
Maddy snatched her up and hurried toward the church, the
only place to hide. There was no time to gain entrance; she
would have to huddle in the shadowy recesses of one of the
side doors. She hoped the huge bulk of the church would
cast enough of a shadow that the visitor would not be able to

discern either her or her footprints.

He drew nearer. Who could it be? As far as Maddy knew, Dacre and Musgrave were gone, and the laborers, such as the smith and stable lads, did not live on the property. She crushed Useless against her chest, and by some miracle, the creature made no sound. The footsteps stopped. Maddy could see the mysterious figure plainly, though it was too dark to identify him in his hooded cloak. He'd halted at the cross and hunkered down, and before long she heard the sound of stones scraping against each other. He grunted with the effort of lifting the loose one out of the way. This man must be Ryder's go-between. Since he would not find her note, Ryder wouldn't see it.

Should she step out and give him the missive? She couldn't risk it. It could be Musgrave, it could be anyone. She simply could not take the chance. After a moment, the man replaced the stone. He got to his feet and hastened back the way he'd come.

Maddy debated what to do, at last deciding to place the note under the stone. Ryder would eventually receive the message and know that she'd at least tried to warn him. She was able to pry the stone up high enough to slip the note underneath without too much trouble, thanks to the efforts of the hooded stranger. Worried that someone might notice the exposed stones, she spread some of the snow she'd removed earlier back over them.

Maddy carried Useless back to her chamber, feeling all the while as though somebody were watching. She shivered, and not only from the cold.

Chapter Ten

In the morning, while they were embroidering, Lady Dacre informed Maddy that Sussex would be arriving at one o'clock. If she cared to meet him, she would be welcome to do so before the private meal.

"Thank you, my lady. It is kind of you to make the offer." And indeed, it was. "But I think not."

Lady Dacre smiled, cocking her head. "He does not bite, you know."

Maddy laughed. "Of course not, but I'm quite certain he would care nothing for an introduction to someone of my status."

"Let me have a look at your work," she said. Maddy handed it over. "It's quite lovely, if a bit...untamed. You have an eye for color and design."

She passed it back and Maddy examined the big splashes of color on her canvas critically. "I see what you mean. When I'm working, I sometimes let whimsy carry me away. I will need more silks and wools soon. Does the market have a stall for such things?"

"Oh, yes. There is a mercer's shop in Brampton, and the proprietor keeps a stall on market day. If you intend to go next time, I will ask you to purchase some supplies for me as well."

"Certainly."

When the church bell rang noon, Maddy commenced putting her silks and canvas into her basket. "Do you require my help in dressing for dinner?" she asked.

"Aye, if you don't mind. Edith is still feeling ill." She rose and Maddy accompanied her to her chamber. Edith had laid out clothing on the tester bed, more elegant attire than the lady usually wore. Maddy helped her disrobe down to her kirtle and smock, which she left on. Over those, she donned a skirt of soft wool, and then Maddy lifted the heavy gown—aubergine velvet with gold thread embroidery along the slashed front—over her head.

Maddy was beginning to worry about making her escape before Sussex's arrival. "I had best be on my way."

"By all means."

"Do you have any work for me to do while you entertain your guest? I imagine the meal will go on longer than usual."

"Nay, I've made no progress on sorting my papers. Read, write letters, get out of doors. Do what pleases you."

"Thank you, my lady. Send for me after your guest departs, if you have need of me."

"I expect I'll want to nap."

Maddy nodded and left. Walking back to her chamber, it occurred to her that this might be an ideal time to search for the letter, while the Dacres were entertaining Sussex. Musgrave was gone to Carlisle. Edith was ill, and the other servants would most likely be busy helping Mistress Derby in the kitchen or serving the food and clearing plates. When would she have a better opportunity? The cook had left a tray in her chamber, and Maddy kept her door open as she ate. She was able to judge by the cook's harried voice, and the subsequent silence, when the meal was being served. After readying herself, she'd got halfway down the stairs before it struck her that she'd better don boots and cloak. The excuse of a walk would seem suspicious if she were not wearing the appropriate attire.

Before leaving her chamber a second time, she spotted her dinner tray and decided to return it to the kitchen so as not to get in trouble with the irksome cook. To her dismay, Cook was standing at the wooden table, a trencher in front of her. "Can you not sit for your meal, Mistress Derby?" Maddy asked, setting the tray down.

"No time to get too comfortable. How was your meal?" She eyed her cynically, since it had consisted of bread and cheese, and a single sweet.

"Thank you for the piece of marchpane. I have a fondness for sweets."

To Maddy's surprise, she laughed. "Never know it to look at you. I do too, but that can be easily guessed by my size."

Maddy turned to leave, but the cook stopped her. "If you've no duties right now, I could use your help. A bit shorthanded, we are. Cath is down with the same thing Edith's got."

Maddy hesitated briefly. She hadn't the time for this. It was urgent that she search for the letter while the Dacres and their guests were eating. But she could not refuse without seeming churlish. This was her chance to get back in the woman's good graces. Who knew when she might need her? "I would be happy to help, although I warn you, I haven't much experience in the kitchen."

"Oh, 'tis a simple task." She directed Maddy to the far end of the long table, where a wheel of cheese, a bowl of apples, and a large pewter serving platter rested. "Slice the cheese and apples and arrange them on this." She gestured to the platter. "Can you do that?"

Maddy nodded and removed her cloak. "Seems simple enough, even for me." She began slicing and arranging, concentrating so hard on her task, time slipped away. Suddenly, at least half an hour had flown by, probably longer. Hurriedly, she placed the last of the apple slices and called to Mistress Derby. "All done!"

The cook walked over with a cloth bag in her hand. "Put these figs around the edges before you go."

Maddy dredged up a smile, hiding her impatience. When she'd finished, she wiped her hands on a cloth and said, "I'll be off now."

Cook was putting finishing touches on the sweets. "Thank you for your help, mistress."

Maddy nodded and hurried out the door before Mistress Derby could think of anything else that wanted doing. At least she'd thanked her.

The temptation to hover outside the door of the dining chamber was strong, but Maddy knew it was too great a risk. And it was doubtful she'd be able to hear their voices through the heavy oak door. Instead, she made her way to the passage comprising the family chambers, and after rapping lightly on the door to be certain she wasn't inside, entered Lady Dacre's bedchamber.

Maddy went directly to the stack of papers where she had originally found the letter from the Duke of Norfolk. To her dismay, the document she sought was not there; nothing in the pile was marked with blue thread. She racked her brain trying to recall what Lady Dacre had done when she'd caught her with the letter. Maddy had dropped the document back on the stack, and her mistress had ordered her from the room. She had done nothing with it in Maddy's presence. Discouraged, she glanced hastily through the myriad other piles of papers, but they all seemed related to the lawsuit or household matters. This could mean only one thing. Lady Dacre had secreted the letter in the coffer.

Perhaps she had forgotten to lock it. Maddy didn't know where she kept it and hurriedly made a pass about the room to see if she could spot it. No luck there. At last she ventured behind the privacy screen, assuming she'd find only her mistress's clothing, chamber pot, and washbasin. Those things were indeed there, but it was a prie-dieu and a tapestry depicting the crucifixion that drew Maddy's eye and caused her to gasp in surprise.

Was Lady Dacre a secret Catholic? Is that why she never removed the cross from about her neck?

If she was, what did that mean? And did Ryder know? But she had no time to speculate further. Hurrying back to the main part of the chamber, she walked the perimeter more slowly. Near the door stood a cupboard she'd overlooked the first time because a cloak was draped over it. Crouching down, Maddy opened the door and found the object of her frantic search. She pulled out the coffer, but before attempting to open it, she cracked the door of the chamber a fraction and listened. Nothing. No voices or footsteps coming this way.

God be praised, the coffer wasn't locked. But the letter was not there, at least not that she could see. *Jesu.* She would have to look through the entire stack. She lifted out the documents, remembering that the letter from Norfolk was marked with blue thread. Unfortunately, so were most of the papers in this stack. A shame she did not have time to study each of them. Any one of them might prove useful to Ryder.

Hastily, she thumbed through the documents, eliminating those that were not letters, ears pricked for any sounds from the passage. She scanned the end of each one, looking for

Norfolk's signature. And finally, there it was, near the bottom of the pile. After replacing the coffer, she rolled up the letter and tucked it into her sleeve. Then she hastened down the passage and the stairs and entered the relative safety of Dacre Hall. She traversed the great hall as though being chased by the hounds of hell, but jerked to a stop when she neared the kitchen. Maddy did not want Mistress Derby to see her. She paused a long while, waiting to hear any signs of the cook working near the doorway. Hearing nothing, she dodged past the long table and up the stairs, her heart thudding all the way.

Useless wandered out from behind the wardrobe to greet her, and Maddy patted her head. "I'll take you outside as soon as I copy this letter, wee friend." Maddy's breathing had finally slowed. After situating herself at the small table that served as a desk, she dipped her quill in the ink jar and copied as rapidly as she could. Her hand was trembling and she struggled to make the words legible. She did not stop to decipher the meaning, which was not immediately clear. There was no time for that if she wanted to replace the letter before Lady Dacre sought her bed. When she was done, Maddy spent a few precious minutes locking up the copy she had made, then tucked the key into her pocket.

Snapping her fingers at Useless, who toddled along behind her, she began to retrace her steps toward Lady Dacre's chamber. When she opened the vicarage door, however, she heard voices, most likely coming from the drawing room. Male laughter, and the soft voice of her mistress. Maddy could not be certain, but it sounded as though they were bidding adieu to each other. *Jesu.* She'd not be able to replace the letter! She could only hope the lady had imbibed too much wine to attempt any work and would nap, as she had indicated she would. Had Maddy left everything in the chamber in its place? When the voices drew closer to the staircase, she grabbed Useless and walked east, away from the stables, but not before glimpsing the earl's horse being led toward the vicarage by one of the lads. It appeared she had gotten away in the nick of time.

Later, she locked Norfolk's letter inside her own coffer, on top of the copy she'd made. She would wait until tomorrow to study it, when the Dacres, mother and stepson, would be preoccupied with their visit to Naworth Castle.

In the morning, Lady Dacre made no mention of yesterday's visit with the Earl of Sussex, and it would have been impertinent for Maddy to inquire about it. They sewed and read but ended early because the Dacres were making the trip to Naworth. Edith had recovered from her illness, and Maddy's services were not required.

She returned to her chamber and let Useless out. At first, Maddy had been afraid the dog would not return if sent out alone, but she always did. Seeing her sitting by the door waiting for her always warmed Maddy's heart. Now, while everybody was busy, it would be a good opportunity to read Norfolk's letter. After making certain there was no one about, she closed her door, unlocked the coffer, and withdrew the document.

1 March 1570

Greetings to my friends in the North.

You may know that I currently reside in the Tower.

My northern affairs were found to be unacceptable to the queen and her secretary, and the gipsy, who had pledged his faithfulness to my cause, quickly capitulated. However, I am confident that my imprisonment nears its end. Our sovereign, wise in all things, will soon set me free so that I may once again provide for and protect those who depend upon me.

The rising in the north was a bad business and has caused the queen to further mistrust the northern citizenry. For the sake of peace and stability, I pray there will be no more challenges to the queen's authority and that nothing will occur to turn her attention to the region.

When I am a free man, I intend to travel north to Carlisle. I yearn to see the thistles bloom in the late spring. Mayhap I will bring my Dacre children with me. They are eager to see their relations and most especially wish to make the acquaintance of the infant.

Anything you can do to accommodate this visit will not be forgotten. I will need your assistance and counsel while I am in the region.

Yrs,
Thomas Howard, Fourth Duke of Norfolk

Maddy could make head nor tail of it. What were his northern affairs? Who was the gipsy? Obviously, he wanted the queen to turn her attention to other concerns and hoped the north would settle itself. But did he truly long to see the thistles bloom? And what infant did he refer to? She was certain this was a cipher, and no doubt Nicholas Ryder would know exactly what it all meant.

She placed the letter back in its hiding place and walked downstairs to let the dog in. She wasn't waiting by the door, so Maddy headed toward the open area that ran alongside the vicarage. There she was, running and gleefully leaping through the snow, playing with some of the mongrels that loitered about the place. Maddy didn't wish to spoil her fun, so she hurried upstairs and retrieved her cloak, finally settling herself on a nearby stone bench to watch the antics. The air was cold, but the sun was strong and there was no wind.

Unintentionally, her thoughts turned to Nicholas Ryder. With all that had been going on the past few days, she'd put him out of her mind.

That Ryder was a handsome man—and fine of figure, too—had struck her right from the beginning. And the more she saw of him, the more attractive he became. Since her disastrous affair with John Musgrave, she had steered clear of men, making up her mind they were not to be trusted, and the fates had been kind to her. Maddy had met no man who interested her in the least, let alone one to whom she felt a powerful attraction. Until now. Until Ryder.

But she was nothing more than one of his underlings, forced to do his bidding unless she was willing to risk execution. She might have been a servant, a beggar, a cunning woman. It mattered little to him. Maddy should be afraid of the man, not attracted to him. When she'd said she disliked spying on Lady Dacre, his expression had changed. His mouth had grown hard, his eyes cold. And then he'd said, "You like it better than the alternative."

Maddy feared her fascination with him would complicate matters, eroding the negligible amount of control she retained over her own fate. At length she grew cold. Whistling for Useless, she made her way back indoors. It was nearly time for dinner.

Lady Dacre and Christopher Dacre left for Naworth Castle directly after the meal. Maddy estimated they would be gone between two and three hours. While they were off gathering plate, tapestries, paintings, and whatever else they deemed valuable enough to strip from the castle, she intended to replace Norfolk's letter. It may be impossible, but she had to make the attempt.

Maddy had heard Edith say she planned to tidy Lady Dacre's chamber this afternoon, so she waited until the lady's maid would have had sufficient time to accomplish that. Given her mistress's proclivity for clutter, this task could take a while. So Maddy bided her time, playing with Useless and tidying her own belongings, before venturing toward the vicarage.

No one was about. The house was silent, as it might be in the dead of night. Maddy tapped on Lady Dacre's door and entered, heading straight for the cupboard and glancing around to make certain she was alone. She lifted the coffer from its shelf and set it down, but the lid wouldn't budge. She tugged, pulled, yanked, even hunted for a hidden spring, all without success. By God's light, what was she to do?

This was taking far too long. Not that Maddy expected them back so soon, but a servant could catch her prowling around in here, and how would she explain herself? And then it struck her. *Keys.* She must find Lady Dacre's keys. Surely she had not taken them with her to Naworth. They were likely to be behind the privacy screen, where she undressed.

But when Maddy searched the area, she didn't see them. Expelling a frustrated breath, she had turned to leave when she spotted the key ring, hanging from a hook on the far wall. Relief washed over her, rapidly replaced by a sense of urgency. She grabbed the ring and rushed back to the coffer. Only one of the keys was small enough to fit the lock. She inserted it, and thank the good Lord, it opened easily. Maddy pulled the document from her sleeve and rolled it in the opposite direction so it would lay flat. With shaking hands, she placed it near the bottom of the stack, roughly where she'd found it. Maddy had just locked the coffer when the door to the chamber burst open. In walked John Musgrave, who froze when he saw her.

She made a split-second decision to brazen it out. He had less right in this chamber than she did. Concealing the keys in her skirts, she said, "What are you doing here? I thought you were still in Carlisle."

"Nay, I finished early. Have you forgotten, my chamber is also in this passage? I heard someone skulking about as I was passing and thought I should check, since I knew the Dacres were not at home."

This was so nonsensical a lie as to be laughable. "That's ridiculous. I wasn't making any noise."

"You shouldn't be in here without Lady Dacre."

"I am helping her sort her papers." Maddy made a sweeping gesture with her arm. "As you can see, she keeps everything in these random piles and therefore can find nothing." She picked up the coffer and put it inside the cupboard, as though she did so daily. After making a show of glancing around, Maddy said, "She was supposed to obtain some boxes for storage, but I see she has not yet done that."

"In which case you should leave."

Not before I return the keys.

Maddy smiled. "Yes, you are quite right. But I must check behind the privacy screen first, in case she's stacked them there." Before he could gather his wits, she'd ducked behind the screen and replaced the key ring. "Not there, either. We should both leave now." She brushed past him toward the door.

"Wait." Musgrave grabbed her arm roughly, and a jolt of fear spiraled through her. Here they were, alone in a chamber with a bed. The last time that had happened, he'd nearly violated her. Still clinging to her arm, he pressed his ear to the door, then cracked it open. Thank the Blessed Virgin, he was only checking to make sure there was no one in the passage. Her heartbeat slowed. Musgrave walked through, and she followed him down the hall.

"I trust you completed your business in Carlisle?"

He snorted. "That's none of your concern."

"Merely a friendly inquiry. I found it interesting that the necessity of your going to Carlisle coincided with the earl's visit." The words were out before Maddy could consider how risky it was to make such a comment.

They'd been walking toward the drawing room. Without warning, he stopped and shoved her against the wall, so hard her head slammed against the plaster and then whipped forward. She cried out in pain. Musgrave towered over her, caging her. "What do you know?" he asked.

"Nothing. I have no idea what you're talking about." He bent down until his face was so close to hers, she could see the broken blood vessels on his nose and the tiny wrinkles beginning to form around his eyes.

His voice was low. "Have a care, mistress. Servants run off all the time. If you were to disappear, Lady Dacre wouldn't trouble herself too much."

Maddy's blood went cold. This was more than an implied threat. She itched to raise her arms and push him away, but instead she clutched her skirts to prevent herself from doing something so futile. "I have friends who would make inquiries."

Abruptly, he backed away, glowered at her one last time, and strode off. Maddy rubbed the back of her head. Her neck was already aching, and she hoped Lady Dacre would not summon her to do any work this afternoon.

• • •

Maddy spent the next morning helping with the booty the Dacres had hauled over from Naworth Castle, making an inventory of all the goods. Every able-bodied servant had been pressed into service, carrying the treasure upstairs and laying it out on a long table in a room Maddy had never been in. Perishable goods, such as loafsugar, dried ginger, and salad oil had already been delivered to the kitchen.

In the afternoon they embroidered. Maddy stole a look at Lady Dacre as she bent her head to her work. She thought it unlikely the lady had noticed that Norfolk's letter had gone missing for a short time. If so, she would probably conclude that she herself had misplaced it. Musgrave had obviously entered her chamber with the intention of snooping and must know if he informed on Maddy, she wouldn't hesitate to return the favor. What was he looking for, she wondered? And what was it he feared she knew?

Lady Dacre was feeling ill the following day. Edith told her she thought the mistress suffered from the same complaint she herself had recently gotten over. Maddy attended Sunday services by herself and dined alone. She did not know where the men were, nor did she inquire. In the afternoon, she walked about the property. The air was crisp, but the sun shone with a brilliant fervor. Because it was Sunday, only a few workers were on hand to feed livestock and tend to one or two sick animals. She caught a glimpse of Christopher Dacre's coursers, Devil and Prince, over by the stables. With a shudder, she walked in the opposite direction.

On Monday, Lady Dacre emerged from her bedchamber looking tired and pale. Maddy read her favorite Bible stories to her, and when she nodded off, sewed. By Tuesday she had fully recovered, and they returned to their usual routine.

That night lying in bed, Maddy thoughts again turned to Ryder. She would see him tomorrow. A pleasurable feeling, more than pleasurable, if she were honest, nestled against her heart. Conjuring up his face threatened to steal her sanity. Those green eyes—severe, judging, but offset, at times, by a sweetness around his mouth. Sleep claimed her with his image still clearly visible in her mind's eye.

Chapter Eleven

Early the following morning, Maddy made a list of the embroidery silks Lady Dacre needed and accepted the necessary coin from her. Because it would require extra time to visit the market, Maddy intended to depart early and requested a simple meal in her chamber. Ever since she'd made up the platter of apples and cheese for Mistress Derby, the cook seemed to be warming toward her. Maddy had asked only for some bread and cheese, but the tray delivered to her chamber contained apples, figs, and several pieces of marchpane as well. Apparently, the woman had forgiven Maddy for her past sins, whatever she thought they had been.

The northern climes were fickle, but now, in mid-March, the snow was rapidly melting, giving way to puddles, overflowing streams, and flooded meadows. The Irthing was running high. Ploughmen would soon be out turning the earth, sowing oats. The road, wet and muddy, was leaving its unwelcome gift on her hem with every step taken by her trusty mount, Eve. There was nothing to be done about it. The sun was shining, the day mild, and she would not allow a muddied hem to ruin her ebullient mood.

The church bells were ringing nones when Maddy rode into the village. She stopped in at the mercer's shop to purchase the silks, both for her mistress and herself, then strolled about the market with her basket, hoping to be noticed by many of the good citizens of Brampton, as Ryder had suggested she do. The square was filled with gossiping housewives, servants, and men drinking ale they'd bought from a stall. No doubt they were talking about farms and enclosure, sheep and horseflesh. Children ran hither and yon, chasing each other. A couple of older boys were poking a dead dog lying in the ditch.

When she arrived at the Ryder house, Nicholas Ryder met her at his door, looking ferocious. "Where is your groom?" he demanded.

"I-I did not bring one." Out of the corner of her eye, she glimpsed Daniel peeking out from between Ryder's legs, smiling mischievously.

"I thought we agreed that you would not come unaccompanied. What is the matter with Lady Dacre, that she allows you to go about the countryside without an escort?" All this before he had uttered a word of greeting, while Maddy was left standing on his front step.

"I'm sure she would have seen to it had I asked. But the truth is, I never thought of it again. I am not afraid, you know, to travel alone." A half-truth at best.

As if God were punishing her for the lie, a giant slab of snow, soft and melting, dropped onto her head from the roof, soaking her hair, bodice, even her skirts. Maddy inhaled sharply, her breath stolen by the shock of the searing cold. Bits of wet snow dribbled down her face. Even worse, some of it forged a chilling trail down the back of her neck.

"By all the saints, why are you standing there?" Ryder hauled her inside and called for a servant. He began brushing snow from her hair and clothing, touching her body in places he truly should not be anywhere near.

Maddy stepped back. "I pray you, sir, stop!" Her host appeared unfazed. Fortunately, a servant came running with a stack of linen cloths in her arms. Ryder grabbed one and made as if to continue assisting Maddy, but she relieved him of the cloth. "Pardon me, but could she"—Maddy looked at the serving woman, whose name she did not know—"take me to a chamber where I might dry off?"

Now discomposed, he said, "Certainly. Margery, escort Mistress Vernon to the blue bedchamber. And find her some fresh apparel to wear. When she is ready, bring her to my study."

She followed Margery upstairs to the designated chamber. The tester bed was hung with deep blue drapes, pulled open, and a Turkey carpet in the same shade of blue covered much of the floor. Margery helped Maddy undress, and she rubbed herself briskly with the linen cloths. Only her hair remained damp. Meanwhile, Margery had laid out a clean smock, kirtle, a lovely embroidered bodice, and petticoats on the bed. While Maddy was dressing, she asked where the clothing had come from.

"It belonged to Mistress Ryder. Susan, her name was."

"Master Ryder's mother?"

She smiled. "No, mistress, his sister-in-law. Master Daniel's mother. The poor lady died while bringing her second child into the world. The babe passed on, too."

Maddy nodded, feeling at a loss for words. Last time, Ryder had introduced Daniel only as his nephew and ward, with no mention of the tragedy that had befallen them. Daniel's father—Ryder's brother—must also be dead.

"I will set your clothes by the hearth in the kitchen, mistress, but they may not be dry before you leave." She passed Maddy a wool shawl to wear about her shoulders.

Ryder was waiting for her in his study. The mood was different this time, more welcoming. Cushions had been placed on the settle, and a tray with hot spiced wine and a platter of dried fish, fruit, and tarts lay on the desk. Getting to his feet, he said, "Pray, be seated. I'll stoke the fire." Busying himself with prodding the blazing wood and adding another log, he spoke no further. When he finished, he seated himself next to Maddy on the settle. Something about his appearance seemed altered—he reminded her of somebody she'd seen before. Before she'd become his captive. But that was impossible.

Maddy was leaning toward the heat of the fire when he spoke. "Are you warm enough?"

"Yes, quite, thank you."

He looked at her sheepishly. "It was rude of me to leave you standing on the doorstep. You have my apology."

"No matter. All is well now. I am grateful to have fresh clothing, since my own was quite soaked through." That reminded her of his hands touching her body, and her face grew hot. When he rose to pour her a cup of wine, she said, "You look different today, Master Ryder."

He handed her the wine and sat. "That is because my hair and beard have been trimmed."

"Ah. Of course." She could see it now but still could not shake the odd feeling of having made his acquaintance prior to their first meeting in the castle.

"What do you have for me today?" Except for the fact that he remained seated next to her on the settle, he was now all business.

"First, will you tell me if you received my message?" She drank a long swallow of the wine, its heat sliding down her gullet to her belly, banishing any cold left from the drenching.

"I did. Thank you for the warning, but I have not had occasion to be in Carlisle of late. The questioning of the captives from Leonard Dacre's raid is finished."

"I have my doubts as to whether Vine himself was actually there. I suspect that he wished to see Sussex no more than I and simply invented an excuse."

"The mysterious Master Vine. Have you had any more threats from him?"

"I'll tell you in a moment. But first, I learned nothing about the Dacres' meeting with the Earl of Sussex. They dined in the small chamber, with the door closed. There were servants going in and out of the room, so I could not loiter." Maddy set her cup down, and leaning close to the fire, ran her fingers through her locks to hasten their drying. Glancing at Ryder, waiting for the next question, she found him staring at her most unnervingly, his eyes glowing softly. He swallowed, his Adam's apple bobbing.

"The red-gold strands in your hair gleam in the firelight, Madeleine."

Disconcerted, she said, "But my hair is brown, sir."

"Aye, but in the light it…" He never finished his thought but gave his head a shake and got on with business. "Some believe Sussex is not as loyal to the queen as he ought to be. The fact that he was dining at Lanercost adds fuel to that fire." His eyes now wore their usual cool expression. Possibly she had been mistaken in believing they'd ever looked any different.

"Why did you not wish to see Sussex?" Ryder asked.

"He was present the day I pleaded for my brother's life before the council. I feared he would recognize me and tell Lady Dacre she was harboring the sister of an executed traitor." Ryder looked rueful, as though he might feel some regret over her brother's hanging. Maddy cast that thought aside—she could make no sense of it—and went on. "I have brought you Norfolk's letter. I made a copy of it." She jumped up to retrieve it. Painstakingly, she had rolled it up, tied it with a cord, and put it in her basket, covering it with a cloth. Glancing about the room, Maddy felt a bit frantic when she didn't see the basket anywhere. She should have kept the letter on her person. If anybody else found it…this was most careless. "I must have set it down when I came in. I was… distracted."

"Calm yourself, mistress. I'll find it." He strode from the room and returned shortly—empty handed. Daniel trailed behind him.

"My nephew was angry with me because I would not allow him to speak to you. He has hidden the basket and will reveal its location only after he is permitted to greet you properly."

Maddy looked at Ryder, then at the boy. He did not seem at all happy to see her. In fact, his small face had turned ashen, and big tears spilled from his eyes. When she knelt down, he came to her, placing his small hand on her bodice and stroking, a little bit like one might pet a dog. Then he did the same with her skirts. "What is it, Daniel?" Maddy asked. "Why are you crying?"

Ryder bent down and lifted the boy into his arms. "You are wearing his mother's apparel. He remembers, aye, Daniel?" The child buried his face in Ryder's chest. "And you bear a slight resemblance to Susan."

The boy must have taken his coloring from his mother. Maddy reached out and rubbed the small back. "Pray forgive me, Daniel. I should have asked you if it was all right for me to wear your mother's clothing. But you may recall—mine was dripping wet." He looked up at her, and she thought the corners of his mouth curved up a tad. "All because your jackanapes of an uncle left me standing outside long enough for a mountain of snow to fall on my head!" Daniel laughed, a squeaky sound emitting from his chest. Maddy looked up at Ryder, who'd raised his eyebrows at her.

"Did you call me a jackanapes, mistress?"

"I'm afraid I did, sir."

"How shall we punish her, Dan? Shall we tickle her? Spank her?" Daniel nodded his approval. Ryder was smiling broadly, and she was beginning to regret calling him such a name. They took a step toward her, and she pretended to cower.

His uncle set Daniel down and whispered something in his ear. The child scurried out of the room, and then there was silence between her and Ryder. To her shame, Maddy was still thinking about being tickled and spanked by him. He was waiting near the door, arms folded loosely across his chest and looking as if he dearly wanted to laugh. Maddy reclaimed the settle and fussed with her hair.

"He likes you."

"Daniel? Do you think so? He is the sweetest child! Although it was very naughty of him to hide my basket."

"If you could see him when he is having one of his childish tantrums, you would not think him so sweet."

Maddy gave him a skeptical look. "I can't credit it."

Ryder shrugged. "He becomes frustrated. And then he loses his temper. But I admit it is a rare occurrence."

An awkwardness ensued, until she finally worked up enough courage to say, "Would you mind if I asked you why he does not speak?" Just then, Daniel burst through the door carrying the basket, and her query went unanswered for the present.

"Off you go, brat," Ryder said. She waved to the child as he left the room. His uncle, having retreated to his desk, was already unrolling the document and paying her no mind. After a few moments, he threw the missive down and she heard him say, "God's teeth, the man is a reckless fool."

"I could not make out the meaning. Is it a cipher?"

He rubbed at his beard with the back of his hand. "A very

poor one, yes."

"Will you not tell me what it means?" Maddy asked, turning up her palms.

"Trust me, it is better that you do not know, for your own protection."

She puffed out an irritated breath. "If I am to be of help to you, shouldn't I be aware of any intelligence that pertains to the Dacres? He seeks their assistance when he comes north. That much I understood. For all we know, he intends to lodge at the priory during his visit."

A knock at the door. Margery stuck her head in and said, "The master will see you and Mistress Vernon now."

Maddy looked from one to the other, confused. Who was "the master?"

Margery left, and she stared at Ryder, a question in her eyes.

"My father," he said with a scowl. "Come. Let's get this over with."

He led her toward the front of the house, to a chamber near the entrance. Why would his father wish to meet her? Maddy had pictured him as an invalid. A doddering old man who needed his son to look after him. Ryder halted abruptly and rapped on the door.

"Come," called an impatient voice.

They entered the room, a large, sunny space with windows on two sides. A sprawling table rested before one set of windows, and an older man—but certainly not doddering—stood to one side of it, poring over a map. More maps covered every available bit of wall. Their entrance did not distract him—he continued his perusal. At length his head bobbed up, and he studied Maddy. He was tall and well built, with shrewd, penetrating eyes. In his youth, he had probably been as handsome as his son. But no more. His countenance was severe, with a hard mouth and deep grooves between his brows.

"So this is our little spy," he said derisively, obviously with the intent of intimidating her.

"Father, may I make you acquainted with Mistress Madeleine Vernon?" Ryder said. He glanced at her then. "This is my father, Francis Ryder."

Not quite the man I envisioned. Maddy curtsied. "Good morrow, sir."

"You did not mention that she was so bonny, Nicholas, but I should have guessed."

Nicholas said nothing.

"My son tells me you're providing him with valuable information."

This seemed to require a response, so she said, "Yes, sir. I am doing what I was asked to do."

He stepped out from behind the table. "What you were *required* to do, you mean. You are well aware of the consequences if you do not, I assume."

His son intervened. "There is no need to threaten Mistress Vernon, Father. She has proved herself to be trustworthy and reliable and quite clever at figuring out what we need to know before I've even instructed her."

"Joining up with Leonard Dacre wasn't too clever, now was it? And she is sister to a traitor, although I suppose she could not help that." He raised his brows, two dark slashes that reminded her of nothing so much as slugs.

Maddy knew his words were intended to get a rise out of her. He was enjoying her unease. But she also knew if she expressed her pent-up feelings, it could be dangerous for her, and possibly for Ryder. So she kept her temper in check and said, "You are correct on both counts, sir."

He barked out a strident laugh, as if that were the last thing he expected her to say. "See that you take the utmost care not to give yourself away. If we are forced to remove you, things will not go well for you."

"Father, she knows—"

Francis Ryder interrupted him. "No need to defend her again, Nick. Although now that I've seen the lass, I understand why you are always so eager to take her side. Just see you don't fall too much under her spell." Again, that harsh laugh, and then he said, "Now leave me. I've work to do."

Ryder bowed, grasped Maddy's arm, and the meeting was over. He hurried her through the flagged hall and only let go when they reached his study. She wheeled on him as soon as the door was shut. "Never before have you said your father was your...your employer. Pray enlighten me, sir."

Chapter Twelve

Nicholas stood before Maddy, uncertain of what to say. How to explain. But first, an apology. "I do beg your pardon for his rudeness." And then he led her to the settle, pushing her shoulders lightly so she would be seated. After tending the fire, he poured them each a cup of wine and sat down beside her.

His gaze on the flames, he began to talk. "As an agent of the queen here in the North, my father needed help. Because his work was covert, and decidedly against the interests of northerners, he was forced to depend on my brother and me from the time we were young lads. Before Richard died, I acted as Father's secretary—writing missives, listening and taking notes on reports from various spies, arranging meetings, and the like. But after my brother's death, Father expected me to assume Richard's duties." Folding his hands, he lowered them between his knees.

Maddy's voice was soft. "And you did so?"

He glanced at her, then back to the flames. "I did as he ordered. Brought prisoners to him and watched many unfortunate souls beat senseless, sometimes even killed, for providing the wrong information, or none at all. As you might guess, this work has increased ten-fold since the rebellion. I have never...taken to it."

"Your father beats people to death before your eyes?" She couldn't hide her disgust. He understood.

"No, of course not. He would not bloody his own hands unless he had no other choice. Richard was more like my father, always strangely fascinated with the whole bloody business. And now I am trapped and know not how to extricate myself."

"Can you not simply tell him you no longer wish to do this work?"

"It is not that simple. I have Daniel to care for. I don't own my own property or have any other home. And I do believe in their ends. What I am sick to death of is their murderous, conniving, deceitful means."

"What exactly *are* their ends?"

"A unified England, ruled over by the queen in all her royal majesty, with no citizens questioning her God-given right to be our monarch."

Maddy cast him a skeptical look. "You sound as though you are mocking the queen's right to rule rather than defending it."

"Forgive me, I've grown cynical. I strongly believe England should be ruled by an English monarch, the rightful queen, Elizabeth. It is the only way forward. The fact that the rebel earls looked to foreign powers for aid...can you imagine what chaos would ensue if Spain invaded? Propped up by the Pope?" He shifted his body so that he was looking directly at her. "But I am much aggrieved over the queen's brand of justice. I did not like the executions of the rebels any more than you did."

"Then you were telling the truth the day you brought me to Lanercost, that you lost friends in the rising?"

"Aye. Men from Brampton I'd known all my life."

She seemed stunned. "So everything you've done regarding me, including forcing me to spy, was on your father's orders?"

He faced her, his gaze steady. "Aye."

"Against your conscience, against your morals, you still carried on because your father ordered you to?" She sprang up and set her cup of wine on the desk. "I must go."

She had judged him and found him lacking.

He had to convince her to stay so he could explain further. Pushing to his feet, he said, "No. It's early yet, you haven't eaten. And I'm sure you have more to tell me."

"I've lost my appetite. And I have told you everything."

Nicholas stepped closer to her. "You said there was more about Vine."

"Nothing significant." She reached for her basket. "Would you summon Margery and ask if my clothing is dry? I will need my cloak."

"Pray, Madeleine, do not run away from me." He placed a hand on her arm, keeping his touch gentle. "Sit down and give me leave to explain."

Maddy searched his face, and he sensed the exact moment she relented. Her lovely eyes softened, and his heart galloped. For whatever reason, she'd decided he deserved a hearing, and he was grateful for it. For her trust. She set the basket down and returned to the settle. "I am all ears."

He gave a brisk nod and continued his tale. "I had made up my mind to leave the queen's business, as soon as the work relating to the rising was at an end. The executions, you see, were beyond what I could tolerate. And when I was at my lowest, wondering how I would endure, you came into my world and threw me off balance."

She shook her head. "I did?"

"I expected you to be a hardened wench. A woman in battle would by necessity be rough around the edges, would she not? Instead, you were brave and strong and...brave." He'd meant to say "captivating," but thought better of it. When he stole a glance at her, her cheeks bloomed with color.

"Why did you keep on with it, then? Why were you cruel to me?"

"Because it would have been the end for you if I had not!" He'd been standing, but now crouched down before her. "Don't you see? What reason could I have invented for letting you go? It had already been decided that you were the one to be placed at the priory. I was merely making certain the correct decision had been made."

"How did they even know of me?"

He sighed, got to his feet, and put some distance between them. "I was your captor. At the battle, I was one of the men who—"

"You! Now I remember. Your hair, your beard. They were shorter, as they are now. That is why I thought earlier I had seen you somewhere before this nightmare began."

Wincing, he said, "Yes."

"After you questioned me, you could have said I wasn't suitable. Had you wanted to, you might have invented a plausible reason for letting me go."

"They were never going to let you go, Madeleine. Do you think they would have sent you home with a pat on the head? No, I fear they would have gotten rid of you, not at the block or the gibbet, but by taking you out of your cell and slitting your throat, then throwing your body into the Eden. No one would have inquired too closely."

She shook her head as if to clear it. "But why?"

His father would rage if he found out what Nicholas was revealing. But, for the first time in years, he cared deeply about something. Someone. He would not hold back, his father be damned. "Why would they let you live unless you could serve some purpose? You were a traitor in their eyes. After executing hundreds, do you think they would have balked at one more? So I did what I could. I made sure your cell had fresh straw, that you had food and drink. I tried to make you comfortable, and as soon as I could, I removed you, to get you ready for this mission."

"But you were so cold to me. I thought you hated me."

"Quite the contrary." He would love to take her in his arms, but he knew she would not countenance it. Instead, he reached out and traced a finger down her face. Her skin was soft as a rose petal. Nicholas wished they had the time, the freedom, to explore what they might mean to each other and follow where that would lead. Maddy held still, her eyes closed. Until suddenly she seemed to realize what was happening. Her eyes snapped open and she drew away.

"What do we do now?"

Grasping her hands, he said, "We finish this. We work out what is going on at the priory—and rest assured, something is—and then we're done with it."

Her expression guarded, Maddy tugged her hands from his grasp. "And will your father let me live? Let me go home?"

"He would not go against me, provided our work is fruitful."

"And if it isn't?"

"It will be. It already has been. Father will be very satisfied when he sees the contents of Norfolk's letter."

"There is no escape for me, is there? You, at least, will have a choice." He heard the resentment in her voice, understood what she must be thinking. Maddy had sacrificed her own freedom to avenge her brother's death, and it had gained her nothing. In her mind, her future looked grim. He couldn't argue; there was no escape for her at present. "I truly must take my leave now. The sun is low."

Sighing, Nicholas rose and summoned Margery to bring Maddy's clothing, but she returned without it. "Mistress, your things are still damp. Especially your cloak."

"Is there a traveling cloak of Susan's she could wear?" Nicholas asked.

"I'll get it." Margery returned shortly with the cloak

and a package tied with a string. "Your clothing, mistress." Maddy retrieved her basket and tucked the package inside.

Out front, a groom led two horses toward them. The palfrey Maddy was riding and his own sleek gelding, Raven. "I am accompanying you," Nicholas told her. "Arguing with me will be a waste of breath." A servant handed him cloak, gloves, and hat, and soon they were both mounted. The groom secured her basket to the side of the horse, and they walked together toward the road. They had not gone far before Nicholas heard a sudden commotion and smiled. It would be Daniel. He should have allowed the lad to say farewell to Maddy, but given the fraught discussion they'd been having, he'd forgotten. They reined in the horses.

The boy was running toward them, his short legs pumping.

Nicholas glanced at her. "Stay put." He dismounted and gathered Daniel into his arms. "Do not cry, Sir Mouse," he said. "You must be a brave knight if you want Mistress Madeleine to pay attention to you." Nicholas settled the boy in Maddy's lap, then steadied her mount.

"You *are* a brave and fearless knight," she said. "I could tell that as soon as I met you, Master Daniel. Or should I call you 'Sir Mouse'?" Daniel smiled, burrowed against Maddy's breast, and then kissed her cheek. Nicholas looked on, musing. After Maddy had kissed the child, Nicholas lifted him down and into Margery's grasp.

"Fare thee well until next time," Maddy called after him, waving. Nicholas marveled over how loving she was with Daniel. There was nothing false about her dealings with him.

As they set out once again, Nicholas said, "It had not occurred to me last time that you probably remind him of Susan." He hesitated a moment before asking, "Do you still wish me to tell you why he does not talk?"

"Yes, if you will." Her anger seemed to have dissolved. As Nicholas knew from personal experience, it was difficult to sustain an ill humor after a hug and kiss from Daniel.

They clip-clopped along companionably, and at length Nicholas began his tale. "Susan, Daniel's mother, died in childbirth a few years ago, along with her baby. A sister for the lad, had she lived. And then my brother, Richard, was killed last year, on the queen's work."

"How sad," Maddy said.

"Aye. After the boy's mother died, he seemed to shrink into himself. At four years old, he'd already possessed a prodigious vocabulary. He continued to talk, although not so much as before. He was altogether more subdued. And then after Richard died, he spoke less and less, until I realized one day he'd stopped speaking altogether."

"Is there anything to be done?"

"Not according to the physician we consulted. He believes, with time, Daniel will find his voice."

"It must isolate him from other children."

"Not as much as you might think," Nicholas said. "There aren't many children about. But he sees them at church, at the market, and on holy days. The other boys seem happy enough to include him in their play."

"You are very good with Daniel."

He was shocked—and ridiculously pleased—that she would pay him such a compliment. "Am I? He trails after me everywhere I go. I believe he fears I might disappear one day, as both his parents did."

"In a child that age, it seems like a logical conclusion. Sir Mouse seems to look upon you as a father."

Nicholas smiled. "Only natural, I suppose. I enjoy playing with him. My father believes I overindulge the boy, but as you've observed, he is an easy child to love."

"That he is. How fortunate he has you as his guardian."

Embarrassed, Nicholas shrugged off her praise. "I hope you will judge me more by my treatment of Daniel than by—"

"The way you've dealt with me?" She met his probing gaze, but she did not yield. She might believe in his devotion to Daniel, but theirs was a completely different kind of relationship. Though earlier he'd sensed she was ready to trust him, he'd obviously been mistaken.

To break the awkwardness, he said, "Now will you give me the rest of your information?"

"Back to the spy business? Truly, there is not much to impart." She related her difficulties with Norfolk's letter. "I stepped behind Lady Dacre's privacy screen while I was looking for the coffer and discovered she has a prie-dieu and a religious tapestry. From the look of it, it might have hung in a monastery at one time. That surprised me."

"Probably from the abbey at Lanercost. The Dacres at the priory are supposed to be Protestant, but many who have pledged themselves to the reformed religion secretly keep to the old faith, as you well know."

"Thomas Vine sneaked into the bedchamber just as I had locked the letter back in the coffer. He gave me such a fright, I nearly screamed."

"Sweet Mother of Christ. What did you do?"

"I acted as if I belonged there and challenged him on what right he had to be in Lady Dacre's chamber. He claimed he heard 'someone skulking about,' which was utter nonsense. In the passage, after we left the room, I commented on the fact that he'd made himself scarce for the earl's visit. I realized my mistake immediately. He is not a man to needle. He slammed me against the wall and asked me what I knew."

Nicholas reined in his horse. "He hurt you? Damn the man! Do not bait him, I beg you. Obviously, he has something to hide and fears you've found him out."

"I told him I had no idea what he was talking about, and he seemed to believe me."

"I do not want you to risk your personal safety, Madeleine.

Swear to me you will not."

She had slowed her mount to a stop and looked at him incredulously. "Sir, that is an extraordinary demand, since you have placed me in a situation which, by its very nature, puts me at risk." When he did not speak, she said, "You need not look as if you are beseeching God to save you from womankind."

"And you need not make things worse by goading him."

They sat there glaring at each other, until finally she spoke. "Very well. I will attempt to refrain from engaging in unnecessarily provoking behavior."

Nicholas nodded curtly. That would have to suffice for now. "We must speed up; the hour grows late."

For the rest of the journey, they moved at a fast clip, only slowing the horses to cross the bridge. The river churned beneath them, full of spring run-off. The water swept on toward its eventual joining with the Eden, strong and sure of itself. Nature had such strength of purpose.

Nicholas rode with Maddy until the priory gatehouse was in sight. "Probably better that I'm not seen. Next time, pray ask Lady Dacre for a groom to accompany you, or I shall ask her myself."

"As you say, sir."

Afternoon had given way to evening. Nicholas maneuvered his horse close to her. In the silver-gray light, he could barely make out her features. "Leave off calling me 'sir,' Madeleine. I think you know my name." And then, against his better judgment, he leaned in and kissed her cheek, allowing his lips to linger long enough for her to know this was not an avuncular buss. "God keep you."

Maddy was nearly to the gatehouse before she turned and looked at him. The light was disappearing, the sky now deep cobalt and violet, with a small crescent moon showing. He watched until she rode under the archway. She did not look back again.

Chapter Thirteen

In the morning, Maddy gave her mistress the silks she had purchased for her at the market. She set about sorting them right away, and once again Maddy marveled at how neatly she kept her embroidery supplies. Compared to the state of her bedchamber...Maddy had no doubt that Lady Dacre slept some nights with papers on her bed, probably flying onto the floor when she shifted in her sleep. It occurred to Maddy that the lady's papers most likely were so disorganized because she could not read them.

She asked Maddy to read out loud some of the old Bible stories, beginning with Moses and the tablets. Since these were so familiar, her mind was free to explore her own muddled thoughts. Thoughts that turned to one Nicholas Ryder unless she exercised a high degree of self-control. Since parting from him yesterday evening, she'd not been too successful.

He likes me. The entire time he had let me rot in a cell, dirty, hungry, and frightened, he had liked me. His father's snide remarks made sense now.

And so she was left to wonder about her own feelings for him.

In the last few weeks, she'd discovered that he was capable of great tenderness, kindness, and patience. That he adored his young nephew and was doing all within his grasp to nurture the boy. Ryder could laugh, even at himself, and was willing to suffer her teasing.

And then there was the matter of that sweet, lingering kiss he'd given her. Reluctantly, she acknowledged to herself she would welcome more from him. Much more.

But he was her captor. Her jailer, the man who controlled her fate. Most likely any liaison with her would be strictly forbidden by the queen, by William Cecil. Even, perhaps, by his father. Ryder had snatched her from the battlefield, held her prisoner, and questioned her, sometimes harshly. And ultimately, he had forced her to spy for him. Whether he was doing this at his father's behest made little difference. Maddy's freedom had been stolen from her.

How can I care for such a man?

He had asked that she judge him not by his dealings with her but by the way he treated Daniel. She didn't think that was possible. It may be conceivable to look kindlier on a foe if moderating qualities came to light, but was it realistic to believe she could ignore everything else?

In truth, she did not know Nicholas Ryder's true nature. He had been one man at Carlisle Castle, when she'd been his prisoner, and a completely different one now. Which of these men represented his real character? He seemed desperate to be finished with the spy business, and yet he was bound by his duty to the queen. What might he be willing to do to achieve his goal? Might she end up as his sacrificial lamb? He implied that he would save her, that his father would not go against him, but she wasn't sure she believed that. In the end, when her usefulness had run its course, what then? Ryder could not guarantee she would escape with her life.

"Madeleine?"

Through a haze, Maddy heard Lady Dacre's voice calling her name. Startled, she jerked her head up.

"Madam?"

"You stopped reading. Is something amiss?"

"Not at all, my lady. Pray forgive me. My mind wandered for a moment."

Lady Dacre's brows knitted. "You look a bit drawn today. Return to your bedchamber and rest until dinner."

"But—"

"Do as I say, my dear. You will feel the better for it."

"You are too kind." After gathering her things, Maddy left before Lady Dacre had a change of heart. Once in her chamber, she cuddled up on the bed with Useless, her wayward thoughts tangling in her brain until, exhausted, she fell into a sound sleep.

• • •

"What news from Carlisle, Master Vine?" Lady Dacre asked.

They were at table, the four of them. The smell of fresh pastries wafting up the stairs had awakened Maddy, and she'd hastily washed her face and hands, donning a finer bodice before hurrying to the small dining chamber.

Musgrave did not answer immediately, as he was chewing a large piece of mutton he'd just sliced. He then swallowed a draught of ale to wash it down and rubbed his mouth with the back of his hand. "A rumor is about that the Scots queen is to return to Carlisle Castle."

Was she mistaken, or had the Dacres exchanged furtive glances? It happened so quickly, Maddy could not be sure. Lady Dacre tore off a piece of brown bread before her next question, as though she needed the time to think.

"Why would they be moving her again? Was she not lately removed to Tutbury?"

"Word is, the purpose is to visit her son. His keepers are going to bring him to the castle."

"Has a new regent been appointed, then?" Lady Dacre asked. "I cannot imagine Queen Elizabeth would allow such a visit until there was a regent." After pausing, she added, "If at all."

"Were I the queen, I would not let her within a mile of her son," Musgrave said.

"And why is that?" Dacre asked him.

Musgrave snorted. "Her child is, after all, the king of Scotland. Mary is a Jezebel, a slattern. The Earl of Bothwell bedded her before Lord Darnley was in his grave. She was big with the earl's child when she was taken prisoner in Scotland."

Lady Dacre spoke sharply. "Master Vine, unless you were present, or privy to information very few people have access to, I doubt you can know that." Her clipped words gave away her irritation, bordering on anger, with Musgrave. "And I would ask that you speak more decorously." She nodded toward Maddy. "We have a maid present."

Musgrave cast her a mocking glance, though he spoke to Lady Dacre. "Forgive me, madam. I was carried away." Only he could know she was no maid, although he may have shared that information with Christopher Dacre on one of their evenings at the alehouse.

Dacre spoke. "Mary Stewart has not proven herself to be trustworthy. Instead of putting Scotland first, she places her personal dilemmas ahead of all else. She has been involved in scandal after scandal, finally spelling disaster for herself." He threw down his knife, obviously disgusted.

Most interesting. Where did Christopher Dacre's loyalties truly lie?

"I am well aware of her faults. But she has long been

handled by men, from the Duke of Guise to Bothwell. Who can blame her for her mistakes when she is being pulled in different directions by her so-called councilors?"

"You will ever defend her, madam," Dacre said. "Ever since she gave you the gold chain you wear."

Lady Dacre's hand flew to her neck and she fingered the chain. A gift from Mary Stewart! Maddy blurted out a question before considering the wisdom of it. "How did she come to give you a necklace?"

Lady Dacre answered readily enough. "I traveled to Scotland several years past for my nephew's wedding. I was introduced to her on that occasion, and we struck up a friendship of sorts. We had certain things in common, you see. Before I departed, she made me a gift of the chain, which I thought exceedingly generous."

What could they possibly have had in common? Maddy knew little about Lady Dacre's history. Perhaps one day when they were alone, she would elaborate on the story, but this would not be a good time to ask. Dare she probe a bit, though, since they were talking about the erstwhile queen of Scotland? Ryder asked her to inform him if she heard anything about the Duke of Norfolk. Maybe the duke's letter had something to do with Mary. Mayhap she was the "thistle" he longed to see.

"If she is freed eventually, do you think she will marry again?" Maddy asked.

After a snort from Musgrave, an unsettling silence fell. Lady Dacre set her knife down and carefully wiped her hands on a napkin. Christopher Dacre was studying Maddy, one hand absentmindedly circling the rim of his tankard. Musgrave was the only one who continued to eat.

"She may never be free again," Lady Dacre finally said. "We can't know." Then she rose from the table. "Finish your meal, Madeleine. I shall be in the drawing room." Nobody spoke as she exited the room.

Maddy did not care for the idea of sitting alone with the two men but was loath to let that show. So she helped herself to a sugar cake—her favorite sweet—and popped a piece of it into her mouth. Closing her eyes, Maddy sighed deeply, savoring the rich, buttery sweet flavor. When she opened them, she found both men staring at her, Musgrave with a distinctly salacious grin. Her face burned with embarrassment. Fortunately, Dacre laughed. "You looked as though the myriads of angels were carrying you to heaven, mistress."

Maddy smiled, relieved that his thoughts hadn't been going in the same direction as Musgrave's. "You must sample one of these if you have not. They taste as if angels made them."

"Maybe the Scots queen will wed the Duke of Norfolk," Musgrave said, dredging up a subject she thought they'd dispensed with.

Dacre shot him a quelling look. "Since they are both locked up at present, that is an odd bit of speculation."

Musgrave bristled. "They are both power hungry, are they not? I do not find the idea so farfetched, that they will gain their freedom someday and make an alliance."

"Keep your offensive statements to yourself, Vine. Don't subject us to them." Dacre shoved his chair back roughly and got to his feet. After a curt bow in Maddy's direction, he departed. Was this an act for her benefit? Indeed, what Musgrave suggested was exactly what the rebels in the north wanted.

Now Maddy was alone with Musgrave, who wasted no time in carrying on with his opinions. "Why do they defend that whore? Because they're secret Catholics. Why else?"

"Why should you care?" she asked, forgetting her promise to Ryder to tread carefully with Musgrave.

He leaned back in his chair, arms folded across his chest, his lips quirked. She knew what was coming. "You, a maid. That's a fine joke."

Maddy could not stop herself from glancing around to make sure nobody else was about. Otherwise, she ignored his slur. "I've been wondering, Master Musgrave, what your true purpose is here at the priory. How a murderous brute such as you ingratiated yourself with Christopher Dacre, and, more to the point, why?"

His hand shot out and grabbed her wrist. "Haven't I warned you to keep out of my affairs?"

His fingers pressed the soft flesh of her forearm, at first almost like a lover's caress. Slowly, gradually, he increased the pressure. She should cease her goading. But Maddy could not seem to stop herself, despite Ryder's admonition being fresh in her mind, despite her own common sense. She cocked her head at him. "*Hmm*. Are you hoping to profit in some way from your knowledge of their affairs? Is that it?"

The pressure grew stronger, until she could no longer feel her hand and fingers. A blind rage possessed her; a thick fog seemed to obscure her mind. She was weary of being ruled by men. Her knife was within easy reach, and she snatched it and aimed it toward his hand. "Let go of me. Now. You know I'm not afraid to use this."

Time stopped. She continued to clutch the knife, her hand shaking. Musgrave could easily have cuffed her with his other hand, but perhaps he was afraid she could stab him faster than he could raise his hand to strike her. She must have looked maniacal. He dropped her wrist.

It was the second time she'd nearly stabbed the man.

Rising, he smirked at her, then very indifferently walked out of the room. Maddy recalled his threat, that he could kill her and nobody would care. He was probably correct in that, even though she had insisted her friends would make inquiries. Would Lady Dacre even care enough to look for her if she simply disappeared? Would Nicholas Ryder? He would know who was responsible.

• • •

Sometime during the night, a messenger arrived, rousing Nicholas from his slumber. Since his father did not summon him, he assumed it was nothing urgent and attempted to go back to sleep, but it was no use. His mind would not settle; he kept wondering if the news the man carried had anything to do with Madeleine.

He lay in his bed and imagined her there with him, naked, that glorious hair spread out over his pillow. Over him. He recalled the softness of her skin when his lips had touched her cheek; the little gasp she'd uttered; the fresh, womanly scent of her. His cock was now on full alert.

God's teeth, he needed a woman. It had been too long. But he hadn't any time lately for such pursuits. Between Daniel and his work, he was lucky to tumble into bed for a few hours of sleep each night, never mind a wench there with him for sport. And right now, he did not believe any other woman but Maddy would satisfy him.

God's wounds, what is the matter with me? As long as he was in thrall to the queen and his father, he couldn't have her.

After a time, Nicholas rose. It was not yet dawn. Shivering in the frigid air, he washed and dressed, then found his parent in his lair. He was not alone.

"Enter, Nick. We have news from London." A man they'd dealt with many times in the past was sitting across the table. They knew him only as Roger, and he was a burly, oafish-looking fellow. But Nicholas had discovered his looks hid a keen intelligence.

"What have you to report?" he asked.

Roger spoke in an accent that belied his appearance. Nicholas had always wondered if he was from a noble family. "Your Thomas Vine is one John Musgrave. He is at the priory on Cecil's business."

Nicholas listened closely while the messenger summarized what was known of Musgrave. The man was an outlaw, well known to the authorities in the north. He'd been brought to Cecil's attention as somebody who might be willing to work for both sides.

"A double agent?" Nicholas said. "He is spying on the Dacres while also feeding them selected bits of information regarding the queen's business?"

"Aye."

"If that is the case, why did Cecil want us to place Madeleine Vernon there?" Nicholas asked, his puzzled eyes shifting from his father back to the other man.

The elder Ryder answered. "Because they needed somebody who could get close to Lady Dacre. There is some suspicion that she and her stepson may be working at cross purposes. Or that one is more deeply involved than the other. Perhaps one of them may be more prone to slips of the tongue."

Roger wasn't finished. "The queen will issue pardons any day now to the northern rebels."

Nicholas must have misunderstood. "Say that again, pray."

"The queen is set to issue pardons. Not just to the northern rebels, but to those who joined up with Dacre as well. This will affect your dealings with the lass." His dark eyes bored into Nicholas.

Francis Ryder tossed a bag of coins to Roger, dismissing him. "I'll take it from here. My thanks."

As soon as Roger had closed the door, Nicholas's father said, "You cannot tell her, Nick."

"So we're to deal with her through lies and deceit? She has a right to know."

"Aye, but not now. Not when we still need her. As soon as she's fulfilled her duty, you can tell her. She owes us, after all."

"I don't like it," Nicholas said.

"There's more, and you'll like it even less."

Jesu. More involving Maddy? "Out with it, Father. What else did Roger have to say?"

His father stared at him for a moment over steepled fingers. "Mistress Vernon's brother is alive."

Nicholas was stunned. "You jest."

"Indeed, I do not. Sources confirmed it. He avoided execution and has been in hiding since. His wife knows, but none other except those who are sheltering him."

"But how is this possible? Madeleine witnessed the hanging."

"I will tell you the details later. Now I am more concerned about you getting word to her about Thomas Vine. Musgrave. She must not antagonize him."

Nicholas hadn't made the shift back to Vine. "I shall have to tell Madeleine. His death—"

"You shall not tell the lass. It would compromise the mission even more than her knowing of the pardons."

Getting to his feet, Nicholas glowered at his father. "She grieves his loss deeply. It is why she joined Dacre's raid—to seek revenge. She must be told."

"I warned you about developing an attachment to her. You know as well as I such a thing is strictly forbidden. How can you be objective if you're besotted with the lass? You're considering her welfare before that of the queen. The country. That's not acceptable. Starting now, you will cease all contact with her and I'll take over myself."

The air crackled with tension. In a voice that left no

doubt as to his feelings, Nicholas said, "Do that and I shall leave and take Daniel with me."

"Empty threat. You've nowhere to go."

"I have friends, Father. People who will help me until I'm on my feet. And frankly, I don't believe you can manage without me."

It was a standoff. They glared at each other until finally Nicholas broke the impasse and spoke. "Madeleine trusts me, and she's proved herself willing to do as I ask. Do you think she would do the same for you?"

"By God, she will if she knows what's good for her!"

"That tactic will not work with her, Father. She must be handled with kid gloves, which is not your preferred method."

His father had also risen, and Nicholas leaned over the table, as close as he could get to the man. "You must let me deal with her as I see fit. We've spent hours together, and I know what works with her."

Francis Ryder abruptly resumed his seat. It was the first time in Nicholas's memory he'd challenged him on something and come out the winner. "Very well. But she can't know about the pardons, and especially not about her brother. Look at it this way. It will only hurt her. Wait until this is over, then tell her. She can't have any contact with him now, but she'll want to, and then what will happen? She'll be worthless to us."

So only a partial winner. "I do not like it. But I'll abide by your judgment on these matters for the time being." He excused himself and left to write a brief message to Maddy. What kept him awake that night, however, was pondering how he might get her out of harm's way.

Chapter Fourteen

In the morning, instead of reading and sewing, Lady Dacre asked Maddy to accompany her while she attended to various housekeeping tasks. They went over accounts with Mistress Derby, spent further time inventorying and dispersing the goods from Naworth Castle, and visited the stillroom, where jars of herbs were lined up in neat rows.

"I must do some compounding," she said. "You may return to your chamber and attend to your own tasks, my dear."

Maddy left the lady to her herbal salves and balms and began walking back toward Dacre Hall. A man moving across the grounds from the abbey came into view. He was not on any path but was simply cutting through mud and slush and stepping around the ruins of the cloisters. Although the day was reasonably warm, he had pulled the hood of his cloak up over his head, and it partially concealed his face. Though he did not acknowledge her in any way, she had the impression it was she he was seeking out. Sure enough, when their paths crossed, he pressed a paper into her hand and kept on walking, now rather hurriedly. Acutely aware this could be a message from Ryder, she pressed her hand into her skirt and did not dare glance at it until she was safely in her chamber.

It was indeed from Nicholas Ryder, who bid her meet him at twilight, at the Roman wall north of the priory. She could not imagine the urgency behind this command. What might have happened that called for a clandestine meeting tonight, instead of waiting for their usual appointment on market day?

After an hour or so of reading and sewing after dinner, Lady Dacre excused herself. Maddy suspected the morning's exertions had taken their toll, and she would be napping until it was time to dress for supper. Breathing a sigh of relief, Maddy set off toward her chamber. When she neared the kitchen, Mistress Derby called to her. She wished she could ignore the woman, but her voice was so loud, Maddy could not pretend she hadn't heard.

The cook had an array of vegetables spread out over her worktable and continued chopping until Maddy stood before her. "Thought you might like to know, mistress. Cath hasn't come to work for a sennight. I sent word round to her family asking after her. They thought she was here."

A sick feeling curdled Maddy's stomach. "Are you sure?"

"That she hasn't been here? Wouldn't I know that?" Mistress Derby looked at Maddy as though she thought her not quite sane. "And what reason would her mother have to lie?"

"Does Lady Dacre know?" Surely if she did, she would take measures to find the girl. Yet she'd mentioned nothing to Maddy, who was feeling ashamed that she hadn't noticed Cath's absence.

"Aye. She said there was nothing to be done, that serving girls sometimes run off with a man, or go home because they don't care for hard work."

"Cath did not seem like the kind of girl to shirk her responsibilities. What do you think?"

The woman shrugged. "Can't say I know, but she were a reliable one. And I don't think she had any admirers, except the one we already know about." She tucked her chin and cocked a brow. "Somebody would have told me if she'd been sneaking off with a man."

Musgrave. Maddy didn't say it out loud, but she knew it instinctively. Somehow, he was responsible for Cath's disappearance. Given what he had threatened *her* with, she feared he may have harmed Cath after she'd refused his attentions. "Did she ever say anything else to you about Master Vine? Did he...harass her any further after we intervened?"

"Nay, she never said naught else about it."

Maddy made up her mind to tell Ryder at their meeting tonight. She would confess everything she knew about Musgrave and beg his help in finding out what had happened to Cath. Meanwhile, she must make some response to Mistress Derby. "I'm glad you told me. I will think on what might be done." The cook nodded and Maddy went on to her chamber.

Near sunset, after making sure Lady Dacre did not require her help, she set off walking toward the wall.

Maddy had not explored in this direction since she'd been at the priory, but everybody hereabout knew of the Roman wall. It could not be far if Ryder had asked her to meet him there. Apparently, he intended to keep to the wall for his ride over from Brampton. It ran east and west for miles. The local citizenry—including those who had built the priory, according to Dacre—helped themselves to the stones to construct their homes and outbuildings, and always had done.

After she'd walked for about ten minutes, Maddy glimpsed the wall stretching horizontally before her, gray and wraithlike. It blended into the gloaming and seemed like God had put it there instead of the Romans. The remnants of a Roman fortification were visible as she approached. Since the wind had come up and it was mizzling a bit, she decided to shelter there while she waited.

Maddy was musing on the purpose of this meeting when she heard muted hoof beats on the water-soaked ground. Stepping out to greet horse and rider, she was welcomed by a nicker from Raven, Ryder's mount.

Ryder swiftly dismounted. "Next time be certain who you are greeting before you show yourself," he said rather sternly.

"Had I not been expecting you, I would have." He grasped her elbow, leading her back inside. Three walls were intact and helped block the wind. Maddy lowered the hood on her mantle and waited for him to speak.

His expression was grim. "I wished you to have this information at once. I have learned Thomas Vine's true identity."

Her heart jumped. "Oh?" she said, attempting to gather her wits. Maddy had remained undecided about exactly how much to confess when the time was right. If Ryder already knew Musgrave's identity, conceivably he knew all.

He did not notice her unease but went on speaking. "His name is John Musgrave. He's a notorious border reiver, a brutal criminal and most likely a killer. I am considering removing you from Lanercost for your safety."

And return me to Carlisle Castle? "Oh, pray do not! This is my only chance to save myself." And to redeem herself. What would happen to her if Ryder carried out this plan? If his father had any say in the matter, which he most assuredly would, she would soon be sleeping on straw again. "Nicholas, I beg you!" Before thinking the better of it, Maddy grabbed hold of his doublet and yanked.

Ryder said nothing, only kept a probing gaze on her. How had she dared to lay her hands on him? Reaching out, he captured them with his own, his sage green eyes searching her face. "Do you still fear I could not protect you? I would keep you from harm, Maddy. You have become very important to me."

And then he bent his head and kissed her. A gentle, exploring kiss. With a soft moan, she leaned into him. His arms came around her, gathering her close, kissing her more urgently. The tantalizing pressure of his tongue seeking hers made Maddy forget everything but the here and now. Nicholas smelled as clean and fresh as morning dew. The soft rustle of Raven's grazing, the wind soughing, the rain drip-dropping off the wall, yes, she was aware of all those sounds. But nothing mattered except the warmth of his embrace and the sensual press of his lips. A fever possessed her, and when he stepped away, she wanted to lure him back. He tasted like twilight: deep, sensual, and a little mysterious.

They laughed, both of them breathless. He continued to hold her arms. "I would very much like to kiss you the night through, but I must tell you the rest."

She nodded. "Go ahead." Maddy hoped she could comprehend it; her senses were still attuned to other things.

All seriousness now, he said, "Musgrave is an outlaw, drafted into service by Cecil as a double agent. In the past year, he was hauled before the Council of the North because of his raiding. He got off with a warning, since they had no proof, as is often the case with these men. Their steel helms cover their faces, and of course they ride mainly at night."

Maddy pulled away from Nicholas. "Which is why he could not be present when Sussex came to Lanercost. He would have recognized Musgrave and exposed him."

"Precisely."

"What is his purpose there?"

"He's been sent to gauge the loyalty of the Protestant Dacres."

"But that is what I am doing. Why must there be two of us?" How she wished Musgrave might be removed.

"It seems Lady Jane Dacre and her son may have differing loyalties. They want Musgrave primarily to keep an eye, jaded as it is, on Dacre."

"Has my mission changed?"

Nicholas shook his head. "Nay. 'Tis unclear to me why Cecil needs two spies at Lanercost, but your duty will remain unchanged. Watch and observe Lady Dacre and take note of questionable behavior on the part of anybody else."

Questionable behavior. Did her suspicions of Musgrave in Cath's disappearance count? When Maddy thought about Cath, she was convinced his ruthlessness knew no bounds. "I found out today that the young serving girl who spurned him is missing. I'm frightened for her, Nicholas, and quite certain it's Musgrave's doing." She explained what little she knew. "Can you do anything to help find her?"

"I'll put some men on it, have them be on the lookout for her—or her body." Nicholas gripped her shoulders. "In the meantime, you must stay away from him as much as possible."

Trembling, she broke away from Nicholas. Now was the time to tell him, yet still she hesitated. What would he think of her? But if there was to be trust between them, there must first be truth. It was up to Maddy to convey it. She drew in a deep breath and said, "Musgrave was no stranger to me."

A questioning brow arched. "I do not understand."

It would be easier said if she were not facing him straight on, so she began to pace. "I was introduced to him in Carlisle, during a Midsummer celebration. It will seem difficult to believe, but back then he cut a dashing figure." She paused and glanced at Nicholas, whose face had frozen. "He was tall, handsome, and seduced me with flattery. I was an innocent girl of nineteen years, completely taken in by it."

"He seduced you? Did he—?"

"Bed me?" Maddy looked at him over her shoulder, wondering if her expression reflected the shame and regret she felt. "Aye."

"God's wounds, Madeleine! It is beyond belief that you lay with that man." Even when he'd questioned her, she did not recall him raising his voice. Not like this.

Maddy turned around to face him. "I cannot apologize for what happened so long ago now, or for the foolish, naive girl who welcomed his attentions. At the time, I did not know what he was. But I am sorry indeed for lying to you about the fact that I knew Musgrave. Knew he was not Thomas Vine from London."

"Why did you keep it from me?" His icy glare sent a jolt of alarm through her.

"The first night I was undecided about what to do. Then, as I grew to…to like you, I was ashamed." She searched his face for a sign of forgiveness, of understanding. But he only looked angry. Betrayed.

Now he grasped her arms and shook her once, fiercely. "How can I trust you after this revelation?"

"I made a poor choice, Nicholas," she said. "I was young and inexperienced. I am telling you the truth now so that there may be complete honesty between us."

He snorted. "What else are you keeping back, Madeleine?"

"Nothing! I swear it."

"How can I be certain you are not weighing information yourself, deciding what I should and should not be told? Perhaps you are feeding me only the bits that will reflect well on you. Or even worse, inventing information you imagine I might find useful."

Maddy's breath seemed trapped in her chest. "Why

would I do such a thing?"

"Mayhap you have your own agenda. One you are keeping secret from me."

Something inside her fell away, and she felt the ache of its loss through her body. "That is a harsh judgment, sir. If you believe that of me, then we are lost. Send me back to my cell."

"In truth, I no longer know what to believe."

Maddy recalled Musgrave's revelations at last night's supper. Ryder probably already knew, but after his accusations, she wished to make certain she did not leave anything out. "Musgrave informed us at the evening meal last night that Mary Stewart was coming north to Carlisle, to visit her son. He did not say when."

His tone of voice reflected his irritation with her. "Yes, I am aware of that. The queen had to approve the visit." He hesitated briefly before saying, "You need not come on market day. It is only a few days hence, and unlikely you will have more to tell me by then. In the meanwhile, I will think on what to do with you." He stepped outside into the wind and mist, and Maddy followed.

He gave her no opening to relate the odd conversation that had taken place among the Dacres and Musgrave during dinner, but so be it. Ryder mounted his horse and said nothing more, and Maddy began to make her way toward the priory. She felt a shriveling inside, all hope drifting away like a patch of mist. From elation to despair in only a few minutes. Aware he was watching, she squared her shoulders and moved swiftly, most desirous of getting beyond his line of sight.

Chapter Fifteen

The more Maddy thought about Ryder's parting words, the greater her agitation. *I will think on what to do with you.* What right had he? Would it be ever thus for her? To live at his direction? Or his and his father's, most likely, until finally they no longer required her services?

There was a small voice inside her that said Ryder's reaction to her confession regarding Musgrave might have sprung from hurt, and possibly jealousy. He might feel she'd been too free with her affections, even though any rational thought about the matter would have proved how ridiculous that notion was. Musgrave was far in her past, long before she had ever heard of Nicholas Ryder. Possibly his reaction was merely concern for her safety. Undeniably, Musgrave was a shady and dangerous man, and she shared a past with him.

In the morning, Lady Dacre said she required Maddy's help in visiting the sick that afternoon. That suited her well. Keeping busy would be a good antidote to the turmoil in her mind. After dinner, they stopped by the stillroom to fill a basket with salves and medicines and set off toward the cottages, a groom following with the overflowing basket.

Menfolk were busy turning the earth, later than usual this year due to the long winter and extraordinary amount of snow. Many of the women were out tending herb borders around flower beds, while their children dashed about, squealing and laughing.

They visited patients with all manner of ailments. Sties, boils, and minor wounds were easy to treat. It was those with chronic illnesses that posed the greatest challenge, for they could offer little help. One such man suffered from consumption and looked to be at death's door.

"Can't nothing be done for him, my lady?" his despairing wife asked.

"I'm afraid there is no cure for what ails him." This exchange was carried out in whispers, so that the afflicted man would not hear. "The best you can do is keep him comfortable and warm. Anise seed for his cough and a poultice on his chest are best."

On their way to the next patient, Lady Dacre said, "I tell her the same thing every time I visit, but she is ever hopeful of receiving more encouraging news. I'm afraid it won't be long now."

After their third encounter with influenza, Lady Dacre admitted she was worried. "It seems an odd time for it, with the spring air so fresh and clear." Soon enough, they found yet another sufferer, a child this time, ill with the same malady. While Lady Dacre spoke in hushed tones to the girl's mother, Maddy remained at the child's bedside, smoothing her hair back and washing her face with a cool cloth. The poor child was racked by a cough that sounded like she might hurl her lungs from her chest. She was feverish and couldn't hold still.

Maddy had kept quiet until now. But a child's pain was the hardest to witness. "Mistress Sloan, have you given her willow bark tea for her fever?"

"She's not got a fever."

"Oh, but she does. Mayhap it just came on. Feel her face; it's quite hot." Lady Dacre placed a hand on the girl's brow and concurred. "Pray bring the kettle, Mistress Sloan. I've willow bark in my basket."

"The air in here seems stagnant," Maddy whispered after the mother stepped away. "Should we crack the door?"

"Aye. Just a little, mind. We do not want too much air to seep in. It may contain the infectious vapors causing this malady."

The child, whose name was Bess, looked to have about six years. The same age as Daniel. Bess had been allotted the parents' bed while she was ill, so her mother could keep watch on her while she worked. Normally, the girl would be sleeping with her five siblings in the only other room.

Bess continued to move restlessly, tossing her covers about and nearly falling over the edge of the bed a few times. Mistress Sloan brought the tea, and Maddy moved out of the way so the child's mother might persuade Bess to swallow some of it. It was notoriously bitter tasting.

The girl would have none of it. It spilled over her mother's hand and the bed clothing. "Go see to your hand before it blisters," Lady Dacre advised her. "Madeleine, you try."

"Me? I doubt she'll take it from me if she will not from her own mother."

Maddy was the recipient of a look that brooked no argument. "As you say, madam."

She blew on the tea to cool it. If it was hot enough to burn Mistress Sloan's hand, it was surely too hot to drink. When it had cooled enough, Maddy raised Bess's prone form into a sitting position, then held her in place with one arm. She weighed no more than a child half her age. With her free hand, Maddy raised the cup. "Pray take a sip of this, little Bess. It will help you to feel better."

Another coughing spasm overtook the child. Maddy was close enough to feel droplets of spittle land on her face. As soon as the coughing had subsided, she held the cup to the child's lips. "Drink the tea for me, Bess." To her surprise, the girl swallowed some. Exceedingly pleased with her efforts, Maddy smiled, and Bess smiled back, if weakly. She continued to drink, until the tea was almost gone. Then, collapsing back to the bed, she quickly drifted to sleep.

"Well done, my dear."

Maddy laughed. "I think she was too weak to protest."

As it turned out, Bess was the last of the influenza cases they visited. Lady Dacre's fears were somewhat assuaged.

· · ·

Market day arrived. Maddy tried not to think about Ryder, who had decided not to trust her even though she'd admitted to an error of judgment in not telling him about Musgrave and humbly apologized for it. She would miss seeing Daniel and wondered if he would be aware that it was market day. Would he ask his uncle where she was?

While stitching with her mistress, Maddy ruminated about trust. What was it, exactly? A gauge of someone's reliability? Their truthfulness? And how did you gain, or regain, someone's trust, once lost? It seemed a rather ambiguous concept to her. Ryder had been taking what she'd told him, for the most part, on trust; now he was calling into question everything she'd discovered on his behalf because she'd withheld one bit of information from him. Could trust exist in love or friendship if it was not absolute? It seemed to her everybody held things back on occasion, even from friends. Even from those they loved.

She might have told Ryder that her own doubts about whether to trust *him* weighed like a stone on her heart at times. Where did his true allegiance, or perhaps obligation, lie? With his father, William Cecil, and ultimately the queen. Why would he fight for her? Why would he protect her?

Maddy exhorted herself to stop thinking about Ryder.

Lady Dacre was surprised when Maddy said she would not be visiting Brampton this week, unless her mistress needed something. "Nay, I do not. It is your free afternoon, so you must do whatever pleases you, my dear." She looked at Maddy fretfully. "I don't like the sound of that cough, Madeleine."

Maddy had awoken with a dry cough that continued to plague her throughout the morning. Since she had no other symptoms, she wasn't worried. "'Tis nothing to worry over. I'll be all right."

"You must inform me immediately if you feel feverish." Sometimes Lady Dacre was so kind to her, she hated herself for deceiving the woman. And she resented Ryder for forcing her to do so.

What would please her most on her free afternoon? Finding Musgrave gone for the remainder of the day so that she could sneak into his bedchamber. Ryder had asked her to stay away from the man, but she hadn't given her word. Besides, she wanted only to search his chamber, not confront him. Who knew what secrets he might be keeping? And Ryder would be pleased if she discovered a new piece of intelligence. When the men rode off after dinner, and Maddy had made certain Lady Dacre did not require her assistance, she set out to do her dirty work. She had to be careful, because Musgrave's chamber was in the same corridor as those of the Dacres. Even though her mistress slept like the dead, Maddy still must use caution.

To her chagrin, Musgrave's door was locked. The door of her chamber did not have a lock, but apparently those located in the vicarage did. She could only conclude that Musgrave did, in fact, have something to hide.

Discouraged, Maddy began to make her way toward the tower and her own chamber. And then she made an abrupt turn back to where she'd come from.

I should search Christopher Dacre's bedchamber.

He seemed a harmless, unremarkable sort of man, and she had no real reason to suspect him of anything devious, other than that overheard snatch of conversation between him and Musgrave. Judging from his comments of a few days ago, he was not overly fond of the Scots queen. But weren't the unobtrusive, silent sorts sometimes the very ones keeping secrets? Maddy stopped midstride, struck by a coughing spasm. When it had finally passed, she proceeded to Dacre's door, working up her courage. Then she raised her fist and rapped softly.

No answer. Silently, Maddy unlatched the door and walked in. Dacre's chamber was a marvel of cleanliness and order. The exact opposite of his stepmother's. Where to start? The wardrobe loomed as the largest piece of furniture in the room besides his bed. Other than his neatly folded shirts, doublets, small clothes, and hose, she found nothing of any interest. Next to the bed a simple oak table stood with a book resting atop it. It was Copernicus's work, *De revolutionibus orbium coelestium*, beautifully illustrated with woodcuts. Maddy hadn't thought of Dacre as a man of scientific erudition. The priory had no library as such; possibly he'd removed it from Naworth. She flipped through it, but nothing was concealed within its leaves.

Near the windows, which looked northwest toward the precinct wall and the road, an escritoire caught the sun. It was an elegant piece, inlaid with marquetry. Something else from Naworth Castle? Papers resting underneath a seashell drew her eye, and she lowered herself to the chair nearby to look through them. The ones on top related to estate business, but it was the last one, on the very bottom of the stack, that piqued her curiosity.

It was a brief missive, unsigned, dated a mere few days since. It read, "Our party to gather at LP on Friday next, 24 March. F, H, and B in attendance."

And she'd thought the letter from the Duke of Norfolk a puzzle! A gathering here, at Lanercost? And on Good Friday, when most folks observed the day of Christ's suffering quietly, praying and fasting. The biggest mystery of all: who were F, H, and B? Obviously, the writer assumed Dacre would know. Maddy committed the words to memory and placed the letter back where it belonged. When she stood, the room seemed to swirl about her, and she nearly lost her balance. She steadied herself and made a hasty exit, before her luck ran out and she was caught.

Hurrying toward her chamber, Maddy pondered the message. The missive could be perfectly benign. But why then was it unsigned? It did seem odd that she would not know of a gathering the Dacres were hosting in a few days' time. And why did the writer use only initials to identify the attendees?

While traversing Dacre Hall, she was forced to stop twice, her body racked with coughs. She was beginning to feel apprehensive. Reaching her chamber, Maddy closed the door and leaned back against the wall, breathing heavily. In the silence, her ears rang loudly, as though someone standing next to her were playing a viol. She detested being sick. It was such a waste of time. But this illness had gotten its claws into her, and she could no longer ignore it. Making a half-hearted attempt at undressing, Maddy found she was too weak to accomplish it. When she finally collapsed upon her bed, she was hot with fever. Every time she shifted, her joints protested. Maddy needed Lady Dacre's ministrations, but she would not know Maddy was ill until her absence at supper. She hoped somebody would have the good sense to look in on her, because she lacked the strength to move from her bed. The last thing she remembered was Useless cuddling up next to her and licking her face.

Drifting in and out of sleep, Maddy lost track of time. Day had slipped into night. Her waking was consumed with coughing and aching and an irresistible urge to thrash about. Lady Dacre hovered just outside her consciousness, forcing willow bark tea into her. Each time, she promptly brought it back up. Her fever raged, and she begged them—Lady Dacre and Mistress Derby—to let her strip to her smock. That lasted until the chills set in; then, they piled the bedclothes high, and still she shook. Mistress Derby speculated on whether she might have the sweat.

"Nay, there's been no sweating sickness in many years," Lady Dacre said. "Besides, she'd be dead by now if that were what ails her. I think it is influenza." Maddy drifted into a dream-plagued sleep on that comforting thought.

She was with Nicholas and Daniel, but she could not make out what they were doing. Daniel's face was distorted as he tried to speak to her. In a different dream, she was on a huge sailing vessel, plowing through a soundless sea. The air was completely still, and an eerie silence prevailed. The ship was taking Maddy away from them, and she wept. When she woke up, her eyes were wet.

Mistress Derby was snoring gently in a chair near the bed. Maddy drank some of the willow bark tea her mistress had left, and then she slept again, this time seeing her father quite clearly, a wool flat cap covering his silver hair, his brow furrowed. She even fancied she heard his voice. Then Maddy realized there was a man in her chamber, speaking to Lady Dacre. "How is she?" he asked. The voice belonged to

Christopher Dacre.

"There is some improvement, but she is not recovered yet."

"Should we send for the surgeon?"

"I don't think bleeding will aid her. It is not that her humors are unbalanced. I believe the fault lies in the fetid air of the cottage we visited, where the sick child lives." Maddy wanted to thank her mistress for ruling out the surgeon, but she was too weak.

"What about Ryder? Should he be informed?"

As though Nicholas would care.

"Let us see how she fares today. If she is still unwell tomorrow, I shall send word."

"That would be best. If he was of a mind to attend her... we can't risk it. The party we're expecting may already have arrived. And it is too late to cancel the meeting," Dacre said. "We will need to wait and hope she improves."

The party. Something about a party floated at the edge of Maddy's mind, but would not venture all the way in. Hadn't she recently heard or read something about a party? It was important, crucial that she remember exactly what it was. She stirred and opened her eyes.

Christopher Dacre was gone. She might have imagined the entire exchange.

"Madeleine!" Lady Dacre said, rushing to her side. She placed a cool hand on her forehead. "I believe your fever has broken. How do you feel?"

"Better, I think." She tried to sit up, but the effort was beyond her and she flopped back down.

"You have eaten nothing since early Wednesday, my dear. Stay as you are until we get some food into you. You must rest."

"What day is it?" Maddy asked, still woozy.

"'Tis Good Friday."

"I do not remember Thursday at all." So strange to have lost a whole day. More than a day. "Thank you for taking care of me, my lady."

"It is my duty to do so, child," she said, seeming embarrassed about Maddy's gratitude. "Now, I shall speak to the cook about some nourishment for you. We must begin with broth, and perhaps a boiled egg."

Maddy nodded, not very enthused about the prospect of eating. Later, Lady Dacre returned with Mistress Derby, who was carrying a tray. They helped her sit up. The cook handed Maddy a cup of water. "Drink, but not too much all at once."

"I am parched. How did you know?"

"Always happens after a fever."

Maddy ate what she could, which proved to be very little, under Lady Dacre's watchful eye. "You will feel more like eating later in the day, my dear."

"*Mmm*," she said, feeling drowsy. She lay back down and promptly fell asleep.

Maddy awoke in the afternoon and found a bowl of custard on her table and another cup of water. The custard had the loveliest texture, rich and creamy, with a mere hint of sweetness. She could not identify the flavor, though it was a familiar one. After devouring the entire bowlful, Maddy decided she was feeling well enough to get out of bed. It was about time; she'd been there since Wednesday afternoon.

As soon as she tried to stand, a wave of dizziness hit. She sank down before she fell and injured herself. In a few moments, she tried again. Better. Cautiously, Maddy took a few steps, holding on to furniture just in case. She found the chamber pot and relieved herself, considering the act a great accomplishment. By the time she crawled back to bed, she felt as though she'd scaled a mountain.

Dozing, she stirred only when Mistress Derby said, "You liked it, then. Thought you might. Good for you, too."

She opened her eyes. The cook was holding the empty custard bowl. "That confection is nectar from the gods," Maddy said, stretching. "I've never tasted anything better. Even sugar cakes."

"There's more where that came from," the older woman said, winking at her. "And where do you think I found the bowl?"

"I set it on the table."

She crossed her arms in front of her chest in mock anger. "That beast of yours was licking it, pushing it all around the floor to get every last bit of custard."

"Oh!" She sat up too fast. Black spots floated in her vision, and she quickly lay back. "I forgot all about poor Useless. She probably hasn't had anything to eat since I was taken ill, poor wee lass."

"Never fear, mistress, I've been giving her scraps. Did you think I'd let her starve?"

Maddy's face flushed, and not from fever. "I didn't think anybody knew about her."

The cook chuckled. "Little chance of that. The girl who straightens your chamber every day is right fond of the creature."

"I'm not in trouble, then? Does Lady Dacre know?"

"She tried to keep her off your bed while you were at your worst, but she never said we should put her out."

"God be thanked. I'm very attached to her."

Smiling, Mistress Derby plumped her pillows and helped her sit up. "I brought you some broth and a bit of bread for your supper. Best to eat on the light side for now."

Then she plunked herself down at the side of the bed. Maddy now doubted her earlier theory that the cook was Musgrave's informant. Not simply because she was friendlier to Maddy than she'd been before, but also because she'd asked for Maddy's help with Cath. And seemed to suspect

Musgrave. Maddy had a hunch that Cath herself might have told Musgrave about her involvement.

The cook brought up the girl's disappearance. "Have you given any thought to Cath's vanishing, mistress?"

Maddy didn't dare tell her she was counting on Nicholas to pursue the matter. Mistress Derby would wonder how her cousin could possibly help, and she certainly couldn't have her telling their employer she'd asked him to assist them. "Nay. There's been no time. When I'm well, I'll see what can be done. Maybe I should have a word with Lady Dacre."

"Nay, she thinks the girl ran off with a man!"

"Truly, I pray she's right about that, as long as it's not Vine."

Mistress Derby bobbed her head in agreement. "Can you eat on your own?"

"I devoured that bowl of custard, didn't I?" The mere memory of it made her crave more. "What was the flavoring? I couldn't identify it."

"It is a cook's right to keep her recipes secret. When you are betrothed, come to me, and I'll tell you."

Maddy ticked up a corner of her mouth. "That could be years." *Or never.*

The cook laughed heartily. "I'd best finish my supper preparations." She was at the door before Maddy could protest.

"Mistress, one more thing. I hate to trouble you, but after supper, could you ask one of your serving girls to bring up some hot water for me? I am greatly in need of a good wash."

"'Tis no trouble. I'll have her bring you a hot cross bun too, but don't eat it all at once."

Maddy stripped and bathed thoroughly, feeling as though she was ridding herself of the last vestiges of sickness. The room was warm. Alice, who had replaced Cath in the kitchen, had built up the fire after bringing the water. "Can't have you taking a chill, now, mistress," she said. Maddy wished she could wash her hair, but that would have to wait. She didn't have the strength for it at present. Perhaps Alice would brush it for her.

Afterward, Maddy donned her smock and wrapped a shawl around her shoulders. Somebody had brought a settle to her room while she'd been sick and placed it before the hearth—probably part of the Naworth booty—and she sat down on it now. Staring at the flames flickering before her in varying shades of orange and cobalt, she thought about Nicholas—the first time since she'd been ill other than in her dreams. Would he renege on his promise to help find Cath, since they'd fallen out? Not simply a falling out. It had been more complicated than that.

Although aware he was angry, and maybe a little jealous, Maddy was glad she'd told him the truth, even if it meant he no longer trusted her. After he had time to think it over, maybe he would not judge her so harshly. Hadn't he said she was important to him, and then stolen her breath with that intimate, sweetly tender kiss? A thrill surged through her, remembering the feel of his lips, the press of his body against hers. If she closed her eyes…

She must have dozed off. Sometime later, shouts and the pounding of horses' hooves roused her from sleep. Hurrying to the window, she glimpsed torches illuminating the night, revealing men on horseback and dark figures running toward the farm. Her heart beat harder, drumming out an insistent warning.

Reivers. It was a raid. *Blessed Virgin, protect us.*

Having no time to waste, Maddy threw on a kirtle, wool bodice, and skirts, all the while casting about in her mind for a hiding place. Raiders often kidnapped women, held them for ransom. Or worse, raped them. She pulled on her stockings and tied them with garters she had to search for and shoved her feet into leather shoes. Before hastening to the door, she grabbed her shawl off the bed. She would proceed cautiously and see what she could see. Perhaps it was not a raid. Maybe there was something amiss at the farm, and the men had gone to investigate.

Down in the kitchen, she spotted Alice asleep on a pallet before the huge grate. Quickly she roused her and whispered, "Reivers." The girl's eyes widened with fear, and Maddy put a finger to her lips. When Alice started to look for her clothing, she stopped her. "You must come with me now. Just bring your shawl. Where is Mistress Derby?"

"She went to Brampton after supper."

Taking Alice's hand, Maddy guided her toward the door leading to the undercroft, the principle storage area for kitchen staples. The girl was trembling with fright. In contrast, Maddy felt the blood pumping through her body and with it, a surge of strength. "We'll hide here, in one of the alcoves. We must lift a couple of bags of grain up and then crawl in behind. Can you help me with that, Alice?"

"Aye." She was the one who knew where things were kept and led them to the bags. They hoisted two of them—the alcove was at shoulder level—both breathing hard when they'd finished. Maddy gave Alice a leg up and she tumbled over the bags. "How're you going to get up here, mistress?"

Heavy footsteps and bellowing voices forced Maddy to a hasty decision. "I'll hide down here, Alice. You must remain in the alcove until it's safe, mayhap until morning. Don't concern yourself about me. If they find me, do not give yourself away. Do you understand?"

"Aye. But—"

If the girl finished her sentence, Maddy didn't hear it. Feeling her way around, she located some butter-filled firkins and ducked behind them. Just in time. In seconds the door banged open and torchlight brightened the room. She hoped they would not bother trying to haul away the heavy barrels concealing her.

But it seemed she had nothing to worry about. One of them shouted, "Nobody in here. 'Tis a storage space." The door banged shut again and they were gone, noisily climbing the stairs to the chambers above. What would they think when they found hers deserted? They would guess she was hiding somewhere and might return to conduct a more thorough search.

Maddy heard Alice call to her in a quavering voice. "Mistress?"

"Stay put, Alice. They may be back." In a few moments she heard them pounding down the steps. From the sound of it, there were only a few men searching the buildings. They did not return to the undercroft.

Leaning back against one of the barrels, Maddy let her guard down a bit. Something was off. What were they looking for? And why hadn't they ransacked this vast storage area, filled not only with kitchen staples, but goods from Naworth as well? By now, raiders should have been hauling at least some of it away.

It was unbearable, waiting like this. After what seemed a very long time, but was probably a quarter hour or less, she pushed to her feet and crept over to Alice's hiding place. "I am going to investigate."

Alice's head popped up above the bags of cereal. "Nay, mistress. What if they find you? They might kill you, or worse."

"I'll be careful. But I want you to remain here."

"Oh, I wish you would not leave me."

"I know. But I must find out what is happening. Perhaps it is nothing, and I can come back and get you out of there." When she said no more, Maddy began to make her way back toward the kitchen door, feeling a little ashamed about deserting the lass.

Chapter Sixteen

When Maddy reached the door, she paused and listened. She heard nothing, except for the rustling of busy mice feet skittering about the undercroft. The raiders might have left a man to stand guard, but she did not think they had. She unlatched the door and pushed it open. The kitchen lay in darkness, silent and empty. Tiptoeing all the way, Maddy headed toward the stairs and ascended as quickly as she was able in her weakened state. She had to retrieve her dirk, which she'd forgotten in her haste to dress.

Back downstairs, she debated whether to exit through the kitchen door leading outside and walk around to the vicarage, or go the usual way, through the long expanse of Dacre Hall. It was more likely that men would be posted outside, so she chose the usual route. Maddy was about halfway down the length of the hall when the door creaked open. A solitary figure carrying a candle was moving toward her, and it was too late to hide.

She would have to brazen it out, as she'd once done with Musgrave. She had her dirk for protection. *Breathe, Maddy.*

Be calm.

"Madeleine, is that you? Oh, you gave me a fright, looming out of the dark like that! I've come to see if you were safe."

Lady Dacre. She looked witchlike with the candle casting its eerie light under her chin.

"I-I heard noises, saw men running around with torches out my window. Is it a raid?"

"Yes, they've gotten away with some livestock. The men have ridden after them. You should not be out of your sickbed, my dear."

The first thought that struck Maddy was how calm the lady was. And the second: she was lying. Her purpose was to ensure Maddy remained in her chamber. The men who'd been searching must have told her she wasn't in her bed. For now, she'd have to do as her mistress bade her.

"No, of course I should not, but I was frightened. I will return to my chamber then, unless—"

"I'll accompany you to your room. You are still weak." Lady Dacre gripped her arm.

"That's not necessary, my lady. I am perfectly able—"

"Nonsense, I'll see you safely back to your bed."

Maddy decided not to protest, but to appear helpless and grateful for the assistance. "Thank you, madam. 'Tis true, I do not have my strength back yet." Maddy entered the chamber first, hoping the scabbard strapped about her waist wasn't noticeable in the near-dark. Useless emerged from behind the wardrobe, and while Lady Dacre fussed over the dog, Maddy removed the sheath and shoved it under the bed coverings.

The woman did not depart until she'd helped Maddy undress and tucked the coverlet under her chin. "Do you need anything before I leave you?"

"Oh, no. Pray return to your own bed."

Then she was gone. Maddy lay there, counting. When she reached two hundred, she deemed it safe to dress and set out for the vicarage once again. Earlier, a welcome surge of strength had possessed her. But now, bones aching, Maddy moved more slowly. She considered returning to her bed—she was not yet recovered from her bout of influenza, after all. But something about this raid smelled rotten, and she intended to find out what it was.

Maddy proceeded more cautiously this time, edging along the east side of the great hall, ready to duck under the enormous oak table if the door suddenly opened. At the far end she waited, straining to hear any sounds of men or horses. After a reasonable amount of time, she went to the door and peered through the window, to no effect. The dark of a moonless night blanketed everything.

No sooner had she pushed the door open and stepped out than a couple of men holding torches came striding her way. This was no raid; it was a gathering. The word tugged at her memory; she had heard it recently. Christopher Dacre had reminded his mother about a "party" gathering at Lanercost on Friday, tonight, but in her feverish state she'd not made the connection to the letter she read in his chamber. Now she remembered. "F, H, and B in attendance." She had thought it strange to hold a festivity on Good Friday.

Maddy leaped back into the shadows. A tall man came into view behind the first two. He moved with purpose, his eyes riveted on the vicarage. She wondered which of the initials he was. One of the torchbearers unlatched the door for him, and he disappeared inside. Unfortunately, the other men did not.

"They'll be a while," one of them said. "Meantime, we can have our fill o' the priory's hospitality over at the stables." He slapped the other man on the back and guffawed.

Had they seen her? She held still, praying they would turn

and march back the way they'd come, from the gatehouse road. She flattened herself against the wall, knocking something free. A piece of stone, loosened over the centuries, had chosen that precise moment to give way, and it was enough to draw their attention. They swung around, and with the light cast from the torches, spotted Maddy right away.

Her skin prickled.

"What have we here?" the brawnier of the two asked. Not that he truly wanted an answer. Bullnecked, he was built like a stone fortress.

His compatriot, much slighter of figure and longer of leg, said, "Why, 'tis a fair lassie!" They both laughed and came closer, to better inspect her. At that moment, she wished she were covered with warts and had crossed eyes.

"Who are ye?" He swung his torch close, and Maddy recoiled, saying nothing.

They looked at each other. Bull Neck said, "Remember our orders? We're meant to—"

"Nay, dinna say before the lass!"

Maybe she could make a run for the stables. It was plain they were both well into their cups. Bull Neck stuck his face close to hers, bolstering that impression with his spirit-laden breath. "Would ye like to take a ride wi' us, lass?"

The other man shook his head. "Nay, we should not."

"Why? We're meant to be reivers, are we not? We should act the part." He handed his torch to his friend, who placed both of them in holders by the door to the vicarage.

Maddy's sense of self-preservation kicked in. *Run. Now!*

She spun, surprising them. Lifting her skirts, she dashed along the grassy area that ran beside the hall. She could get to the stables this way, and since they'd come the other way, perhaps it would disorient them.

Maddy heard Long Legs call to his friend. "Get the horses, man. I'll catch her."

She zigzagged, hoping to confuse him, and that ploy seemed to work for a while. His curses rang out. But luck was not on her side this night, and her strength was waning. Tripping over a low hedge, invisible in the dark, Maddy fell face-first onto the cold ground, air whooshing out of her. "Oof!"

The man giving chase hauled her up and did not let go. She was gasping, trying to catch her breath. All too soon, Bull Neck returned with the horses. He passed a wine skin to the other man, who drank a long draft before handing it back. Maddy tried to yank her arm from his grasp, but it was no use. He was too strong, and she, too weak.

"Lovely night for a ride, eh mistress?" he said, jerking her toward the horses.

The events of the evening were beginning to take their toll. Since Maddy had fallen, her head was spinning, and she feared she might faint if forced to sit a horse. Her cheek was stinging—when she touched it, her fingers came away bloody. No doubt she'd landed on something sharp when she hit the ground. Maybe if they knew she was sick... "Pray sir, allow me to return to my chamber. I have been ill with influenza these past few days. I have no strength for riding."

They glanced at each other. "The lassie found her voice. Dinna ye worry, because ye'll no' be doin' anything but hangin' on," Long Legs said.

"But—" It was useless to argue. They weren't listening. Long Legs mounted and his friend tossed Maddy up behind him. She refused to put her arms about his waist but clung to his doublet instead. It hung loose, because, unlike Bull Neck, he had no fat on him to speak of.

Once through the gatehouse and on the road, they whipped their horses into a gallop, slowing only when they crossed the bridge. She squeezed her eyes shut. It was dangerous to ride at this speed on such a black night, for both horse and rider. A loud buzzing in her ears made her dizzy, so she rested her head against Long Legs's back. After a time, he called out to Bull Neck, and their pace slowed. They must be halfway to Brampton by now. Lulled by the motion, Maddy fell into a stupor, and for a time, was blessedly unaware of her predicament.

Eventually their voices roused her. The horses had slowed to a walk. "What're we to do wi' her?"

"Ferniehurst said we're no' to harm anybody. From the look and sound o' her, she's gentlefolk."

"Aye."

"Here's as good a place as any to dump her," Long Legs said, right before he shoved her off the horse. Another ignominious fall to the earth. Though it jarred her, the ground was yet soft and still covered with last autumn's leaves. Maddy lay there, too exhausted to even cry out. Though she hated showing such weakness, it might be wiser to let them think she had passed out.

"She's no' dead, is she?" Bull Neck asked. That was the last thing she heard before they galloped off, back toward Lanercost.

Not dead, but Maddy felt as if she might be dying. If she stayed where she was, the first traveler on the road tomorrow might find her cold, lifeless body. She had to be close to Brampton, and if she could summon the energy to walk the rest of the way, she could find Ryder's house. He would take her in. Even if he was still angry with her, even if he did not trust her, he would take her in.

• • •

In the middle of the night, a pounding on the front door awoke Nicholas. Since his father was in York, he'd best see who it was. Wearing only his nightshirt, he rushed downstairs.

When he approached the door, he saw that a servant had already flung it open. He heard a pathetically weak voice—a familiar one—cry out. "Help me." And then, "Pray, let me in!" Nicholas pushed the servant aside, and his worst fears were confirmed.

"Maddy! God's wounds, what's happened to you?"

She was shivering so hard her teeth were clacking together. Without another word, he picked her up and carried her up the stairs, giving orders all the way. "Wake Margery and bid her come to the blue chamber. Bring hot water and clean cloths. Extra blankets, too." Maddy was so light as to seem boneless.

Nicholas laid her down on the big tester bed and unfastened her cloak. "Are you hurt, sweeting? Jesu, whoever did this to you will answer to me." Her face was scratched and bleeding in a few places, but not enough to account for her extreme weakness.

"Cold." That was the only sound she uttered, other than feeble moans every so often.

Nicholas began piling blankets over her. "We must get you warm. You will be warm," he said. In a few moments, Margery entered with a basin of water, linen cloths draped over one arm.

"I'll take that," Nicholas said. "Leave us, pray. Wait outside the door."

He wet a cloth and wrung it out, then sat on the edge of the bed. "You are covered with grime, Maddy. Let me wash your face."

She nodded. For the first time, her eyes focused and she appeared to know where she was. Who *he* was. Gently, he stroked the warm, wet cloth over her face. She moaned, and he ceased immediately, afraid he'd hurt her. But she said, "Don't stop. Are you an angel? Nay, perhaps the devil."

That made him smile, but it did not diminish his rage.

"Only a man, Maddy. Can you tell me what befell you? How did you get this cut on your cheek?" Nicholas tried to keep his voice soothing, even though he wanted to kill whoever had done this to her.

Gradually, her chills subsided. But still her voice shook when she spoke. "Some men were chasing me. I fell."

"Who? Who was chasing you? Can you remember?"

"Aye. Long Legs and Bull Neck."

Nicholas laughed. "I believe you are delirious. There will be time enough later for you to explain." He dipped the cloth into the basin and swept it over her face again, then moved lower, wiping her neck. The candlelight lent a soft glow to her skin. He laid his cheek against her forehead.

"Wh-what are you doing?"

"Checking to see if you have a fever. You are burning with it, Maddy."

"I-I've been sick. With influenza."

"Aye. Margery will provide a remedy for it. But that is not what brought you to me."

"Nay. Would you wash my hands, Nicholas? They are filthy." Maddy closed her eyes and drifted while he lifted each hand, one at a time, moving the cloth over them, then up and down each finger, even cleaning the dirt from her nails. When he finished, Nicholas kissed the center of each palm. He did not think she would remember. Then he summoned Margery.

"Margery is going to undress you," he told Maddy. "Your clothes are soiled. And then you must sleep."

"Where will you be?" she asked, a note of desperation in her voice.

Squeezing her hand, he said, "Don't be afraid, Maddy. I'll be close by."

What she had endured this night, on top of suffering from influenza, he did not yet know. But he would get it out of her and would not rest until he'd found the villains who had caused her such pain. Nicholas studied her face while she drifted off, dark lashes sweeping across the tips of her cheekbones. Pulling a chair over to the side of the bed, he covered himself with a blanket and watched her until his own lids grew heavy and he dozed off.

. . .

Hours later, Maddy awoke, an uneasiness gripping her. Where was she? The faint light of dawn had crept into the room, and she heard the early morning songs of thrush, robins, and chaffinches. Propped on her forearms, she glanced around. Ryder was sleeping in a chair nearby, his head lolling on his chest, a blanket wrapped around him. She lay back down until sleep once again carried her away.

The next time she woke up, the sun was streaming in. Ryder was gone, and she thought maybe she'd dreamed his being there. But she glimpsed the blanket draped over the chair and decided he'd been real enough. It made her happy, knowing he'd watched over her. But she didn't wish to dwell on it overmuch. His moods seemed to change unpredictably, and God only knew whether he would be gentle, loving Nicholas or judgmental, curt Master Ryder when next she saw him.

Before long, Margery tapped lightly on the door and entered. She set a tray down on the table near the bed. "And how're you feeling this morning, mistress?"

"You didn't bring me anymore of that vile brew you forced me to drink last night, did you?"

She laid a hand on Maddy's forehead and gave a satisfied grunt. "I did, but I'll not make you drink it again unless your fever comes back." After she'd bathed Maddy thoroughly and helped her into a clean smock, she said, "Might you be able to eat something?"

"As long as it's not pottage." Maddy didn't think she

could ever eat it again, after that brute Wolf had forced it on her at Carlisle Castle.

"Nay, that would not sit well on your stomach, you being ill with the influenza. Can you sit at the table, mistress?"

"I think so." Cautiously, she swung her legs over the side of the bed and remained there until she felt steady enough to stand.

"Here, put this about your shoulders." It was a lovely cloak, made of fine, soft wool and embroidered with flowers around the neck and hem. It must have belonged to Daniel's mother. Margery laid out the meal on the small table. Fresh strawberries and cream, manchet with butter, broth, a tankard of ale. The sight of it gave Maddy the last bit of strength she needed to stand up and walk.

"Master Ryder will see you while you are eating, if you feel well enough, mistress."

She glanced down at her attire. With the cloak, she was decently covered. "Aye. Tell him he may come." When Margery turned to leave, Maddy stopped her. "Thank you, mistress. Much as I hated that tea, I suspect it lowered my fever."

In a few minutes, Ryder strode in. "Good morrow, Maddy," he said, studying her. She sipped at the broth and let him look. "You are feeling stronger?"

"Pray, be seated." She gestured to the settle, which he pulled around so that it faced the table. "Would you share my meal? It is far too much for me."

"Nay, I've already eaten." He had washed and dressed, and appeared so handsome, Maddy had to look away. His beautiful green eyes shone bright; his curly dark hair and beard were both neatly combed. The shirt and leather doublet showed his broad shoulders to advantage—best if she concentrated on eating. She needed her strength.

Face resting against his hand, Nicholas watched while

she ate. Just when she was beginning to feel uncomfortable, he said, "Who are Long Legs and Bull Neck?"

She sputtered, half laughing, half choking. "Did I mention them last night?" Maddy thought maybe he was angry, but he was smiling. "My captors. That is what they looked like, so it was easiest to think of them with those names."

Nicholas laughed. "I thought you were delirious. How did you come to be taken by them?" He leaned forward and wiped something off her cheek with a cloth.

"I…they were reivers. Or they wanted me to think they were, at first. But then one of them said to the other, 'We're meant to be reivers; we should act like them.' Those weren't precisely his words, but close enough."

Nicholas's hand was suddenly gripping hers, gently. "Can you start at the beginning, Maddy? Do not leave anything out."

And so, with his hand clutching hers, at times stroking it with his thumb, Maddy gave him an account of all that had happened last night. When she was finished, he said, "What makes you so sure it was not a raid?" He let go of her and helped himself to a piece of manchet.

She sighed, frustrated. "I must have left things out. It was all so confusing, and I didn't feel well."

"We can finish later, if you wish to rest." He got to his feet.

"Sit down, Nicholas." Impatiently, Maddy motioned toward the seat he had vacated. "I'm quite well." He did as she asked, although she'd expected him to argue. "I did not think it was a raid because, aside from what I've already told you, they didn't actually take anything. Except me."

"You're sure about that?"

"Lady Dacre said they made off with some livestock, but I think she was lying. I saw no evidence of it. They weren't dressed like reivers—no steel bonnets, no padded leather doublets or breeches. And there wasn't a lance in sight."

"*Hmm*. And they planned it for Good Friday, a day they knew most folk would be in their homes. Why would they want you to think it was a raid?"

"Most likely to conceal the fact that they were meeting with the Dacres." Then Maddy remembered she hadn't told him about the short letter she'd found in Christopher Dacre's room. She had related only last night's events. "There is something more I've not yet told you."

"Which is?" He cocked a brow at her.

"After our meeting at the wall"—she couldn't look at him when she mentioned it—"I decided to search Musgrave's chamber, but it was locked. I passed Dacre's chamber on my way back down the passage and it struck me that I should have a look in there instead."

"And you found something, I take it?"

"A strange missive. It was very…concise." She paused, because she had to rack her brain to recall what it said. So much had happened since.

"Maddy?" Ryder said.

"Wait a moment. I am thinking. Directly after I found it, I went down with influenza." She leaned her forehead against the heels of her hands, finally looking up. "This is not it exactly, but close enough. 'The gathering on Friday will go on as planned. Attending will be F, H, and B.' No signature."

"You said the two who took you were Scots?" When she nodded, he said, "So the initials most likely stand for Ferniehurst, Hume, and Bucceleuch. The lairds suspected of sheltering the rebels."

"Aye! Long Legs mentioned Ferniehurst by name. Said he'd cautioned them not to hurt anybody. That must have been the tall man they led into the vicarage."

"Did you see the other lairds?"

"No. But they may have been there. Perhaps Ferniehurst

arrived late, after the others." What did it all mean? Maddy's head was a jumble of disparate facts that did not make sense. She pushed herself up from the table, suddenly feeling a great need to lie down.

Nicholas was on his feet in an instant. "I have exhausted you with my questions. Come, let me help you to your bed."

"I am not usually so frail," Maddy said, embarrassed by her weakness. "There is much more to discuss."

"But not now." At the bedside, he removed the cloak from about her shoulders. She felt her cheeks burning, as she wore only the smock underneath it. Nicholas leaned in and kissed her forehead, the barest tickle on her skin, before she lay down. "I shall call Margery in to close the drapes and help you with the bedclothes."

Maddy wanted to ask him where he would be, but he was gone before she had the chance. It wasn't that she was frightened. She was not, not any longer. When Nicholas was near, her mind—her soul—hummed with a higher degree of awareness. Colors seemed brighter, voices louder, taste more acute. At the same time, she felt buoyant and light. Maddy wasn't strong enough to fight these odd, opposing feelings, nor did she want to. She could only succumb.

Chapter Seventeen

Something warm and soft was burrowing into her. The sensation was pleasant. Maddy smiled, thinking it was Useless. Then she remembered she was not at the priory. The burrowing creature giggled, and she knew who it was.

"I must remember to thank Master Ryder for bringing my dog—I did sorely miss her." Maddy petted him—Daniel, not Useless—and more giggling ensued. "*Mmm*. Good girl."

"Daniel. You were not to wake her." Nicholas's voice came from somewhere across the room. He was probably at the table near the window, where they'd sat this morning. She heard the crinkling of parchment.

"Master Daniel, is that you? And I thought it was my wee canine friend." He grinned at her, his hair tousled, his eyes mischievous. "You do slightly resemble a dog, now that I look upon you."

Daniel sat back on his heels, held up his arms like paws, stuck his tongue out and panted. "You are funny, Sir Mouse." Maddy stretched and yawned. "What time is it? Have I slept all day?"

"I heard the church bell ring two a short time ago," Nicholas said, now much closer. She did not dare glance up at him, with her tangled hair and sleepy eyes. "Come, brat. Mistress Vernon will want to wash and dress. You may see her later."

Nicholas lifted Daniel into his arms and they left. Fortunately, she'd remained under the bedclothes, because Nicholas stuck his head back in. "Shall I send Margery to you?"

"Aye, pray do." Nestling back into the bed, Maddy smiled to herself, until a sobering thought struck her. Where was Nicholas's father? No mention had been made of the man, and it made her uneasy. After all, he had threatened her—said things would not go well if they were forced to remove her from Lanercost. It was a rather vague threat, but a threat nonetheless. So while Margery was helping her bathe, she asked. "Is Master Francis Ryder at home, Margery?"

"Nay, mistress. He has gone to York. Left yesterday." Since it was unlikely she would know when he would be back, Maddy did not ask. York was quite a distance. If he left only the day before, he would not return anytime soon. One less thing to worry about.

She felt renewed after bathing and washing her hair. When she was dressed—in more of Susan Ryder's apparel, no doubt—Margery bid her sit by the fire while she combed her wet locks.

"You have a fine head of hair, mistress," she said. "Thick and shiny."

"And unruly. I'm afraid I pay little attention to it. But I do thank you."

She set the comb down. "Are you hungry?"

"Something to eat would not go amiss," Maddy said. "And drink. But I would very much like to go downstairs."

"Let me ask Master Ryder." She bustled out of the

chamber before Maddy could stop her. Must one seek his permission for everything? She wandered over to the window. The prospect offered up a wide expanse of green, with archery butts on one side, and on the other, an enormous garden with an abundance of blooming flowers and a path meandering around it. An inviting place to stroll.

"Are you sure you are feeling well enough to leave your bed, Madeleine?" She hadn't heard him enter.

"Are you so tyrannical with your servants that they require your approval for everything?" Maddy asked, ignoring his question. "It must occupy a great deal of your time."

"Such sarcasm. And I thought you were ill."

"I'm not ill, Nicholas," she said, turning. "Only a little tired, still."

He held out his hand. "I'll take you down to the drawing room, if you will hold on to my arm."

She rolled her eyes, but in truth was glad for the strength of that arm. Maddy had never been in the drawing room. It still bore a woman's touch, and she suspected both Nicholas and his father steered clear of it, each staying in his own domain. A fire was burning in the grate, and Nicholas led her to a cushioned settle positioned near it. Margery entered and lowered a tray to the chest in front of the settle. Maddy felt like the Queen of Sheba.

"I've never been so pampered."

"Aye, well, it will be of short duration. Do not become accustomed to it." His voice was teasing.

Margery left, and Maddy sipped from a cup of clary. Nicholas buttered bread and sliced cheese for her. "Eat, Maddy, or I'll feed you myself."

"Like your man at Carlisle?" She gave him a cynical glance, even though his comments had been said in jest. His eyes darted away and he rubbed his beard. She'd embarrassed him and felt moved to apologize. "Forgive me. I know you were joking."

"It is I who should apologize to you. I am sorry for what you endured there."

"Let's not talk about it. Not now." She brushed a lock of hair off her face. Since Margery had admired her somewhat wild tresses, perhaps Maddy should ask if she would give it a trim. "What happens now? Will I return to Lanercost?" Even asking the question made her heart thump, but she tried to keep a measured tone of voice. If she did not return, what else awaited her?

"We shall see. I wrote to Lady Dacre this morning to let her know you would be remaining with us until you regained your health. Even though I'm sure she already knows, I explained how you came to be here. I noted you had sustained some minor injuries and suffered a relapse of influenza but were recuperating well."

"So now we wait?"

"For her response, yes. Would you care to hazard a guess?"

Maddy chuckled. "What are the stakes? If I guess correctly, will there be a prize?"

He gazed at her a long time before saying, "I might kiss you again, if you would let me."

Oh. Heat suffused her face, and other, more private places, too, and then she laughed. "That, sir, would be a prize for you, not me."

Nicholas sat down beside her. "You did not enjoy my kisses, then," he said, teasing her.

Like a foolish, lovesick girl, she could not suppress her smile. Before she could gather herself, Nicholas seized her hands. "Maddy, forgive me if I've upset you. But I do want to kiss you again...and do other things with you as well. Does that shock you?" He lifted her hand and lightly kissed her fingers, sending a jolt of heat through her.

Say something. Maddy wanted to but was utterly tongue tied. So instead of speaking, she raised her hand to his face and caressed it. His beard was surprisingly soft to the touch. She found this degree of touching was not sufficient. Without giving it any thought, she raised her other hand to his face as well. Nicholas held perfectly still, watching her, waiting to see what she would do next. "Come here," Maddy said. "Come closer." He complied, and she kissed him.

Opening her mouth slightly, she invited his tongue to taste her, as she wished to taste him. A dazzling brilliance nearly overwhelmed her, but from pleasure rather than fever. Maybe this was a different kind of fever. Before she'd had enough of him, he pulled away.

"You are not well yet, sweeting." He smoothed her hair, his fingers caressing her sensitive scalp and making her want to say, *I am well! I am well!* He kissed her once more, lightly, on the lips, and moved away. The man possessed a great deal of self-discipline.

"Back to my question. What do you think Lady Dacre will say?"

Maddy clasped her hands together tightly. "That depends on information we do not have. Does she suspect me? Is she worried I overheard something? Or saw Ferniehurst entering the house? If so, she will dismiss me. She might say my health is too fragile to assist her."

"There is another way of looking at it. If she suspects you, she—and Dacre—may want to keep a close eye on you. For that reason, they may want you back. I mislike it."

"You are misliking one thing or another most of the time, Nicholas." He looked so discomfited, she couldn't hold back a grin.

"Not I." When he registered the skepticism on her face, he laughed and said, "Perhaps, but only when you are involved."

"I know her well enough to judge the true meaning of her words. She is fond of me, in her way, Nicholas. Strange as it sounds, I like her, too. It pains me to think she is involved in some perverse plot against the queen."

He didn't speak, but the slight lift of one side of his mouth gave away his feelings on the matter.

"I know what you're thinking," Maddy said. "But she has come to rely on me. She likes having me there to help with her correspondence, to assist with her household tasks, to visit the sick—"

"And why would she not? You ease some of her burdens, make everything simpler for her. That doesn't mean she genuinely cares for your welfare."

Maddy exhaled a long breath. He was most likely right, but she hated to acknowledge it. And how could he really know? It was she who had spent so many days by Lady Dacre's side.

"Enough talk of this," Nicholas said. "We need not decide what to do until we hear from her." He cut into a blackberry tart and popped a bite into his mouth, then fed her a piece. Juice ran down her chin, and before she knew what he intended, he'd leaned in and licked it away. And then their lips pressed together, and the tang of blackberries was as potent as if she still had them in her mouth.

"*Mmm. I adore blackberries.*" *And your kisses.* While they were devouring the tart, Maddy heard a scratching on the door.

"That will be Daniel. Do you feel strong enough to see him?"

"Aye, of course."

"Come, Daniel," Nicholas said.

Daniel pranced into the room with all the natural exuberance of a boy his age. He was pretending to ride a horse and trotted about the room two or three times before his uncle called a halt to it.

"Mistress Madeleine will take her leave if you don't behave like a gentleman when she is about, nephew."

"Would you like a bite of tart, Daniel?" Maddy asked. When he nodded, she sliced him a piece, which he devoured in a few bites. "You remind me of my own nephews. They love to play at riding horses, too." He gave her a quizzical look.

Ryder said, "How many nephews do you have, Maddy?" Somehow he'd perceived this was what the boy wanted to know.

"I have two. Andrew and Edward. And I have a niece as well. She is called Martha."

"Are they Daniel's age?"

"Martha is the eldest. One of my nephews, Edward, is a few years older than Daniel. Andrew has but two years."

Daniel smiled and tugged on her hand, and she concluded he'd learned enough about her relations for the time being.

Nicholas intervened. "No, Daniel, Mistress Madeleine must rest."

He stomped a foot and looked petulant. "What does he want?"

"He wants you to come outside with him. Yes, Daniel?"

The boy nodded and continued to tug on her hand. Maddy rose, maybe to prove she was capable of standing on her own. "The day seems fine. Why can we not take a turn about your garden?"

"I sense this is a battle I will not win," Nicholas said. "Daniel, fetch Mistress Madeleine's cloak." After the child had skipped from the room, Nicholas turned to her and laid his hands on her shoulders. "I have something to say to you, Maddy."

He looked so serious, his green eyes holding her gaze. She waited, her stomach fluttering. Was he about to reveal her fate if Lady Dacre did not want her back?

"Can you forgive me for my behavior when we met at the Roman wall? Be assured, I *do* trust you. At no time have you given me reason not to."

Ah. An apology. She hadn't expected it. "Why did you lash out at me?"

He looked sheepish. "I am ashamed to admit it, but it was a simple matter of jealousy. The thought of you lying with Musgrave made me furious. And wretched."

Her cheeks flamed. *Not as wretched as it's made me.*

He went on. "That a maid of your...your admirable qualities would find such a man attractive vexed—vexes—me exceedingly.

"I was young, Nicholas. Too childish still to grasp what he really wanted of me before it was too late. I have regretted it ever afterward, most especially now, when I find myself living in close quarters with him."

"You do not, that is, there is nothing...?"

"Are you asking if I still think him desirable?" Maddy couldn't help it; her lips twitched and Nicholas noticed.

He gave her the gimlet eye. "You are making sport of me, Madeleine."

And then she laughed out loud. "How could you possibly suspect me of such a thing? You know I despise the man, as he does me. And I'm more than a little afraid of him."

"God's blood, I wish this were over!" Nicholas stepped away from her, one hand on his hip and the other rubbing his beard. "I hate to think of you trapped in that house with him loitering about. He may be Cecil's man, but he is the kind of agent who has no scruples. I've run into them before—my father has had men like that working for him."

"Let us not talk of Musgrave." She came up behind him and ran her hand lightly down his arm. "Perhaps before Daniel comes racing in you could enlighten me about my 'qualities.' The ones you find admirable."

He turned carefully, as though he did not want to break her hold on him. But before he could speak, Daniel burst through the door. "Later," he whispered, just before Maddy leaped away from him.

. . .

Daniel led the way outside, marching them through the glass house Nicholas used for forcing blooms. A profusion of roses, white and dusky rose and vibrant red, spilled out of containers.

"Is this your doing, Nicholas?" Maddy asked.

Pleased at her interest, he nodded. "I grow them in here during the cold months, the rest of the year in the garden."

"Will you tell me what they are?"

"Most are damasks and gallicas. And a few albas. They're the white ones."

She walked over to a pot that caught her fancy. "I've never seen anything like this. They're lovely." The petals were striped—pale pink and a true rose color in a single bloom. Nicholas took pride in the gorgeous blossoms, still unique enough to draw interest from those who saw them.

"That is a *Rosa mundi*, said to be named for Rosamund Clifford, mistress of—"

"Henry II. I know the story. 'Tis said Queen Eleanor had her poisoned."

"Or did the deed herself. But alas, I believe it is all a myth."

"So it wasn't named for her?"

"It was. That much is true." He grasped her arm then. "Come, let's go outside while we still have the sun."

Daniel, unleashing his formidable energy, was running before they'd even stepped through the door. "Will you be all right if I play with him?" Nicholas asked. "There is a bench just there." He pointed toward the garden.

"I'll amble about for a bit. If I feel dangerously close to swooning, I shall sit on your bench." She raised her brows at him.

"Very droll, mistress. If I see your prone form on the ground, I may just leave you there." Nicholas couldn't stop gazing at her, drinking her in. Her beauty never ceased to enrapture him. It was a heady combination of glossy hair, striking blue-green eyes, and luminous skin. He badly wanted his hands on her body, and Maddy's on his. By God, if he could only get rid of Daniel for a few hours...never mind. Not possible.

"Ha!" She waved him away.

He acknowledged with a healthy dose of regret that what he wanted to do with Maddy, how he'd come to feel about her, was absolutely forbidden because of his work for the queen. He only dared violate it because his father was away.

What would happen when he returned? Nicholas chose not to worry about that at present. He would deal with it when the time came.

After shedding their doublets, Nicholas and Daniel began with Daniel's favorite game—chase—which Nicholas was persuaded the lad subjected him to simply to wear him out. After that, it was wrestling and rolling about on the grass. Daniel could have kept on forever. Finally, Nicholas called a halt. "Off, ruffian!"

The lad started to protest, but his uncle said firmly, "Enough for now, Daniel." He helped the child put his doublet back on, whispered something in the lad's ear, then walked toward Maddy while slipping into his own doublet. She was watching him, and he took the opportunity to allow her a long look. Moving slowly, he lifted his shoulders to adjust the garment to his form. Her cheeks turned rosy and she averted her gaze. Nicholas grinned. Daniel was racing toward the archery butts, and she turned her attention to him.

"Do little boys ever simply walk anywhere?"

"Nay." Still breathing hard, and not only because of the horseplay, Nicholas lowered himself to the bench. "I told him he could shoot while we talk. Are you warm enough?"

"Aye. The sun feels wonderful. While I was watching you and Daniel, a vivid picture of my father and Robert playing in much the same way caught me by surprise. Bittersweet..." Her voice trailed off on a sob.

He put his arm around her shoulders and drew her close, and she laid her head against his chest. "I don't have a handkerchief with me, but you are welcome to my sleeve," Nicholas said.

That made her laugh. "I'll use my own—handkerchief, not sleeve—if need be, but thank you for the offer."

"Do you often think of your brother, Maddy?" Nicholas wasn't sure why he asked. Perhaps because she was trusting him. Confiding in him, and it felt damned good.

Maddy straightened up. The flood of emotion, and the accompanying tears, seemed to have ebbed. "Oh, aye. Every day. We had an unusual bond from the time we were children. Robbie was a sickly child, spoiled and cosseted by my mother, with me as her willing accomplice. As he grew older, he took full advantage and somehow managed to dance through life without accepting responsibility for anything."

"Such as?"

"It began with little boy mischief, like the bee attack, among other pranks."

"The bee attack?" Nicholas repeated. "That needs explaining."

She nodded. "Aye. He was ten at the time. Robbie interfered with the swarm, and of all people, his tutor happened to be outside taking the air. The poor man was stung dozens of times. Rob convinced me Master Ripley smelled like manure, and that was what had attracted the bees."

Nicholas tried in vain to stifle a laugh, then apologized.

"Nay, I understand. 'Tis funny, if you were not the one called to account for it. Looking back on it as an adult, I'm certain my father suspected I was covering up Robert's misdeeds, so there was no caning. But I was made to work side by side with the shrewish wife of his tutor, in her brew house, for two weeks. I hated her, but even worse was the stink. To this day, my gorge rises if I smell the malt."

"There is one aspect of this I don't understand," Nicholas said. "If your father suspected...did your mother also? Why were you all complicit?"

Maddy shrugged. "From the time Robert was young, no older than Daniel, I began to take responsibility for many of his misdeeds. It was my job to keep him on the straight and narrow path, and if he strayed, it was because I failed in my duty."

Nicholas was incredulous. "Did your parents expect this of you?"

She sighed. "'Tis hard to explain. My mother lost several babes and consequently became an invalid. Father was too busy to give Robert much guidance, so it fell to me. I accepted it. We all did."

"And as he grew older?"

"His mischief progressed to more serious offenses. Stealing from the neighbors, setting fire to their hayricks, even poaching. At some point, it became impossible for me to take the blame. My father never would have believed I'd committed certain of Robert's crimes. And yet, I continued to come to his aid when he begged me for help or advice."

"He married quite young and even had children," Nicholas said, perplexed. "That does not seem like something a man with his tendencies would do."

"How do you know that about him?"

Damnation. He should not have revealed what he knew. She would not like the answer. "Before we assigned you, we thoroughly investigated your family."

To his surprise, she did not seem angry, or even irritated, but took it in stride. "Ah. To answer your question, he married Kat because she was with child."

"So that was the way of it. Was he a good husband? Father?"

"Aside from evenings at the alehouse with his friends now and then, I believe so."

Nicholas squeezed her hand. "That is a good memory to keep." No matter what he'd promised his father, it was time to tell her the truth about her brother. "Maddy," he said, and heard the peculiar ring to his voice.

But she ignored him, still lost in her memories. "Thinking of Robert, I can't help comparing him to you, Nicholas." She turned and looked directly at him. "You have shouldered so much responsibility. I never glimpsed in my brother any signs of the devotion you show Daniel. But I think he was faithful to Kat and protective of the children."

Nicholas barely heard the last part of that, so stunned was he by her compliment. "You believe I show devotion to my nephew? That is high praise. I don't deserve it. I had little choice in the matter."

"Nonsense. You could have paid somebody to take him in. You give everything to Daniel. You hold nothing back. Without you, he would be alone in the world."

That she admired him provoked a visceral reaction he felt all the way to his loins. "I wish I could kiss you right now. But I do not think I would be able to stop with a kiss."

"Nicholas!" He'd made her blush, and he hoped not only from embarrassment.

Laughing, he rose and pulled her up. "Come. Time for you to rest." He accompanied Maddy to her chamber and kissed her lightly before taking his leave.

He was already wondering when he could kiss her again. Hold her. Make love to her.

. . .

It rained during the night. The pitter-patter of the drops against the windows woke Maddy, then lulled her back to sleep. Easter morning dawned fresh and warm, but she could not persuade Nicholas to take her out. He and Margery insisted she needed one day more to rest. Uncle and nephew attended services, and afterward, Nicholas sequestered himself in his study. Was he considering her options, mulling them over, arguing with himself about what would be best for her? She read to Daniel, played with him, but could not keep her mind from drifting toward the closed door, wondering about her future at Lanercost or elsewhere.

Something else was bothering her, too. Yesterday's conversation with Nicholas was plaguing her like an itch that needed scratching. She vowed not to think about it. Surely it would come to her on its own.

The midday meal was a mouthwatering banquet of the meat withheld during Lent. Thick slices of beef, roast pig, all manner of fowl—guinea hen, duck, even swan—accompanied by spring vegetables and strawberry tarts with fresh cream. Eating proved to be the greatest exertion of Maddy's day.

At last it came to her. Nicholas had never told her what he wanted when he'd said her name in that odd voice.

Chapter Eighteen

Maddy and Nicholas were seated in the drawing room when Margery brought in the long-awaited missive from Lady Dacre. Daniel had been in and out, but now it was quiet. Maddy was sewing, working on a piece of embroidery designed and partially stitched by Daniel's mother. Nicholas had given her leave to have any of Susan Ryder's things she desired, and she'd found a treasure trove of fabric and silks in a chest in the blue chamber. Maddy was beginning to feel as though Susan was her second self. Or she hers.

Every so often, she looked up at Nicholas. After Easter, they had established a comfortable routine, and Maddy believed he enjoyed the peaceful times they spent together as much as she did, each of them with their heads bent over their work. Today he had been studying a map and reading various letters. He did not say, but Maddy felt sure these must have been from his father. A couple of times she'd caught him staring out the window, as though what he was learning upset him or required him to come to a decision.

"A letter for Mistress Vernon," Margery said, handing it

to her.

When Nicholas leaped to his feet, acting as if he might snatch it from her, she held up a hand to forestall him. "I'll read it out loud," she said, wondering if Christopher Dacre had written it for his stepmother. While Maddy broke the seal, Nicholas waited, arms crossed across his chest.

28 March 1570

My dear Madeleine,

I do heartily apologize for what befell you the night of the raid on the Lanercost property. My stepson and I were certain all the reivers had been chased off, and thus I was confident you would be safe. As you will remember, I saw you back to your bed myself. Had you remained there, I do not believe your abduction would have occurred. Nevertheless, I am most distressed over your suffering at the hands of those brutes and am only grateful the harm they inflicted on you was not worse.

I hope your recovery proceeds apace and you will soon be well enough to return to your duties here at Lanercost. I find I can hardly get along without you, my dear. You have made an old woman quite dependent on your kind offices.

Pray inform me of the date you may return to us.

"She signs it, 'With regard, Lady Jane Dacre.'"

Nicholas huffed a sardonic laugh. "She regrets what happened, but obviously believes you brought it on yourself because you did not stay in your bed." He paused, then said, "What think you, Maddy?"

"It is her way of scolding me for not doing as she bid.

She truly wants me back, I'll warrant." Maddy said this while fighting a niggling voice reminding her of Lady Dacre's actions the night of the raid. She'd been certain her employer was involved in whatever was going on.

Nicholas looked skeptical. "Has she asked herself why you did not remain in your bed? Why you were prowling about when you were still sick and weak? Does she wonder what you were up to? This is what worries me." He rubbed at his beard. "She may have guessed you were spying."

"Perhaps she'll talk to me about all of that upon my return," Maddy said, somewhat defensively. "I can explain what I was doing."

"Truly? What will you say?" Before she could answer, he walked over and came down beside her on the settle. "I have reservations about your continuing employment at Lanercost."

"But I am close, so close, to discovering something truly significant! I've already obtained much information that has been useful—Norfolk's letter, Lady Dacre's religious leanings, Dacre and Musgrave's mention of the Scottish lairds. More. The fact that the raid was a ruse for a meeting between the Dacres and the lairds."

Nicholas frowned and shook his head slowly. "Something is brewing. Things are coming to a head, else how to explain the clandestine visit with Ferniehurst? I am not sure it is safe for you to be there when the endgame is afoot."

Maddy wanted to go back to salvage her pride. To atone for Robbie's death. For Ann Dodd's. And to redeem herself in Nicholas's eyes. She had misread and misjudged so many things in the last months. She'd been impetuous and foolhardy and badly needed to see this through to the end. "Pray, do not forbid me to return, Nicholas. What else would you have me do? What fate would befall me, then?"

He pulled her up and held her close. "Do you think I

would allow any ill to come to you? I would send you home, back to your family, first."

Maddy thought of her lonely, depressing existence in the home of Robbie's in-laws, where she was not valued except as one who looked after the children. With her brother dead, they owed her nothing. No, she did not wish to return to that life, although it was preferable to imprisonment. "What would your father say to that? Only a few weeks ago he threatened me, said things would not go well for me if he had to remove me from the priory. I cannot believe he would not have some say in the matter of my...of what was to become of me."

"He is not here, Maddy, as you must know. And I don't expect him back for some time. He is a hard man"—he gave a harsh laugh at that—"but he will not gainsay me on this."

Maddy studied him and saw that he was sincere in his belief. "Why not?"

"Because we have discussed it. I told him that if he did not allow me the authority to deal with you according to my own conscience, I would cease my work for him. I would take Daniel and leave. He pretends this would not matter to him, but underneath his sometimes harsh exterior, he cares about us."

Maddy was dumbfounded. She thought of what he'd told her, that he had no land, no money of his own. And yet he would go this far to protect her. "Oh, Nicholas." She placed her hands on his chest and looked up at him. He leaned down and kissed her. Not a friendly, reassuring brush of the lips, this, but a deeper, more sensual kiss that surprised them both. Maddy welcomed it.

He broke the kiss and pulled away long enough to assess her feelings on the matter, though how he could have been in doubt was beyond her understanding. Then he pressed his lips to hers again while his hands played down her spine, cupped her buttocks, and drew her close enough to feel his arousal.

Daniel chose that moment to burst through the door.

They leaped apart. The child seemed not to notice what they'd been doing. Obviously excited, he held out a palm on which a small toad rested, eyes bulging.

Maddy had to suppress a giggle. "Pardon me," she said. "I am not overly fond of toads and will remove to my chamber." On her way out the door, she heard Nicholas tell Daniel to find Margery and show her the creature.

"You have my permission to visit the stables, too. And let the toad go, Daniel. It belongs out of doors."

Maddy paced about in her chamber. Would Nicholas come to her? She might die if he did not. Surely that was why he was so deviously getting rid of Daniel. Finding Margery, showing her the toad, pestering the stable lads—all of that would take at least an hour. The door clicked open, and she spun around.

There stood Nicholas on the threshold. He was as braw a man as she'd ever seen. His body overpowered the doorway. Holding quite still for a moment, he watched her, as though he thought she might turn him away. His eyes were full of want, and maybe a little madness. Maddy ran to him. He lifted her into his arms and steadied her while she wrapped her legs around his hips. He slid her skirts up, to make it easier for her.

"Are you sure you are well enough for this, sweeting? You have been so ill. I do not wish—"

"Hush. To the devil with all of that."

He sat on the upholstered chair and she straddled him. They kissed, over and over. Soft, lush, kisses. Kisses that were in no hurry. Nicholas moved his hands up her calves and thighs toward her bottom, and then removed them to stroke her face tenderly. "You are beautiful, Maddy Vernon. You are so beautiful. I want you with my whole being."

"Aye."

Then he lifted her off his lap and began unfastening her bodice. Maddy undid the fastenings of her skirts, and he helped pull her kirtle over her head, so that she stood there wearing only her smock. When he made as if to lift her up to the bed, she protested. "Off with your clothing, Master Ryder."

A roguish grin spread across his face, and in a moment he was naked as the day he was born, his organ hard and pressing against his belly. The beauty of him made Maddy gasp: his body formed and hardened by labor, with wide shoulders, sinewy chest, flat abdomen—and the aforementioned part. Nicholas closed the distance between them, backing her up toward the bed. "Have you looked your fill, mistress? Do I pass muster?"

In answer, Maddy pulled her smock off and let him see her. She was on the thin side since she'd been sick, but she was not ashamed of her body. Her breasts, though not large, had a roundness to them, and her nipples were a rosy color. She judged her legs to be shapely, tapering down to slim ankles. From the look on Nicholas's face, her nakedness met with his approval.

After yanking the bedclothes down, he lifted her to the bed and crawled in. Her coupling with Musgrave—and she hated herself for thinking of him at this moment—had been quickly over. It had consisted of him pushing into her and thrusting until he'd spent.

But Nicholas put her pleasure above his own. His kisses were precious offerings. His hands stroked all over her body—her breasts and buttocks, arms, shoulders, and belly. Everything inside her came alive, and when his hands drifted down between her legs, she gasped, because that was exactly the place she felt hot and wet and quivering with need.

When she could wait no longer, she grasped him and

brought him inside her, and they teetered toward the edge together. Maddy peaked first, then wrapped her legs around him, pulling him down and down into the spiraling joy along with her. She felt his seed flow into her, but something had burst from her and into him, too. Her better self, the part she had been closely guarding for so long. It belonged to him now.

Maddy had fallen deeply asleep, and when she awoke, it was to the soft drumming of rain on the roof. Nicholas was gone. On the bed table was a jar bursting with the striped roses, the *Rosa mundi*, with a note underneath. She reached over and extricated it.

> *Another kiss shall have my life ended,*
> *For to my mouth the first my heart did suck;*
> *The next shall clean out of my breast it pluck.*

She recognized Thomas Wyatt's verse, and smiling, held the page to her breast until she heard sounds in the passage and realized Margery would soon be tapping on the door and entering to help her dress for supper. And here she lay, completely naked. Margery would know. Maddy's cheeks flamed, but she spared no more time for lovesickness. She jumped from the bed, slipped on her smock, then went to the washstand, poured fresh water from the ewer into the bowl, and washed herself. Then she pulled on her kirtle and hastily dragged up the bedclothes and smoothed them into place.

If Margery suspected anything, she never let on.

• • •

The following morning was fine, and at last Nicholas agreed to take Maddy riding. She had been housebound for too many days and longed to venture out into the spring air, alive with the earth's reawakening. They rode toward the Irthing and, in no hurry, walked their mounts side by side so that they could talk.

Since yesterday afternoon, it had been difficult not to break into a blissful smile whenever she laid eyes on Nicholas. So she was glad for this time alone, away from Daniel, away from servants. Nobody had voiced any concerns about their going off unchaperoned, for which she was grateful.

As soon as they reached the river, Nicholas slowed his horse and she did the same. They leaned toward each other, and he grasped the back of her head, pulling her into the rapturous kiss of new lovers. They sat for a moment with their foreheads resting together until finally the horses grew restive, then journeyed on in harmonious silence for a mile or two along the river.

Nicholas broke the silence. "We did not finish our conversation regarding your return to Lanercost, Maddy. Lady Dacre will be expecting an answer."

"Will you not advise me?"

"Let's stop here and refresh ourselves," he said in answer. Her question hung between them. Maddy spread an old coverlet over the grass and Nicholas laid the food out—cold beef, manchet, cheese, sweetmeats, and a skin of wine.

The sunlit river sent up gem-like sparks of light, and the vibrant green of new leaves shimmered at the tips of the branches overhanging the water. She spotted a hawk soaring above them, zeroing in on his prey.

"This," Maddy said, "is a perfect day."

"And you are feeling well? Fully recovered?"

She tore a piece of bread from the loaf, unsure how to answer that. In her body, she was well and feeling more fit by the day. But her mind was unsettled and would remain so until she was certain of her future. "I want to go back to Lanercost, Nicholas. I know you don't think it wise, but hear me out while I explain."

He finished chewing a portion of beef before replying. "I am disinclined, but by all means, have your say."

"'Tis as I said after I received Lady Dacre's letter. We are right on the cusp of something big, something significant. You agreed with me. All my work thus far will be for naught unless I am there to discover it and bring it to you."

"But in so doing you put yourself at great risk. *I* put you at great risk." He threw down the piece of bread he'd been about to bite into and brushed crumbs off his hands. "These people are ruthless, Maddy. The more I learn of them, the more I see it."

"Your man, the one who looks beneath the stone for messages from me. Could he stay close by the priory, so that if I needed help somebody would be nearby?"

Nicholas shifted, looking impatient. "If you are held prisoner, how would you get word to him?"

"If a day passes and he doesn't see me—"

"By then it could be too late!"

She gave up all pretense of eating. "You didn't seem to mind before, my being there. You were willing to 'put me at risk,' as you state it."

"I always minded. And now the situation has grown more dangerous. The fact that the Dacres held a secret meeting with the lairds tells us that." He scrubbed a hand across his face. "I have been in this business long enough to sense when the action is heating up, and I believe that time is now."

"And that is exactly why I need to be there. I'm your conduit for information about whatever their next moves are."

"And precisely why I do not want you there!" Nicholas got

to his feet and strode away from her. Maddy wasn't making any headway, and she would have to bare her soul to him to make him understand. She rose and followed him.

"Nicholas." Maddy laid a hand on his arm until he turned from his rigid stance and looked at her. "My brother was executed because I could not keep him safe. My attempt to seek revenge for his murder was…foolish at best and suicidal at worst. This is my only remaining chance to atone for his death."

He looked stricken. "That is what this is about?" He raised his brows in astonishment. "You've nothing to atone for, Maddy. How can you think thus?"

Her voice broke. "You're wrong. Weren't you listening to me when I explained? It was my job to protect Robert, and I was negligent. Not paying close attention. Otherwise, he never would have joined up with Northumberland." She stepped back, blinded by tears. "And I am responsible for Ann Dodd's death, too."

Nicholas answered, his voice firm but gentle. "Your brother was a grown man with a wife and children. How could you be to blame for his folly? If his own wife could not sway him, how could you?"

"Kat came to me and begged me to convince Robert not to join, for the children's sake. By the time I talked to him, it was too late. He'd already made up his mind and wouldn't listen to me." Tears were streaming down her face now, her voice quivering with emotion. "I should have stopped him. I should have found a way. And I had no business inviting the Dodds to take part in the raid with me. It was senseless and tragic."

Nicholas pulled her to him. "Hush now, Maddy. You shall go back to Lanercost if it means so much to you. I'll find a way to be more vigilant. As you felt responsible for your brother's safety, so do I for yours." He stroked her hair, kissing the top of her head and uttering comforting sounds. Stepping a little away from her, he said, "You were the best of sisters, sweeting. Never think otherwise. And you did not force the Dodds to accompany you on the ill-fated raid."

"Do you truly believe so?"

"Aye, because it is true. Your brother did not deserve a sister such as you." He drew her back into his embrace, and soon, something stirred within Maddy, and apparently within Nicholas, too. They did not speak but hurried to their picnic spot. With one hand, he swept the food aside and grabbed the coverlet, and they dashed off to the shelter of a stand of trees, away from the river path. Margery had found her a riding dress in Susan's wardrobe; she needed Nicholas to unfasten it. He made quick work of it, then undressed to his hose while she pulled off her kirtle.

Nicholas removed her smock and cast it aside, then began a slow perusal of her body. After they lay down together, he pleasured her between her thighs in a way she hadn't dreamed of, and when he entered her at last, she rose up and kissed his lips. Capturing her in his arms, he whispered love words until he found his release inside her. Afterward, he hugged her body against his, back to chest, dropping soft kisses on her neck. They dozed for a while in a haze of soft sounds. The river gurgling over stones, birds calling, tree branches rustling softly in the breeze.

When she awakened, Maddy rolled away from Nicholas, who was snoring softly, and slipped on her smock. She did not think anybody was about, but she made sure before venturing over to where they'd eaten. She found a clean cloth in the basket and walked toward the river to wash. Stepping gingerly, as she knew the stones could be slippery, Maddy moved out into the frigid water until it rose just above her ankles, then dipped her cloth. She washed her face, neck, and arms, dipped the cloth once more, lifted her smock, and cleaned her female parts. Out of the corner of her eye, Maddy glimpsed a flash of white downriver a short distance from where she stood.

Straightening, she craned her neck, trying to see what it was. Something had snagged in the bushes hugging the riverbank. It was bigger than she'd first thought. Knowing she would not be content until she found out, Maddy tossed the cloth onto the bank and moved cautiously toward the splotch of light. Now she could see something dark and voluminous as well. A tight knot formed in her stomach, her instincts signaling danger before her mind became fully aware of it. Slowly, cautiously, she kept going. Closer, closer, until she made out a long form, and oh, Blessed Virgin save her, a submerged face. Or what had been a face. And the splendid blond hair streaming around it. Maddy screamed, a full blown, earth shattering, frightened-out-of-her-wits scream. Turning, slippery stones be damned, she ran, or tried to. She fell before she'd taken five steps, and by that time, Nicholas was in the water and heading toward her.

"What is it, Maddy?" *How had he gotten here so fast?* He raised her up from the water, a wild look on his face.

"Over there," she said, pointing. "It is Cath. Musgrave has murdered her."

Chapter Nineteen

Maddy huddled in the ladies' drawing room, as she'd come to call it, sipping hot spiced wine. Even though a fire was blazing in the hearth and Margery had draped a shawl around her shoulders, she could not stop trembling. Squeezing her eyes shut, she tried to banish the memory of Cath, poor, dead Cath, from her thoughts, but it simply couldn't be done. The scene was imprinted on her mind.

After Nicholas had taken a look, he guided Maddy back to shore and helped her dress. Then he said exactly what she had not wished to hear. "You must ride back to the house and send two men to me."

"Nay, I cannot go alone. You go."

He clasped her shoulders firmly. "I'll not have you staying here by yourself. The person who did this could be lurking somewhere nearby. I will wait here while you ride back to Brampton."

"But—"

"Do not say you would rather remain here alone while I ride off, because I will not believe you."

In the end she had simply nodded, and Nicholas boosted her into the saddle. "There is no reason to rush—we cannot help Cath now. Ride at a reasonable pace. Margery will know who to send."

"When will you be back?"

"I cannot say. I'll ride over to see Master Carleton after we retrieve her body from the river. He's the justice of the peace and must be notified." As soon as Maddy had reached the house, she alerted Margery, and had been sitting in the drawing room ever since.

Maddy heard a light tapping at the door. "Come."

Daniel walked in. She was happy to see him, badly needing a diversion to make the day seem ordinary and unexceptional. "Greetings, Sir Mouse." He crawled into her lap, more subdued than usual, as if sensing she was not herself. He seemed content to stay there for a while. In fact, it was Maddy who finally said, "'Tis too beautiful a day to waste indoors. Shall we go outside?"

And that was where Nicholas found them. Crouched down behind some shrubbery, Maddy heard him before she saw him. She and Daniel were in the middle of a game of hide-and-go-seek. Peeking out from the foliage, Maddy saw the boy run to his uncle, putting a finger to his lips. Nicholas hoisted him into his arms, and the two of them began to search for her.

"Could she be here?" Nicholas said, "behind this tree?" Then, "Ah, not here. I should have known even this huge tree is not large enough to hide one of her wide girth."

A laugh escaped her chest, and some of the darkness lifted. Showing herself, she said, "So I am wide of girth, eh? You make me sound like a mare rather than a lady."

Nicholas dropped Daniel to the ground and shooed him toward the archery butts. "I am glad to see you in good spirits, Maddy. Come." They sat on the bench, turning to face each other. "Master Carleton is taking charge of the investigation," Nicholas said. "He will want to question you."

"I didn't look closely at Cath's body after I realized what it was. Not close enough to discern any marks or wounds. How will the authorities be able to tell she was murdered and did not simply drown?"

Nicholas's eyes drifted away, and she could see he was considering how much to reveal. "She had bruises on her neck indicating she was strangled," he finally said. "And many lacerations on her body, although 'tis hard to tell if those resulted from her time in the river or a beating."

Tears welled in Maddy's eyes. "How frightened she must have been. She was so young, Nicholas." He grasped her hand and held it tightly while she wrestled with her sadness. "Who will tell her parents?"

"Carleton has that unhappy duty."

They were quiet for a brief time, this act of murder colliding with what Maddy had earlier deemed a perfect day, sneaking in without warning and violating them.

"I know this will be difficult for you, given your feelings about John Musgrave," Nicholas said, "but I must ask you to try very hard not to be judge and jury in this case, Maddy. When Master Carleton questions you, you must tell what you know without accusing anybody. The justice of the peace will weigh the evidence and determine if it is sufficient to make an arrest."

"But I am sure beyond anything that Musgrave is the devil who did this! Are you asking me not to reveal what passed between him and Cath?"

"I did not say that. Only that I want you to relate the dealings between them as you observed them, including your own intervention, without giving your opinion."

"Are you saying I should not tell him Cath was frightened and came to me for advice?"

Nicholas heaved an impatient sigh. "No, of course not. Only that it is important for Master Carleton to be objective, to consider the facts. All the facts. As much as you would like to think it, we cannot know that Musgrave is responsible for Cath's murder until Carleton looks into the matter and reaches his conclusions."

Unexpectedly, a harsh voice interrupted them. "What is she doing here, Nick?"

Francis Ryder had returned.

Maddy did not rise or acknowledge him in any way. If he would be rude to her, she would treat him in kind. Nicholas stood and said, "It's a long story, sir. How was your journey?"

"My journey be damned," he answered. "I want to know what has transpired in my absence, and why the wench who's supposed to be at Lanercost in the service of her queen is here in Brampton."

"Come to the library with me, Father. We can talk there." Not another word was spoken by either of them as they strode away. There was much to relate. Maddy doubted she would see Nicholas again until supper. She walked over to Daniel and the two of them practiced their shooting until evening was nearly upon them. Maddy's prowess with the bow would become legend if she continued to hone her skills with such frequency and exactitude. Daniel, too, was turning into quite a marksman.

"Come, Daniel," she said. "We must wash before our meal." He took her hand and they ambled toward the house together. In the dim light, she glimpsed Nicholas coming toward them. Soon he drew near enough for her to make out his grim expression.

"Nephew, Margery is waiting for you upstairs. Go find her." His voice and manner brooked no argument, and the little boy ran off. They entered through the glass house, and Nicholas stopped her. "My father wishes to speak to you. I've told him everything, including what happened today."

Maddy nodded, then followed Nicholas toward the library. She had known this idyllic time with him would come to an end. Nothing so happy lasts long, at least not in her experience. Today's nightmarish discovery of Cath's body had been only the beginning. And now this. There was no use asking what the man wanted of her. It would be an interrogation, with more threats thrown in to frighten her. Her knees trembled, and she clenched her hands together. *Stand your ground, Madeleine. Nicholas will back you up. Didn't he say so?*

Upon entering the room, Maddy was surprised to see Francis Ryder seated on a chair before the fire instead of standing in an intimidating posture. She curtsied and said, "Good even, sir."

"Pray be seated, Mistress Vernon. My son tells me you have been ill."

"Aye. But I am well now." Nicholas led her to the cushioned settle.

"Unfortunately, your illness does not change your circumstances, nor the urgency of your mission at Lanercost. Your presence there is required, now more than ever. Since Nick tells me it is your wish to return, this should not be too much of a hardship for you."

"I did wish to return, it is true. Until today, I was certain of it. But after finding Cath's—the serving girl's—body, I am fearful. John Musgrave—"

"Is also on the queen's business and under a direct order to stay away from you."

Shocked, she asked, "Has he known all along of my reason for being at Lanercost?"

"He was not informed until recently. I wish you to bear in mind that we currently have no proof he is culpable in the death of this serving girl."

"Nicholas told you of the dealings between him and Cath? And of my involvement?" She glanced at him, then back to his father. "And that he tried to rape me?" Nicholas winced, but this was not the time to spare anybody's feelings.

"My son told me a while back of Musgrave's threats against you. As I said, he has been warned."

Maddy thought for a moment, staring into the fire. Everything she'd told Nicholas earlier still held true, yet she was reluctant. A deep unease had taken root in her, and she knew it was largely due to Cath's murder. Could there be a connection between her demise and whatever else was going on at Lanercost? She remembered how Lady Dacre and her stepson had looked the other way when Musgrave was seducing Cath, instead of offering her their protection. Maddy did not have all the pieces of the puzzle yet. She would have to return to find them and put them all together. For now, she would keep this notion to herself.

"Mistress?"

Francis Ryder's voice, surprisingly gentle, called her back to the moment. "I'll return, even though my instincts are warning me not to."

"You have little choice in the matter, as you have not yet discharged your debt to the crown. There is more work to be done before you may regain your freedom."

Ah, this was the Ryder Maddy had expected. Should she tell him that's not what Nicholas had said? Before she could decide, he spoke up, looking at her earnestly.

"You don't have to do this, Maddy. As far as I'm concerned, you have earned the right to refuse. You've given us much valuable information, intelligence that has carried this investigation forward."

Francis Ryder gave his son a hard, cold glare. "This is my operation, Nick, and I say Mistress Vernon must continue to do my bidding. This matter is not finished, is it?"

"And I say it is too risky," Nicholas said. "There are other ways—"

Maddy interrupted. "If I go back, I want to know everything, starting with what was in Norfolk's letter. You must have some inkling of what they are planning. I need to know what that is, especially at this stage."

Father and son exchanged a look. "Go ahead, Nick."

Beard rubbing ensued, a gesture that was becoming dear to her. "You will insist on this, then, Maddy? I cannot stop you?"

"I must finish it, Nicholas. For all the reasons I explained earlier." If his father had not been present, she would have gone to him and thrown herself into his embrace. She needed the reassurance, and so did he.

"Very well, then. Norfolk's letter. It was a poorly designed cipher meant to inform the Dacres that he would be arriving around the time of Mary Stewart's trip to Carlisle. He warned them about any further action against the queen that would arouse suspicion or bring unwanted attention to the region. He also implied he would require their assistance upon his arrival in the North."

"If I remember correctly, he seemed to believe he would be released from the Tower by the time of the visit. Has that happened?"

"No," the elder Ryder said. "At this point, I think we can rule out his showing up here."

"He could escape," she said.

"Highly unlikely. He is too heavily guarded. Oh, the queen will release him at some point, but I do not believe she's prepared to take that step yet." Francis Ryder had an almost unnatural stillness about him. He showed no outer sign of worry or hesitation, only an overarching self-assurance.

"What should I be watching—and listening—for?"

Nicholas was quiet, letting his father do the talking.

"That's the tricky part. I'm afraid we don't know much more than we ever have. Your instincts are good. Rely on them."

"So—nothing. You can tell me naught, other than I should not expect Norfolk to show up?"

"Father," Nicholas said. His voice held a note of warning. A challenge. "Tell her the rest."

That earned him a glower from his parent. "The less she knows, the more honed her instincts will be. If she is anticipating one thing only, she may miss something else."

"Believe me, sir, I will be mindful of any piece of information, no matter how trivial, no matter if I do not fully comprehend it."

After eyeing her for a moment, he said, "Fair enough. We suspect something is afoot to coincide with Mary Stewart's sojourn in Carlisle. But we don't know what or when. The Dacres are a party to this, which is the reason they staged the false raid as a cover for meeting with the Scottish lairds."

"That sounds rather vague. Can you tell me anything more?"

"Aye, we can," Nicholas said. "We think there may be an attempt to abduct—rescue, in their eyes—Mary while she's in Carlisle for the visit with her child. Any piece of intelligence regarding that possibility will be of primary importance."

His father jumped in. "But herein lies the problem." He leaned forward, regarding Maddy closely. "We're not at all certain about that. And to muddy the waters further, that is not the only thing we must be on the lookout for. Allies of the Earl of Moray, Mary's late brother and erstwhile regent, may take this as a prime opportunity to assassinate her, so that she will never be restored to the Scottish monarchy or have any influence over her son. And then we have the Marians, Mary's staunch supporters, some of whom are accompanying her on this trip and may use the opportunity to make their own mischief. We simply don't know at this point."

Nicholas rose. "We've said enough, Father. An attempt

on Mary's life should not concern Mistress Vernon. Lady Dacre and her son would most likely be involved only in the rescue plot and may be working with the Marians in that." He turned to Maddy, looking weary of the whole business. "We'll soon find out. With your help."

When had this become so complicated? She got to her feet and paced away from them. "By God's light, I have less chance of discovering the truth than finding the threepence in the Christmas pudding."

Francis Ryder scowled at her. "If you are not able—"

Maddy interrupted. "When will I return? Do we need to inform them first?" Nicholas moved to gaze out the windows, silent.

"We'll send a missive tomorrow. You'll leave the following day. Is that satisfactory?"

"The letter should be from me," Maddy said.

"I agree. See to it after supper."

She nodded. Ryder stood to leave. He actually honored her with a short bow, but that meant nothing. She didn't trust him anymore than she ever had. He needed her now, but at the end of this, would he let her go? Or would it suit his purposes better to rid himself of her because she knew too much? From all Nicholas had revealed, and what she'd witnessed herself, he was ruthless enough to do it. Maddy sat back down, looked at Nicholas, and said, "Well."

He eased down next to her. "How I wish I had never gotten you into this," he said, his voice ragged. "If only you had not taken part in Leonard Dacre's raid—Dacre's folly."

She put a hand on his arm. "How many times I have wished my brother hadn't joined the rebellion. But I can't change the fact that he did."

With a tormented look, he pulled her into his arms. "Maddy, dear Maddy. How shall I keep you safe? And how shall I do without you when you are away?"

Fear, and the uncertainty of their future, trembled in the air between them.

After the evening meal, Maddy composed a letter to Lady Dacre. It was simple and concise, stating that she was now well and would be returning two days' hence.

Nicholas insisted on accompanying her to Lanercost, but dread was her true companion. It seemed to be mounted behind her, nudging her, in case she forgot just where she was headed. The day was overcast and pale, hazy light cast a pall over everything. Even the river looked brown and dull. Maddy insisted they part ways before reaching the gatehouse. They dismounted, and Nicholas grasped her arms. "Get word to me right away if you feel endangered, Maddy. My father was right about using your instincts. If you feel threatened, there is most likely a good reason for it."

She nodded. Her sense of apprehension was mounting, and she wanted to be on her way and finish this. Face whatever dangers were awaiting her. "Will your man be close by?"

"Always."

She started to pull away, but he wouldn't let her. "Kiss me, sweeting."

Maddy framed his face with her hands and did as he asked. *Ah.* The sweet press of his lips. The soft bristles of his beard skimming her face. He tasted of mint and smelled like...himself. Whatever else the Dacres might do, they could not steal these sweet moments.

I love him. Parting from him is the last thing I want.

Abruptly, she let go. "Adieu, Nicholas."

"May God keep you safe, Maddy."

She rode away from him, blinking back the tears she didn't want him to see.

Chapter Twenty

Maddy arrived mid-morning, and Lady Dacre was there to welcome her back. She seemed gratified to see Maddy, and they spent the time before dinner at their work while the older lady shared news of the tenants, staff, and servants. Sadly, Maddy realized she no longer trusted her mistress. All she could think was: *there is plenty going on here you are keeping hidden from me.* No doubt Lady Dacre felt the same way. It was strange that Maddy could enjoy her company, and yet at the same time distrust her. Logic told her she had to be involved with whatever dark deeds were in the offing. But for the moment, Maddy must carry on as though all was normal.

She was surprised to see both Christopher Dacre and John Musgrave at the midday meal. The latter simply nodded in greeting, but Master Dacre was more welcoming. As well as full of questions, which he asked between bites of salad and swallows of ale.

"And how do you fare, Mistress Vernon?" he asked. "Is your health restored?"

"Aye, I am perfectly well, sir." She deftly deboned the

turbot on her trencher, acting as if the matter of her well-being was trivial.

"My stepmother and I were most distressed that the raiders made off with you, especially given the state of your health. It must have been quite a ride they took you on."

At this she looked up. "Indeed. I pleaded with them to leave me be, told them I'd been ill, but they were determined to carry on, for whatever reason." Maddy wiped her hands on the serviette draped over her wrist and chewed a bite of fish, drenched with a savory cream sauce.

"And they dropped you near Brampton?" Dacre asked. His tone was accusatory, as if she had planned her own kidnapping. Had wanted it.

She set her knife down. "Aye. 'Dropped' is a good word for it. They shoved me off the horse. I recognized where I was and made my way to my cousin's house. I suffered a relapse of the influenza, and they took care of me. I also had many cuts and bruises, but nothing serious."

"So your cousin's letter said. How is it, mistress, that they seized you? My stepmother said she had tucked you into your bed herself." The idea that because Lady Dacre had helped her back to bed made her somehow invincible was ludicrous, but both mother and stepson seemed to feel strongly that if Maddy had remained there, she would have been safe. She felt like arguing the point but desisted. He was waiting for an answer, studying her over the rim of his tankard.

She and Nicholas had discussed a response to this query and decided she should be as truthful as possible, because they did not know what her captors had told them. "Very true, sir, but I could not sleep. The commotion beneath my window frightened me. I wanted to see what was happening."

"Where were you when they caught you?" he asked.

Maddy was beginning to feel uncomfortable. She'd anticipated a few questions, but not this grilling. "I had just stepped outside the hall when they came along. I stayed in the shadows, but a small piece of stone broke loose and gave me away. And that was that."

Lady Dacre pointed her chin at her son. "Enough, Christopher. I am quite sure Madeleine does not wish to relive her terrifying experience."

No sooner had Maddy gulped some ale, feeling relieved that the questioning was over, than Lady Dacre said, "I am only grateful the same fate did not befall you as befell our Cath."

The sight and smell of the food was beginning to nauseate her. Maddy had not expected anybody to mention Cath's death, at least not right away. And if she'd wanted to ask her about it, why had she waited until now to bring it up, when they'd had that time alone earlier? Surely it was not something to be discussed during a meal.

"We heard you and your cousin discovered the body," Dacre said.

"We did. It is not a pleasant thing to recall." Maddy was beginning to tremble, and she wrapped her arms about herself to stop it.

"You simply happened to be riding along the river and came upon it?" he asked.

His words and their implication angered her and made her defensive. "We certainly did not go looking for it. Her body was…it was snagged on a bush, partly submerged. It was horrible, grotesque." She shoved her chair back and rose stiffly. "I will join you in the drawing room shortly, madam."

Maddy raced down the stairs and into Dacre Hall, her heartbeat keeping pace. Pray God Mistress Derby would not see her, for she knew the cook would want to talk. What was happening here? Why were they interrogating her? And mentioning Cath, whom they hadn't given a fig about when Musgrave was harassing her. Calling her "their Cath." It made Maddy sick. She was beginning to believe Nicholas had been right about returning to Lanercost.

She could draw only one conclusion. They were trying to intimidate her. Threaten her in some way. It was clear they thought she was up to no good. But did they suspect the worst? That she was a spy? And how easily Maddy had fallen into their trap. She was angry with herself for losing her composure and fleeing, because it only made her look guilty. Much better to have remained at the table and ridden out the storm. After nearly ten days with Nicholas, she needed to relearn the skill of subterfuge around the Dacres and Musgrave, who had remained oddly silent throughout the whole exchange.

Approaching the kitchen, she slowed her pace and lightened her step. The cook was nowhere about, and Maddy climbed the stairs with a sense of relief. When she entered her chamber, Useless squirmed out from behind the wardrobe to greet her. Gathering the wee dog into her arms, Maddy allowed a few minutes of slobbery licks and kisses. This was obviously the only creature at the priory who cared to show her some affection. Someone—Mistress Derby and Alice, probably—had taken good care of Useless in Maddy's absence. The animal was looking on the fat side. Maddy had the feeling the beagle would be her only friend in the coming days.

A footman had carried her things up, and she busied herself putting them away. Nicholas had insisted she bring Susan's clothing with her. When she balked, he'd held her by the shoulders and said, "Allow me to make you a gift of this apparel, Maddy. It is of no use to anybody here. At least take the traveling costume and the skirts and bodices you have been wearing during your time here." She had finally given in.

Maddy let enough time elapse for Lady Dacre to have

finished her meal and attend to her other needs, and then, with a sense of disquiet, she made her way back to the vicarage. The lady was already seated, with her work in her lap. She wasn't sewing, though, but sitting quietly, her gaze fixed on some indeterminate spot. Obviously musing on something.

She started when she realized she was no longer alone. "Madeleine, my dear, forgive us for our clumsy questions. We should have seen your distress. Are you feeling better?"

Maddy would not apologize for her hasty departure from the dining room. She nodded and said, "Would you like me to read to you?"

"No. I want to talk to you about something."

Maddy's heart lurched. *Pray God, not more questions.* She fumbled in the basket for her embroidery and waited.

"You will be shocked to hear it, but while you were gone, I began the tedious job of organizing my papers, with Christopher's help." She laughed at the expression on Maddy's face, and that helped ease the tension between them. "I've barely made a start. Are you still willing to help me with the sorting and storing?"

Maddy smiled. "Of course. I'm sure if we work together, it will soon be done. When do you wish to start?"

"Tomorrow, after dinner. My stepson and I will spend the morning separating the private documents."

Maddy nodded. "Very well." They worked companionably until Lady Dacre excused herself, saying she wished to nap before supper.

"Perhaps you would like to do the same? Despite being well, I'm sure you have not fully regained your strength."

Maddy bid her good afternoon, and as soon as she left the room, beat a hasty path to her chamber. The last thing she wanted was to be caught alone by Master Dacre, who seemed to have turned chillingly suspicious of her. She tried to relax, but her mind was a like a boiling kettle. If only it would distill her muddled thoughts into something coherent, so she could study them from every angle until she understood. At length she gave up on resting, donned a cloak and boots, and made her way outside.

The weather had not improved, but at least it wasn't raining. Maddy walked past the church, then toward the gatehouse. Vivid spots of color brightened the landscape here and there on this April day, daffodils and daisies, and lady smock, beginning to spread its silvery whiteness across the meadows. In the orchard, crab apples were showing off their rosy blooms and brilliant green foliage. Before long she glimpsed somebody emerging from the stables and moving toward her. With a start, she thought it might be Nicholas's man, with a message for her, but Maddy shortly recognized Musgrave. She stopped, wondering if she should retreat. But it was too late; he knew she'd seen him.

"Mistress Vernon," he said. "I didn't expect to find you out and about."

Prior to the midday meal, she had not seen him in quite some time, and once again his exceptional stature and rough good looks struck her. He sounded more cordial than she'd yet experienced, rather like the Musgrave of old, making her suspicious. What did he want of her?

"Nor I, you. I wouldn't have come this way if I had."

"Come now, mistress, can we not be friends? Judging from the conversation at dinner, you might be in need of one."

"And you truly think you could be a friend to me?" Maddy took a step back and folded her arms across her chest, watching him.

His expression darkened. "Walk with me a moment, if you please."

She did not please, but curiosity got the better of her, so she fell in beside him. When he turned toward a stand of trees, she hesitated. Did she really want to be alone with this man, out of view of everybody who might offer help if it were needed? But Maddy sensed that something had changed with him, so she decided to trust him, despite her grave misgivings.

When they were well out of sight, he said, "What do you know about the supposed raid?"

This surprised her, and she needed time to gather her wits. Stalling was in order. "Where were you that night? I didn't see you."

"Not that it's your concern, but I was in Carlisle. I only heard what happened when I returned. And I learned you'd been ill, then taken by the so-called raiders."

"Why do you doubt that it was truly a raid?"

He puffed a weighted breath. "Workers. Servants. People talk, you know."

Still unsure of how much to reveal, Maddy said, "It seemed real enough at first. Mounted men shouting, others running about with torches, and…fires burning here and there. Lady Dacre said they'd taken some livestock, and Christopher and some of the laborers were giving chase."

"And then?"

"And then nothing more seemed to happen. I can't be sure, though. When I tried to find out exactly what was occurring, a couple of ruffians jumped out and grabbed me."

"Did you notice anybody in particular? Men you'd never seen before, who…seemed a cut above your ruffians?"

Could I trust him? Francis Ryder said he was here on the queen's business, but Nicholas thought him the kind of agent without scruples. She pretended to think about it, finally shaking her head. "It was dark, and there were several men about. I could not see their faces, could barely make out their forms. Alice and I hid from them in the undercroft. I heard their voices, but they were none I recognized."

Musgrave gave a grunt of frustration. "I think you're holding out on me," he said, stepping closer, his voice threatening. "We're on the same side here, you know."

Maddy faced him squarely. "I've no idea what you are referring to."

"Do you not? You're lying, mistress. In the days to come, you may have need of a protector, and that cousin of yours is at some distance. Maybe you'll decide to trust me if your life is endangered."

That raised her ire. "As you protected Cath?" she asked, before considering the wisdom of such a question.

A dawning awareness passed over his face. "You think I killed her, don't you?"

Maddy refused to meet his eyes, and he grabbed her arm. "Answer me!"

Her belly felt as if it were pushing up into her chest. "Didn't you? Who else if not you?" She tried to look defiant, but more than likely only looked scared.

To her surprise, the bluster seemed to drain out of him. "She was found in the river. I had assumed she drowned."

"Nicholas—my cousin—said there was evidence to the contrary."

Musgrave's large frame seemed to shrink. "I admit I tried to seduce her. I wanted to bed her. But I would never have hurt her. By God's blood, I-I cared about her."

Maddy eyed him closely. Her intuition said he was telling the truth. She could hardly credit it, but his manner and the sadness in his eyes persuaded her of his sincerity. Either that, or he was a very accomplished liar and knew the trick of sounding genuine. Best to be skeptical. "So you say, but you were violent toward me. Why not to her?"

"I was drunk the night I came to your chamber. I barely knew what I was doing and am heartily sorry for it."

"That was not the only time you threatened me with physical harm," Maddy reminded him.

"And I suppose you'll never forget. Or forgive. I often

act without considering the consequences, and then I regret it." He drew close and stabbed the air with his finger. "But mark this. I did not kill Cath, mistress." He paused, his eyes flashing. "I think I know who did. In fact, I'd stake my life on it."

Maddy was so taken aback, she could only stammer out, "Who, then?"

"You work it out," he said, striding away.

"Wait!" But he kept on going, ignoring her. "You'll have to tell the justice of the peace," she shouted, but he was too far away to hear. What a fool she was, yelling like a fishwife. Anybody loitering close by might have heard her.

He seemed like a changed man, implying he wanted her forgiveness. Was he frightened of someone? Cath's killer, possibly. Musgrave attempting to extract information from her seemed all topsy-turvy. He too suspected the raid had been staged. Maddy had not wished to tell him she'd seen one of the lairds entering the vicarage. Musgrave was a double agent, after all, and how did she know what he might tell the Dacres about her? Deflecting his questions with her implications about Cath's murder had seemed the wisest course.

And there was a conundrum. Musgrave claiming he hadn't done it, but he knew who had. She must contrive a way to get him to name the villain who murdered that lovely young girl. Most astonishing of all, John Musgrave seemed to have had a genuine liking for Cath.

• • •

Over the next few days, Maddy and Lady Dacre spent their afternoons working in her chamber among the piles of papers. She claimed to have sorted through them and pulled out anything private. But it looked as if a whirlwind had spun through the room, lifting documents and tossing them back down willy-nilly.

"How do you want to organize these, madam?" Maddy asked when she first encountered the mess. "By subject? Date? Or possibly by a name?" Whatever she decided, it was going to be a daunting task.

"Oh, dear, we hadn't gotten that far. What do you think?"

After pondering for a moment, Maddy said, "If I get to work, the best method will come to me."

Lady Dacre gestured to a stack of documents. "You may begin with those." Then she turned to a different stack and began marking parchments with embroidery silks.

The first papers Maddy encountered were either copies of letters Lady Dacre had sent to her solicitor, or letters from him. "All this correspondence with your solicitor. We can arrange those by date and put them together in one box, according to the topic. A name can serve as a topic when appropriate."

"Ah! Excellent plan." Lady Dacre motioned to the papers on the mantel. "There are the statements from various people attesting to Sir Thomas's state of mind."

"We can file those under 'witness statements.'"

"Madeleine, perhaps you have a calling to the bar!"

Maddy laughed. "The last time I took note, the Inns of Court were strictly a male preserve. I would only qualify as a clerk, in any case, but I don't believe women are welcome in that work, either." After a short time, Lady Dacre left the chamber to consult with the steward about suitable storage for the papers.

Maddy stood and stretched. Her back muscles were aching after sitting for so long, bent over, studying the documents. No sooner had she sat down to resume her work than the door opened. She glanced up, expecting to see her mistress, but instead Edith came through. "Sorry to disturb," she said. "But I must ready my lady for her trip."

Maddy nearly blurted out, "What trip?" but quickly judged it might be wiser to act as though she already knew. "Of course. I suppose you have much to do."

"Aye. Besides her own things, my lady has gifts for her grandchildren. She likes to take them little trinkets when she visits. 'Tis not often she gets to see them."

"I expect not." Grandchildren? Lady Dacre had never mentioned any. Would these be William Dacre's children? Maddy did not think so. His stepmother was on such poor terms with him, surely she wouldn't be paying him a visit.

"How many does she have again? I can never remember." Maddy hoped it was more than one or two, or her comment would make her sound shamefully dim. She pretended to continue working, so her interest wouldn't appear overly great.

Edith paused in her advance to the wardrobe. "Mistress Mabel has three little ones, a boy and two girls, and Mistress Jane has two, both boys."

"And she's visiting Mistress Mabel this time." Pure conjecture on Maddy's part. As it turned out, she'd guessed right.

"Aye, near Carlisle. Well, they both live thereabout. Their father, you know, was Constable of Carlisle Castle. The girls used to play there when they were bairns."

Maddy's head was spinning. Lady Dacre had been married to the constable of the castle? This was the first she'd heard of it. Why did she never speak of it, or of her daughters? Early in her stay at the priory, she'd told Maddy all about William Dacre and her troubles with him, and how she got on with Christopher, but she'd never mentioned her own children.

"So long ago, now, that she was married to him," Maddy said. "I can't recall his name."

Edith readily supplied her with the necessary information. "'Twas Sir John Lowther, mistress." She lowered her voice and stepped closer. "And don't say I told you, but they never married. They lived as man and wife for many years, though."

"I see." Stranger and stranger. Lady Dacre had been the mistress of Sir John Lowther and had birthed two daughters by him. He had been the constable of Carlisle Castle. After she'd been widowed, if one could call it that, she had married Sir Thomas Dacre.

"When did he die, Edith? Sir John, I mean."

Before she could answer, Lady Dacre entered the chamber. No matter. Maddy didn't truly need to know.

"Any luck?" she asked.

"They are looking for containers, but it will be tomorrow at the soonest. We may as well be done for today. It's nearly time to dress for supper."

"Very well, but let's make sure the papers we already sorted stay that way. Where shall we put them?" Edith knew where there was an empty coffer and ran to retrieve it. Carefully, Maddy laid the documents inside, in crisscrossed piles.

On the way back to her chamber, a thought that had been hovering at the back of Maddy's mind now came to the fore. Who would be better equipped to know the layout of the castle than a woman whose partner had been the warden, whose children had played within its walls? No wonder Lady Dacre was crucial to the plot, if indeed a rescue of Mary Stewart was in the offing. As yet, however, Maddy had found no solid evidence of any such plan. She could only watch and wait.

Chapter Twenty-One

Although Maddy did not have anything of much importance to report, she guided her horse toward Brampton and the Ryder home on market day. She wanted to dance for joy at the thought of seeing Nicholas again. Did he feel the same? Was he in his glass house tending the roses, all the while thinking of her? As he requested, she'd brought along a groom this time. But they no sooner arrived than Nicholas dismissed him, saying he would escort her home. Like a lovelorn maiden, she struggled to suppress a blissful smile.

He grasped her hand and pulled her toward the library, so fast she could hardly keep pace. The corridor echoed with their laughter. Once he'd closed the door, he pulled her into his arms and lowered his head to kiss her. She stepped away. "One moment, pray. Is your father here?"

Nicholas looked at her, his eyes dusky with need. "My father? He is in Carlisle today. What do you want with him?"

"Nothing," she said, grabbing hold of his doublet and pulling him close. "Nothing at all." When she thought they might both be overcome with the frenzied passion of lovers who had been reluctantly separated, there was a knock at the door. A timid one, which meant Daniel had noticed her arrival.

"Curse that child," Nicholas muttered, though she knew he didn't truly mean it. "Come, Daniel."

He burst into the room and ran to her. Burying his face in her skirts, he hugged her legs tightly and wouldn't let go. She glanced at Nicholas with a puzzled expression, but he only shrugged. What had caused this heartfelt display of affection? Kneeling, Maddy embraced the lad. "Did you miss me so much, Daniel?"

His head bobbed up and down. "I missed you too, Mouse. Oops, I mean Sir Mouse." Maddy heard a muffled giggle. What have you been up to since I left?"

He stepped away and pantomimed shooting an arrow. "Ah. You're soon going to be more skilled than I. What else?" Now he looked at his uncle for help.

"We rode along the river a few days ago and did a little angling, didn't we, nephew?"

"Any success?" she asked, facing the boy.

He nodded and pretended to throw fish up on the bank. "And did you eat them for your supper?"

Daniel hesitated, so Nicholas said, "We threw some back and brought the rest home. Cook prepared a tasty trout pie for us." Daniel rubbed his belly and they all three laughed.

Nicholas placed a palm on his nephew's head. "Mistress Maddy and I have business to discuss, Daniel. We shall come and find you when we've finished." Without protest, the child left the room, but not before giving her a wistful glance when he reached the door.

She looked at Nicholas, her eyes telling the story of how woefully she'd missed him. His lips brushed hers, briefly. "Let's talk first and be done with business quickly."

Ah. So he had missed her, too. "Aye. Well, then. I'm

afraid I haven't had time to discover much. What do you know of Lady Dacre's background?"

Nicholas led Maddy to the settle before the hearth, though no fire burned today. "*Hmm.* She was raised in Carlisle. I do not believe she ever married before she wed Sir Thomas Dacre." His eyebrows shot up. "From your expression, I collect my information is wrong. What have you learned?"

Could it be they truly didn't know about Lady Jane Dacre's former husband—lover? "You are not aware that her first husband was Sir John Lowther, once the warden of the castle? Growing up, her daughters played in the bailey. She herself must have a thorough knowledge of the grounds and the layout of the castle."

"John Lowther was her first husband?" Nicholas sprang to his feet, obviously agitated. "Sweet Christ, how could we have missed this? Musgrave should have been aware."

"According to Lady Dacre's maid, they never wed, but lived together as man and wife for years."

"Something so vital! We searched the records for any mention of a marriage and found nothing. We should have pursued it further, questioned what she was doing all those years." He brushed vigorously at his beard. "It's she who will know how to gain entry to the castle. And she probably knows every possible chamber where Mary Stewart and her son are likely to be housed on their visit."

"Undoubtedly. Lady Dacre was Lowther's mistress. Fancy that! She seems such a proper lady, I have difficulty believing that state was acceptable to her."

"Had she never told you of her daughters?"

"Not one word. I'm certain that was deliberate. She didn't want me to know, possibly because she would have had to reveal who their father was. Eventually, I would have worked out her connection to Carlisle Castle." Maddy paused, musing. "When I was your...guest...at the castle, Joan told me Mary had stayed there once. Wouldn't they put her in the same chambers as before?"

He shook his head. "Too many people know their location." Resuming his seat, he said, "This makes it even more likely that the Dacres are involved in a plot involving Mary. How did you discover it?"

"Coincidence." Maddy related everything Edith had told her, including Lady Dacre's upcoming trip to visit her daughter.

"She will be in Carlisle when Mary Stewart arrives, and make no mistake, there is a reason for that. They—whoever they may be—need her help at the castle. Well done, Maddy." He smiled, looking as though he'd like to rub his hands together in glee.

"I cannot truly take any credit, since I found out purely by accident."

"Have you learned anything else?"

"Nothing at all about any attempt to liberate Mary. If they're planning something, they're hiding it well, at least for now." Maddy glanced at the tray bearing food and drink. "May I pour us some wine? You may be preoccupied with other matters, but I'm ravenous."

"Of course, you must be hungry." Nicholas filled their wine glasses, and she laid out cheese, bread, cold mutton, and berries. "My first day back was…interesting. The Dacres, Christopher in particular, grilled me at dinner, to the point that I almost felt fearful."

Nicholas paused, a piece of mutton halfway to his mouth. "About what?"

"The night of the raid. Why hadn't I stayed in my bed? Where was I when they captured me? Where did they drop me? Dacre's tone was biting, as though I were to blame for my own abduction. In hindsight, my guess is that they were trying to figure out if I'd seen Ferniehurst."

"Did they actually put the question to you?"

She broke off a piece of manchet. "They stopped short of that, probably hoping I'd inadvertently reveal it. Then they started in on me about Cath. I'm afraid my equanimity deserted me, and I fled from the room. I couldn't bear hearing them talk about her, as though they had truly cared what happened to her."

Nicholas took her hand, kissed it, and said, "I'm sorry, sweeting. The situation seems to be worsening, becoming riskier for you. I don't like it. If you feel you're in imminent danger, don't wait to get word to me. Leave. Brampton is well within walking distance."

"If I left suddenly, they'd probably come after me. They would assume I'd learned something incriminating. I must try to behave as though all is normal, even if I'm frightened."

Apparently not satisfied with her answer, Nicholas adopted the look of a schoolmaster dressing down a disobedient pupil. "If you believe you have reason to fear for your life, get out of there. You can sneak out under cover of darkness, if necessary, and walk along the Roman wall. There are places to conceal yourself if it comes to that. Safer than the road or the path. Promise me you will do so. I'll hear no argument on this, Maddy."

She cocked her head at him, even though he had an excellent reason, in this case, to order her about. "Very well, I promise."

"What of our friend, Musgrave? Where was he during this?"

"He was there but did not speak a word. You'll be interested to know, however, that he accosted me while I was out walking. He asked me what I knew about the raid. It seems he also thought it was contrived."

She related her conversation with Musgrave, Nicholas listening intently.

"So he must sense danger as well."

"It would seem so. I scoffed at his being my protector, though. I said, 'Like you protected Cath?' I regretted the words as soon as I'd spoken them—"

A scratching at the door. Nicholas looked up, irritated. "Pray, let him join us," Maddy said. "I believe he must have feared I was not coming back, judging from the way he clung to me earlier."

"I tried to reassure him, but apparently, that did not quell his fears." He walked over to the door and opened it. "There's a rodent about, Mistress Madeleine. What shall we do with him?"

"Leave the door ajar, sir. He'll smell the food and fall into our trap." Nicholas came back and sat beside her. They ate quietly for a while, pretending not to notice the small form sneaking into the room and nearing the table. When a little hand reached out and tried to filch a strawberry, Nicholas pounced.

"Aha! I've got you, you little rat."

Daniel, laughing, wriggled out of his uncle's grasp, shaking his head vehemently.

"That's no rat, Master Ryder," Maddy said. "That's a mouse. A harmless creature. Let's feed him."

Daniel crawled up between them and shared their collation, until finally they'd all eaten their fill. Then he stood up on his sturdy little legs and tugged on their hands. Maddy glanced at Nicholas. "Outside? Do you want to go outside, Daniel?" she asked. "I sometimes wish you would say out loud what it is you're thinking, for I have never heard your voice, you know."

Everything stilled. Nobody moved. Daniel and Nicholas were both staring at her as though she'd grown a pair of horns. Surely his uncle had talked to Daniel about his lack of speech. Had he never tried to gently coax the boy into talking?

Nicholas shrugged, and suddenly, normality resumed. They followed where Daniel led, toward the glass house.

"I fear I have not cleaned up in here as thoroughly as I normally do," Nicholas said. "Just before you arrived, I was propagating." Maddy almost laughed. The word sounded indecent. She knew it meant reproduction, but obviously he was referring to the roses. Indeed, the room was in disarray. Containers were strewn about, some filled with soil, others empty. Soil was sprinkled all over the floor, too. Knives, small pruning shears, other tools lay on one table, and three or four pots of rose bushes on another. "Daniel," Nicholas said. "I need your help. Will you sweep for me?"

The lad marched directly to one corner, where a straw broom was kept, and got to work. Maddy helped Nicholas pick foliage up off the floor. "From the pruning," he said, looking rather sheepish.

When they'd finished cleaning up, she asked him if he would explain his propagation method. Nicholas was passionate about his roses and willingly shared the techniques of grafting and taking cuttings, as well as his opinion about which method worked with greater efficacy. "Cutting is easier, but grafting produces heartier roses."

"You love doing this." It was a joy to see the tension lifted from his brow. His whole face shone with enthusiasm.

"I correspond with other growers, and we share information about propagation techniques, soil composition, and the heartiness of various bushes. At present, all of us want to get our hands on roses grown in the Orient. 'Tis said they breed new varieties in a multitude of colors. Even orange. I hope one day to grow and sell them locally."

Daniel wasn't looking, so Maddy clasped Nicholas's face with her hands and kissed him soundly on the mouth. "It makes me happy to see you engaging in something that gives you such pleasure."

He held firmly onto her arms, not letting go, and leaned down to whisper in her ear. "*You* give me pleasure, sweeting. Let's go upstairs." His words held a slightly desperate tone. "There's time."

Maddy was tempted, but in fact, the afternoon was waning. And there was Daniel to consider. "Nay, you know we cannot. I must be on my way. I have still to make a stop at the market." Resigned, Nicholas heaved a sigh and went off to ask Margery to bring her things.

Daniel, perhaps sensing the change in mood, had wandered over and was looking up at her. She stooped down to tell him she was leaving, fearing he might be upset. He hugged her around the neck, and Maddy felt tremors running through him, then heard his sobs. "Don't cry, little mouse. I will be back soon." When she stood, he clung to her skirts, and she bent down and lifted him into her arms. He was surprisingly light. In that way, they walked out into the central corridor leading to the front of the house, where they met Nicholas.

She looked at him, brows raised, but he was at a loss as much as she. Maddy walked into the drawing room and lowered herself to a chair, Daniel in her lap. Nicholas followed, setting down her basket and cloak. "Can you tell us what is wrong, Daniel?" Maddy asked.

But Daniel did not speak. He would quiet at intervals, but whenever she attempted to rise, his gulping sobs resumed. They broke from deep within his chest. When there seemed no end to his tears, Maddy glanced at Nicholas and said, "I am going to give you to your uncle now, Daniel. 'Tis time for me to take my leave. The people I live with will worry if I am not home for supper." Kissing his temple, she whispered, "I'll see you again soon, love."

Maddy pried the child's arms from around her neck and handed him over to his uncle. Hurriedly, she donned her cloak and grabbed the basket. "I will be fine on my own, Nicholas. You must stay with Daniel." He walked her to the entryway with the lad clinging to him. By the look on his face, she knew he was torn. He'd planned to accompany her back to the priory.

At the door, Nicholas kissed her cheek and said, "God keep you safe, Maddy."

"And you." Tears welled in her eyes, and she turned quickly so neither of them would notice. Leaving them was like a physical pain, but there was naught to do about it. Maddy's horse waited at the mounting block, and she mounted without assistance.

As she rode off, it struck her that she hadn't told Nicholas what Musgrave had said about Cath. That he knew who killed her but refused to name him. After Daniel had interrupted them, she'd forgotten.

Market day was winding down. Maddy strolled around the stalls and purchased a few items—a darning needle, a small painted box, some hairpins—and looked longingly at others. A lace handkerchief and a pair of tawny stockings made of fine yarn. Alas, she didn't have the coin for either. Wanting to quench her thirst before she left, she wandered over to the alehouse and asked for a tankard at their outdoor stall. Several citizens, both men and women, were milling about, drinking and talking animatedly about something. Maddy moved to one side, not wishing to be caught eavesdropping. But as it turned out, she could not help overhearing them and picking up on the subject of their excited babble.

Pardons.

Pardons for those who had joined the northern rebellion. Apparently, some were in hiding while others rotted in prisons. They had not all been executed.

She edged a little closer.

One goodwife was crying with joy. "It is over. My boys can come home now." Overcome, the woman leaned on a friend until she'd recovered.

"But all the ones put to the block or the gibbet," a man said. "What about them? Too late for them, isn't it?"

Another man snorted. "Only God can see to their pardon."

Maddy thought of Robert and hoped he'd met a deity who was forgiving. More forgiving than his queen had been, though from the sound of it, she'd recently decided to show more mercy. Two questions sprang to mind simultaneously, and their implications were so powerful Maddy's breath caught. Emboldened, she hurried up to the group, not caring to whom she addressed herself. "Pray pardon me. What about those who joined the Dacre raid? Are there pardons for them, too?"

The man nearest to her scratched his chin, looking around at the others. It was plain he did not know. But somebody else piped up. "The sheriff made the announcement in the square, in Carlisle. I was there. Aye, them, too." Voices rose again, and if she were to find out anything else, she must be quick.

"Sir. When was this announcement made?"

"Why, Monday last, mistress. But the sheriff said the decision had been made weeks ago. News came late to the north, like usual. The queen and her advisors say enough folks have been punished."

Indeed. Maddy could feel herself growing pale, feel the strength seeping from her body, as though she were dying. The man who'd answered her question said gently, "Come, mistress, and sit down. You don't look well."

She let him escort her to a bench. He carried her tankard

and urged her to drink. It was the last thing she wanted, but it would probably help revive her. She gulped several swallows and thanked him.

"You have somebody, then, who can come home now?"

"Nay. 'Tis too late for him." His brows raised in a question, and Maddy realized her query about the Dacre raid did not make sense in view of what she'd just told him. "Too late for my brother," she amended. "But I have a...friend who took part in Dacre's raid." He patted her shoulder and walked away.

Too late for Robbie, but not for me.

How long had Nicholas known, and why hadn't he told her? After a few more sips of ale, Maddy passed a coin to the lad who had been tending to her horse, mounted, and headed back to the Ryder home. Strength was returning, and with it a blind rage.

It only took a few minutes to get there. A sense that the world was falling in around her, on top of her, made her chest ache. Maddy hardly waited for the groom to help her off her horse. She raced to the door and with the flat of her hands, banged on it with all her strength. So hard her palms stung and would probably bruise.

• • •

Nicholas got to the door on the heels of a servant, whom he shoved out of the way.

"Maddy, what is it? What has happened?"

She did not answer but brushed past him and marched directly to the library. Dread pooled in his belly. She was angry, not afraid. As soon as the door thudded shut behind them, she wheeled on him. "When did you intend to tell me about the pardons?"

He stared dumbly. "The pardons." It was not a question,

but a delaying tactic.

"Don't play the lackwit with me, sir. You never told me the queen was doling out pardons. Did you and your father think to keep it a secret from me? To get out of me what you could before I found out?"

That was exactly what they'd done. What his father insisted they do. He stepped closer to her. "Not a secret, exactly." God's breath, that sounded pathetic.

"What, then? What would you call it?"

Nicholas knew it had been wrong, so wrong, to keep this from her. "My father thought it would further complicate things if you knew. I was going to tell you when all this"—he waved a hand through the air—"was over."

"Your father! You must always do his bidding. So you do not deny you withheld this information from me?"

The comment about his father set him off. "My allegiance is to the queen, not my father. Recall, I all but told you, Maddy, when I said it was your right to refuse. I knew if you chose not to return, there would be nothing Father could do about it. It was you who insisted on going back. You and he were in agreement on that."

She grabbed his arm. "Because I believed my freedom, possibly my life, was at stake if I did not complete the mission."

"Be that as it may, I told you it was your decision to make. In fact, I urged you not to return to Lanercost because I believed the risk was too great."

"That was before we'd found Cath's body. Afterward, when I told your father I was hesitant, he implied that I—we— must finish the job at Lanercost. That there wasn't a choice." When Nicholas didn't respond, she asked, "How long have you known? About the pardons?"

He deflected the question. "Have you listened to a word I said? You are quibbling, simply because I never used the word 'pardon.' What I offered meant the same thing."

"An official pardon, issued on the queen's authority, would have changed everything, Nicholas. You know that."

Truly, he did not believe the pardon would have made a difference to her, so determined had she been to find redemption. "Would you have given up, if you'd known?" This time he moved faster than Maddy, grasping her arms, giving her a slight shake. "No. You'd never have stopped, and all on account of your worthless brother, curse him. Your brother, who is alive, hiding near Carlisle these many months." He let go of her and stepped back, so abruptly she nearly fell.

Now he'd gone too far. He hadn't meant to break it to her like this, when they were both half-crazed with anger. Maddy's face crumpled with the shock. "What? Is this some preposterous new ploy to force me to do as you bid?"

Nicholas sat down, leaning his forehead into his hands. "I knew this would end badly," he muttered to himself. Then he looked up at her. "Sit by me. You must hear this."

Maddy didn't argue. She wouldn't, with something so vital at stake. She settled herself beside him, and he allowed himself to hope nothing would change between them.

Nicholas turned toward her. "Robert was not executed. He bought his way out of it."

She gave her head a shake. "That is a lie, invented to further confuse and control me. I witnessed his execution."

"Are you certain of that? You saw a man who resembled your brother. Was it you who prepared his body for burial?"

"No. I never saw him after he…afterward. Kat insisted on doing it herself. She thought it would be too painful for me."

"Your sister-in-law made sure you did not."

She massaged her forehead, as if that might help clarify matters. "How is it possible to 'buy your way out' of an execution?"

"Generally speaking, it is not. But in your village—

Rickerby—the list was short. The executions of four men, your brother being one of them, were stayed."

"On what grounds?"

Nicholas hedged. "Does it matter? Your brother is alive, Maddy. Why concern yourself with the details?"

"It matters to me. You have deceived me in all ways imaginable; pray do me the honor of telling me the truth about this."

Nicholas rose and put some distance between them. It would be easier to reveal the truth if he weren't so near her. Every word he spoke was driving them farther apart. "To gain their freedom, Robert and the others each had to find someone—a ruffian, thief, or worse—to die in their stead. I don't know it for a fact, but I'd wager coin changed hands as well."

"My brother bartered another man's life for his own." Her voice was as flat as a schoolboy's declining Latin verbs. "That's what you're saying?"

Her face was a mix of sorrow and ire, and he could hardly bear to look at it. "That is the crux of it, yes."

She stood, shook out her skirts, and made for the door. "Wait," Nicholas said and she paused. "I have tried to tell you more than once. Remember the day in the garden, when I asked you about Robert? I very nearly gave you the truth of it then. It pains me to see you hurt. That's why—"

"Don't! You couldn't tell me because you knew how it would make you look in my eyes. I came to your door, sick and despairing, and begged for help, yet still you let me believe Robert was dead, even though you knew how it grieved me. How you must have laughed when I said I wanted to atone for his death, knowing I'd soon be granted a pardon." A brittle sound tore from her throat. "I told myself over and over that you were my enemy, that I should never make the mistake of thinking of you as anything more. And then I foolishly disregarded my own counsel."

"Don't leave like this, Maddy. You are not yourself, and that makes you vulnerable. Stay the night here, and we can sort this out in the morning. I'll send word to Lady Dacre that you've taken ill."

"Stay here under the same roof with you? With the man who put duty before love? The man who used me, seduced me, and betrayed my trust? I'd rather spend the night in a hovel along the road." She grabbed her cloak and wrapped it around her shoulders. "Pray call for my horse."

Nicholas knew he could do nothing to sway her today. She needed time. When he thrust the door open, it nearly slammed into Daniel. He'd obviously been listening to their conversation, and if he did not comprehend it, he recognized the implications.

Maddy stopped in her tracks. Daniel's eyes were big and round, and though he wasn't crying, fear and confusion reigned in his gaze. Nicholas tried to pull him close, but he wouldn't allow it. Maddy was standing in the doorway, and it was to her Daniel directed his attention. He opened his mouth, and Nicholas heard a whoosh of air burst out. Felt it. Daniel's lips pressed together. "M-Ma-Maddy." The child's eyes darted back to Nicholas, as though seeking permission to speak to her.

Daniel had spoken for the first time in a year.

Maddy dropped to her knees, the better to hear him. "D-don't g-go. St-stay here w-with us."

Chapter Twenty-Two

Maddy thought it wiser not to show too much elation at Daniel's speaking. It might frighten him. She yearned to look at Nicholas but would not let herself. "How wonderful to hear your voice, Daniel," she said.

Maddy rose so that Nicholas could take her place. He had waited for this day a long time, despaired of its ever coming. Kneeling, he clasped the boy against his chest, burying his face in Daniel's hair, laughing and crying all at once. This immediately brought tears to her own eyes. She didn't want to weep, not now, when she must leave and never return. Maddy tiptoed down the hall while uncle and nephew rejoiced together.

Margery was there to open the door for her. "Did the little one speak?"

Maddy smiled. "Aye."

"'Tis a miracle from God!"

"Mayhap it is, Margery." She hurried outside and summoned a groom, who ran off to get her horse. While waiting, Maddy debated whether to go back in and bid Daniel farewell. He would be disappointed if she did not, but the last thing she wanted was to see Nicholas again. Before she had time to decide, the two of them hastened through the doorway.

"Daniel wishes to make his farewell."

The child nodded hesitantly, as though he wasn't entirely sure. "W-will you come back?" he asked. His words sounded tentative, as if he wasn't convinced anybody but himself could hear them.

Maddy nodded. "Aye, to see you." *Will I?*

Nicholas set him down and turned to give orders to the groom. "Escort Mistress Vernon to the gate at the priory, John, and watch until she is safely inside." He bent down and spoke to Daniel then. "I must speak with Mistress Vernon alone. Go inside to Margery. She might like to hear you talk."

Maddy kissed Daniel's cheek. "I'm so proud of you for trying out your voice. Talking after all this time took courage. Now I know for certain that you are a brave knight, Sir Mouse." He smiled, hugged her around the neck, and ran inside.

When she rose, Nicholas was watching her, cheeks wet with tears. If things between them had not changed so drastically, she would take him in her arms and hold him close. They would celebrate together. But now that would not serve. He was the best of fathers for Daniel, but never again could he be anything to Maddy. Neither friend nor lover, but simply a man who had wronged her. Betrayed her. His work for the queen was more to him than she could ever be.

He reached out for her hand, but she shook him off. Regardless, he spoke. "Maddy. Forgive me for my errors in judgment. My sins and my failures. Forgive me for not being completely honest with you."

She shook her head. "I cannot. Not now. Maybe never."

He nodded, seeming to accept the finality of her words.

"Do you intend to leave the priory?"

"I'll remain until I solve the mystery of Cath's murder. After that, I'll most likely go home. My relations may believe me dead." Ironic that she'd thought her brother dead all these months, and he probably thought the same about her.

"Pray don't do anything rash. Get word to me, or the justice of the peace. There is nothing you can do on your own."

"I'll get word to Master Carleton when I leave the priory. That is, if I find out anything. 'Tis doubtful I will." She glanced at the sky and saw that it was growing late.

Without another word, Maddy stepped to the mounting block, and the groom helped her up. He led the way out onto the road. She did not look back.

John trotted ahead, leaving Maddy free to examine the discordant thoughts spinning through her mind. *Robert is alive.* She should be rejoicing, but instead she could only shake her head over it. The way in which he'd saved his life, by sacrificing another man's, was repugnant to her and told her he hadn't changed. That the aftermath of Northumberland's fiasco had taught him nothing. Why hadn't Robbie simply gone into hiding, as countless others had, when he realized the queen's justice would be swift and merciless? Instead, he sent some poor soul to his death. As it turned out, Robert must have had to secret himself anyway, since the entire village had seen him swing and thought him dead. Maddy hadn't asked Nicholas, but maybe her brother had remained in hiding until the pardons were issued. Afterward, others would have been making themselves known, too.

He should have realized that pardons would one day be possible. *Once a fool, always a fool.* She did not relish the idea of going home to live with Robert, Kat, and their children in the same house as Kat's parents. If only they could get their land back. Maddy could perhaps live in one of the tenant's cottages by herself. Sadly, she would not wish to be in Robert's company for some time to come. There *was* a slim chance she could plead her case with the Council for the return of her family's land. After all, she had spied for the queen and discovered much valuable information. Shouldn't that count for something?

In the aftermath of their dispute, Nicholas had mentioned nothing about the work she'd been doing for him and his father at Lanercost. Maddy was grateful for that, because she had no idea what she'd do if she stumbled across a significant bit of intelligence. Ignore it? Feign total disinterest? Even if she pretended otherwise, she was still invested in the outcome of all of this. Still drawn to deciphering the machinations of the Dacres. If a crisis arose, she would need to rely on her instincts to guide her. Given the situation between them, she hoped Nicholas and his father had no further expectations of her.

One thing she knew for a certainty. Never again would she feel responsible for her brother's actions. Or those of anyone else.

All the way home, Maddy had been watching the setting sun. Now, while she rode under the gate and into the garth, day was easing into night. Dread welled up inside her. Tonight, bone weary and in very low spirits, she wished only to bathe and have a meal sent to her chamber. But she knew she would have to sup with the others; they would think it odd if she did not make an appearance.

She entered the hall and approached the kitchen, the warm fragrance of roasting meat and something else, something sweet, floating toward her. Pleased that she'd not encountered Mistress Derby, she made haste up the stairs to her chamber. In a very short time, freshly washed and hair tidied, she hurried to the vicarage. The others were waiting for her in the drawing room, the two Dacres drinking wine, Musgrave quaffing ale.

"My dear, sit, sit," Lady Dacre said. She waved a hand, nearly spilling her drink. "Christopher, pour Madeleine some wine." Maddy wondered if her mistress perhaps had imbibed too much.

Dacre poured the burgundy liquid into her glass from a ewer. She thanked him and took a swallow. It was excellent, rich and warming.

"How was your visit with your cousin today, mistress?" Dacre asked. He and Musgrave were standing, looming over her and Lady Dacre.

None of them had ever asked her about what she did on market days, so the sudden interest seemed suspicious. "Satisfactory, thank you. I stopped by the market on my way back, which is why I was so late. Everybody was talking about the pardons for the rebels." Maddy hadn't intended to raise that subject, but neither did she want to talk about Nicholas.

"We've heard the news," Dacre said.

Musgrave gave a mocking laugh. "The queen finally decided to show some mercy."

"Tell us about your relations, Madeleine," Lady Dacre said. "What do they do?"

Maddy sipped more wine to relieve her dry mouth. Never had she given any thought to what she might say if they asked about Nicholas. She racked her brain to recall what they'd talked about the day he'd brought her to the priory. "Do?"

"Aye. Are they farmers? Do they own livestock? What is their livelihood?" asked Lady Dacre.

"Nay, they are not farmers. They live in Brampton, in the town. My cousin, Nicholas, grows roses. They are quite beautiful; I'll bring you a bouquet next week." She was talking too fast.

"And what about Francis Ryder?" Dacre asked.

"I haven't seen much of him. He's from home quite often," Maddy said, trying not to stammer. "On business, I suppose."

"But you do not know what that might be?"

"I haven't felt it was my place to inquire." Hoping the wine would have a calming effect, Maddy finished what was left in her glass and set it down. Their sudden interest in Nicholas and his father was chilling.

"It's been rumored in the past that he was an agent of the queen," Dacre went on. "What do you know about that?"

Jesu.

Hands shaking, she folded them in her lap and hoped they would not notice. Lacing her voice with skepticism, she said, "Nothing, sir. It's never been mentioned, at least not in my hearing." Impulsively, she decided to tell them about Daniel, just to turn the conversation. "Nicholas is a good man. He is raising his nephew, who was orphaned after the death of both his parents."

"How kind," Lady Dacre said. In a few moments, they adjourned to the dining room and, praise God, nothing further was said about the Ryders.

"Madam, will we continue our project?" Maddy asked.

"I am afraid I shall be away for a time, Madeleine. I have some business to attend to."

"I see. When do you leave?"

"Not for a few days yet, so we can continue with our work until then."

Maddy nodded. The visit to her daughter. If Nicholas was correct, the conspirators needed her in Carlisle when the plan to abduct Mary Stewart was put in motion. That was the true reason for her trip.

Lady Dacre fell asleep in her chair after supper. The men

had disappeared. Maddy summoned Edith, who roused their mistress and bundled her off to bed. Leaving the vicarage, she went in search of Mistress Derby, who was cleaning and polishing and putting away the last of the trenchers and serving pieces. Maddy had not yet spoken to her about Cath, and no doubt the cook was wondering why. She threw down her cleaning cloth and motioned her toward the worktable, where two stools stood. Without preamble she said, "You found Cath's body."

Maddy nodded. "Aye."

"Tell me the truth about how she died."

Maddy related a shortened version of the sad tale. "Master Carleton, the justice of the peace, is investigating. When he questions us, we must answer truthfully, without making accusations."

The older woman didn't speak but watched Maddy with a keen eye. "I talked to Thomas Vine about Cath," Maddy said.

"And what did that varlet have to say?"

"He thought because Cath had been found in the river, she had drowned. He swears he didn't kill her."

Mistress Derby's chest puffed out like a robin's breast in the cold. "The filthy liar!"

"I thought so too, at first. You may not credit it, but I could have sworn he was telling the truth. It was in his expression, something around his eyes and mouth. A flicker of genuine sadness."

"*Hmph.*"

"In the end, he claimed to know who'd done it. But he wouldn't tell me. He said I should figure it out for myself."

"Because he's the murderer! You know it as well as I, poor Cath was afraid of him."

Maddy listened patiently. Maybe if she'd been there and heard what Musgrave said, she wouldn't be so determined to lay the guilt at his feet. Maddy had been the same way with Nicholas, unwilling to consider that while Musgrave may be a reiver, a thief, and a violator of women, those sins didn't necessarily make him a murderer.

And speaking of reivers...she hadn't planned to, but it seemed an opportune moment to ask the cook what she knew about the raid. Musgrave had said he learned what happened from the servants. It would be wise to proceed carefully, though. While Mistress Derby now considered her a friend, Maddy was all but certain she would be loyal to the Dacres over her.

"Mistress, you were not here the night of the raid, were you?"

The cook's gaze dropped down to the table. She picked up her cleaning cloth and rubbed it across a spot that looked like it was etched into the rough wood. "Nay, I was not."

Maddy had always thought it strange that she'd gone off somewhere after supper that night, when darkness had already fallen. "Where did you go?"

"Not that it's any of your affair, but I went to Brampton to visit my sister and her husband. He's been ailing, and I'd been putting it off. Lady Dacre prepared some remedies for him in the stillroom."

"So late in the day seems a strange time to venture out."

Mistress Derby made no response to that but jumped off her stool and began to wipe down the table with long, vigorous strokes, still not looking at Maddy. She could press her, but that would only make her angry. She'd learn nothing more from her tonight.

Maddy slid off the stool and shook out her skirts. "Good even, mistress," she said, making her way toward the stairs.

"Wait!" the cook called.

Maddy stopped but did not turn around. Perhaps whatever she had to say would come easier that way.

"Lady Dacre told me earlier that day it would be best if I took myself off after supper. And if you ever say I told you so, I'll swear you're a liar."

Maddy turned her head slightly, so the woman would know she'd heard. "Thank you, mistress." And although she longed to pry further, she continued up the stairs and into her chamber.

While Maddy undressed and washed, she thought about the Dacres' questions. They were suspicious—of both her and the Ryders. Perhaps she should write a note to Nicholas and warn him. If the Dacres had unraveled the truth, wouldn't they anticipate an attempt to stop them from carrying out their plan? Nicholas and his father might be in danger.

And so might I.

Sleep was a long time coming that night.

In the morning, Lady Dacre embroidered while Maddy read to her, a dark depressing passage written by Sir Thomas More when he was facing certain death. "A Godly Meditation." It seemed an odd selection. She was still puzzling over it when Edith stepped in and announced a visitor.

"Master David Carleton," she said.

Oh, no. With all that had occurred yesterday, Maddy had nearly forgotten about being questioned by the justice of the peace. A gray haired, older gentleman entered the room and wished them good morrow. He and Lady Dacre obviously were acquainted. "How is your family keeping, sir?" she asked.

"They are all well," he said, smiling. "And I have two grandchildren now. How fare—"

But she cut him off before he could finish his question. Obviously, he'd intended to inquire about *her* grandchildren. With Maddy present, Lady Dacre could not let that happen. "I collect you are here to make inquiries about the death of our servant, Cath Bell?"

He seemed flummoxed and took a moment to gather himself. "Aye. I must question each of you separately. Is this a convenient place?"

She nodded and put her work away. "Begin with Mistress Vernon. I shall be in my chamber. Madeleine, fetch me when Master Carleton is ready for me."

When Lady Dacre had gone, Maddy said, "Do be seated, sir." She dropped her embroidery into her basket and turned to face him.

"This should not take too long, Mistress Vernon." He was attempting to put her at ease, and she appreciated the gesture. "I understand it was you who found the body of the unfortunate young girl."

She nodded, and he went on. "Can you describe exactly how it happened?"

"My cousin and I had brought a picnic to the river. He was packing up our things, and I decided to walk along the riverbank before we rode home."

"Go on."

"After a few moments, something caught my eye. I tried to ignore it, but my curious nature wouldn't allow it. I plunged into the freezing water to investigate." Swiftly, she related the remainder of the story.

"*Hmm.* And you recognized Mistress Bell immediately, would you say?"

"Not immediately, no. Not until I was closer did I realize it was Cath, by her clothing, and especially her hair."

"Did you know her well?"

Maddy thought about that. "No. But she'd had a problem recently, and I had helped her with it."

"And what was the nature of the problem, mistress?"

This was the part she dreaded having to recount. As Nicholas had suggested, she would stick to observations and avoid judgments. "Cath was very young," Maddy began. "A friend of the family who is staying here was trying to seduce her. I could see she was frightened by this man's attentions, and I intervened."

He cocked a brow. "What form did your intervention take?"

Maddy explained that she'd urged Cath to speak to Mistress Derby, and that the cook had agreed to remove the girl from serving duties.

"The gentleman in question is?"

"Thomas Vine. He is still here, as far as I know."

Master Carleton opened the pen case he'd brought with him and extracted a quill, ink jar, and rolled parchment. He flattened the paper and wrote down Vine's name. Then he asked Maddy to repeat the cook's name, and recorded that, too. "How did Vine react to your thwarting his...intentions?"

"He was angry with me for interfering, but I don't know what passed between him and Cath."

"Did he threaten you or the serving girl?"

"He told me to keep out of his business. I said I'd go to Lady Dacre if he didn't stop harassing Cath. Or if he threatened me. It was not a pleasant conversation, but to my knowledge, nothing more happened between them."

"And then?"

"And then one day the cook told me Cath hadn't been seen for a week."

She heard a scrape across the flagged floor of the gallery. Was somebody listening? She kept her eyes riveted toward the sound, hoping whoever it was would reveal himself, but nobody did.

"Do you think Vine murdered her?" Carleton asked, inclining his head toward Maddy.

How to answer that? She'd been so sure, but no longer. Drawing a deep breath, she plunged in. "I thought so at first. But now I have my doubts." She gave him the gist of her conversation with Musgrave, emphasizing the man's shock and sadness. "If he was acting, he should join a company of players. He was that convincing."

Jotting more notes, he glanced up at her and said, "Thank you for answering my questions, Mistress Vernon. Would you summon Lady Dacre?"

Maddy curtsied. "Certainly." As she passed the open entryway to the gallery and stairs, she glanced around. But it was empty.

From the window in her chamber, Maddy saw Master Carleton ride off before dinner. It seemed scarcely enough time to have questioned all the others, but that had been his intention. Nobody mentioned his visit during the meal, but neither of the Dacres, nor Musgrave, seemed perturbed.

After they left the table, Lady Dacre said she would sew for a while before her customary afternoon rest. Maddy followed her to the drawing room, and when they were seated said, "Is there a carpenter on the estate, my lady? If so, you might have him build something for the storage of your documents."

"Oh, why didn't I think of that? Clever girl! But I can't fit anything else into my chamber."

Maddy laughed. "No, indeed. But isn't there an unused room you could claim for yourself? Perhaps one of the chambers off the gallery? That way you could remove all of your business papers from your bedchamber so the room would be more comfortable."

"*Hmm*." She tipped her head up. "Yes, there are one or two chambers that would serve. I am afraid they are both sorely in need of cleaning and rearranging, however. We will see to that after my trip."

"Aye." Dare she slip in a question about the lady's trip? It might seem odd if she weren't the least bit curious. "Where are you going, madam?" Maddy tried to sound spur-of-the-moment, leaning over for her embroidery as she spoke.

"To Carlisle, to tend to some business that demands my attention. It has to do with properties left to me by my late husband."

"Ah," Maddy said, concentrating on her stitching. A vague answer, but one she would have to let stand.

At length, Lady Dacre sought her bed and Maddy returned to her chamber, pondering what to do with a few hours of freedom. She felt too restless to sleep. Useless jumped up beside her, and she scratched the pup's ears and petted her while she thought. The little dog seemed full of energy, so a walk might serve them both well. The day was warm, with scattered, billowy clouds obscuring the sun every so often. Maddy carried a basket, thinking she would pick some wildflowers. She gravitated toward the Roman wall, which of course reminded her of Nicholas and the first time he had kissed her.

And then she had ruined the lovely moment by confessing she'd known all along who Musgrave was, and worse, that she'd lain with him when she was a girl. Nicholas had claimed he could no longer trust her, but later apologized for that, admitting he'd only been hurt and jealous. It wasn't long before she drew near the Roman fortification where she and Nicholas had sheltered that night, and the sight of it made her heartsore.

Snapping her fingers, she called to Useless, who had run off in pursuit of a rabbit. It was then she heard a horse and rider approaching. Scooping up her dog, she hurried inside the fort before she could be seen. Voices drifted on the wind. Clearly, there was more than one rider. Huddling against the stone wall, out of sight, she hoped they hadn't spotted her.

Maddy had expected them to turn off toward the priory, since there wasn't much else nearby. But they raced on past. Whoever it was, they were traveling at a fearsome speed. There was an opening in the wall, and cautiously she peeked through. One of the riders was Dacre; the other one she could not immediately identify. And then realization hit. So great was the shock, she felt exactly as she had the day she'd fallen into the icy river.

No. It can't be.

But it was. If Maddy hadn't recognized him by his posture, the way he sat his horse, his mount would have given it away. The elegant, sleek gelding, moving across the land in long, sure strides, carried Nicholas Ryder on his back.

Chapter Twenty-Three

The days passed in a haze. Maddy could not engage fully in anything, images of Nicholas flying past on his horse alongside Christopher Dacre unsettling her. What business did they have? Where were they going? Was Nicholas secretly working for the other side? No matter how he'd deceived her, she could not believe he would betray his father—or indeed, the queen. His life would be forfeit. Or was Dacre a double agent, like John Musgrave? She could not make sense of a meeting between Nicholas and Dacre. Seeing them together rekindled the urge to be gone from Lanercost. Desperately alone and confused, Maddy questioned why she remained here. If only she could solve the puzzle of Cath's murder, she would leave the priory—the Ryders, William Cecil, and the queen be damned.

She and her mistress continued to work on their project. Nothing of any significance turned up among the papers Maddy sorted. She was morose and withdrawn, so much so that one afternoon Lady Dacre said, "What is troubling you, Madeleine? You are not yourself lately."

Maddy didn't know how to answer. There was a long silence. "I don't think I've ever fully regained my strength since my illness," she said, making this up on the spot.

"Influenza can leave you feeling out of sorts for weeks, and you had a relapse, don't forget. I leave tomorrow, so you'll have some extra time to rest while I'm from home."

Maddy rolled her shoulders, trying to work out the stiffness. "What would you like me to do while you're gone, my lady? Shall I get started on cleaning out one of the chambers for your use?"

"I don't think you can manage that on your own," she said. "Why don't you go on with the sorting, and we'll work on the other task when I'm home, with the help of a servant."

Maddy thought physical labor was just the diversion she needed but didn't press her. Only God knew what might happen while her mistress was away. Maddy may not be at the priory much longer if the plot to abduct Mary Stewart came to fruition. Her stomach grew a little queasy when she considered possible outcomes, one being the necessity of arranging a hasty escape from Lanercost. If she could not—what would Dacre do with her? Would he simply ride off and leave her here with no explanation? Lock her up in one of those unused chambers? Since the Dacres' interrogation of her after she returned to the priory, she'd felt uneasy. Frightened. Not only for herself, but for Nicholas as well. She had decided not to warn him. He and his father were in charge of this operation, after all, and were most likely keeping a close eye on the situation. Perhaps that's why Nicholas had been riding with Dacre. She no longer knew what father and son expected of her, if anything, and she wasn't sure what she could do about any of it.

In the morning, Maddy and Lady Dacre broke their fast together, as they'd become accustomed to doing. Afterward, she asked Maddy to accompany her to her chamber. She assumed the lady had some further instructions to impart before her departure. Edith was there, packing up the last few personal items, and was dismissed by her mistress. That seemed odd.

"Sit, Madeleine," she commanded, gesturing to the bed. She herself remained standing.

"Will you not sit too, madam?"

She didn't answer, only began to speak. "You know, my dear, how much I prize loyalty."

Maddy blinked, smiling hesitantly. "Aye, my lady. Of course."

"We have become more than mistress and retainer to each other these last few months, do you not agree? More like friends, or even family." She did not give Maddy time to answer, which she was glad of. "Your loyalty to me, to the Dacres, will soon be tested. You may find yourself having to…to make a choice. Pray do not disappoint me."

If only she'd had warning of this meeting, she might have been prepared, known what to say. Something that implied understanding yet was noncommittal. Instead, Maddy fumbled for words. "I-I am not sure what you mean, my lady."

Lady Dacre heaved a sigh and turned away. "Recall my love for the story of Naomi and Ruth. I admire Ruth's pledge to remain with her mother-in-law, with no thought for her own wishes or desires." She swiveled toward Maddy. "Do you think you can be my Ruth, Madeleine?"

Now Maddy was feeling decidedly uncomfortable. A little seed of anger planted itself in her belly, and she rose. She was taller than her mistress. "That depends, madam, on what you are asking of me. I care little for my own wishes and desires. But if loyalty to you means endangering somebody else, I cannot be certain what I would do. What choice I would make." Maddy kept her gaze fixed on Lady Dacre, and they remained that way, eyes locked.

"Fair enough. That is all I can expect, I suppose." She opened the door, dismissing Maddy.

"Fare thee well, madam. Have a pleasant journey," she said as she exited.

• • •

After the disaster with Maddy, Nicholas had remained in a foul temper. He should have been elated because of Daniel finding his voice, but the way in which it happened would haunt him. The child had only spoken because Nicholas and Maddy were quarreling. In truth, it was far more significant than a mere quarrel.

Over the past days, Nicholas had written a number of notes to her—all undelivered—and even ventured toward Lanercost himself, hoping to catch a glimpse of her. That was how, to his consternation, he'd encountered Christopher Dacre and ended up racing along the wall with him. Of all the asinine actions he'd taken, that qualified as one of the worst. When he'd run into the man, he had to invent a reason for being in the neighborhood. He said his horse needed exercise, practically inviting Dacre to suggest a competition—which Nicholas had won handily. But the only thing he'd wanted had eluded him. To find Maddy and convince her to see reason and forgive him.

He turned his attention to the man sitting before him. Nicholas had to know what was happening at the priory, and John Musgrave should at least be able to tell him if Maddy was safe. Though he'd like to throttle the villain for the way he'd treated her, he needed to keep this discussion cordial to get the information he sought.

"Musgrave—if that's what I should call you—I summoned you here for a report on the affairs at Lanercost. What can you tell me?" Studying the other man, he could understand why women might find him attractive, in a rough, brutish sort of way. Especially, when he'd been a few years younger.

"Lady Dacre is leaving today for Carlisle, to see her daughter. But I suspect she has other motives."

"Such as?"

"You know the Scots queen is currently at the castle?" When Nicholas nodded, he went on. "Lady Dacre knows the place intimately, having lived there with Lowther, raised her bairns within its walls. If anybody can figure out where the queen's chambers are it's her."

So Musgrave had known about the lady's past. "You believe the plot is on to capture Mary and her son, then?" The other man nodded, and Nicholas asked, "What makes you so sure?"

"Everything and nothing. Lady Dacre's jaunt to Carlisle, the so-called raid, the sudden taking on of extra laborers. But nothing's been said, and I've found no clues in any correspondence. Despite doing everything possible to be a friend to Dacre, I've learned only trivial bits from him. He imbibes little, so his tongue is never loosened by drink. He's a little too circumspect, if you ask me."

"Allow me to make sure I understand. You believe the scheme is going to be carried out, but you do not know the particulars. The when or how of it. Although if Lady Dacre has left for Carlisle, we can assume it will be soon."

"Correct. Scottish lairds are involved, but I don't know who. I wasn't there the night of the raid, but I believe it was cover for a meeting with one or more of them."

There would be no harm in confirming that. "Ferniehurst was there. Madeleine saw him, but no other."

"I knew she was holding out on me! That little—"

"I would guard my words when speaking of Mistress Vernon, were I you," Nicholas said, his voice steel.

Musgrave smirked. "Of course."

"My gravest concern at present is for her safety. You will do everything in your power to see that she comes to no harm."

"At the expense of the mission?"

"Aye. At the expense of the mission. She comes first."

Just then, Francis Ryder burst through the door, glowering at both men. "No, Nick. She can't come first."

Nicholas was aware his father had arrived home late last night, but he hadn't yet seen him. He did not wish to have this discussion with Musgrave present, but it seemed unavoidable. "Madeleine knows all, Father. She discovered it on her own. The pardons. Her brother. All of it."

"That's as may be. I'm sorry for it, but we're at the most crucial point of this mission, and the merest suspicion we're on to them could ruin months of careful work and planning. Some of which the lass helped us with. Madeleine Vernon is a very determined woman. Do you think she would want to see it all come to nothing?"

"Since she learned of our deceptions, she's no longer vested in the mission. Would you be, in her shoes? Her only interest now is in finding out who murdered Cath Bell."

His father looked livid. "For both your sakes, I pray that's not the case." He turned to Musgrave. "Return to the priory. If you see anything to indicate Mistress Vernon is in mortal danger, send word to us immediately. Otherwise, carry on as usual."

"I assume you know that Dacre and his stepmother suspect both of you," Musgrave said. "They questioned Mistress Vernon about you when she returned. She handled it well, but it was obvious they thought she was lying."

"She told me. Did Dacre say anything to you about it?" Nicholas asked.

"Nay. He couldn't, not without revealing why they grilled her."

On his way out the door, Musgrave paused. "I can tell you who killed Cath. Or who I strongly suspect. Dacre. Christopher Dacre."

God's wounds. "Does Madeleine know this?"

Musgrave shook his head. "Nay."

Nicholas got to his feet. "You must inform her immediately. Stay close to Dacre and don't allow him to be alone with her. Do you understand?"

"Aye. I'll do what I can."

When he'd left, Nicholas turned and scowled at his father. "We must talk," he said.

Francis Ryder claimed the chair Musgrave had vacated. "You've lost sight of your duty in this mission, Nick. I should have made good on my threat and taken over the handling of the Vernon wench."

"But you did not. I've simply come to my senses. Maddy's safety is my primary objective. To get her out of Lanercost before any harm befalls her. If we do not hear from Musgrave by tomorrow, I'll ride to the priory and retrieve her myself."

"God's breath, Nick, I told the man to get word to you if she was in danger. If we hear nothing, that's a good sign."

"I don't trust him. For all we know, he's working for Dacre."

His father sighed. "I warned you about becoming involved with the girl."

"It's too late, Father. I love her. Just as Richard loved Susan, as you loved Mother. It is not something to turn on and off at will. It simply is."

His father said nothing; he only looked heavenward as though to beseech the Almighty for aid. Nicholas ploughed ahead. "After this is over, I'm done serving the queen. It doesn't suit me."

"I can't force you, Nick. But what will you do?"

"Marry Maddy, if I can persuade her to accept me. Raise

Daniel. Your grandson started speaking while you were away, largely due to Madeleine."

Francis Ryder actually smiled. "That is good news indeed."

"I want to import and grow roses. Sell them. I think there is enough money to be made in the endeavor to support myself and a family."

"When this mission is over, we can discuss your future."

His father was right. No use speculating on a life with Maddy until the Dacres and their accomplices were caught and she was safe...and in his arms.

• • •

After Lady Dacre set off for Carlisle, Maddy spent some time sewing. Ripping out more stitches than she sewed forced her to abandon that pursuit. Lady Dacre's words kept repeating in her head. *Your loyalty will soon be tested. Can you be my Ruth?* On Maddy's first morning at Lanercost, she'd wondered if that was how the woman viewed her. Had she been trying to instill that faithfulness, that loyalty in her, right from the beginning?

Maddy had the feeling she'd failed the test. Rather than pledging her unquestioning devotion, she'd attached a caveat. She would not endanger anybody else. Lady Dacre hadn't liked that answer, and had coldly released Maddy, not even responding to her farewell. Well, then. At least she'd stood up to her, and she was glad of it. Maddy would not be blindly loyal; nor would she pretend to be. What she had said, however, must have been a sure indication to the woman that Maddy suspected she and her son were up to no good.

She dined with the men. Without Lady Dacre there to steer the conversation, they were quiet. After they'd eaten their last course of fruit, cheese, and marchpane, Dacre said,

"What shall you do with your time while my stepmother is away, Madeleine?"

She didn't like him calling her by her Christian name, did not recall granting permission for him to do so. "I intend to continue working on organizing your stepmother's papers."

"Is this something she has approved?"

"Aye. She is well aware of what I am doing."

He nodded. Maddy wished she were bold enough to say she'd lately observed him riding with Nicholas. She would love to hear his response. Or evasion. But he may think she was spying on him, which she was, of course, even if it had been accidental. After the meal, Maddy retired to her chamber to refresh herself and let Useless out. They walked toward the stables, in time to see Musgrave and Dacre ride out together. Perhaps they were off to a meeting with Nicholas to engage in some devious scheme. Her rational mind told her this was a ridiculous idea, but nothing made sense anymore.

Her thoughts soon drifted back to that odd meeting with Lady Dacre this morning. She'd all but said a major event was about to occur. Something that would test Maddy's loyalty to her and the Dacre family. Maybe she should try to find out exactly what was afoot, although what she would do with the information, she did not know.

Back inside, Maddy rested on the settle, which had remained in her chamber since her bout of influenza. Useless hopped up beside her, and she absent-mindedly scratched behind the pup's floppy ears while considering what to do. Making a mental list of everything she knew for a certainty might be helpful before trying to gather more information.

First, the raid. There was no question that it was an attempt to cover up a meeting, most likely with one or more of the Scottish lairds. Ferniehurst might have been recognized, if he'd arrived in the light of day. And if Maddy hadn't been convinced before, Mistress Derby's admission that Lady Dacre had advised her to vacate the premises that night persuaded her. Ever since Maddy had returned from her stay at the Ryders', the Dacres had acted suspicious of her, as though they no longer trusted her. They'd questioned her upon her arrival, and again after market day last week.

Lady Dacre had asked her to read aloud Thomas More's "A Godly Meditation." It had seemed like a warning, now more than ever after her peculiar lecture about loyalty. For that was what it was. She'd had no intention of revealing anything, of allowing Maddy to know why she was demanding her loyalty. And she'd expected nothing from Maddy other than acquiescence.

And how did Cath's murder fit into all this? No longer sure Musgrave was the killer, she was, nevertheless, no closer to finding out who had done the cruel deed. Curse Musgrave, why couldn't he simply have told her? Was he protecting somebody? Perhaps himself. If he revealed who the killer was, and that person found out, Musgrave's life could be endangered.

Since Lady Dacre expected her to be working in her chamber while she was in Carlisle, Maddy was certain she would have asked Christopher to remove any incriminating documents. It was his chamber that might yield something. This was her opportunity, with both men gone. Edith had accompanied her mistress, and the other servants always completed their work in this part of the house before the midday meal. She would have the vicarage to herself.

Maddy gave Useless one final pat and descended the stairs as soundlessly as possible. The kitchen was quiet, the cleaning up from dinner finished. Mistress Derby and her staff were probably having a rest. The vicarage itself was deserted. When she reached the passage with the bedchambers, she paused. She'd better have a reason for wanting to speak to Master Dacre, in the event he'd returned. She could tell him about the plan to use a vacant room as storage for his stepmother's papers and request his help in choosing a suitable one.

Maddy rapped lightly on his door and waited. The sound echoed in the empty hallway. She knocked once again, and after a moment had passed, unlatched the door and walked in. The chamber looked much the same as before, with everything in its place. Only this time, there were no papers stacked on the escritoire. No book on the bed table. The man lived like a monk. Or a Puritan.

It was almost eerie, as though a spirit resided here. A being who owned no earthly possessions and left no trace of himself in the room. She peered out the window to make sure there was no sign of the men riding in. A groom was leading a horse toward the smithy, but that was the extent of what she could see.

Mayhap there was something in Dacre's wardrobe she'd missed before. Maddy swung the doors open. The same neat piles of clothing sat on the shelves, a fussy man's arrangement. No doubt he required the servants to place them that way. A more thorough search was in order. Hastily, she unfolded all his apparel and shook each item out. She found nothing, and then had to waste precious time refolding all of it as precisely as she'd found it.

Her eyes drifted to the bottom of the heavy piece of furniture. Maddy hadn't examined it closely the first time. Hunkering down, she pulled out a pair of boots, shined and ready for the master's feet, and a pair of formal shoes. And then she spotted it. Pushed way to the back, behind the footwear, was a small wooden coffer. She pulled it out and set it on the floor. Before examining it, she walked over to the door and listened, then cracked it and checked the passage. Nothing.

Maddy brought the coffer, carved from mahogany and bearing the Dacre crest, over to the escritoire and into the light. She tugged at the lid, fearing it would be locked. But it opened easily. Obviously, Dacre stored odds and ends here. She began laying them out on the writing table. A penknife, a man's signet ring, a miniature of a stern-visaged man. His father, Sir Thomas? A few pins and points. There were no letters or other papers among the assortment, and thus nothing useful to her. Maddy wondered why he bothered to hide the small chest in the back of the wardrobe, especially since he used it to hold everyday items.

Lifting the coffer, she examined the underside of it to see if it had a hidden compartment. She found nothing. The remaining contents shifted, and when she set it back down, Maddy noticed a strip of bright blue at the bottom. She tugged on it, pulling it free; it was a length of ribbon. Hair ribbon. Alarm bells went off in her head. She had seen it before. Squeezing her eyes shut, she tried to visualize it in someone's hair. When it came to her, she had to sit down on the bed. It was Cath's. Nobody else at Lanercost had ever worn a ribbon of that vibrant shade. *God have mercy!*

"I hated having to kill her. She was such a pretty lass."

Maddy jumped up and spun around. Christopher Dacre stood in the doorway, his close-set eyes boring into her. She'd heard nothing. Not a footstep, not the door unlatching. How could she not have sensed his presence?

She was trapped.

"This is what comes of snooping, mistress. You inevitably find out something you would have been better off not knowing." He closed the door and moved into the room.

Maddy stood there staring at him, then blurted out the first thing that leaped into her head. "Why did you do it?"

He shrugged, as if murder was no great matter. "Unfortunately, she overheard a conversation between my stepmother and me. The subject, if generally known, would have put us in great peril. I had no choice, really."

"You had no choice but to murder a young, innocent girl? Loathsome coward! I would not have believed it of you."

He let out a laugh, then plucked the ribbon from Maddy's hand. Motioning to the bed, he said, "Sit down, mistress."

Could she make a run for it? Not yet. She'd wait until they left this room. Certain he would not keep her here, she complied with his request.

"If I'm a coward, you, my dear, are a fool. All those visits to your cousin. Each time I was certain you would not return, especially after the raid. But you kept coming back. I had to ask myself why. The obvious explanation was that you were a spy, and your so-called cousin an agent of the queen."

"Let me go," Maddy said. "I'll return to my home near Carlisle and tell no one about any of this. Nothing I do can bring Cath back."

He snorted, as she'd been sure he would. But she had to try.

"You must tell me everything you know, all the information you've already passed along to the Ryders. How much do they know? If they've planned anything to compromise our scheme, they'll need to be dealt with."

In the same way he'd dealt with Cath? Maddy stared at him defiantly, not saying a word.

"I could call the sheriff in. I caught you stealing from me. You know what the penalty for thieving is, don't you?"

Hanging. "You couldn't risk it. I would tell them you killed Cath."

He smirked. "But you have no evidence. Why on earth would I commit such a heinous act? And whom do you think they'll believe? A pathetic nothing of a girl whose brother was executed for treason, or me, a landowner and law-abiding citizen?"

So they had known about Robbie all along. "I would not be too certain about your reputation with the authorities. After all, Leonard Dacre is your close relation. And I am not without connections."

Dacre scoffed at that. "Carleton already questioned me, and he's pronounced me innocent." He stepped closer to her, hatred beaming from his eyes. "I've already killed once. I can do it again." He flexed his fingers, as though he couldn't wait to set them about Maddy's neck. She had some time, though. He sought information only she could provide, and the longer she could hold out, the longer she'd stay alive.

When she remained silent, he grabbed her arm and yanked her up. "Come. I have a place to put you that might encourage you to talk." Dacre thrust open the door, not seeming to care who might be about, and marched her to the end of the passage, through the drawing room, and into the gallery. They stopped before one of the rooms Maddy had suggested to Lady Dacre as her workroom. She tried to wrest herself from his grasp, but his grip was far too strong. He unlocked the door and gave her a nasty shove. She fell hard on her knees, and an icy tremor of fear arced through her.

"I shall return soon. It would be more convenient to know what you told the Ryders, but not essential. In fact, it may be easier to simply get rid of a troublesome little meddler like you, and Ryder and his father as well." He was gone before Maddy could gather her wits enough to respond.

The door latched and she heard a key turn in the lock. The room was dark as a moonless night, and her eyes required a few moments to adjust. Sitting back on her heels, she forced herself to breathe deeply.

In. Out. Have courage, Madeleine.

Even though Maddy knew it would be futile, she banged on the door with her fists and yelled for help. But there was nobody about who might hear her. She was wasting precious time. When that door opened again, she had to be prepared.

She was in a windowless chamber, but after a while she could make out shapes. To her left was a small bed, pushed against the wall. On the other side, a table and chair. Maddy got to her feet, slowly. Her knees were bruised, but not truly injured. Reaching out to the objects on the table, she identified them by touch. An ink jar. Quills. A candle in a holder—but no tinder. She moved toward the back wall where a high cupboard stood. An oddly shaped object rested on top of it.

By exploring with her hands, Maddy ascertained that it was helm-shaped, with rough iron bands curving at intervals toward the base. The center band forked into two parts. She ran her fingers around the circular base and found a piece of iron, about two inches long, just below the opening created by the forked bands. Maddy jerked her hands away. Something akin to the way she'd felt when she heard Robbie was to be executed sent her to the bed, where she dropped like a stone. A thick, heavy pressure in her chest made it difficult to breathe.

Maddy had seen a woman wearing such a device in the market square in Carlisle when she was a child. Her father had pulled her along by her hand so fast she'd stumbled. Horrified and fascinated all at once, she'd kept turning her head to watch. "Why does the goodwife have a cage on her head?" she had asked. He had explained it to her later.

"What you saw today was a cruel and inhuman punishment. The poor woman was wearing a scold's bridle, lass, to prevent her from talking. And to shame her."

"Does it hurt, Father?" she'd asked.

"Oh, my dear child, I imagine it does." His eyes had looked sad.

As a small child, Maddy had pictured the woman over and over. The nightmares had begun after Robbie had told her the bit had sharp spikes on it. She was no longer sure what was real and what she'd dreamed. Always, when Maddy conjured the woman, her eyes streamed tears and her face was contorted into a grimace of excruciating pain.

The object on top of the cupboard was a scold's bridle.

Chapter Twenty-Four

It was vital that she escape this room, this prison, before Dacre returned. The door. *Check the door.* Perhaps it hadn't latched properly. The lock might be rusty; the mechanism might have failed after years of disuse. The resounding click Maddy had heard, however, made her doubt that possibility. Nevertheless, she spent several minutes bearing down with all her strength on the lever—it proved to be immovable—and then feeling her way about the chamber to locate anything she might use to substitute for a key. *Nothing.* There was nothing.

Could there be a window she hadn't noticed? Concealed in some way, so no daylight could penetrate? But after a thorough search of the back wall, she knew no window existed, except in her wasted hopes. Dropping to her sore knees, she crawled around the perimeter of the room, examining the floorboards, ending with a search under the bed. She came up empty-handed. This chamber was more Spartan than Dacre's own.

Periodically, Maddy banged on the door and screamed for help.

Beads of perspiration had broken out on her forehead from all her exertions. She couldn't think of anything else to try. Giving in to despair, she lowered herself to the bed and wept.

After several minutes, Maddy wiped her eyes and dripping nose on her sleeve. Dacre could walk through that door any time, and she was no further along in an escape plan. Fear and desperation were getting her nowhere; it was time to collect herself. She got to her feet and began to pace. Thinking came easier when she was moving.

Dacre wanted to know what she'd told the Ryders. The fact that he didn't already know convinced her his ride along the Roman wall with Nicholas had been happenstance. Although her faith in Nicholas was not completely restored, she'd obviously rushed to judgment in thinking he might be working with Dacre. Maybe she'd been too hasty in judging other matters as well.

How best could Maddy help Nicholas without risking her own safety? She could claim that he and his father had only a vague idea that the Dacres were planning something. Surely that would not be enough for Christopher Dacre to kill them. It was highly unlikely he'd believe her, though, and she might be forced to reveal more. And if she did, what would that mean for her? Once Dacre had gotten the information he needed, he would have no further use for her. He'd shown he was willing to kill to keep his secrets. The deaths of two young women, both employed at the priory, might appear suspicious, but Dacre was resourceful. He would devise a way to absolve himself of guilt.

The other alternative was to reveal nothing. Then what might happen? Maddy could think of several possibilities, none with a favorable outcome. She didn't believe he would kill her immediately. He might withhold food and drink or beat her. Or he might put the scold's bridle on her head.

If Maddy held out as long as she could, it would buy Nicholas some time. Time to find a way to foil the Dacres' scheme. But most important of all, she might save Nicholas's life. And her own. And then what she'd been dreading happened. The key turned in the lock, and Dacre entered. Maddy was sitting on the bed, her hands folded, posture upright. He was carrying a taper, its flame guttering with the movement of the door. After lighting the candle on the table, he walked over and set the other one down next to the scold's bridle. Maddy pulled her gaze away and stared straight ahead.

"Been contemplating your future, mistress?" he asked.

She said nothing.

He stepped closer. "Mark this, Mistress Vernon. Time is running out, both for me, and most perilously for you. In case you were depending on your cousin's messenger to save you, put that from your mind. He's been...dispatched."

"You killed him?" she said, incredulously.

"He got in my way." Dacre's eyes were cold, heartless. "You're a smart lass, and I'm sure you've put all the pieces together and figured out our little scheme. We ride tonight to Carlisle to steal away Mary Stewart and her babe. We're taking them to Scotland, to a safe haven, until she can be restored to her throne—and wed the Duke of Norfolk. Someday she will succeed Elizabeth as Queen of England."

By God's light, they'd gotten it all right! Her jubilation was short-lived, given her perilous situation. To buy some time, and satisfy her curiosity, she said, "I thought you did not care for the Scots queen. You disparaged her that day at dinner."

He huffed a laugh. "She's a harlot, like so many women. But she is the rightful successor to Elizabeth." Maddy wondered if the man had been crossed in love and thus judged all females harshly.

"I have a problem you can help me with," Dacre said. "I

need to know if I must deal with Ryder and his father first. As our scheme won't be set into motion until midnight, we have plenty of time to take care of the Ryders beforehand."

"The Ryders should be the least of your concerns," Maddy said. "It is the king's men you should fear. Those who support Mary Stewart's child as Elizabeth's successor. It is my understanding they may attempt to assassinate Mary while she's in Carlisle." This was a transparent effort to deflect suspicion from Nicholas and his father, one she was sure Dacre would see through.

And he did, even though he looked nonplussed for a few seconds. "Cleverly done, mistress, but we've ruled out any threat from that quarter already. Now, tell me of the Ryders."

"They know nothing. 'Tis true, Francis Ryder works for the queen on occasion. But he is no longer young, and the queen doesn't rely on him as she once did."

"Why do I not believe you?"

Maddy shrugged. "That is your prerogative."

He came over and stood unnervingly close to her. "All those visits to Brampton. Do you expect me to believe you weren't reporting on everything that went on here at Lanercost? That you haven't been reading my stepmother's letters and eavesdropping on conversations? And you told the Ryders nothing about what you saw the night of the raid?"

"May I remind you, I was ill the night of the raid. And I thought you and my cousin were friends. I saw you riding together along the wall the other day."

He laughed. "Purely coincidental. We ran into each other on the bridle path and decided to race. A foolish pastime, I grant you, but one we men find hard to resist."

So their meeting *had* been unplanned. Though Maddy felt tremendous relief at having her suspicion confirmed, she was ashamed of believing Nicholas might be part of the plot. Without warning, Dacre grabbed a hank of her hair and pulled so hard tears stung her eyes.

"You're hurting me."

He laughed. "That is the point, my dear. Your pain will only increase if you don't provide me with the answers I seek."

"You mean the answers you expect." A whimper flew out of her mouth as he gave her hair another a hard yank. "If you're convinced I'm lying, why don't you proceed accordingly?"

"Because your cousin could be laying a trap for us. For me and my little band of Scots. Our position is…precarious, to say the truth. You must know, I cannot leave anyone alive who knows of our intentions. My mother and I could never return to Lanercost—that would mean arrest and execution. We would be forced to live out our lives in some hut in that pathetic excuse for a kingdom to the north of us. Cold, and most regrettably, poor."

Finally, he let go of Maddy's hair and moved to the cupboard. Leaning against it, he aimed his gaze at her, his eyes points of light in the candle's flame.

"Do you know what a scold's bridle is, Madeleine? Some call it the branks."

She nodded. Her mouth had gone too dry to speak.

"I thought you might. Perhaps you hadn't noticed—it was so dark in here—I have one, right here in this chamber. For years, my stepmother was the mistress of John Lowther, constable of Carlisle Castle. She refers to him as her 'husband,' but we all know he never wed her. According to her, the castle has a whole array of torture devices. She found this one of interest and brought it with her as a small token of her years with Lowther."

"A gruesome object in which to place sentimental value."

"It is, I agree. Fortune smiles on you this day, Madeleine. You are going to try it on, and you can tell me—when you are once again able to speak—how you would assess it as a means of punishment."

Maddy felt as she had as a child, when her father had taken her to have a tooth pulled. Limp with fear. What if she couldn't breathe? The bit, pushed to the back of her mouth, would cause her to gag—and then what? But she would rather bear it, all of it, than beg for his mercy. He would never grant it, in any case.

"I must find someone to assist me. Pray excuse me for a short time. While I am away, I urge you to reconsider telling me what I seek to know."

In deep despair, Maddy sat hugging herself while Dacre was gone and thought about her plight. An unexpected feeling of calm washed over her. A few months ago, she had set out to seek revenge on the queen by joining Leonard Dacre's raid. Her actions had been rash, and her present situation was a direct result of what she'd done. The only good that had come from the failed raid was Nicholas.

Nicholas was ever his father's man, even as he swore he would no longer do his bidding. He hadn't told her about the pardons. Even more hurtful, because it was crucial to her happiness, he'd kept from her the fact that Robbie was alive. Yet Maddy still cared about him. Even loved him.

There was much in Nicholas to soften the hard edge of her anger with him. Qualities demanding her admiration and respect. He was doing the best he could for himself and his nephew until he could cease his work for the queen. When she'd seen how he was with Daniel, playful, yet fiercely protective…her heart had fairly leaped in her chest. She would not reveal things to Christopher Dacre that would endanger Nicholas's life. Now, looking death in the eye, what had once seemed unforgivable became trivial. It was an unbearable sorrow to her, that she may never see him again. If she could, Maddy would forgive him unconditionally.

Maddy heard the door opening and steeled herself for the

worst. Dacre walked in with Musgrave, who neither looked at her nor spoke.

"Have you had a change of heart, mistress?" Dacre asked. She shook her head.

"Stand up, then." Maddy did as he asked. When he walked over to get the bridle, she bolted for the door. Musgrave saw her, but he made no attempt to stop her.

She raced down the hallway, Dacre's furious words to Musgrave catching up with her. "What's the matter with you, fool? You let her get away."

Maddy heard their footsteps thumping behind her, but she had a decent head start. She dashed around the gallery and made for the stairs. Sensing freedom within her grasp, Maddy pushed the door open and plunged through. She came to a sudden and precipitous halt when she saw what awaited her. Dacre's coursers, Devil and Prince, growling and ready to spring.

God have mercy.

She lunged to one side, and Devil sank his teeth into her ankle. Screaming in pain, Maddy barely noticed when Matthew, the blacksmith, appeared and said, "Off, Devil!" The dog immediately obeyed.

She tried pleading with the smith. "Pray help me, Matthew. Dacre intends to hurt me."

"Sorry, mistress. He is my employer and I must do as he says. I have a wife and little ones to think of."

"You will get in trouble with the sheriff. That could result in dire circumstances for your family." By then her words were futile, as she heard Dacre and Musgrave approaching.

Without a word, Dacre took one arm, Musgrave the other. Blood from the dog bite flowed into Maddy's slipper, causing her foot to slide about. Within minutes, she'd been dragged back to the chamber from which she'd so recently fled.

"Sit," Dacre commanded. Maddy obeyed.

Musgrave stood guard over her while Dacre picked up the scold's bridle. It appeared small, and for a moment, she hoped it would not fit over her head. But that proved to be no problem for Dacre. He forced it down until it pressed against both sides of her head like a vice. Maddy's nose fit through the opening between two of the bands. When he started to shove the bit into her mouth, she balked. "Wait! May I have a drink first? My mouth is so dry."

Dacre seemed to hesitate, and Musgrave said, "What harm could it do? I'll fetch some water."

Dacre objected. "No! I don't trust her. She's trying to trick us again." Turning to Maddy, he said, "Open your mouth."

She pressed her lips together and tipped backward until she fell, the contraption on her head banging against the wall and jarring her senseless. Dacre dragged her upright and forced the bit against her lips until she tasted blood. Enough was enough. Maddy opened her mouth and he shoved the bit in. Even though it wasn't more than a few inches, it felt enormous, and she gagged repeatedly. Now completely helpless, Maddy teetered on the edge of hysteria.

Musgrave grabbed Dacre's arm. "God's breath, man, are you sure you want to do this? She could die, then you would have two deaths to account for."

She was going to be sick. Bile rose in her throat, its acrid taste reminding her again of that day so many years ago, when she'd had a tooth extracted. Her mother had told her to breathe through her nose. Maddy did so now, and while she could not seem to stop the sobs issuing from deep within her chest, at least she felt less nauseated.

"Leave off, Musgrave." Dacre jerked out of the other man's grip. "Stand up," he said to her. She did, swaying on trembling legs. "Hold her steady," he instructed the other man.

Musgrave gripped her shoulders while Dacre fastened

the padlock on the device. To do so, he had to pull the circular band tight, making the pain excruciating. Maddy looked up at Musgrave and was surprised to glimpse sympathy in his eyes. Maybe he could not help her now, but perhaps he would return later and free her.

When the job was done, Musgrave helped her to the bed. He pulled out a handkerchief and tied it around her ankle to stanch the bleeding from the dog bite, and that small kindness moved her to tears. Dacre was already at the door. "We shall see if you feel more like talking after you've worn that a few hours."

Maddy tried to scream a retort, forgetting she couldn't move her tongue. It came out as a grunt, and Dacre laughed as he and Musgrave walked out of the chamber. Left alone, she could only be grateful the bit did not have spikes on it. And that he was not dragging her around a public square by a rope around her neck.

She could not find a comfortable position. If she lay down, the bands pressed agonizingly against her head. Sitting rigidly seemed to be the only way to make the pain bearable. Her breathing finally slowed, and she felt herself drifting into a trancelike state.

Maddy came to her senses when her head began to list forward. By now the pain was acute, as if somebody were driving spikes through her skull. She thought she might pass out from it. Better to lie down, regardless of the pain, so that if she blacked out, she wouldn't keel over.

The door pushed open, and Dacre walked in alone. He got directly to the point. "I'm giving you one last chance to talk, mistress. You may save yourself by telling me what Ryder and his father know. And then I'll remove the bridle."

Maddy sucked in a deep breath. After he released her from this contraption, what then? He'd said earlier he couldn't allow anybody to live who knew that he and Lady Dacre were the primary conspirators. She shook her head, hoping that would indicate her continued unwillingness to talk.

And then Dacre went into a rage, shoving Maddy to the floor and kicking her in the ribs. As he walked to the door, his booted foot struck her in the head, and pain reverberated through her skull. The last thing she heard before losing consciousness was his hateful voice. "I could kill you now, but I think I'll just leave you to rot here."

Maddy drifted in and out of awareness. Did anybody other than Musgrave, and probably Matthew, even know where she was? In a final, desperate attempt to attract attention, she roused herself and banged the cage on her head into the immovable oak door—once, twice, three times. But it was of no use. In the end, she settled on the floor, because the hard surface kept the scold's bridle stable and lessened the pain.

Death now seemed inevitable, and yet she could not give up. As long as she was still breathing, she could not surrender to this ignominious end.

Chapter Twenty-Five

In her few lucid moments, Maddy thought of Lady Dacre and wondered how deeply she was involved in this enterprise. Up to her ears, Maddy suspected. There had been numerous clues. The fierce guarding of her private papers. Her obvious devotion to the old faith and her defense of Mary Stewart. Her expectation of Maddy's unquestioning loyalty. And her trip to Carlisle.

Time dragged on.

Surely, Dacre and his followers had set out for Brampton by now, and even if she'd had the means to escape, it would be too late to warn Nicholas. If he and his father were killed, what would happen to Daniel? Maybe a kind servant would care for him, or his mother's family would take him in.

Without warning, Matthew appeared on the threshold, not even bothering to close the door behind him. Why would Dacre have sent him to her? To see if she still lived? To dispose of her body had she died? Possibly the smith had undergone a change of heart and now wished to help her. But a small frisson of doubt kept her still and silent. Mayhap he had come here for another purpose entirely. Maddy let him believe she had swooned. Since she was lying on her side, she did not believe he could see her face clearly enough to know her eyes were open and watching him.

He held a dagger in one hand and was running a thumb along its edge, testing its sharpness. *Jesu*. He intended to kill her. No sense pleading for her life; she'd tried that with him already.

The smith leaned over the table, probably to slide the candleholder closer, the better to see his prey. Warily, silently, she pressed her left hand into the floor and pushed herself up. Then she kicked out her leg and wrapped a foot around Matthew's ankle, yanking with all her strength. The fellow was sturdy and muscular, and odds were against her, but she had caught him off guard and at just the right moment, when he was a bit off balance. He yelped in surprise, and then fell spectacularly, banging his head on the corner of the table before he sprawled onto the hard, flagged floor.

His head was bleeding profusely, but Maddy did not stay to see if he was alive. She grabbed his dagger and, after a precautionary glance out the door, hurried through the gallery and down the stairs, skidding to a halt at the bottom. What if the dogs were still standing guard? Though she abhorred the thought, she'd be forced to use the knife. She eased the door open. Nothing. No dogs or humans were about. Entering Dacre Hall, she made for the kitchen, her heart pounding against her ribs, breathing labored.

As she neared the kitchen, Maddy heard voices. Friends or foes? The higher register of a woman's voice came in short bursts, and she recognized it as Mistress Derby's. *Praise God.* Reaching the threshold, she waved her arms about. When that did not suffice, she banged her head against the doorjamb.

Mistress Derby's head flew up from her work and she

rushed to Maddy's side, with Alice right behind her. "Oh, my dear girl," the cook said. She put her arm around Maddy's shoulder and guided her to a stool. "Never did I dream he would do this to you. Hold you prisoner, aye, I believed it of him. But this?"

Alice's chest heaved, sobs breaking out, but after a stern look from her mistress, she covered her mouth and tried to compose herself.

"How long have you...been like this?" the cook asked.

Maddy shrugged, then held her hands wide apart, to indicate a long time. She was consumed by shame, hated that they bore witness to her humiliation.

"We need help to free you, lass. I have no key for the padlock. I shall send Alice for Matthew."

Maddy shook her head, waves of anguish washing over her. "Not Matthew, then. But who?"

She tried to say Thomas Vine, by which name the cook still called him, but could not. Mistress Derby understood her predicament. "I will say some names and you squeeze my hand if that person will do."

The problem, of course, was that Maddy could not assess the involvement of anybody else. Musgrave was the only man she trusted, and he might have ridden off with Dacre. When finally Mistress Derby said his name, and Maddy gave her assent, she looked skeptical. "That villain?"

Maddy squeezed her hand harder and tried to nod. The cook turned to Alice and said, "Find Master Vine. Tell him to come with a hammer and chisel."

He might not be on the property, but they would know soon enough.

After Alice left, Mistress Derby said, "It won't be long now, dear." Then she launched into a litany of self-castigation. "I should have known, should have guessed. Everybody around this place has been acting odd of late. Going off to secret meetings. Asking me for extra food, for no reason I could work out. Whispering all the time and ending their conversations when I came near."

Maddy grasped her hand and patted it, to let her know this was not her fault. "When you were not at supper, I feared something was amiss. I asked the master where you were. He said you were indisposed." She lowered her head, as if ashamed. Maddy tapped her arm and she looked up again. "I was busy and did not check on you right away. When I finally had the time, I hurried to your chamber and discovered you weren't there. I feared, then, that something was terribly wrong. I could see Master Dacre and lots of other men were preparing to ride out, and I bid Alice to help me look for you, but we'd no luck. We could not find you anywhere.

"I don't know who all those other men were, but no doubt it was them who required the extra food. What they're up to I have no idea, but it's nothing good, I'll warrant. Must be why Lady Dacre took her leave."

Alice and Musgrave burst through the door, Musgrave carrying the required tools. Mistress Derby glared at him, which, under the circumstances, did not seem prudent. "Can you break the padlock?" she asked.

He ignored her and spoke to Maddy. "Pray forgive me, mistress, for my part in this. I was making ready to rescue you. I had to let Dacre think I would ride with him and his men." The cook pressed her lips together hard, for which Maddy was grateful. Whether Musgrave told the truth or not, she could not judge. But as long as he freed her, she didn't care.

"*Hmm*. How best to accomplish this?" He seemed to be talking to himself, but Mistress Derby said, "You need her on a hard surface. Let's lay her down on the floor, on her side." Then to Maddy she said, "This will hurt like the very devil, lass, but then it will be over."

She and Alice helped Maddy lie down on the unyielding stone floor. "You must hold her still," Musgrave said to them. "I want to break it with one blow." Alice leaned hard on her shoulder and legs, while Mistress Derby held onto the cage with a fearsome grip. Maddy couldn't have moved her head even if she'd had any remaining strength to do so. She prayed his aim was true.

In the end, it required three blows.

The pressure eased immediately. They helped her up and guided her back to the stool. "Wrench the sides apart as far as you can," Mistress Derby directed. "We must have room to get the bit out before we lift the bridle off." Alice offered to help, but Musgrave waved her away. He pulled, grunting with the effort, and the cook drew the device forward, far enough to extract the bit. Without delay, they lifted the cage off Maddy's head. For a moment, she could not move her tongue. Everybody was staring at her, waiting for her to speak. After several attempts, she was able to wiggle her tongue, and thus to form one word. "Water."

"Oh! We should have thought of that," Alice said. She left, returning in seconds with a ewer and cup. The girl helped Maddy drink a few sips, and afterward Maddy squeezed her hand gratefully.

"Do you think you can walk?" the cook asked. "We must get you to your chamber and into bed. And you need some patching up." She and Alice made as though to help her, but Maddy stopped them.

"Nay. I must warn my cousin." Her tongue was thick and not working well, and the words came out garbled. She could tell the others weren't sure of what she'd said.

"Come now, you can tell us everything once we have ministered to your wounds."

This was not going to be easy. Maddy repeated what she'd said before, as clearly as she could, and now they understood.

"You're doing nothing of the kind," Mistress Derby said. "You can barely walk, let alone sit a horse."

And then, for the first time, Musgrave spoke up. "You cannot go alone, mistress. I'll ride with you."

"Thank you, John." It sounded like, "Ank oo, Ohn."

Shock emanated from the cook. She must be told the truth of the matter, so Maddy revealed it, her tongue limbering up as she spoke. "Mistress, this man's name is John Musgrave, and he did not kill Cath. Christopher Dacre did that."

When she started to protest, Maddy stopped her. "He told me so himself, right before he brought me to the room where he held me prisoner. Now, I need your assistance binding my wounds and changing into a riding costume. Will you help me?"

The cook nodded, apparently too shaken to argue.

"I'll ready the horses," Musgrave said, "and meet you right outside the tower when you are prepared. But first I want to know exactly how you escaped from that room." The three of them eyed her suspiciously. Perhaps they thought she had supernatural gifts.

"I haven't time to explain now," Maddy said impatiently.

"Give us the gist," Musgrave insisted.

And so she did, ending with, "Somebody should check on Matthew. I-I might have killed him." All three stared at her in disbelief, until she nearly jumped from her skin. "We must be on our way, John!"

He nodded, obviously suppressing a smile. Glancing at the two women, he said, "If one of you could gather some bread and cheese and a skin of wine? I am sure Mistress Vernon needs some sustenance."

"I'll do that," Alice said.

Mistress Derby grasped Maddy about the waist, and haltingly, they made their way up to her chamber. Maddy located her riding apparel while the older woman ran back downstairs to collect the supplies she needed to tend to Maddy's wounds. While she washed and bandaged the abrasions, Maddy told her a little of what she thought the Dacres were up to, evading all questions about how she was privy to this information. Every so often, the cook made little noises of sympathy, especially when she bathed Maddy's mouth and the worst of her head wounds. Best not to mention her bruised ribs. "One of Matthew's dogs bit me when I tried to make a run for it. Would you—?"

"Look at that!" The cook untied the handkerchief Musgrave had used as a tourniquet. "It's still oozing blood. I knew having those evil beasts around would bring harm to one of us someday."

At last it was done. Maddy stood up, and between the two of them, they managed to get her out of her torn and filthy bodice and skirt and into the riding costume.

· · ·

Musgrave was waiting with their mounts. Maddy had strapped her scabbard and dirk around her waist and prayed there would be no cause to use it. They debated what route to take.

"We should ride along the wall," he said. "That will give us the best vantage point—we might look down and see exactly where they are."

"No! It will take too long to get up there, and it is too circuitous. I am sure they took the Roman road, so they already have a substantial lead."

"Bear in mind there are only two of us. If we approach them from the rear, they will hear us. Which in turn means we will be dead before we can reach for our weapons. Warning Ryder should be our chief concern, not accosting Dacre."

He had a point. When Maddy hesitated, Musgrave said, "There is the path on the ridge. It is not ideal, but it sits above the road. It's more accessible than the path along the wall."

Maddy had been on that path the night of the raid. "Good plan. What are we waiting for, then?"

Musgrave helped Maddy mount, every one of her wounds crying out as she landed in the saddle. "Can you shoot a bow?" he called, holding one up.

"At a target. But I can't ride and hold one at the same time." *Especially not with bruised ribs.*

"Take the quiver. I'll carry the bow."

At last they were off. They trotted over the bridge, but once they'd gained the path, Musgrave shouted "Hiyah!" His horse sped up to a canter and hers followed. Galloping would get them there faster, but the terrain was a bit uneven for it. Maddy hoped Dacre had not set any sentries along the way. Musgrave carried the bow out to one side in an impressive show of one-handed horsemanship.

There was still plenty of daylight left, yet it was eerily dark along the wooded path. It wasn't long before Musgrave reined in and beckoned to her. The woods had given way to a clearing. He was gazing down toward the road, but there was nothing to see. "Dacre and his men must have already passed."

"Let's go," Maddy said. "We've no time to waste." In only a few moments they neared the end of the path and slowed the horses to descend from the ridge. When Musgrave looked confused, she said, "Follow me."

They had to cross the road to get to the market square. Only a few people were about. Shops had already closed. Tethered horses stood in a line outside the tavern. When they got to Church Street, she held up a hand. "I think you're correct in assuming Dacre and his men are already there. What should we do?" All along, Maddy had imagined herself arriving ahead of Dacre, riding up to the front door and banging on it until Nicholas answered and she could warn him.

"How far down the road is the house?"

"A half mile at most. Not far."

Musgrave studied her. "I could ride down there and have a look."

It was time to pluck up her courage. And summon what little wisdom she possessed. What would serve them best? Maddy was no longer the foolish, impetuous girl who had joined Leonard Dacre's raid. She was capable of reasoned, cautious action, and she wanted to prove it to herself, and to Nicholas. "That would probably be best. Can you see the stand of yew trees? Let's take cover there. You should probably walk the rest of the way."

"Aye."

They walked the horses a good way into the trees and dismounted. Musgrave wore a rapier, and she was certain he had a dagger in his boot. That was where he'd always carried one.

"I'll leave you the bow. If I do not return—"

"I shall come. Pray, don't tell me not to. The house is across the road. 'Tis the only one."

He hesitated before setting off, his eyes on her. "It is thanks to you the justice of the peace did not arrest me. You have my gratitude." And then he was gone, before she could respond. Maddy watched his progress. He remained in the cover of the trees a long time, finally crossing the road where the woods ended. When he was too far away for her to make out his form any longer, she paced from tree to tree, agitated, the pine needles soft beneath her feet. She hefted the bow, practiced pulling the string, nocking an arrow. Her ribs screamed in agony. Maddy could only hope that when a heightened sense of urgency kicked in, she would be able to focus on her target and ignore the pain.

For a long time, she waited. When Musgrave didn't

return after what she judged to be another quarter of an hour, Maddy decided to find out what was happening. Nicholas might need her, and what good was she doing, cowering here among the yews? Following Musgrave's example, she stayed in the woods as long as possible, finally crossing the road toward the house.

All appeared normal, if rather too quiet. Laborers would have finished for the day, but nobody else, neither a groom nor a stable boy, loitered about. Maddy darted from tree to shrubbery, trying to conceal herself. If Dacre and his men were here, they'd left their horses somewhere else.

Not satisfied, she sneaked up to one of the windows and peered in. It was too dark inside to reveal anything. If all was as it should be, why hadn't anybody lighted candles? Where was everybody? She was mulling this over when a commotion coming from behind the house claimed her attention.

Shouts. The clank of steel. A scream.

Maddy hurried to the rear of the house, the bow bouncing against her side. A skirmish was underway in the Ryders's back garden, a place where she had known such tranquility. Pulling her hood up, she ducked behind the ancient oak, the one with such an enormous girth, and hoped nobody noticed her. Cautiously, she peeked around the tree to observe the action. For several helpless moments, Maddy watched, trying to sort out who was who.

The Scots were dressed like border reivers, in padded leather doublets and steel helms. She spotted Francis Ryder, in the midst of a rapier fight with one of them. He seemed at a disadvantage, without armor or helm. Musgrave fought with another man, rapier in one hand, dagger in the other. To her horror, a few bodies lay on the ground.

Where was Nicholas?

And then she spied him. He wasn't wearing his doublet, which would at least have afforded him a small degree of protection. His hair was slick with perspiration. He and Dacre were in combat against each other, also with rapiers. Dacre grasped a dagger in his other hand. She kept her eyes riveted on them. At the moment, neither seemed to have an edge. Maddy stepped back behind the tree and nocked an arrow. She wanted to be ready if she had a chance to take a shot at Dacre. Then she peered around the tree once again.

Nicholas had the upper hand. He was younger, stronger, and more fit. But his opponent had two weapons, a distinct advantage. After another series of attacks and counterattacks, Dacre suddenly crossed his weapons. When Nicholas lunged, Dacre fended him off with a downward thrust of his blades. Nicholas's body was now completely exposed. And then, the unthinkable happened.

Daniel jumped out from behind a lilac bush and screamed. "Uncle! Uncle Nicholas!" Nicholas turned and Dacre landed a hard kick to his stomach, felling him. From where she stood, Maddy could hear him struggling to breathe. Dacre stepped on his middle with one booted foot, holding him in place. But instead of running him through, Dacre began talking. To Daniel. His voice was too low for her to hear, but his intent was obvious. He motioned to the boy with his dagger. Nicholas did not dare move. It was down to her now.

She stepped out from behind the tree and pulled her hood down. "Daniel! It's Maddy. Run to me!"

Without hesitation, Daniel charged over to her.

He clung to her skirts, and she knew he would not let go. Dacre looked at her, and she could see a flash of recognition and shock pass over his face. Distracted, he forgot about his foe long enough for Nicholas to struggle to his feet. Maddy was not about to gamble on how long the distraction would last. While Dacre was gawking at her, she raised her bow and shot him square in the chest.

He dropped like a deer in a hunt.

Clutching Daniel's hand, she ran to Nicholas. He gestured toward the house and said, "Get inside! I must assist my father." He threw himself back into the fight before she could answer. Not the greeting she'd hoped for, but he was in the middle of combat, after all.

A moment before they reached the door, she heard a howl of terror. Wheeling around, she glimpsed John Musgrave pinned to the ground by his attacker, but fortunately, Nicholas ran the man through with his rapier. Musgrave leaped up and the two of them went to Francis Ryder's aid.

This was nothing Daniel should be witness to. It looked as though they would soon defeat the enemy, so she grabbed his hand and they dashed inside.

"Is Margery here?" she asked the child. They went to the drawing room, where Maddy quickly found tinder and lit a few tapers. A fire was laid in the hearth, and she lit that, too. There was a chill in the room, and a fire would provide both warmth and comfort.

Before Daniel could answer, Margery swept into the room. "Master Daniel!" she cried. "You disobedient child! You were meant to stay inside with me, where it was safe. I am very angry with you." Her actions belied her words, as she lifted him into her arms and hugged him until he began to wiggle. She eased him down, and only then did she see Maddy.

"Mistress Vernon. What are you doing here?"

"It is a long story, and one best saved for another day." Suddenly, Maddy felt all the energy drain from her body. She needed to sit before she collapsed. Lying down would be even better.

Maddy lowered herself to the settle. Margery walked over and took a closer look at her. "What has happened to you, mistress?"

"I...may I lie down, Margery? I am not feeling quite

well."

Margery settled Maddy upstairs in the same chamber she'd stayed in before, and afterward, brought her the willow bark tea she so detested. After drinking it, she fell into a deep, dreamless sleep.

• • •

Hours later, Nicholas crept into Maddy's chamber. Weary to the bone, he had neither washed nor refreshed himself in hours. Margery said Maddy had been injured, that her face bore wounds. He needed to reassure himself that she was all right. He sat on the bed, and she stirred and then rolled over so that she was facing him.

"Nicholas? You are safe, then." She sounded groggy, barely awake.

"Aye, 'tis over. Dacre still lives, even though your arrow was true." He chuckled. "Well done, Maddy. Unfortunately, the padded doublet he wore allowed him to survive the hit. What did he do to you, sweeting?"

"I can't...talk of it now, Nicholas. Tomorrow."

"In the morning, I am sending you and Daniel to a friend in the village. My father and I will be riding to Carlisle at first light. But I will visit you when my work is done, and then we will talk."

"Aye." Her eyes drooped shut.

Had she understood anything he'd said? Nicholas leaned over and kissed her forehead. "Adieu for now, my love." But she was already sleeping.

Chapter Twenty-Six

The next morning, Margery and a male servant escorted Maddy and Daniel to the home of Widow Lettice Samuel and her two children. Maddy did not see Nicholas or his father, who had already left for Carlisle with their prisoners.

This arrangement was fine for Daniel. He thrived on playing with the widow's children, a boy and a girl near his age. Maddy had never seen him so happy. But it was not such an ideal situation for her. She wanted to know all. Everything that had happened with the Dacres. And what about the plot to kidnap Mary Stewart? Had they foiled it?

Even though she was badly in need of rest and time to heal, Maddy was restive. The Widow Samuel was kind and tended to her needs in much the same way Margery had. Young and quite lovely, her hair was the color of ripe barley. When not in company, she disliked hiding it under a cap, and it trailed down her back in all its golden splendor. It struck Maddy that the widow would make a fine wife for Nicholas. Daniel would have a family, and her children would have a father. How well did she and Nicholas know each other? He'd had no qualms about sending them to her. Dwelling on this was nonsensical, but the idea was like a pesky fly buzzing around. Maddy couldn't rid herself of it.

• • •

The aftermath of the clash with Dacre and his men occupied all of Nicholas's time for several days. His visit to Maddy was much delayed, although he knew she and Daniel were in good hands. Lettice showed him to the drawing room, and after he thanked her—a friend since childhood—she left the room.

Maddy sat alone, the sun streaming through mullioned windows. Kneeling before her, Nicholas took her hands in his and said simply, "Maddy." Then he examined her thoroughly, lightly touching each of her wounds. He sensed her shame that he was seeing her thus, her scabby mouth and the sore, red patches on her head.

"How did you get these wounds, sweetheart?"

As soon as he asked this, the tears began to flow, and she buried her face in her hands. Nicholas gently pried them away. "Tell me, sweeting."

Maddy managed to choke out, "Scold's bridle."

He suppressed his burgeoning rage. It would solve nothing. When he spoke, his voice was mild. "Can you tell me more?" Nicholas found his handkerchief and blotted her tears. She nodded and told him what had happened from the time Dacre caught her snooping in his chamber until her escape. He was sure she'd left out many details, but he would learn them soon enough.

"Mistress Derby, Musgrave, Alice—they saved me. I will be ever in their debt."

"As will I." Anger and frustration burned in Nicholas's chest, that Maddy had suffered so. And he hadn't been able to prevent it. "I am heartsick at what you endured at that man's hands." With tightly controlled fury, he leaped to his feet and prowled about the room. "Curse the man for a fiend! Dacre killed the poor serving girl and nearly killed you. I wish he had died. But he lives yet, though he is not in good condition."

"Where is he?"

"They have all been transported to Carlisle Castle. We've caught Lady Dacre, too."

"Their scheme did not go forward, then? Mary Stewart remains in the queen's custody?"

"Aye. Turns out their plan was loosely contrived. We've learned there were Scots who were meant to meet them near the castle. Ferniehurst, Hume, and their ilk may have been among them. When Dacre didn't arrive as planned, they fled over the border, no doubt."

"How did you locate Lady Dacre?"

"Her other stepson, William, the one suing her, was quite happy to tell us where she might be staying. She's proclaiming her innocence and demanding to see you. She says you will vouch for her." When Maddy gave no response, Nicholas said, "What have you to say to that?"

"I pray you will show her mercy. I've no doubt that she is a Catholic and a supporter of the Scots queen as Elizabeth's successor. But it is hard to judge how deeply involved she was in the plotting, and whether Dacre coerced her."

"You are too good, Maddy."

"Not I. But most of the time I was at the priory, she was kind to me. In my mind, her gravest sin was not protecting Cath. And that makes me wonder if I, too, could have done more to save her. She was a sweet, innocent girl."

"I know 'tis small comfort, but I do not believe either you or Lady Dacre could have prevented Dacre from killing her."

"What will happen to Lanercost now? Will William Dacre finally be able to claim it?"

"Legally, he has no right to it."

"Which means the queen will have yet another new property," Maddy said sardonically.

Nicholas could not deny it. "I can make you no promises regarding Lady Dacre's fate."

"I understand, but I hope you will take into consideration what I've said."

"Be assured I will." Nicholas had calmed down enough to sit next to Maddy. "You saved my life, sweeting, and most likely Daniel's as well."

She did not answer immediately, and when she spoke, her voice trembled. "After Dacre put me in the branks, he seemed to feel he could tell me anything. I'm convinced his plan was for me to die in that room. I was afraid...so afraid." She paused, visibly straining for control. "Since that last day at Lanercost, I can't seem to cease weeping. I-I am heartily sorry for it."

"Never apologize to me, Maddy." He leaned forward and brushed strands of hair off her face, damp from tears. "What prompted him to put you in the scold's bridle?"

She hesitated; for some reason, she was reluctant to tell him. "He demanded to know if you and your father were aware of his scheme. And whether you would be laying a trap for him. I refused to tell him."

Nicholas's expression softened. "You tried to protect us. And you suffered for it."

"I had hoped to free myself in time to warn you, but he had too much of a head start." Looking wretched, she dabbed at her eyes with his handkerchief.

Nicholas reached for her hand, smiling. "I understand you felled a man nearly twice your size."

Maddy gasped. "I forgot all about Matthew. Is he dead?"

"No. He's at the castle with the others. How did you manage it?"

She explained.

Nicholas tipped her chin up and kissed her scabby lips, very gently. "What you bore at the hands of that villain...and even afterward, you risked your own life to save ours. You did all this, and after I hurt you so deeply. I—"

The door swung open and Lettice came through carrying a tray laden with food and wine. Very poor timing on her part. But what could Nicholas do but invite her to sit with them, and it was not long before the children burst in. "Uncle Nicholas!" Daniel ran to him, and he pulled the boy onto his lap. Before long, Daniel wriggled from his uncle's grasp and went to Maddy, cuddling up at her side. Maddy was quiet, leaving Nicholas and Lettice to carry the conversation, mainly with insignificant remarks about the children and neighborhood. Nicholas wished it were he, not Daniel, nestling against Maddy.

She ate little, and he guessed she had not yet regained her appetite. Her recovery would take time, and he must accept that. After partaking of the meal, Nicholas rose. "Fare thee well, and thank you, Lettice." Then, gazing only at Maddy, he said, "God keep you safe." She inclined her head slightly. Nicholas motioned to Daniel to come outside with him.

He hunkered down in front of the boy. "Since I cannot be here, I would like you to watch over Maddy. Can you do that?"

Daniel nodded solemnly. "Aye, Uncle. I hate that man for hurting her."

Nicholas pulled him in for a hug. "I know, son. So do I. Now it is our duty to protect her."

He let the boy go, mounted, and guided his horse to the road home. His love for Maddy swelled in his chest, until it grew so full as to be uncomfortable. She was hurt, and not only bodily. Quiet and withdrawn, Maddy seemed so distant. What if she hadn't forgiven him his betrayals? Perhaps her time imprisoned in that room with the scold's bridle on her head had made her less likely to forgive him. If not for him, she would never have been at Lanercost. Would never have ended up in the clutches of Christopher Dacre.

He must do whatever was within his grasp to show her, by both word and deed, how very much he loved her.

· · ·

On market day, another visitor arrived. Mistress Derby, toting a basket filled with food, judging from the scent floating toward Maddy. By this time, she was feeling stronger physically, and her injuries were healing well.

"May I bring some refreshment?" Lettice asked. "Perhaps some ale or wine to accompany whatever smells so good in that basket?"

"Thank you, mistress. You are very kind." Maddy's appetite was returning gradually, and when the cook spread out a veritable banquet on the table, her mouth watered. Cold fowl, fruit tarts, bread, cheese, and her favorite sweet: sugar cakes.

After the widow had come with the ale and gone away again, and they each had filled their trenchers, Mistress Derby said, "We heard what you did. Shot an arrow at the master and saved both young Master Ryder and his little nephew. Dacre got his due, for what he did to you. And poor Cath."

"I believe I thought only of saving Nicholas and Daniel," Maddy said. A sugar cake beckoned. Maddy snatched one and took a bite. *Divine.*

"And Matthew, the brute. He told Master Ryder he'd come to the chamber to save you, the lying swine. I still don't trust Vine. Musgrave, that is."

"He was working for Francis Ryder, Nicholas's father, all along. Even Nicholas didn't know at first. I doubt we'll see him again. In the end, he did the right thing." She hesitated a moment, because she knew Mistress Derby wouldn't credit what she intended to say. "To be honest, I've half a mind to believe he was in love with Cath and sincerely grieved by her death."

"*Hmph*. I guess we'll never know." With a sly look she said, "You were no ordinary companion to Lady Dacre, were you?"

Ducking her head, Maddy smiled. "Nay, I was not." The cook accepted that, nodding in acknowledgment.

"What will you do, Mistress Derby?"

"Stay on with my sister in Brampton until I can find new work. And what about you, Madeleine?"

"I am…returning to my family." She could not say "going home." Kat's family home was in no way Maddy's home. "I've a brother I thought was dead, a sister-in-law, and a niece and nephews. It is where I belong."

"*Hmm*. Are you sure about that?" She canted her head at Maddy and looked skeptical.

An uncomfortable feeling settled in her chest. "Why wouldn't I be?"

"A certain gentleman seems more than passing fond of you."

Heat spread through her, and she couldn't feign ignorance. "Nicholas? We were thrown together because of the work I was helping him with, but nothing more." Maddy could barely swallow.

"If you could have heard the things he said about you when he came to Lanercost…he sounded like a man besotted."

Stunned, Maddy could barely contain the emotions swelling in her breast. Nor could she look directly at the woman, or she would guess. "We had a falling out. He lied to me about some important matters."

"There is such a thing as forgiveness, Madeleine. It is

highly underestimated by people who are inclined to hold grudges and make themselves miserable. You should consider it."

Maddy nodded but was unable to answer.

"I brought your things. They are in cartons—the widow had her servant carry them to your chamber."

"My dog! Is anybody looking after Useless?"

"Don't you worry, mistress. We've been taking good care of her."

"Thank you." Maddy wished she could have her little dog with her, but that seemed too much to ask, given that Lettice had already taken in both her and Daniel.

They rose and began clearing away the food. When she was ready to leave, Maddy said, "Thank you Mistress Derby, for coming to my aid. I might have died wearing that…device. I will never forget what you did."

If she was not mistaken, the older woman was blinking away tears. "Stop, now. 'Twas nothing. The best way you could thank me would be to heed my advice."

After Mistress Derby had gone, Maddy retreated to her chamber to rest. Lying on the bed, she thought about what her friend had said about forgiveness. Did Nicholas think Maddy hadn't forgiven him? She supposed it was possible. Nothing could be right between them until they'd both aired their grievances. Maddy believed he owed her a truer explanation about the matters he had kept secret, both Robbie's death and the pardons.

Yet when she'd learned Dacre wanted to kill him, nothing else had mattered except saving him. When she had been locked up in that room wearing the scold's bridle, she had thought she might never see him again. She recalled thinking that if given the opportunity, she would forgive him without a moment's thought or hesitation.

How she would love to know what he'd said about her to

Mistress Derby.

• • •

The days passed and Maddy grew stronger. She offered to help Lettice in the stillroom, with the preparation of her decoctions and salves. And in the nursery as well. Her little daughter, Meggie, was sweet as a sugar cake. One morning when Maddy awoke, the wee girl was standing next to her bed. Maddy threw the coverlet back and Meggie crawled in with her. Feeling her warmth, inhaling her sweet smell—both made Maddy wish for a bairn of her own someday, an intense sensation that caught her by surprise.

Maddy volunteered to tend the herb garden, largely so she could be out of doors. Daniel and his new friend, Simon, Lettice's son, could run free as she worked. In the late afternoon, Maddy would return to the house with the scent of purslane and mint on her hands. In the evenings, she sat by one of the windows and embroidered, completing the project Daniel's mother had started before her death. Maddy fashioned it into a cover for a cushion, stuffed it with goose down, and presented it to the widow to thank her for sheltering Maddy these last few weeks.

She sensed her time here was almost at an end. Healed in body, Maddy was ready to return to Carlisle and her family. It was no use fretting over it; she'd nowhere else to go. Nicholas had not visited again, so she was surprised one morning when Lettice called to her. "Master Ryder is here," she said, smiling.

"Oh?" she was in the drawing room playing a game with the children.

"He wants you outside, my dear."

Maddy smoothed her skirts, ran a hand through her hair, and made for the door. Daniel followed, but the widow stopped him. "Not now, Daniel."

When Maddy stepped through the doorway, Nicholas was standing there, looking so handsome in the morning light. He was holding a wiggling creature in his arms.

"Nicholas! You brought my dog. Thank you." She stretched up and kissed his cheek, and he passed Useless over to her. "Oh, how I've missed you, lass."

"I should bring you a gift every day, if that is how you will thank me."

She could do nothing but smile foolishly.

Nicholas put a hand on her arm, and now his expression grew serious. "I've brought somebody to see you," he said. When his gaze drifted toward the corner of the house, Maddy's followed. Her brother stepped forward, into the bright sunlight.

"Well met, dear sister."

She was frozen to the spot. Her hand flew to her chest, where her breath seemed to be caught. Nicholas hadn't let go of her and began speaking softly. "All is well, sweetheart. Greet your brother."

Maddy set Useless on the ground. And then she ran to Robbie and threw herself at him. He wrapped his arms around her and they clung to each other, both of them weeping. When at last Maddy stepped back, she noticed that Nicholas had withdrawn.

"Let me look at you." Robbie had aged and did not appear hearty. Obviously, his ordeal had affected him. He had lost his youthful vigor and was too thin.

"I've come to take you home, Maddy," Robbie said.

"You what?"

"You will make your home with Kat and me for now."

Anger pinched at her, but she restrained herself. "I am not prepared to leave. I haven't packed my belongings."

"A servant will help you."

It disappointed Maddy that she had no choice in the matter of her leave-taking. Had Nicholas conspired in this? Was he so eager to have her gone? Her limbs felt heavy, as though lifting them would be painful. This had been inevitable, and it would do her no good to protest. Maddy had thought herself resigned to it, but now that it was upon her, she could hardly bear the idea.

Reluctantly, she summoned a smile. "Do come inside, Robbie, and take some refreshment." He hesitated briefly, but finally followed her to the door.

Maddy couldn't look at Nicholas but stated to nobody in particular that she must supervise her packing. It would be awkward for Robbie, having to converse with Nicholas and the widow in her absence, but she couldn't help that. All the belongings Mistress Derby had brought her were still packed in the wooden cartons. Fleetingly, Maddy wondered if these were the containers the steward had built for Lady Dacre's documents. A serving girl had the rest well in hand. Maddy riffled through the clothing in search of a traveling costume, and the girl helped her change into it. When they were done, she surveyed the bedchamber. In truth, she was only trying to delay her departure. She was quite sure they'd packed everything.

Downstairs, they'd reverted to that age-old subject, the one everybody turned to when all else failed. Children. Robbie was telling Lettice about his own little ones. Nicholas was holding Daniel, speaking to him in a low voice. Mayhap telling him she was leaving.

She drew in a deep breath, but still could not get enough air. "My belongings are packed," she said. Robbie left to help the servant carry them downstairs. Maddy went to Lettice and kissed her cheek. "Thank you for all you have done for me, mistress. It has been a pleasure to reside here with you and your children." Meggie, who must have sensed what was happening, began to wail. Lettice quickly kissed Maddy, then lifted her daughter into her arms. Maddy bussed her plump cheek in farewell, and then turned to Nicholas and Daniel.

Robbie had gone outside, and Lettice, signaling to her son, departed as well.

Maddy reached out a hand to Daniel. To her astonishment, he batted it away. "Daniel!" Nicholas said, before turning to her. "He is much saddened by your leaving."

"I understand. No need to explain." She looked at the small boy who meant so much to her. She had filled a void in his life, and he had loved her absolutely. Maddy didn't blame him for feeling angry with her—he must believe she was abandoning him. Helpless to say anything that would make things less hurtful, in the end all she could say was, "Pray forgive me, Daniel." She wanted to hold him close and tell him she loved him, but that would not help. And she doubted he would permit it. Nicholas lowered him to the ground, and he ran off to find his companion.

That left Maddy alone with Nicholas. He looked at her, and his eyes seemed to hold a great sorrow, barely contained. "You're sure this is what you want, Maddy?"

She nodded, not looking at him. If she looked at him, she would cry. Did he not know if he asked her to stay, she would? Did he truly believe she wished to leave him and Daniel? But if he would say nothing, neither could she.

He lifted her hand and held it to his cheek. "Fare thee well, then, sweeting." He bent his head toward her. She moved closer to him, anticipating one last kiss. Indeed, yearning for it.

"Maddy, we must be on our way." Robbie stood in the doorway watching them.

She nodded. "As you say."

Nicholas accompanied them outside. The day was overcast, and no doubt rain would give them a good soaking before they were too long on the road. Robbie climbed onto the wagon bench, astute enough to give them a moment.

"Farewell, Nicholas. And thank you."

"God keep you, Maddy. I will hold you in my heart."

He helped her climb up to the bench, beside her brother, and handed Useless up. Robbie clucked to the horse, and they were off. Maddy did not turn around. If she glimpsed Nicholas one more time, she might be tempted to leap down and run to him.

• • •

Nicholas cursed himself for a fool. Letting her go had been the most difficult thing he'd ever done. But how could he do otherwise? After observing Maddy's reunion with her brother—he could not entreat her to stay with him. Didn't she deserve some time to work things out with Robert? Given all that she'd related to him about her brother, the action he'd taken to save his skin would not have sat well with Maddy. Perhaps they could heal the rift between them in the coming days.

A wiser man than Robert might have taken a different approach with his sister, however. Judging from Maddy's look and demeanor, she had resented his abrupt manner of informing her she was leaving with him, rather than asking if she wanted to. Or if she was ready.

Nicholas did not wish to be separated from her. Not for *any* length of time. Their days together in Brampton had been idyllic. After their lovemaking, he'd felt himself drowning in her, and everything in his life had seemed slightly off-kilter since she'd left. Ever since the night they first dined together at the castle and he had glimpsed her in the soft glow of candlelight, Nicholas had known she was a rare beauty. But she possessed an inner radiance that surpassed anything physical. Maddy could be strong and stubborn, yet she was the kindest person he knew. She could not forgive herself for her perceived sins, yet she was forgiving of everybody else. She had advocated for Lady Dacre, even though the woman had stood by, silent, while her stepson planned to kill Maddy. Nicholas suspected that only a few days would pass before she absolved her brother of his sins and they were as close as they had ever been.

She had given herself to Nicholas without hesitation. She was the woman he wanted by his side for the rest of his life.

But to his frustration, he remained uncertain as to his own status with Maddy. They'd had next to no time alone together. Had she forgiven him for foolishly placing duty above his love for her? Duty was only part of it. In truth, his worst fear had been hurting her, and then losing her because of it.

Nicholas planned to visit as soon as he could without intruding on the siblings' reconciliation. And in the meantime, he intended to petition the Council of the North to regain the Vernon lands and property.

For the present, he must summon every bit of restraint he possessed to soothe his visceral longing for her.

Chapter Twenty-Seven

Maddy spent her days at the home of Kat's parents sewing and mending children's apparel, entertaining her niece and nephews, tending the herb, vegetable, and flower gardens, and doing whatever else they required of her. As before, she was perhaps one step up from a servant. She did not mind as much, though. Kat's mother and father managed to be civil, no doubt at Kat's urging. And keeping occupied every waking hour prevented her from thinking overmuch of Nicholas.

On the way to Rickerby from Brampton, Robbie had conveyed, in a stilted manner, his sorrow over her recent troubles. After that, they had spoken little. Although she wanted to confront him about what he'd done to save his neck, it wasn't the right time. Not so soon after they'd been reunited.

From all appearances, Robbie was no longer the irresponsible ne'er-do-well he'd been in the past. He rose at dawn and worked all day with the animals, in the fields, or in the carpenter's shop, under the direction of Kat's father. Maddy would have expected him to chafe at such a lack of independence, but he seemed to have made his peace with it. Perhaps he was as hopeful as she that they would someday regain what was rightfully theirs. Soon she must write to Nicholas about how to make an appeal for their land and property.

Some evenings Robbie spent in the local alehouse, but she believed it was with Kat's blessing. Maddy maintained a distance between herself and her brother. What he had done was repugnant to her, and she didn't know if she could ever forgive him.

One morning when she and the little ones were picking fruit in the orchard, Robbie came by to do some pruning and cleaning up. They'd had a ferocious storm a few nights before, which had cracked branches and scattered damsons and quinces across the ground like billiard balls on the baize.

Nearing them, her brother said, "Children, pick up the fruit and put it in the basket." Maddy had noticed that they were quite obedient to him, and now they began to do as he instructed with no argument.

Apparently, he had something to say to her. She lowered herself to a stump Robbie motioned toward. He'd made no effort to engage her thus far, but maybe he was as uncomfortable with the awkwardness between them as she was. "We must talk of what happened, Madeleine, if we are ever to be true brother and sister again."

Maddy nodded in agreement. "What have you to say for yourself?"

"You are angry with me about what I did to save my life." It was not a question.

She gazed steadily at him. "How could you? You, of all people, had no right to judge anybody!"

"Would you rather I had died that day?"

"Of course not. But you could have run off, concealed yourself somewhere before the queen's men had a chance to track you down. Many did."

"Make no mistake, I had planned to do exactly that. But in the end, there wasn't time. When the opportunity arose, I had no choice but to seize it."

"You should have considered the consequences before you cast your lot with Northumberland. Then you would not have had to make such a choice."

"Aye, hindsight is always sharper, is it not? Rumors were circulating about the way a man's life might be spared. I found a wastrel, a criminal who was willing, for coin, to take my place. He wished to bestow the money on his family. He said he had no hope of redemption in this life, and mayhap sacrificing himself for me would give him hope for the next."

"Poor, pathetic creature!"

"Aye."

Leaning over, Maddy rested her head in her hands. When she felt his hand on her arm, she looked up and was shocked to see his eyes glossy with tears.

"Do you think I do not suffer for what I did? I am mortally ashamed, Maddy. I am working hard to gain God's forgiveness, and that of my family. Pray, give me a chance. Without your forgiveness, I don't think I can carry on."

"Mine? Why?"

"Because you have always been my guardian angel. When I was a lad, it was you who protected me, saved me from Father's punishment in scrape after scrape. And I disappointed you over and over again. When I married Kat, I beat down my wild impulses, especially after the children came. But the chance to do something exciting—dangerous, even—called to me. I was a fool, in every respect."

Maddy felt a hard shell around her heart begin to break apart. "If you were a fool, then so was I. Do you think it showed good sense to run off and join Leonard Dacre's raid? It was a reckless, senseless act. It led to all the troubles that followed."

His next words surprised her. "I am in awe of you for what you did. But you were hurt by it. For that, I blame myself. And Kat feels responsible, too, for not telling you I was alive. You would never have put yourself in such peril had you known the truth."

"It was entirely my decision."

Robbie scowled. "And Ryder. Turning you into his spy. If it weren't for the fact we likely need his help to get our land back, I'd challenge him to a duel."

Maddy grabbed his hands. "Oh, no, Robbie, you misjudge him. He has been forced to work for his father, but he wants free of it. Nicholas is a good man, believe me."

He smiled. "So that is the way the wind blows, eh?"

A blush stole over her face. "I doubt anything will come of it, brother. You need not concern yourself, or tease me about it, come to that."

Maddy rose, and he did, too. "Perhaps it is time to stop blaming each other—and ourselves," she said. "If you require my forgiveness, you have it. And I will pray for you, Robbie."

He embraced her and kissed her cheek. They watched his children for a moment before he called to them. They lugged the basket over, proud to show him how much fruit they had gathered.

• • •

Nicholas made it a priority to help Maddy regain the Vernon land and property. From the time he'd first questioned her at the castle, she'd made it clear it was the only thing she truly desired. And he wanted her happiness above all else. The day after he'd said farewell to Maddy, he petitioned the Council of the North to appear before them to plead her case.

The Council usually met in York. But they had

administrative business in Carlisle and summoned Nicholas there instead, to the Guildhall. That saved him a long, costly journey. His father agreed to accompany him.

"Are you uneasy about this, Nick?"

"I suppose I am," he admitted. "For Madeleine's sake."

"I believe you may set your mind at rest. This is simply a necessary formality."

"I hope you are right."

His father frowned. "You are aware, of course, that because she is a female, the land will be given not to her, but to her brother."

"Aye. I mislike it, but it is the best outcome I can hope for."

Surprising him, his father said, "I do believe you love that lass." The man was actually smiling.

With every fibre of my being. But does she love me?

No need to share his deepest feelings with his father. They'd never had that kind of relationship. So Nicholas simply nodded in agreement and smiled back.

The Earl of Sussex was still the president of the council. When Nicholas was called, he described in detail the work Maddy had done at Lanercost and how she had been instrumental in ending the conspiracy to abduct Mary Stewart. He was less voluble on the topic of Robert Vernon, but he described him as "reformed" and "regretful of his actions."

In the end, Sussex, looking stern of visage and sounding the same, said, "It appears that Mistress Vernon successfully carried out a difficult assignment beneficial to the queen. Her brother also has...paid his debt. We will confer and give you our decision within a fortnight."

"I am most grateful, my lord." Nicholas did not see how Sussex could advise the Council to deny the petition, given that he himself may have been involved in the plot.

Now he would bide his time until they handed down their decision.

. . .

Maddy's tasks kept her occupied from dawn to dusk, rarely allowing her the luxury of a wandering mind. Yet there were quiet moments, especially in the evenings, when she and Kat sat with their work. It was then that clary sage eyes and curling dark hair made their way into her thoughts, at times causing her to pause, her needle stilled, staring at nothing. Nicholas had once told his father that if he did not allow him to deal with Maddy on his own terms, he would take Daniel and leave. But hadn't he said he lacked the wherewithal to do so? How did matters stand with him now? Of one thing she was certain. He wanted to end his involvement with the queen and her doings.

Nicholas Ryder's affairs are none of your concern, Madeleine.

She did not dare to believe in a future with him. Recently, Robert and Kat had introduced her to a yeoman at a village entertainment. Wealthier than most, he was a widower with two children. They hadn't said so outright, but she would have had to be witless not to see what her brother and his wife wished. To turn over responsibility for her to somebody else. The man was nice enough, with a pleasing countenance. But he did not stir her blood.

Some weeks after she'd last seen Nicholas, Maddy and Kat were preparing to make a call on one of the tenants whose children were ailing. Together they had readied a basket of meat pies, fruit, bread, and cheese. Maddy tucked in a few balls for the boys and a cloth doll for the girl. Kat had gone to fetch her basket of remedies, and Maddy was waiting for her outside, playing with Useless. Glancing up at the sound of a horse approaching, she could not make out who it was at first. But it wasn't long before she recognized Nicholas. She did not know why he'd come, but the mere sight of him made her heart leap.

He dismounted and strode toward her, his smile wide. "Good morrow, Maddy," he said. "Is your brother about?"

"I'll send one of the children to find him," she said. "Come inside, pray, and take some refreshment."

"I shall wait here."

She nodded and hurried in. Martha was sewing with her grandmother, but Edward and Andrew, Maddy was informed, were in the back garden playing soldier. She sent them in search of their father, then returned to Nicholas.

"Why have you come?" she said. His eyes were fair dancing.

"I'll explain when your brother is present. How do you get on, Maddy?"

She shrugged. "'Tis not much different than before, but I have grown accustomed to it. What about you?"

Before he could answer, her brother strode around the far end of the stables and hastened toward them. "Ryder," he said, nodding. "Will you come inside?"

Nicholas again declined the offer. "I stopped only to inform you both that I petitioned the Council on your behalf, and they have decided in your favor. The Vernon land and property are to be returned to you." He brushed a hand across his beard. "I must warn you—I do not know what remains of your furnishings, plate, and the rest." Maddy thought of Naworth Castle, and how the Dacres had looted it. It was likely the Vernon home had been plundered, too.

"We care not for that," Robbie said. "This is good news indeed!" Laughing, he lifted Maddy off the ground and twirled her around.

After he set her down, Maddy said, "You have our thanks, Nicholas. This is very good news indeed. I meant to write to you about it, but I have been busy with the children."

Nicholas looked uncomfortable. "The queen had given it as a preferment to one of Hunsdon's men. He and his family will have to remove their things."

"Have they been told?" Robbie asked.

"I'll be paying them a visit soon. I believe you should be able to take possession within a fortnight."

Kat joined them then, and Robbie informed her of the news. Smiling, they embraced and then went away, whispering to each other. It had most likely been difficult for them to live with Kat's parents. Selfishly, Maddy had never truly considered that.

She turned back to Nicholas, who said, "Will you ride out with me, Maddy? I have something I wish to say to you."

His expression was solemn.

She hesitated only a moment. "Allow me to speak to Kat. I was to accompany her to visit a tenant."

Maddy soon had things squared with her sister-in-law, who insisted Martha could take Maddy's place. "No doubt she will be thrilled to give up her sewing."

Nicholas did not care to wait while another horse was saddled. "You will ride with me," he said, rather arrogantly. After he mounted and settled himself, he reached a hand down to her. She grasped it and set her foot upon his in the stirrup. With little effort, he pulled her up in front of him.

Which was a very fine place to be. He wrapped an arm about her waist, holding her against him. She relaxed into his solid chest, so close she could feel every breath he took.

"Shall we ride to the river?" he asked.

She nodded her assent. The air was redolent with spring fragrances—rain and sage and pine.

Nicholas suddenly broke the silence. "Will you go with them?"

"Aye. I'll live in one of the tenant's cottages, if Robert

will allow it."

The arm encircling her grew firmer. "What? They'll reside in the house, and you, in a tenant's cottage?" He shook his head. "It is only due to you that your family is getting the land back at all."

Irritation got the better of her. "What did you think would happen? I am a female. None of the estate belongs to me—only to Robert. I'll be grateful to have the cottage, where I can live on my own."

"I mislike it."

Awkwardly, she twisted around to look at him. "At least I shall have some degree of privacy and a place to call my own. And a garden. I shall insist upon a garden. Mayhap more than one."

"You will not be happy."

Maddy expelled a breath sharply. "Truly? Perhaps you are right. As you once suggested, marriage might be best for me. There is a wealthy man in the village who has expressed an interest. If I marry him, I can live in a fine house and have servants to do all the work. And I'll have children of my own to mind. God knows I've enough experience caring for other people's." Her throat thickened, and she felt on the verge of tears.

By God's light, why did I say such a ridiculous thing? No doubt Nicholas would be the first to bestow his good wishes.

Neither one spoke again.

Their route took them past property owned by the Dodds. Someday, after her own wounds were healed, Maddy would find the courage to visit them and ask their forgiveness for involving Ann in Leonard Dacre's raid. At present, they would still be grieving, and they would not welcome her overtures. One day soon she would find Ann's grave in the churchyard and lay some flowers on it.

Maddy felt a fullness in her chest. Weeping would relieve

it, but she refused to cry in front of Nicholas. She had been trying to avoid self-pity, attempting to put the horrors of her final day at Lanercost behind her. And now she must put all hopes of a future with Nicholas behind her as well. She refused to speculate on what he wanted to say to her. Probably a final farewell.

When they arrived at an area of the Eden popular with anglers, Nicholas dismounted and helped her down, then hobbled the horse. Squirrels chittered in the branches above, and she gazed at the river. The water pooled here, forming a pond, and fish liked to hide in its depths.

"Maddy." He was looking at her most intently. "There are a few things I neglected to tell you."

"Oh?"

"I sent William Cecil a letter and recommended mercy for Lady Dacre. As the queen's agent closest to the matter, I believe they will give strong weight to my opinion."

Maddy smiled. "Then I am in your debt." She hesitated a moment before saying, "I'm surprised that you placed so much trust in my judgment."

He reached out for her hand. "It was you who lost all faith in me, and for good reason."

"You are mistaken. I never lost faith in you." Perhaps she should let go of his hand, but she could not.

"Did you mean it, about wedding that fellow in the village?"

"Should I?"

"Do you want him?" He stepped closer to her. "Has he kissed you like this?" Nicholas crushed her against his chest, wrapped his arms around her, and placed his lips upon hers in kiss full of yearning and desire. She trembled with feelings pent up for too long.

He drew back and studied her, a bit of desperation in his eyes. "My dearest Maddy. Marry me, sweeting. Marry me.

I love you, more than my own life." He paused to catch his breath. "You said you would tend gardens and look after your children. Let it be our gardens, and most definitely our children. We will have as many of both as you like." He drew back and looked at her, smiling, hope glowing in his eyes. "Five or ten, if that will make you happy."

"Truly? I don't think I'll need that many."

He threw back his head and laughed, a joyous sound. "Come. Before you answer, sit here with me for a moment." He tugged her down to the riverbank. "Do you think you can ever forgive me for not being truthful? At first, my cursed duty to the queen stopped me. But when I knew I loved you, I should have been honest with you. I feared if I told you about the pardons, I would lose you. I wanted you to be free, and yet I wanted to hold you close. Can you understand that?"

She couldn't speak. Not yet.

"About your brother. When I learned he was alive, I should have informed you immediately. My father was against it, and since telling you would have meant revealing everything Robert had done, I knew it would hurt you. How could you live with it? Especially while staying at Lanercost? I convinced myself you were better off not knowing. It was wrong of me and causes me great shame and sorrow to think of it."

When still she didn't speak, Nicholas said, "I understand if I am too late. If begging your forgiveness comes too late."

Maddy shook her head, vehemently. "Oh, Nicholas, I forgave you long ago."

A smile tugged at his mouth. "After you took the shot at Dacre to save me, I allowed myself to hope that might be the case."

"I had a great deal of time to think when I was locked up in that room and feared I might die. I was desperate to see you, to tell you I forgave you a thousand times over."

"Jesu, Maddy, I've been waiting so long to hear you say it."

With that, he pulled her down, until they were lying side by side. For a time, they were consumed by their ardor and fierce desire for each other, and the world simply drifted away. Nicholas loosened her bodice enough to remove it, and then pushed down the straps of her kirtle and smock to free her breasts. "You are so beautiful, my Maddy." He caressed her, teased her, until she thought she might die of pleasure.

Nicholas unfastened his doublet and removed it, then tugged his shirt off. Holding her against his bare chest with one hand, he raised her skirts with the other. He slid a hand upward until he reached her core. Maddy had been waiting for this, hungry for his touch, needing it more than she'd known. His familiar, clean scent and the feel of his skin drove her to the edge. He was her light and her dark, her beginning and end. All she was now and all she would become.

And then he entered her and they began to move together, locked in their tight embrace. Nothing could separate them now. The intensity of her release consumed her, and she buried her face in his neck until Nicholas found his release deep within her.

After a while, when they lay peacefully together, Nicholas said, "You are the bravest lass I've ever known."

Maddy laughed. "Or the stupidest."

"Never." They both sat up, and he helped her straighten her clothing while relating more news. "I've told my father that I will no longer work for him or the queen. I've had my fill of it. Nearly losing you was the last straw."

"I'm glad, for your sake. But what will you do? Where will you and Daniel live?"

"My father has given me the house. To my great surprise, he said I deserved it because I am raising Daniel. All the money his country estate earns is to be mine as well. He has removed to London, to serve the queen there."

"We will have our own home," Maddy said.

"Ah, then your answer is yes?"

She laughed. "I have missed you so, and Daniel, too."

"And we have been miserable without you."

Tears welled in her eyes, and she made no effort to stop them. "I love Daniel, Nicholas. How could I not?"

"And do you love his uncle then, too, lass?" He looked as though he were not quite certain of the answer.

"How could you doubt it?" Maddy asked, putting him from his misery. "Why did your father have such a change of heart?"

"He received a reward from the queen for thwarting the plot to capture Mary and arresting the conspirators. A grant of land and money. Knowing my father as you do, you must be aware he would not give up his home without the promise of something grander."

"But he could have had both. Kept the land in Brampton and added the gift from the queen." Maddy did not say it, but in the future, she wouldn't put it past Francis Ryder to once again draw his son into his intrigues. To use this gift to make Nicholas feel he owed him something in return.

"Since the glory and rewards should by rights go to you and me, I believe he felt this was my due. I did not expect it, and I'm overjoyed that we're to have our own home. Humble though it is, it's a step up from a tenant's cottage," he said, a smile in his voice.

Somewhere, the queen's enemies schemed against her. Her own machinations continued, abetted by her councilors and countless other men in her thrall. It was an endless cycle, and Maddy thanked God they would no longer be part of it.

Instead, they lay on the riverbank wrapped in each other's arms, the water lulling them and a fresh May breeze grazing their skin. Maddy could have remained there forever, but a pressing matter beckoned. Nicholas drew her up beside him and they rode home together, so that he might ask Robert for her hand.

Epilogue

Everywhere Maddy turned, there were roses. White, pink, yellow, even orange. And the striped *Rosa mundi*, the one she thought of as their rose. Hers and Nicholas's. In the year since they'd wed, her husband had undertaken the painstaking work of importing and cultivating roses to sell. Business wasn't yet thriving, but it was growing. Nicholas was content. He maintained his correspondence with other importers and growers, and it occupied much of his time.

Maddy got to her feet, no easy task these days, and placed her knife in the basket she carried over her arm. It was filled with roses for the house. Rubbing her back to ease the pressure, she glanced up. Nicholas was striding toward her. Even from this distance, she could see his furrowed brow. He worried about her. The child was due any day, and he was jumpy as a cricket.

She smiled, and by the time he reached her, he was smiling, too. "You are well, sweetheart? Our daughter isn't ready to greet the world?"

"I'm fine, Nicholas. And I don't think the babe will arrive

today." Daniel, her husband said, was like a son to him, and why wouldn't he wish for a girl, who would be just like her mother? Maddy had ceased pointing out that he may not get what he wanted.

"Is Daniel coming?" The boy had developed a keen interest in the rose bushes and sometimes fussed over them more than his uncle. "We should have our meal before your visitor arrives," Maddy said. Nicholas took the basket from her, and they started for the house, the little beagle, Useless, prancing after them.

As she had predicted, her husband continued to be drawn into the queen's work. Whenever mischief was suspected in the north, his father called upon him to investigate, since he himself was now in London. Most of the time, it amounted to nothing much and could be easily dispatched. Only occasionally did the work demand more time and attention. Maddy enjoyed assisting her husband by reading documents, studying maps, and offering her counsel. Nicholas depended on her advice, and she admitted to feeling a degree of pride in that. What would happen if an assignment from Francis Ryder involved greater risk and danger, she could not say. Thus far, that had not happened. But she was confident she and Nicholas would decide together whether to take on weightier matters.

Daniel skipped alongside her and grabbed her hand. The three of them ambled toward the house together. In these moments, so ordinary and familiar, Maddy felt deep joy and contentment. After the turmoil of the previous year, she had never expected to be so happy.

Nicholas leaned down and whispered in her ear. "I love you, sweeting."

Yes, always.

Acknowledgments

I am most grateful to my editor, Erin Molta, for her commitment to each book she edits. In all matters, both large and small, she never misses a thing. And thanks also to the Entangled Publishing team of behind-the-scenes professionals who do so much to bring each book into the world.

Thanks also to my agent, Jill Marsal, who believed in this story from the first. She is such a pleasure to work with!

Ceil Boyles, Meridee Cecil, Claudia McAdam, and Lisa Brown Roberts critiqued an early version of *Mistress Spy*. Many thanks to them for their insights and suggestions.

And always, a special thank you to my husband, Jim, for, well, everything.

About the Author

Pamela Mingle found her third career as a writer after many years as a teacher and reference librarian. Her love of historical romance was nurtured by Jane Austen, and her novels have all been set either in the Regency or Tudor periods. Many long walks in England, Scotland, and Wales have given her a strong sense of place around which to build her stories. She is the author of *Kissing Shakespeare*, *The Pursuit of Mary Bennet*, *A False Proposal*, and *A Lady's Deception*.

Learn more about Pam and sign up for her newsletter at www.PamMingle.com. She enjoys hearing from readers and would love to connect with you on social media.

Also by Pamela Mingle...

A FALSE PROPOSAL

A LADY'S DECEPTION

Discover more Amara titles...

THE FIANCE FIASCO
a novel by Maddison Michaels

In the heart of Naples, amateur archaeologist Brianna Penderley's terrible Italian has her accidentally becoming engaged to two men at once. Of course, Daniel Wolcott—the tightly wound Earl of Thornton and the only man ever able to vex her—shows up to rescue her. Swept up in a perilous adventure, Daniel and Brianna must work together to survive their time in Italy. Now if they can just avoid killing each other.

HOW TO TRAIN YOUR BARON
a *What Happens in the Ballroom* novel by Diana Lloyd

When Elsinore Cosgrove escapes a ballroom in search of adventure, she has no idea it will lead to a hasty marriage. Now she's engaged to an infuriating, handsome Scottish baron who doesn't even know her *name*! But Elsinore is determined to mold her baron into the husband she wants. Quin Graham is a man with many secrets. If another scandal can be avoided with a sham marriage, so be it. Only his fiancée isn't at all what he's expecting. For reasons he's unwilling to explain, the last thing Quin needs is to fall for his wife.

A RAKE'S REDEMPTION
a *Rake* novel by Cynthia Breeding

To escape an arranged marriage, Inis dresses as a boy and stows away on a ship bound for London. Before long, she's working as an indentured servant in a livery stable, only to then be lost in a game of cards to a rakishly handsome lord who seems to enjoy bucking convention as much as she does. Keeping her identity secret becomes more important than ever when Inis hears of Lord Alexander Ashley's feelings regarding aristocratic ladies and his outlandish idea to prove a servant can be taught to be every bit as ladylike as those born to it.

CPSIA information can be obtained
at www.ICGtesting.com
Printed in the USA
LVHW01s2329021018
592222LV00001B/5/P

9 781725 134683